NEW DIRECTIONS

New Poetry 2004

JOHN ALLMAN
LOEW'S TRIBORO. Evocative poems, via film noir, about New York in the '40s and '50s. "Allman's poems move quickly, immediately, with imaginative range and energy" —*North Dakota Quarterly.* $14.95 pbk. original.

JIMMY SANTIAGO BACA
WINTER POEMS ALONG THE RIO GRANDE. New work by the celebrated Latino writer, Champion of the Int'l Poetry Slam, and winner of the Before Columbus Int'l Hispanic Heritage Award. $12.95 pbk. orig.

INGER CHRISTENSEN
BUTTERFLY VALLEY: A Requiem. Trans. from the Danish by Nied. A collections of four eloquent works: including the title poem, "Watersteps," "The Poem of Death," and "Meeting." $13.95 pbk. orig.

LAWRENCE FERLINGHETTI
AMERICUS, BOOK I. New poetry which stalks our literary and political landscapes in the tradition of Whitman and Williams. "Viva Ferlinghetti!" —Garrison Keillor, *The San Francisco Chronicle.* $21.95 cloth

THALIA FIELD
INCARNATE: Story Material. An enthralling new work by one of America's foremost experimental writers. "Playful, subversive, and intense." —Carole Maso. $15.95 pbk. orig.

JAMES LAUGHLIN
BYWAYS. Edited and annotated, with an Introduction by Peter Glassgold. The long awaited memoir of the late founder and publisher of New Directions, written in a swift poetic line. $35.00 cloth, $19.95 pbk.

NICANOR PARRA
ANTIPOEMS: How to Look Better & Feel Great. Antitranslation and Intro. by Liz Werner. "A poet with all the authority of a master"— Mark Strand, *The New York Times Book Review. Bilingual.* $14.95 pbk. orig.

W. G. SEBALD
UNRECOUNTED. Trans., with a Note, by Michael Hamburger. Sebald's epiphanic poems paired to Jan Peter Tripp's lithographs. A keepsake of one of the greatest writers of our time. "Magic" —Susan Sontag. $22.95 cloth

DELMORE SCHWARTZ
SCREENO: Stories & Poems. Intro. by Cynthia Ozick. Classic poems and stories by one of America's beloved writers. "Absolutely uncompromising in his own literary instincts"—Alfred Kazin. An ND Bibelot. $8.95 pbk.

MURIEL SPARK
ALL THE POEMS OF MURIEL SPARK. Available at last — villanelles, rondels, epigrams, and ballads. "Her poetry is sparse, exact, and intellectually controlled." —*Library Journal.* $13.95 pbk. orig.

ELIOT WEINBERGER, EDITOR
THE NEW DIRECTIONS ANTHOLOGY OF CLASSICAL CHINESE POETRY. One of the Best Int'l Books of the Year 2003" —*TLS.* "The best anthology of 2003" —*Contemporary Poetry Review.* $15.95 pbk.

 Please send for free complete catalog.
NEW DIRECTIONS, 80 8th Avenue, NYC 10011
www.ndpublishing.com

COMING UP IN THE SPRING

Conjunctions:44
AN ANATOMY OF ROADS: THE QUEST ISSUE

Edited by Bradford Morrow

Leaving home is a dangerous business. Whether it's to walk across the street or travel to another continent, one never returns the same.

Our spring issue, *Conjunctions:44, An Anatomy of Roads: The Quest Issue*, will explore in fiction and poetry the fascinating, complex process of defamiliarization as the ultimate path to knowing oneself.

John Barth contributes an astonishing, hilarious novella entitled "I've Been Told: A Story's Story," which may be the ultimate quest narrative in that the story of a quester is narrated by the quest itself. Young British writer and Booker Award finalist for his first novel, *If Nobody Speaks of Remarkable Things*, Jon McGregor offers a story of a distraught man who travels to an unnamed island in search of his lost father. Newcomer David Schuman's story "Miss" is an eerie modern desert journey in which a man— with his daughter, who believes she is a cat—encounters the mother who abandoned him, working in a twilight zonesque diner in the middle of nowhere. "Kronia," by fantasy writer Elizabeth Hand, details a love story that may or may not have actually happened over the course of decades all around the world. Joanna Scott, Lara Glenum, Rikki Ducornet, and two dozen other writers join us on this journey of the mind.

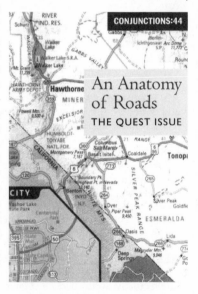

Subscriptions to *Conjunctions* are only $18 for more than eight hundred pages per year of contemporary and historical literature and art. Please send your check to *Conjunctions*, Bard College, Annandale-on-Hudson, NY 12504. Subscriptions can also be ordered by calling (845) 758-1539, or by sending an e-mail to Michael Bergstein at Conjunctions@bard.edu. For more information about current and past issues, please visit our Web site at www.Conjunctions.com.

CONJUNCTIONS

Bi-Annual Volumes of New Writing

Edited by
Bradford Morrow

Contributing Editors
Walter Abish
Chinua Achebe
John Ashbery
Mei-mei Berssenbrugge
Mary Caponegro
Robert Creeley
Elizabeth Frank
William H. Gass
Peter Gizzi
Jorie Graham
Robert Kelly
Ann Lauterbach
Norman Manea
Rick Moody
Howard Norman
Joanna Scott
Peter Straub
William Weaver
John Edgar Wideman

published by Bard College

EDITOR: Bradford Morrow
MANAGING EDITOR: Michael Bergstein
SENIOR EDITORS: Robert Antoni, Peter Constantine, Brian Evenson, Pat Sims
WEBMASTER: Brian Evenson
ASSOCIATE EDITORS: Jedediah Berry, Micaela Morrissette, Eric Olson, Alan Tinkler, Patrizia Villani
ART EDITOR: Norton Batkin
PUBLICITY: Mark R. Primoff
EDITORIAL ASSISTANTS: Caroline Dworin, J. W. McCormack

CONJUNCTIONS is published in the Spring and Fall of each year by Bard College, Annandale-on-Hudson, NY 12504. This issue is made possible in part with public funds from the New York State Council on the Arts, a State Agency. Special thanks to Peter Straub and Friends of *Conjunctions*.

SUBSCRIPTIONS: Send subscription orders to CONJUNCTIONS, Bard College, Annandale-on-Hudson, NY 12504. Single year (two volumes): $18.00 for individuals; $25.00 for institutions and overseas. Two years (four volumes): $32.00 for individuals; $45.00 for institutions and overseas. Patron subscription (lifetime): $500.00. Overseas subscribers please make payment by International Money Order. For information about subscriptions, back issues, and advertising, call Michael Bergstein at (845) 758-1539 or fax (845) 758-2660.

All editorial communications should be sent to Bradford Morrow, *Conjunctions*, 21 East 10th Street, New York, NY 10003. Unsolicited manuscripts cannot be returned unless accompanied by a stamped, self-addressed envelope. Electronic submissions will not be considered.

Conjunctions is listed and indexed in the American Humanities Index.

Visit the *Conjunctions* Web site at www.conjunctions.com.

Cover design by Jerry Kelly, New York.

Photograph of Ronald Johnson, from 1965, reprinted by permission of the Literary Estate of Ronald Johnson.

Available through D.A.P./Distributed Art Publishers, Inc., 155 Sixth Avenue, New York, NY 10013. Telephone: (212) 627-1999. Fax: (212) 627-9484.

Printers: Edwards Brothers

Typesetter: Bill White, Typeworks

ISSN 0278-2324
ISBN 0-941964-59-0

Manufactured in the United States of America.

TABLE OF CONTENTS

BEYOND ARCADIA

EDITOR'S NOTE

THE TWELVE PORTFOLIOS that make up *Beyond Arcadia* are representative of how flourishing is the world of contemporary innovative poetry. The poems here are technically fluent, even masterful, but they are also—from poet to poet, poem to poem—spirited and spiritual, moving and witty, political and philosophical, meditative and exuberant, dark and radiant, provocative and unfailingly compelling. Each of the twelve poets is distinct in approaching image and idea, how the word and line and page work, yet all are equal in their artistic ambitiousness.

The process that brought these portfolios into being was very straightforward. I was curious to learn what some poets whose own work I have admired over the years are reading, what they'd come across recently that moved and interested them. So I asked them all to solicit an unpublished manuscript by a favorite younger poet they consider especially promising. A poet who has published perhaps a book or two, or none at all—someone whose writing should find a wider audience. All of the selectors have generously provided an afterword about their selected poet.

Readers, who I hope will discover some new voices here, and maybe even some new favorite poets, are invited to think of each contribution as an individual chapbook, sans covers, of course. With that in mind, I hope you enjoy the thirteen volumes you now hold in your hand—a dozen folios of vital new poetry and, following that, an issue of *Conjunctions*, as well.

—Bradford Morrow
New York City
16 September 2004

Hours
Christian Hawkey
—Chosen by John Ashbery

HOUR

I mark the spot.
I make an incision.
On the exhale
I make an incision.
The hand is mine
that marks the spot
that makes the incision
on the exhale—slowly—
in the folds.
In this way I fold
myself inside
the folds, cutting deeper.
A noxious odor escapes.
My goggles fog.
I was afraid
I might wake you
although you're watching
me awake: an apple
hangs muted
by the beauty
in which it hangs
among the other apples
wrinkled by thoughts
frozen in the ground
of autumn. I mark
the spot. I make
an incision.
A yellow bird escapes
& clamps its beak

on the end of my chin.
I can't shake it off.
A partially chewed
action figure
climbs up my sleeve.
My lips tremble.
I throw them away.
& behind my lips
an orchard wilts.
I say orchard
& the orchard
wilts. I say wilt
& Thou arrives
with tiny birdcages
swinging from his eyes.
This is how it was
packaged. This
is why I cut into it &
suctioned the clouds
out of the sky & the
three black crows
that thought they
owned it, which is
part of their packaging.
In order to be opened
exhale completely
fold your lungs
into a knot & cast them
into the winter
of a long sewing.
This will almost
be enough.

HOUR

—For T.S.

Come back here—zzt, zzt—you have my
stem cells, you have my fluids,
chemical & otherwise, exchange & movement of,
love . . . blue sparks
a blue waterfall falling
between us: something soldered,
soldered open: laughter
a series of tunnels
along our temples
a green green lawn ripples & bucks
beneath our feet O
we were shining shining
in the chemotherapeutical
afternoon. Selah.
We're still alive.
Selah. We're chewing.
We're taking things in.
We're moving at the speed of goats
over the lush & rioting landscape
leaving a desert in our wake
& pieces of our underwear
& lovemaking
& a few placental sacks,
partially nibbled. Hard to stomach
with one stomach. A goat has five.
Between us, six, & the sixth
is always empty
to remind us
we're alive: a syllable, churned
& eaten clean
until its interior—zzt, not quite—
shines through: chrome horses
riding without eyes into the mouth of a sun.

HOUR OF SECRET AGENTS

The code word, he whispered, just before
letting go, was code word. Asshole,
I thought, watching his head
get smaller and smaller until it ended
in a puff of dust. Where it began,
I thought again, and spun around.
The landfill stretched on for miles.
I heard the voices of lost products beneath me.
My wheelbarrow was missing a wheel. A red bird
flew by, as if on a mission to flee this landscape
as soon as possible. The charred body of an infant
crawled out from a plastic bag. I stepped back,
covering my mouth. It crawled
a little further, then collapsed.
A prerecorded voice announced it was feeding time.
I masticated my last handful of Brazil nuts
but it took forever; by the time I finished
I'd forgotten what I was doing and swallowed.
Nobody wanted you anyway, I shouted,
when it began to cry. My wheelbarrow
was missing a wheel. I'll never get out of here.
It was just a barrow. I flipped it over
on top of the infant. "Ancient graves,"
I wrote in my notebook, "are where the living
feel most alive." A bulldozer
started up, two mounds over. Seagulls
swarmed its yellow bucket raising
piles of blue surgical gowns
to the sun. The skin on my face tightened.
The bird with the red breast flew by again
precisely in the same direction, which confused me.
The rubber soles of my feet were burning.
Coils of smoke rose between fissures.
From the tip of a far-off mound
a CD-ROM repositioned the sun
straight into my eyes, although it could have been
a signal, the permission I was waiting for,
the sign I was clear to return, was once again

unknown, or no longer known, a night sky,
the honesty of stars, a bowl of glass oranges
centered on a table, centered in a room,
a room that had never been opened
or if it had, by a trembling white glove.
The infant was still crying in its makeshift grave.
The red bird flew by again, this time in my mind.

HOUR (BLUE YODEL #1)

Sewn inside a left hip a highway
paved with the blue tongues of coyotes
a song a blue song
I am far from
the sound of your pupils

a shower curtain the color
of your body behind it I
remember a candy that left your lips
& when it left your lips
turned blue &
the mannequin at the front of science class
with its blue, detachable liver

my heart in high school was constantly
popping out it was OK it was
plastic anyway & Rhonda
the bruise above your right eye
was the center of a blue storm
I wanted to walk through & would have
I'm sorry I walked up to you & tried to lick it

Christian Hawkey

HOUR OF A MOUTH PACKED WITH FLOWERS

and heated into glass. I put my lips to the wall and blow a window
and my eyes take for themselves what they need, a blue triangle, sky.
I hang it inside. I tell myself it's only a lie
which is better, lying there with sand in my mouth
than telling the others about a sky. There are no "others."
My lungs don't like this. Neither does the Emperor. He wants his robes,
he wants his little hat back, the one that makes his eyes bulge.
Sometimes when he falls asleep at the throne I remove the pillow
from under his feet. His legs dangle & we all laugh, coughing quietly.
& when a fleck of saliva makes its way
to the corner of his mouth I resist
licking it off; a province
could disappear, struck down by drought, it's that easy. O where
in these kingdoms red with the clay of sunsets
pasted onto our brows
& these wires threaded with copper
listening to our every desire as if it were a need
can I rest with my blue triangle and maybe, if the light is right,
wrap my heart inside it, a soft cloud. The sky unspools over these borders
like a two-ply roll
of toilet paper; who pointed
my genitals toward the rising sun? And why this
stone set in my chest,
cavity I cannot reach to breathe upon, or polish.

Christian Hawkey

HOUR

Some pores open only to accept electronic rain
& in the end, defects litter the lawn
like plane wreckage, smoking a little
with the histories of evening skies.
I'd like to swallow a piano & kiss you
with no lips, banging our teeth
right down to the bones what music
isn't best but broken, somewhere,
along the auditory spine. We
must not wait for the sand machine
to make sand, the wave machine to make
waves, mechanical seagulls colliding
repeatedly in midair above our heads
& the sun malfunctioned & never set
so we got fried, our pores sweating beer cans
& even the horseshoe crabs maneuvering
their little tanks in & out of the waves
seemed to avoid us. The idea of a snack bar
almost killed us right there. Then it
withdrew over the waves all the way to the
horizon, where it stopped, & crouched down,
waiting . . . we swam out to the offshore oil barge
& frolicked under its huge platform, touching
its giant pylons in the cool shade & with the soothing,
underwater sound of mechanical pumping
we made love in the heavy water, the lifeless water,
the kind of water we could smear on each other's faces
& in smearing, drown.

HOUR

From high shelves I took down
laughter without a sound it was late
faces opening on the television
dew collecting on the small hands
of squirrels some creatures move
every time they blink a few inches
I opened my eyes you were my wife
hand a little lower on my spine
although always the presence of tires
burning holes through the night some creatures
move a few inches each time they flinch
these are the hardest to shake hands with
if you walk slow enough people will
stare at you give you money perhaps weep
we scattered at the first sign of rain
but Strom simply stood there
water gushing from the holes in his shoes
I would like to be a drainpipe
any way to serve the rain
imagine a squirrel wrapping its hands & feet
around your neck some people
are made entirely of neck-matter
yellow cones used to divide highways
& the beauty of Parmigianino is that he painted
the Madonna from the perspective of the infant
Christ sucking on a breast looking up
at the high tower rising to a little shelf
where the face sits the one with a smile
that fits perfectly across her mouth like a label

Christian Hawkey

HOUR (UTOPIC)

Incoming: field strafed by fireflies.
Incoming: sand shelled by enemy waves.
Landmines whisper sideways underground.
A horseshoe crab is a beautiful helmet.
I extend my limbs entirely into the air
& a sleeping flock of pink flamingos
explodes into morning, the sun stained red
behind outstretched wings, dew
burning off my flak jacket of grass.
Let the Age of Evaporation begin:
the mouths of animals have names.
At night the jaws of turtles creak open
to collect rain, heat lightning
reflected in their wide, sad eyes.
A tear falls. A turtle tear! Two musk deer
shiver across a meadow, dusk,
a brief firefight of fireflies, our names
appear & disappear, like that.
Alison I stored in a bottle in the ground.
I'm standing on a love song. I can hear it tick.
I'm standing in a field with one leg tucked up
into my chest, craning my neck around the necks
of birds, their beaks dipped in ink,
a feather wrote the first word, language
came from the sky, a secret whispered
into a hole, the hole shaped like a bottle,
the earth filled with glass, our names
cool into eyes, I hold mine in my hands:
love song. Evaporation. Let the countdown
begin—pink night eclipsing
a yellow sun, a glass beach
shattered by a chrome-tipped wave,
two glass eyes blown apart
in my hands. . . . A head dents the grass.
Three holes swirl with strings of white mist.

HOUR (WATER IN THE EAR)

We exchanged looks—all three of us—
& mine was totally better: it had rose-colored sequins
glued along the hemline & the word sneezeweed
in one pocket & an open window
with the sound of cows ripping through spring grass
filtering through it. We were filtering through it.
We were filters. We had to use our tongues to remove
the pollen collecting in the corners of our eyes
which were oversized, slightly joined, lidless.
A squirrel mounted the bottom of a drainpipe
& waited there, expectantly. It was kind of sexual
although Morty observed it was "just a rat
with a beautiful ass; in fact, in the original Latin . . ."
We exchanged looks again & this time
blonde women in gold jumpsuits
handed out birds with brand names
sewn into their breasts. Their beaks
were frozen open. I'd never seen a bird pant.
I threw it up into the air but it
dropped softly to the cement
so I stomped on it—I don't know why—
such is the nature of instinct & the
vertical surge of skyscrapers, porcini mushrooms,
the invisible teeth of lichen, sinking into a stone,
how blushing is one part sincerity, one part stupidity,
the clarity of a line of drool
swinging from an infant's
glossy chin. . . . From such a distance
it was hard to tell why he
whacked the side of his head
against the air. He paused, & we all paused with him, listening.

HOUR

I was lying on my side, in a ditch,
soaking my flanks in bog water
with my head propped up, on an elbow,
highway a few inches from my nose.
Semis thundered past like sexual urges.
The grass flattened its ears. My body shook.
I was humming a song. This was my spot.
Tadpoles are a form of punctuation.
Frogs hide inside commas. A whooping crane
landed & began showing off its legs.
Birds go for the eyes, I thought,
so I looked away, humming a song
about looking away, about looking back,
about my fingers wrapped around the flesh
that holds the ribs down to the hips
& hot mangoes rotting, the ground littered
with yellow suns, drainpipe
where the field ends, its dark ooze
the greenest earth. A man walks by
with a giant crucifix on his back
—ALASKA BY SPRING!—cars
speed up to pass him, which makes sense,
even the whooping crane leaves without a sound.
My jaw is wired shut. I'm humming a song
about cleaving, the body drifting apart & what
keeps us from dissolving at the first
drop of rain, my left flank almost
marinated, a sprig of rosemary between my lips,
robots have been dispatched to remove me,
all fruit mirrors the sun, a black seed
against my heart, a black car
driving past, buffeting my chest
& a cell phone lands, right in front of my face:
"It's all right," I whisper into it, "a French donkey,
called a Poitou, whose long ropes of fur
drag along the ground
was also used, in the mid- to late eighteenth century, to polish floors."

HOUR (WITH ONE HAND INSERTED IN A TIME OF WAR)

We dug with our hands & hand shovels.
We dug with our spatulate feet,
& with torsos as our only circumference
we dug a maze. A maze of passageways:
Level Three the Maternity Ward, April
with knees on either side of her chin.
Some thoughts are no wider than a chest.
Some thoughts are no wider than a chest,
heaving. On Level Six a green parrot opened
its red beak & it reached us, seconds later,
as a roar. Our eyelashes cringed, & lashed back.
We named it the Level of Roaring Parrots
& turned back to our work, carrying sewage out
by moonlight, the buckets light each night
& getting lighter. A gas lamp flickered
beside a makeshift waterfall. Ceilings
of soil shook soil. Joo plucked her eyebrows
with her eyes closed, a kind of faith. &
from the mouth of an infant a cracked nipple
slipped—what minerals are my lips
or packed vegetation my eyes—black coals—
how darkness changes darknesses each time
I blink, & blink again, Level One's filling
with tear gas, swing through the Level of
Eternal Foliage & seal it off—April you there,
Yes, I'm here, October's on the Level of Yellow Orioles
Warbling High in the Shadowy Summer Woods
& Gungjeong was last on the Level of Indentations
Left Behind by Falling Snow & should we
stand guard at the Level of One Hand Raised
to Block the Lemon Seed of the Sun
or should we push off, down the tunnels,
dig a hole in the side of a wall & wait?

HOUR

The hole was not aware it was a hole
until it was uncovered. Then it became

a manhole, which I fell through,
over & over. I tried to move the hole

but there was another hole
beneath it, which I fell through,

over & over, an O. This
was my blow hole. I breathed through it.

I took the hole inside my hole
& became the space I fell through.

Sunlight, when I opened my mouth to laugh,
leaked out of my throat. A crow

leapt from a branch
& curved into my sternum—exiting,

seconds later, behind my knee. The crown
of my head slid open to receive the sky.

I was filled with holes. I was falling.
I tried to form a word but it was only a long,

endless moan, a moan with no bottom,
a sound I'd never heard before, rising up

from the ground: the moon rose,
& it was pocked with holes, & the stars

opened, one by one, the roof of the sky,
& I was making this sound—I couldn't stop—

it had nothing to do with me, it was holed up
inside me, I was just a rim, or a hole without a rim,

which isn't a hole at all but a   This,
I thought, is a thought I can fall through, & it stuck.

HOUR

My chest is a kind of topsoil
it always slips off in the rain
it has drawers for every insect
I tuck my head into my sternum
a rapid beak nibbling is the
most efficient form of preening
there are glands in my cheeks
I know nothing of how they work
although I am drawn to rubbing them
against the tips of car antennae
fence posts the end of a big toe
often I bite the skin of my arm
and let go the indent is a circle
of books my skin is a shelf
submerged in the air it marks
the border of an island
how happy for the land to have an eye
a string of islands is a beautiful sight
the ocean uses them to spy on us
this puddle just winked at me
Donald doesn't like me anymore
his chest is in my teeth
he reads me to sleep at night when
the wind floats the house out
from under my skin into the stars
eating so many holes
in the island the sky the weather
a sweater falling apart in my hands

HOUR

There was a lump
in the landscape

tho it had no throat
it spoke to those who

got on their knees
to listen to it

a titmouse
landed & instantly

vomited on it
blowflies

swarmed in &
stuck to it

some thought it was a
hidden camera

& therefore wept
all over it

in this way it
came to be a mound

ON CHRISTIAN HAWKEY

HAVING READ AND LIKED Christian Hawkey's collection, *The Book of Funnels,* I asked him for some poems I could send along to *Conjunctions* for this issue. Surprise! The new ones were different! As far as I could remember, the earlier ones were made up of longish lines that sometimes formed funnel-like shapes. The fourteen new ones were mostly skinny and had "Hour" in the title. I'd forgotten how part of what makes a poet's work exciting is its being different from the earlier stuff one grew accustomed to. Poetry has to be in continual motion to stay the same. The Red Queen observed something similar, and added, "If you want to get somewhere else, you must run at least twice as fast as that."

What has stayed the same is the space and the people in it, who are more like discrete body parts or geometrical shapes interacting strangely—licking, touching, piercing, moving toward and away. "His legs dangle & we all laugh, coughing quietly." The landscapes are like dumps, though of course no two dumps are the same; even a single one is a mass of contradictions. Hawkey's are like the "C & D" ("construction and demolition") variety that always threaten unprotected real estate. Indeed, in "Hour of Secret Agents" a CD-ROM is positioned on a far-off mound. In "Hour," a "lump / in the landscape," after suffering various indignities, "came to be a mound."

So moundhood is about the best thing that can happen to a landscape. Similarly, if you're hungry, you'll be lucky to get a handful of Brazil nuts, traditionally the last nuts in the jar to be eaten. If it's love you're after, consider this:

> . . . we swam out to the offshore oil barge
> & frolicked under its huge platform, touching
> its giant pylons in the cool shade & with the soothing,
> underwater sound of mechanical pumping
> we made love in the heavy water, the lifeless water,
> the kind of water we could smear on each other's faces
> & in smearing, drown.

Despite the shortage of food, scenery, and even complete human beings, all is not hopeless, since hope was never part of the deal to begin with. We rub along. Actions are begun and partially completed:

Christian Hawkey

> We're moving at the speed of goats
> over the lush & rioting landscape
> leaving a desert in our wake
> & pieces of our underwear
> & lovemaking
> & a few placental sacks,
> partially nibbled.

In "Hour of Secret Agents," "The code word, he whispered, just before / letting go, was code word." In another "Hour," "This will almost / be enough." And almost enough is, of course, enough, which in turn is as good as a feast. Better, in fact, for being no more nor less than what it offers to the observer: a glass that is simultaneously empty and refreshingly full.

—John Ashbery

From Plummet
Frances Richard

—Chosen by Martine Bellen

SOUNDS

~~~~~~~~~∧∧∧∧   = thundersheet on-air; horizon static; synesthesia for lightning

{ {   } } = time lag

/////   = giddyap; tongue clicks behind the molar

∧> ∧>   = whirrrrrrrrrrrrr; small body in departure/ landing; wings at close range

- - - - - - - - - - = self-explanatory fall; also not-falling

METEOR

layer of coolness wrapping up the hot so it can float

an accessible surface

thunder is an accessible surface ~~~~~~~∧∧∧∧

meteors

cooling by one degree or two every million years.

~~~~~~~~∧∧∧∧

on the liminal hill, silhouetted/serrated rim

of this inverted bowl we call the

~~~~~~~~∧∧∧∧

25

counting as it speeds,

bruise light on the vector.

hail the gauzy/sharpened hills, irregular

ubiquitous horizon, representative, always troping

and impervious to closeness, existing to make sense of

space, a mama. electromagnetic

billowing, raindrops

as ones and zeroes alternate as they

penetrate the upper

leaves or ground, clot

~~~~~~~~~∧∧∧∧

craven dog under the bed scrabbling

curved & piebald nails, moth

cruises pale with huge false eyes, bedraggled

of its pollen suit, novel/realistic feeling of self-

gratified melancholy, sitting on a porch or car with windows

rolled ajar, consumed, retract

retract into the narrow slot/invisible

interstice, highbeam

stroke. black county road unwinds

through wide back country, recurrent

respite from the noise.

prickles of static transit

burnished off the air, & now non-light-spill

afterdark is where the waves of piercingly

vague knowledge start
to pour out from the weeds. the vista says
hi, orphan, but that's
pleasurable, keen, added
value of the temperature, motif of
spattery rain
~~~~~~~~~~^^^^^

I do not cry out in
words but you say my name

~

if they found no weapons, no bad
chemicals in the hills, if bronze
hadn't happened, old fantasy
of elements loosed from molecular
Lego locks, dispersed
by magic chaperones, replaced into their undisturbed
geology, soothed
back to bed in virgin planet, return to your homes.

loosestrife field, a totally dismantled
& atoned-for/healed K, Wal, EZ Mart

old oil coiled back
into its gusher, vein
subsides and pulls
the crustal blanket

Frances Richard

up ~~~~~~~~~^^^^^

~~~~~~~~~^^^^^

the chassis

melts. you hunkered down

with accidence, waterlily, fiberglass, & sonic

data about the reptile, all

permeability ~~~~~~~~~^^^^^

late night, the radio call-in show, such an ingenious

and not-well-read hope. when it is wrong

to seek being comforted, and when wrong

not to, or to belong

the angry mother of all ~~~~~~~~~^^^^^

meteors on occasion coming right

through the ceiling.

magician sky

flings, nonterrestrial matter lodges

chunky in the dining-room plaster wall, a football-sized bruise

on the sleeping woman

~~~~~~~~~^^^^^

magnesium flash on the vanishing

point, city lurking plangent

in its glare

over the rise

THE GRASS WAS VERY CLEVER

shooting darts of its self-propagating split-grain
sturdiness into your socks, the fog came up
and clonked field-grazing rabbits extremely gently on the head.

Host of pie plates flashed along your fence to wow
the deer, the road unpaved itself and tilted
frighteningly toward ruts rain wrought in surreptitious

time, but recently, because the lupines know.

Blind hairpin. Dogleg into first gear gully-dip til sun scours you

from sleep into aridity. Swish-hush of sliding doors. A spider.
A tanker or a subway bores its way
into the hallucination of *wert thou my enemy*

O thou my friend

and calculates the distance in an emanating
shadow from its core. *How we achieve [that]
is a matter of consultation and deliberative—deliberation; when I say
I'm a patient man, I'm a patient man.* The grass

is armed, it is just using

your motile leg as an expedient.

Frances Richard

SNAKE

In fog a little circle of clarity
travels close, I am its center
pre-Copernicanly

a snake came to my water trough

not exactly, but I wore my brown leather sandals
on the sere, vital path, hurried through a hazeless, variegated stretch
of chufa sedge and tule and common rush where earlier the mystical
sides of dark had mooned me

{ {long-distance

conversation about how or whether/where radicality &
apathy might usefully be subject

to pastiche} }

it was hot out
my gross-motor function synced perfectly to the stubble ribbon

of the trail, my heart
unquestioningly pumping as I trotted in my short polar-fleece vest
because the fog

had recently burned and lifted in a languorous
cessation that was also a sharp snatching back, a gasp, a reeling in
off this hillside, the heavy
air inhaled

by the Pacific that discharged it, and/or relinquished
by the inland whose overnight sun-storage was immense

{ {conversation about "principles"} }

30

Frances Richard

abruptly the snake

---

in ochre and gold faded diamonds

a baby one with its triangular head poked out, its
chilling suppleness of hot-dirt-colored length extended
straight across about one-third of path, its nether tip occult still
between the narrow, close-grown, tall, tawn stalks of sedges,
timothy, ricegrass

     transfixion

         { {   {   }   } }

                      I stepped

       back

              to motionlessness

     it stayed invisibly
     breathing in its place

and then drew forward as if pouring along a downslope microtectonically
known to its underrings of muscle, from between the cool lea
of grass stems to full length on open ground and I saw its pearly
nubs of growing rattle, its tail

freely on the chopped root ends of thick growth on the path and the narrow
cylinder of space it had emerged through seamlessly

Frances Richard

{ {imagining imminent
mass-scale dissemination or
           upheaval, slow-moving
                       toppling} }

we held

the hot blue currents
of totally cloudless sky wheeled
over us and behind the everywhere light, constellations changed
a day's worth of degree in orientation

then the baby changed
its mind, reversed
and doubled, arabesqued
into a palpitating filigree of dusty marked gold, lifted
its head and climbed as if siphoning
into the higher shade edge of grass

my upright body waited and a very tranquil, diffuse, cool vapor
of adrenaline emptied out and numbed and filled the cavity
of my chest

            the baking-oxygen taste
            of barely shifting breeze was in my mouth

                  and the snake did not go back into the grass, a fissure
                  of cracked and hardened graphite-leaden mud bordered
            the path, and with an absolute skimming plunge it entered headfirst
                  and for the length of its whole body and much
                  farther, until the streamer of clear space

behind it

had been swallowed

into the long abyssal narrow crack
in the earth

and I walked a little bit
fast but mostly normally on, looking down
at my toes in my brown sandals, thinking how do I in my

diffident electricity attend to

species danger

2 ANGELS/ ASPECTS

1.

Aspects from the spectral
analysis of things—I do not know

this [settled state]
    [sovereign area]
    [a people]—look,

it has
two angles

        bluejay ,,,,,,
        bluejay ^> ^>

ads in dew or photographed
at close-up saturation, things aglitter

Frances Richard

          SUV parked
          bluejay

          ///// ^> ^>
          recycling

Flap from 2D into 3, swell and breathe
and then cardboardify.

Cheerful nylon banner
on the porch with

          [Santa] [tulips]
          [Easter bunny] [pups]

how many
discrete objects make this

household. Number
[T-shirts] [paperclips] as special providence

in the fall of
[bluejays] [airplanes]. All hold

conditions, shiver in them
slightly, Mars lights splashing

blue to red to blue on the white
day. Belief that "brittle" described

how Jell-O moves.
Thought about

what could the
"donzerly" light be.

34

2.

Or roam or surf. The war
idea redux.

Jamming the channels—then become a person
stricken like heavy

machinery, who has gone a long
meanwhile without

verbs. Become a thing
person. Garden

hose, ice
scraper with bright bristle brush. Wheelwell.

Grease. Carbonless double pink and goldenrod
sheaf—

Misreading, in the
not-yet-speaking child,

"cynicism"
for "animism" and

"loose" for
"loss."

1.

Hysterical
with tenderness or

radiant from entertaining
drone. Lubricant

of false
choice, hours

Frances Richard

in a terminal where nubbled
carpet, plate-glass

replicate. Diesel
fume or fry fume

[ghetto] [meadow]
[pasture] [blaster]

bluejay ,,,,,,
bluejay ^> ^>

Opaque—

2.

Folding
discontinuity or copula

in hinterland
made awkward, narrowcast.

Syncline or
anticline. The aspects

shove the rock upthrust
back flat into aeons and just outside

the sliders
environment begins. A skitter

on the roof, the warm
dishwasher—

Frances Richard

"NOT EPIPHANIES, BUT DILEMMAS . . ."

young mother, young
artificer

glass chimney coated in lampblack, guttering
flame, like Abe Lincoln's ma
dead of the milk-sick on corn-shuck, Illanoise, Indiana, Kaintuck

and the book stood up, dragonfly
wing on the cabin floor, yea, and it spoke to
me straightly (Olaudah Equiano the captive held

the book to his ear like tame
ocean and waited for speech)

aloud in my mind in the *Muttersprache,* straight out my finger-ends/tongue-tip
where script worn by science and prolegomena flashed
greenly at night

on the journey, the exit, cried oh

wait, I didn't mean *science*

Just that we flew up so high, in the weave
of her mouth and weird phosphorescent stuff gullied
in the mome rath outgrabe, in the rocking chair there

by the window the Palmolive Beacon would slash at us
pillar and tinkle of fairy dust (*ting!* turn the page) and in family

archives lie multiple stories relating
how I learned to read

Frances Richard

PLUMMET

Wake as we hang suspended in speed over Greenland.

Brown glacier-sawed rocks and a river of muscled ice
dumping its most severe output
into the sea

Like a jagged wealth
of stale gingerbread, iced, clastic with
frosting and studded with whitish erratics, on the doily of chaotic cake-ice

hewn fantastic geology

in the chopped china plate of the sea

No outskirts or compass like this one, banished to the
    TOP OF THE WORLD, MA! à la
paradise—lonely, inhospitable, lonely, a proof out of
Frankenstein, or how the landmass in Dante shrinks

away horrified from the
crashing-in plummet of the gigantic
sulphurous beauty of the body of Satan cast out

IT IS DRY ON THIS AIRPLANE and hard to breathe, muscle cramps
    seize the leg

~

Loved with a somewhat
unconditional love.

It plunges in, meteor
from the ether, booted out

of its universe niche. Abandonoholic
attraction to the burning cold

lake. Titanic and ripped, hard
as a paragon, angrier. Hyacinthine

38

and leonine, shower of sparks
fucking the air as it falls.

I would like a seltzer with lime, please.
I would like a curved view of continuous day to the edge.
I would like to be laid with my cheek on the fluff
of that cloud heaped like dollops of massive cream shot through
    with coral pink
instance of sunrise as we speed away without seeming
to move—

~

The altitude air
is a mouth, a Pangea of personal
everywhere, and the carved prong of Greenland has to start
somewhere, the left coast of nothing defines itself by abutting this rock:

For hours there was only Atlantic, a monotony you could get used to,
    on which
you had come to rely. And then BAM! the stale devil's food cake
of nude mountainous continent jutting
abrupt from the sea—

Hewn by topographical features, basalt shaped
by water that won't act like water, that's implacable
                stiff
                adamantine
                inimical
                hard

        but ductile, sinuous, snaking
        down, cutting the gullies, dragging its blade
        in the crustal dirt, slicing a washout

        and pouring its thickened white rivulets into the sea
        THE GLACIER IS GOING RIGHT INTO THE SEA
        back to indefinition, a waste of its form, a reunion

Frances Richard

as if rock were angry at water, and wanting to separate, flinching away
as if water clung to and clawed at and pressed on the undilute rock

                                                        a fragile tinge
                                        of hot pinkish gold fading
                                                    into the lining
                                                        of that voluptuous
                            cumulus

~

brrrrrrrrrrrrrrrrrr the drone
that so successfully levitates us

brrrrrrrrrrrrrrrrrr the cold
we flout, immune as we cruise through

brrrrrrrrrrrrrrrrrr the fear
of failing to keep impervious, of falling, finding our

selves stranded on that pinnacle without scale, marooned, abandoned
on that surface quarantined in outlaw sea

~

                    Sole rebel monster, icy

entity that touches down
along the surface, runs with it, leaps
preternaturally over chasms and fuses
suffering with ringing preference

inclement embryo

                            reject, reject
                            reject, reject

the proud
limbs and pectorals, veinous bicep

40

of the glacier choosing
to spiral off, streak
past, the stubborn emotive proto-plate
techtonics that gather angrily
up and hurl
away

What about
the outward and downward motion of repetition?

What about
the mind is its own place?

And the Lucifer face all deeply
scarred by cataclysmic

fall, withdrawal from intoxicating
grace, and how they lied and named

desire for this giant island in its barren flinty
uncomplication

GREEN

~

The indicator light
still glows, the aisle telescopes
THIS MUST THOU EAT, and I ate the world

   —it was granular, dry, in sharp crumbs, it poked
   the membranes and abraded them, stuck
   in the gorge and gagged a bit, but sweet

   disappearing

speck pushed away by constant engines, swallowed in
albumen atmosphere

41

Frances Richard

NOTES

The grass was very clever: "wert thou my enemy, O thou my friend" is Gerard Manley Hopkins, from the sonnet beginning "Thou art indeed just, Lord . . ." The second italicized voice is George W. Bush, quoted in the *New York Times*, August 22, 2002, p. A1.

"not epiphanies, but dilemmas . . .": Abraham Lincoln's mother, Nancy Hanks, died of "the milk sick" (passed to humans via cows' milk and caused by a toxin in white snakeroot weed) in 1817, when her son was nine years old. The story of Olaudah Equiano and "the trope of the talking book" appear in Henry Louis Gates, Jr., *The Signifying Monkey: A Theory of African-American Literary Criticism* (Oxford University Press, 1988).

Plummet: Satan's face is described in Milton, *Paradise Lost* I, 596-621. "Top of the world, Ma!" is Jimmy Cagney in *White Heat* (1949). Description of landmass withdrawing from Satan's body is in Dante, *Inferno* XXXIV, 122-6. "The mind is its own place" is *Paradise Lost* I, 254. "This must thou eat, and I ate the world" is from an account of a dream by Ralph Waldo Emerson, in Robert D. Richardson, Jr., *Emerson: The Mind on Fire* (University of California Press, 1995).

ON FRANCES RICHARD

IN THE LINE "thunder is an accessible surface ~~~~~~~~~^^^^^ "
(from "Meteor"), ~~~~~~~~~^^^^^ completes a semantic proposition. How would one syntactically diagram this line? How
does a reader verbalize the word "thunder" as opposed to
"~~~~~~~~~^^^^^ "? Or in the poem "2 Angels/Aspects," might one
read "donzerly" light and hear "dawn's early" light? Read "cynicism" and think "animism"? Richard's delightfully complicated
poems probe the secrets that lie hidden below the surface of sound,
word, referent. Here sound becomes an accessible surface. She exposes what we hear as opposed to what we say, exposes the synapse
between sound and meaning. She lovingly honors nonverbal verbiage
as well as verbal precision.

Frances Richard tells me that in *Plummet*, she writes "about falls
of all kinds, from Icarus to bombs," yet as I read these poems I am
reminded of the unearthing of space and natural history—". . . the
fog came up / and clonked field-grazing rabbits extremely gently on
the head"—how interdependent nature and technology have become, "SUV parked / bluejay"—how ultimately we don't fall but
transform into space and light, "a fragile tinge / of hot pinkish gold
fading / into the lining / of that voluptuous / cumulus."

These poems are situated in history—personal, political, religious,
and literary. In them Richard converses with her forebears, in one
instance inscribing a variant of D. H. Lawrence's "Snake." Her
snake, like his, is the gold venomous type, only hers is a baby. Hers,
too, like his, disappears into a dark hole in the earth, but in Richard's
poem ". . . the streamer of clear space / behind [the snake] / had been
swallowed / into the long abyssal narrow crack / in the earth."
Richard's space is eaten by mother earth. The poem "Plummet"
cites a dream Emerson had in which he said, "THIS MUST THOU
EAT, and I ate the world." In the poetic field drawn by Richard, "The
altitude air / is a mouth, a Pangea of personal / everywhere . . ." The
space of the mouth, the place where sounds are formed, is the privi-
leged transitional space of these poems. It is the orifice that leads us
to the interior land on which Richard's soundscapes are carved.
"Plummet" concludes with "speck pushed away by constant
engines, swallowed in / albumen atmosphere." We are swallowed
back into our history, into an interior child space. We return to the
albumen of an egg.

Frances Richard's poems return us to a beginning and offer an

43

Frances Richard

alternative path to tread on. "Snake" draws to a close with the poet in a state of contemplation, distinct from Lawrence, who, at the end of his poem, throws a clumsy log at the snake, regretting that he heeded "voices of [my] accursed human education." Clearly Frances Richard has her human education in mind and *Plummet* is her response to it. But, unlike Lawrence, she has nothing to regret. Her poems embrace the wisdom of her fathers without forfeiting twenty-first-century concerns of time, space, and prosody while not sacrificing the human instinct to feel awe and to honor. When reading these poems, which present a fully realized vision in perfect pitch, we find ourselves in a world that embraces us and that we embrace, one that swallows us and that we swallow, a world that at times appears cruel, but is rich and powerful and plentiful so that even as we plummet, or read "Plummet," we similarly - - - - - - - - - - -.

— *Martine Bellen*

Six Poems
Peter O'Leary
—*Chosen by Nathaniel Mackey*

THREE MIGRATIONS

I. CRANES/(*gruidæ*)

Migrating, not an ancestor of, not a proto-crane,
but a crane, already in
V formation with other cranes, riding on the humid tropopause, splitting
the unworldly symmetries of lenticular
altocumulus on the crest of a leewave of airflow
over the emerging Sierras—: it's

47 million years ago. Eocene air bloats with nitrogen, numinous
with oxygen. The earth adrift below the crane
is iceless. Cenozoic patterns of land abide intact
in the saran cortex; its movement
remains there, a map of continents
migrating.

Everywhere stilts line the marshes. Grasses pervasive. That
grallatorial shoreline.

II. (HWHY)

Those whited regions where you go to hide from God.
Their *lumen mysterium*. Remember: the name of God
in a torrential firestorm of starbirth
spallated, flecked. Vast solitude of that name, its gravity.
In the deserts, men have kept the name. Devising from its bits
liturgies. Followers of an eremolatrous God who
loves the waste for its nowhere, contemplating
its originary light, who spelt it:

𝈕𝈐𝈑𝈎

Peter O'Leary

They kept the Tetragrammaton in paleo-Hebrew lettering even
as the Jewish book-hand style of the Herodian period flowed.
But the living can praise thee even as thou wearest the oldest alphabetic
robes. *Even those who stumble can laud thee* but we
cannot imagine thy consonance except as it clatters in
our hoariest nomination. *The LORD has heeded the voice of those who love*
HIS NAME.

    —wondrous, knowledge & insight . . . wondrous firmaments . . . in the
      essence of light, splendor of every
    form of wondrous spirits . . . . . . godlike beings, fearfully powerful, all . . .
      utterly holy . . . praise
    lifted up . . . their wings . . .—

Toil. Fresh wine & fresh oil. Months, years in a treeless desert.
Writing. Copying & praising. A hidden knowledge of God
spooled in a clay urn in a cave. Ripples of liquid alkali evaporate
in scorching sunlight at the bottom of the world.
Circa 30–50 CE.

1956, in Cave II at Qumran, scroll IIQPs^a was discovered
in the Judæan Desert. It was unrolled
in 1961. Thickest surface of any of the scrolls—calfskin, perhaps, & not
sheepskin. Writing on the grain side. The scroll contains 28 incomplete
columns of text. A liturgical collection of psalms & hymns in noncanonical
order.

Embedding אֲדֹנָי for God.

Names are immigrants from the past. "You
are more Jewish than you realized."

III. Lux Contemplatio

There is a change and migration of the soul from this world to another.
                                 —Plato

Since the time of the human decision to cultivate grasses, to harvest
sunlight, to feed on ruminants, in the Levant
where the growers of seeds thrived, developed cultures, "as to cult
as well as production"; since the time

46

11,000 years ago of forgoing nomadic life—opening us
to tooth decay, cholera, malaria, influenza, plague, hemorrhoids—;

since the time three millennia ago the Jahwist
on tanned calfhides stroked the Hebrew uncials that showed
God as an alphabet forming a man from earth-ash, from mud;

since the time in 1911 when Amundsen left Frauheim Base
with twelve dogs pulling each sled

since December 14 when he set foot on the earth's antipodes
measuring sun with sextant

there is no place anymore for us to migrate. The need
yet remains.

Antarctica means now an interior domain. Curiosity
about our inner life increases. A nomad's desert God is an inward
generator. Our outward movement yields our soul's circumincession,
its insitting

in rotation with the divine abeyance,
in contemplations inrapt in spirit
meekly abiding in an inward beholding to know ourself
in the inward virtues of the soul which *the soul hath in continual experience,*
illumynynge
the light of *verry knowleche.*

Prayer is our migration; stillness is our movement.
These continents of insight adrift in our midst. Thoughts,
rifted, rise
& fall.

Come then to the house of your own knowledge:
strive to confine
your incorporeal being within
your bodily house.

Peter O'Leary

THEOPHANIES

—*For Pam Rehm*

I. A LITANY

For Abraham, it was numberless sands, shapeless stars, a voice dropped into the porches of his ear.
For Sarah, it was a vacant womb at ninety filled.
For Hagar, it was promise & desertion. A human jealousy she bore.

For Moses it was his stuttering tongue. Vitreated, unconsuming light of the Backside.
For David, it was slaying & entempling. The wish to carry out Will & Law in his inward parts.
For Absalom it was incest, a gibbeting in a tree's crook.
For Solomon it was a mindful absorption.
For Elijah it was thirst & flame.
For Elisha it was baldheadedness, child-mauling she-bears at this beck.
For the Book of Job it was the introduction into the world of an enormous woe. Disequilibrously.

For Isaiah it was mortal terror on seeing the Enthronement.
For Jeremiah it was an experience of the divine as devastating shock.
For Ezekiel—he lived when the Buddha did—it was to be so afflicted with anxiety as to not stop trembling;
to be forbidden to mourn his wife's death;
to be forced to eat excrement, for months.
For Daniel it was to stare into the sun as if midnight;
to see God at last more than two millennia later through Freud's shaded hypnagogic eyes.

For us it is that massive Book, its pages we wore out turn over.

II. AN ELEGY

—*In memory of Mark Krupnick (1939–2003)*

It's a mystery of the God of Abraham
in whose aura a choral amen

echoes that awful name "I Am."
All our life we gain no time

in the ornamentation. A hymn
of the mystery of the God of Abraham

—once sung, once loved—lost its claim
in the bright steady lumen

burning that frightful name "I Am,"
whispered in the prophet's sacrum,

an emptiness in the kingdom's crown,
its mysterium. The God of Abraham

endures latter-day sym-
bolic species, soulful or warm or known.

Echoes. Full of awe, I name, I am
an adorer of the blame-

less emanational forceful indwelling mystery of the God of Abraham

echoing the awe he named I Am.

III. A CATASTROPHE

> *Butt nowe they desyre a better, that is to saye a celestiall. Wherfore god is not ashamed of them, even to be called their god: for he hath prepared for them a citie.*
>
> —*The pistle unto the Ebrues*, XJ. Chapter, Tyndale trans. (1526)

Subdermal lightning, vascular airstrikes, suture-loosening trepanation of
    thunder—:
photophobia. In the prayer-ruins, a body worries the episcopic inner-seeing
necessary after this disaster. Heavenly meteorite that pocks the private surface
blisters the mirror of your contemplation.
Spirit-weather drives us in. In.

Withdrawing God sucked back from the light rendered like fat from a goose.
  Her
excess is my simmering lipids. Cushion of St. John's wort
he rattled onto, chamomile aroma he
floated from. The utterance was agony,
sorrow. A catanyctic sigh. Life.

In one way or another fear is absolutely indwelling—:
you fear you only use this moment to forget
nothing from within is outside God.

A heart crumbles in heartbreak. Drones of rain

ensue. History.

The World.
Its receding, unreachable innerness.

HYMNOS

The icon is a copy & the image is a man.
God mirrors the schism with xpc in Word-Made-Flesh. An echo
body. Its distortions buzz with *epistrophe.* Golden

luminosity infolded, inverted into that
densest atmosphere expanding. Archaic echoes of
light refracted, sounded, engrained in air, in flesh,

in wood, in word. As God to xpc so light to icon, so
mind to image sound depths radiance embalms in a
syrup of aura, an amber the protozoan

insectiform swims through on frozen hinges. Like a book
hasped in brass buckles, locked but no less emanant for its
closed cover of uncreated energies pulsating

on the prolongations of a generative syllable.
Void. God. Mirror. Schism. xpc. Star-spalls. Vivid static. Uplift.
Inward, made flesh. The icon abiding is the image.

The copy is the world, formed in likeness, given difference
even the summer leaves refract in shadows vibrating
through the windows staining the aisles that lead to paradise,

realm of golden penumbra an icon in symbol
embodies, represents. To be before the world, before
the light showering into it. Source & reflection both.

The difference between icon & image inflates in a
circuitry of innerness, metaphor, & dream. Coils
of depth, taxied by messengers of the imagination,

spiral, braid, plait the name of God they wind down into
primal molecule adorned with a crown of electrons.
The body, bronze with atoms, is the icon, theophoric.

*

The Holy Spirit moves through the image's vibration,
descending through celestial hierarchies, tiers of angel-
matter, compressed elements, sound-tracked with tungsten pings &

filamental slurs of information: humming strings, dark
plasma. In the world on molten waves of heat rides
the Paraclete, yielding a sap as he passes through light.

Holy Spirit is oil. A seal. Oleoresin. A
myrrhic cool in condensation. An empire Enoch
coins. Sojourning scriptural species. Anointed. Oiled. Sealed.

Harvest the uranium of mystical language; bind
its instabilities into radiating tensions.
Accelerate all the words into smashed atmospheres: God's.

*

Peter O'Leary

The name of God's star is redemption & the sickness of
the hopeless it relieves in the distant light it sheds
shadows the future with briefest glow of the kingdom

haunting all our work. *Scientia.* Ignorance of
Hebrew. Mystery language, mystery people. Stranger
in Greek reassembled in Cyrillic. Byzantine

filagree holding those relics of alpha, omega—
its celebrant, its homilist, its healer. An icon
contains a nacreous imago of energy burning

with starlight, platonic & evolving from that heat &
incandescent speed with & out of which God uttered
holy logos, polarizing in a beam of myth

the Word, glistening in firmament, shivered within
complex radiance & error: eros. Blackness beyond
night in our innermost ear where we listen in absolute

ink of binding silence, crucial emptiness of prayer.
My God is alien, speaks an alien tongue whose pass-
word is bafflement. Shibboleth of zeros. *Love. Love me*

as my father, he warns. *Love the other, love the utter-
most stranger.* Diligence. Proximity. Awe-harvester.
Uranium of mystical language. Unstable Lord.

*

Traumas of light exceed the visible barrier,
pool in the gouges of icons, evaporating what
gold loosens in the oxidation. God is above all

the name for the pressure to be alive in the world, to
be open to further pressures & their vexations.
Vinegar. The mind flooded by excitation. Breakdown.

Theopathy. Gall to eat. A growing love of God.
The openness that is a loneliness. *Touching the Al-
mighty, we cannot find him out. Shaddai*—we cannot

attain to him. *Tabret.* Brimstone scattered upon his
habitation. *Brooks of honey & butter. The honey
in the pulp.* Breadth. Icons. Icon & man in unison.

*

Piety—: barbs of it. Lent in the private tendence of
brotherhood, monk to monk. Luminous cone rising out of
the icon. Vanilla lather for washing his hands. Light

focused into the isotone, adamantine. Layered.
Not harmony, not augmentation. Only splendor, its
consubstantiation, its peerlessness. Andrei Rublev

admitted nothing to transcendence not even as he
sculpted from its energies, facing annihilation.
Nothing more private than God could intervene, nothing

he cared to share more than such privacy. He spat into
his hands, warmed them by rubbing them. Light was tinge. And the tinge
was prismatic, holy. He adored the light & painted.

AWE

–For John Taggart

I.

The reverencer enters the dreadcomb: HEAVEN—he plunges to the
    depths of the Earth,
ore pools thunderfoam inward within shadow, a fermentated
liquid & soul—: genuflection.
Feel the full weight of air exalted bearing down onto your shoulders, your
head, bow before it. Falling into the brilliant residence, work
shades the churches' interiors, spirit mirroring their umber hulls the
    acolytic eye
dives through, gold-glazed, in an ordeal of divination.
What is your bird, your weird?
Angel-formed domes of air, their height an antipodal pit of earth, winged
with exquisite plumage: thrones, crowns, inwoven with Adamant, with

threads of African saffron, bow to the ground, sepulchral, exultant.
Apseward, ranked on the nave-walls, in rising hierarchies drawn
with original lutrescence,
abounding figures ascend, look down. Consumed in aura, they join with
& depend on what spreads this light
bearing it up like pillars. *Caritas* looks onward into centuries
from the depths the light the Godshape hives in,
abides in,
rests on.

II.

Reverence is a language its grammar tacticians occultate in lexicons &
permutated Laws pulsating to us from some simultaneous realm. Moses—
an originator—
feared the God in a cloud undulating softly a pillowy Brownian motion
through the darkness. That horrid nimbus.
And his adherence to its unforeseen reflections. But his Law
is a kind of direct speech. His prayers
made the legends on the atlas of paradise, dusted with pumices
culled in the angelic ossuaries, stacked with pellucid femurs & skulls of
    gold-leaf,
apprehensible.
Deception is a poetry buried in linguistics. Our language scientizes during
    our
apneatic sleep. Praise the poets
who phosphoresce the grammars only cautiously; uplift
their images as artisans did the saints,
but leave your jars of spent oil along the pediments.
Where they spoil.

III.

> *a plume of smoke, visible at a distance*
> *in which people burn*
> —George Oppen, "Of Being Numerous"

Revere the *Sea of Substance*, gold indefinite radiation
of the background. At Pisa, the depth is Cimabue's tesserated head & xpc
rises beyond it.
Magnitudes. Corridors of Islamic math interpreted toward the altar. In the

Dome
of the Rock space
is gem-cut. Facets
make light
interesting. Thus, God.

What do I love in the world to make my palms sweat in the mass? The
  sense
of daily suffocations burying me
in calms,

terrors? The problem of awe is one of darkness, sustainer & encloser.
  Suave
consciousness I hope reflected in the apse.
Rising tiers of saints I remember.
The body's lamp is cosmophotic, the eye of prayer who sees it in its
cryptopatric cell, the heart—luxosomatic—
a thesaurus. Treasure
mysterious entries, hallow the secret father whose
tenebrated lumen breaks up
looming.

How great is such darkness that it pools & flumes? It's our tremors &
  ecstasy
at the tomb. The linenless benches within.
The bone robe. The boy.
And the fear we feel in two thousand years, saying nothing,
fleeing the scene.

—See Mark 16:8

Peter O'Leary

WITNESSING IS THE SAINTS THEMSELVES

—*For Fanny Howe*

But there exists not only the visible world (albeit in a spiritualized mode); there is also the invisible world wherein the divine blessing, like metal melting, streams in the deified reality.

—Pavel Florensky, *Iconostasis*

Whatsoever is manifest, that thing is light. The soul in paraphrase is
   sentenced
to hissing static, a robed basement florescence, the pit
of a feeling   •   plunging it into the next deepest reality—

DIVINE DARKNESS:CALIGO DIVINA

Beyond my belief God coiling abides wound inward into fangled
densities, strobed
in ash of *logos*—burnt from XPC—fireflies
irradiate in micropulsions, sculpted dusk minutiæ, tiny
sprent lights.

Theopath   •   admit it

Gold is not a color but a tone.
The icon is executed upon light.

56

Does this make the icon—thus constituted—available
to a blind man, spiritually
or otherwise?

Take the Orthodox Church at Ráckeve, founded by Serbs emigrated
to the grasslands of Hungary
along the Duna. In 1487.

Toward this church I had sympathetic precognition. From the guidebook
where I saw it depicted   •   in my thought
something remains within
withdrawn.

When all the images have been categorized, captured, named   •
    a photic
aphasia, a lightless
passive feeling toward God excited
in contemplation   •   sounding God.

As depths.

You enter a church as you worship an icon. You worship
an icon as you enter a cave.

Ráckeve is a monolith of niveous zinc, sinless rising
out of the world. The black door
is all shadow.

Against the Prussian blue of the day.

57

Through the dark hole of the door you enter the space
of the soul, its cleansed
external sheltering the thickened blessing of the internal. That infolded
   vastness.

The sky is all the saints   •   the Last Judgment
is eternal present & XPC
is multiplied,
fully formed in each of the rapidly involved two dimensions
of Heaven
dwelling in propulsive room—:

the Earth.

Transfigured   Θ   crucified   Θ   born
incarnated in saintly avatars.

A votive totality in carefully hewn proportions. Were I
not camera-goggled snapping
surprising digital simulacra of the inside I would

have knelt into the privacy of a wall-eyed prayer
an astigmatic speculum
shining its inaccessible light on my quietism.

We live in a semipermeable anopsia where the species of saints is the
   translucency
of an insight, a chromatism,
a grace.

Peter O'Leary

UNCENTERING

che col tuo lume mi levasti
—Paradiso I.75

An arch
of your speech
in the newness of the sound & the greatness of the light bows its
    transhuman shadow
across the *beatitude* of river & birth.
The world. Patiently metabolizing sunlight.
Cicada-buzz the plumey air is buffed with. Remembering you
through a fogroom of summer. Incessant rising & sinking of the
    atmosphere slurry
interpretation into weatherwatching. Air. Condensation. Motion. An
    oceanic flame
of dawn crystal streamers falling from the clouds
oxygenate. Humid morning world in the middle of the land—a
    weathercell. Drawing
light like a singularity.

Thunder unearths abundant nightmare ore: the boy
quavers, woken. Stays up for hours, uncomforted. Fear is a light
hot as a cone of flame, not so quickly snuffed. Dread,
a geology, lingered in the gathered layers
of the body, a kind of time. Grief,
not so much a weather as a metaphysics of prediction, prophecy's
    revenant-brother.
The clouds, inseminated with *aqua vita*, roil into mood; everpresent,
    gloriated. Anthelioned.

All things have order, informing the universe like God.
Eternal value encodes growth into every cell, every helix, every pattern
where it tends. Order is not destiny. Rather, inclination.
It moves us nearer or farther from our origin.
Your impulse in me is a weather. Your best idea a feeling.
Your being is a forecast.
An outlook.
It permeates every motivation, adhering the earth together,
bearing fire to the moon.
Mindlessly. Love is the mind. Erotic or compassionating.

Peter O'Leary

The climate of your living hurries into rotations spun by the winds,
hyperheated by pyrocumular torches, from the vast forest fires you
   sparked

a great telluric bonfire   •   your whole art.

Our lives are the air's where the songs stream.

Even as you cannot bear it you are borne by it
into circulations. Song
unwinds you. And the living light
spreads from cloud to cloud.

Struck by the rogative plaints I'd issue,
I pause. It's clear.
The clouds bunch, foil.
I miss you.

—Paradiso I.103-41

ON PETER O'LEARY

IN "THICK DARKNESS," an address on poetry and spirituality deliv-
ered in 2003 at Westminster Presbyterian Church in Buffalo, Peter
O'Leary (following in the footsteps of one of his poetic models,
Robert Duncan, who delivered a sermon, "Crisis of Spirit in the
Word," there in 1982) spoke of "darkness visible . . . both appearance
and transparence." He cited Dante's "dark wood" and Pseudo-
Dionysus's "darkness of unknowing" on his way to declaring,
"Toward such darkness I would have my writing tend. In the light of
this gloom, I want my writing to be *pneumatic*, or *insufflating*. . . .
Insufflating means 'breathed out from within.' . . . In my mind a
pneumatic poem must be in accordance with Olson's breath-based
projective verse. A poem comes then from the lungs, which I believe.
Just so, a poem can have a visual breath. In paring down his language,
in anagrammatizing words and ideas, in demonstrating how to *see*
words in order to begin to transform them into poetry, Ronald Johnson can teach us, as he taught me, the act of breathing with the eye."
   O'Leary initiated a correspondence with Johnson in 1992 and
visited him several times in San Francisco. Mentored by him until
his death in 1998, O'Leary, at Johnson's request, became his literary
executor and has edited two posthumous volumes of Johnson's
work, *To Do As Adam Did: Selected Poems* (Talisman House, 2001)
and a collection of last poems, *The Shrubberies* (Flood Editions,
2001). In addition to his work with Johnson, O'Leary's education
includes several years at the University of Chicago, where he received an A.B. in English in 1990 and from whose divinity school he
received a Ph.D. in 1999, specializing in religion and literature. Born
in Detroit in 1968, he has lived mainly, in recent years, in Chicago,
a city whose architectural wealth has proven significant to his work
(Louis Sullivan's Holy Trinity Russian Orthodox Cathedral in particular); he has taught at the School of the Art Institute of Chicago
since 2000 and for briefer stints at Columbia College, DePaul
University, and elsewhere. Also significant to his work has been
travel, such goings and seeings as a lengthy stay in Greece in 1994,
especially on the island of Patmos, where he first encountered
Orthodox iconography, and a year spent in Vienna in 1997–1998, his
first deep immersion in opera.
   As his poems in this issue of *Conjunctions* make evident, Peter
O'Leary is a religious, iconographic poet, seeking, as he puts it in
"Thick Darkness," to "revive an aspect of the religious sciences"

Peter O'Leary

in and through his work—"a risky undertaking," he admits. Citing
Mandelstam's assertion that Dante's work belongs to the *futuram*,
he goes on to say, "To write religious poetry is to remake the future
in our present image." It's heartening to find the future in such
erudite, adroit, resourceful hands.

—*Nathaniel Mackey*

Twenty-Five Poems
Graham Foust

—Chosen by Robert Creeley

WHY I AM NOT A PAINTER

The most difficult beautiful

thing I think
to paint would be

a close-up, a close-up of

a single square
of toilet tissue

floating

in a bowl.
Or so I'm told.

No matter, my bad.

This heart of earth of mine
can only hear

is only yours.

Graham Foust

JUMP

A wind comes. We stand in it.
We stand in said wind
and under starlight,
much of which might
well not exist.

Word for dead
for word we are
the distance, flames
in snow. God,
the body is odd—

the most remote and unacceptable
of luxuries, in fact. I think
think think once
in a while.

BALMORAL

Things'll get
all right,

the infield strangely green.

I can't tell you
who'll win,

who'll suffer,

how old
I wish I were.

It's always this—

just shoved into something
I never could have made.

Graham Foust

MALL

soft as some blood
begins a corridor
of things

and what to your wondering

eyes should appear,
should stand perishable
there—

hard flowers, an hour, your film

WAKING LATE ON HALLOWE'EN

I'm just grinding
some iris here,
when who demands
my aid?

Sung up from the far-
off interest of sleep
is an insect-sudden music,
a pain-blue light.

Shadows cross, cross
and uncross,
as absent
to what finds them.

Night reads the day to me.
Orange children steering
through the street scream
screams.

Graham Foust

HEREIN

A sober-dumb someone at home,
you'd like
to just injure these dishes, fist
a towel.

That backyard brain of mixed sticks
means nothing.
This pissy fence is nothing, un-path
to other grass.

You look up and gutted
of waves,
afford morning. You are blind
as a mouth.

You are
inconsequentially shrill.

IN THE SPACE PROVIDED

On a near-
suicidally clear
day of wind—

a day like
a day like

television—

I wake to find
that summer
has been detonated.

World is automatic.
That tree's a gust

of blood.

SHIFT CHANGE (THE OLD PINK, BUFFALO, NY)

I'll have
whatever shadows

you say
I've been having

for the last
blank elixir

of your unborn
afternoon.

Or human jam,
my body

of parts back, thanks.
That

and your nourishing
shove.

SUBURB

Thrown-
up glyph

of moon
your smile

is savagely
exact.

HUFFY

August, the dull end
of summer where I'm
from—I've a grill, shrewd
tools, a bag of glue,
some Neil Young. The world
eats what it orders.
My neighbors cough and
wave and wave and frown.
Your youngest cousin
weaves by on a shit-
to-bed ten-speed, two
crutches tucked under
his too-white right arm.
This is to refer
to almost falling
from falling. It's a
dream I'm not ashamed.

MORNING BELL

to space's constant
swallow comes

a small
unslaughter—

a song for once
a sliver

Graham Foust

AFTER ARETHA FRANKLIN

Baby, I know

but not much,
enough.

We are two
breathing people
in a room.

The rest, the rest

is as emphatic,
scratched out.

The meaning of a cruelty
is its hurry,
its use.

GOOGLE

All the fish look shitty
on their ice today,
the fruit like a dull
pile of metal.

A dead bag commutes
between the street
and the trees.

The sky goes
both its ways.

I never find you.

Graham Foust

DAY JOB

What's it *not* like?
I'm all memory,

plight.

The poem is
the poem's

is a snag.

And breath's the boned-
in thought—

I don't wonder.

The unconscious
is structured like

a bladder.

FORMAL

Pretend you don't bleed. Pretend
to not bleed. Pretend
not to bleed—

run cold water on it.

And doubt lights up
like some sudden and
unnecessary good.

ELIMINATIVE

Near some crawling bruise
of river,
it went something like:

"I couldn't see, and did."

Bad guitar, my sad capacity:
I guess that's just
how that bird sings

to vanish me. How day and the bank disagree.

Leaking away,
I'll drop you,
shape.

Go ahead and feed me that hole.

TO A BROKEN PAY PHONE

You,
you bored totem,

are out of your face.

I, too, riot
to hear

if I can hear.

Graham Foust

SURRENDER

This next one's the first. The rain's there.
Lie down in these names, these stems of names.

Spring screams us clean.
The sun's making sense in the west.

Afternoon unfolds into another kissless corner.
What is is lost space, a little wind.

A ventriloquist, then.
Some no one, autumn-close.

Stay.
Go home.

Throw your arms around me.

BOOK

itself
and whatever

else
you were doing

ANALYTIC OF THE BEAUTIFUL

An anapest of shadows, a stutter
there of sun. Alone, over,

we hover at
our door.

This house isn't falling, but we keep it
like a leaf. After glass after glass,
what's the opposite

of closet? The opposite of prism
or of plastic?

This is a waste of good dusk. Just
fuck me. Just help me put
the wind herein

to mouth to mouth
to mouth.

LEAVE IT TO MY GHOST TO KNOW ME

No lover like
the body,
no traitor

like same. The touch.
The fuss.
The little millions.

KID A

What are you painting,
saying, making
as plain—

afraid, frayed, playing
pained—
a business?

The radio?
Rainwater?
Cake?

A contraption from which
we'll back away
not unafraid?

What with all that waste
to get to: Make it up as you fade.

ANALYTIC OF THE SUBLIME

Limping like flames
along awkward
rock

not me, but naked
replicas
of me.

A hallway of faltering
parts
I can't shadow.

Me
and naked replicas
of me.

VACATION

A brawl
of water, the sea
is not radiant.

One window, light
licking at
its slits.

A brawl of water
is all
I ever wanted.

One window,
light licking at
its slits.

CLOUDS

Such things as
the law

fall on us.

There are nameless shapes.
There are tears

of understanding.

"Here,
        catch."

Not a map in the world.

Graham Foust

On Graham Foust

Curious one should think of the way that trickles of water would then find paths down the edge of the street after rain, the way one would squat for hours contriving diversions, little dams of twigs and pebbles, bits of stick, dirt, paper. Then float leaves on the current still persisting, watching the progress of them either end up in a cul de sac, else sail off in proverbial glory. I was supposed to be getting home after school, but this was far more interesting.

Graham Foust's poems are "far more interesting" and find their way through like impedances, moved on by just such currents. Think of the myriad "rhetorics" that overlay our speaking. "Hey there!" "Sir?" And so on, not to mention all the frames and habits, which (that!) make saying anything (something? *some* thing?) so freighted. There is also the *pace* as in W. C. Williams's "The old horse dies slow . . . ," if you know that poem. These poems move in close to luxuriant circles, round and round each particular syllable, neither hurrying nor dragging behind—just there. At times there seems an almost physical presence to them, a third dimension, which is substance.

There are years between us but we meet nonetheless in these places, thinking ("I think / think think once / in a while")—*thinking*. In fact, he's the first person who ever moved me to look up the etymology of that word *think:* "tong-. To think, feel . . . Old English *thancian,* to thank . . ." Anyhow, methinks I owe this poet thanks for fact of us both finding wit in stone and much else. He feels, therefore he knows.

—*Robert Creeley*

Twenty-Six Poems
Sarah Lang
—*Chosen by Forrest Gander*

I.

It is 4 a.m. It is early morning. It is summer and so it is
already light. And it is warm. You have everything.

A field guide, not given to overstatement, lists broad,
strong wings. Folding blueberries into batter; the dog's nose
is up my skirt. The taste of benzodiazepine and/or paroxetine.

We had chemistry if not a future. You tell the story. Your hand within
hair's reach. In comparison I'm largely asexual. I am largely asexual. Eating
berries saved from batter. It would have never occurred to me. The feeder
near empty. The dew not evaporated. I wish you wouldn't wear that.

Sarah Lang

What I must look like. A red glass bowl. A spoon. I am not
pregnant. You say I would look beautiful pregnant. The low taste
of dried apple. The juice of an orange run down my wrist.

If this fails, I will have nothing. I will have left nothing.
Oh, with the way I've been sleeping, I mean.

———————

We broke this body in a pact. For all
your intentions. We made a deal. You and I.
We had a sort of contract involving this body.

This doesn't mean you're off the hook.

the fruit, flower of
the shape
the use of

I'll not be the woman come wading. Come pant legs cuffed.
Come delivering.

Trucks go by. Thunder goes by.

Which is precisely my point. Your hand cool glass. The kids thrown
out in the yard. We're out of tomatoes.

Your tucked starch. Think I don't know my own line of youth. Not
so fast, mister smarty pants. Slipped into family.

Shake my head. Drag you and that cheap kayak in.

―――――――――

The taste of methamphetamines. I'm clean out of apologies.
Proceed. Your lawn art: steel sculpture, the odd bowling ball
and pin. The postal service threatening you. Shovel. Light
through thinly sliced rhubarb, a pear, bread. Asthenia. Cutlery. A thin
waist. Water over plate. Over ceramic basin.

Sarah Lang

What placed you here. What is reflex, light,
we live in your memories; I squint in your
figurative shadow. Tea you can handle. The light
a great battle. Tell you what, finish something.
The feeder, the chickadees with a great
precision. Oatmeal for itching; onion
for insects. A prayer of determination as though
there were other kinds. Protect this meager shell.

––––––––––

Hadar before Antares. Altair before Acrux. There is art
you can't touch. Can't learn right up into. Look

point by point. You calculate with precision. I accept
your eager trot. I probably sing you. My skin

a stretched hide. Upward from the cheek. Of taste
conjured. If talent fails. What is real, what is hallucinated

emotion. A house, a bicycle, an uneven brick walk. What
is present, proper. The way I've been sleeping.

A shell. A kettle as symbol of calm broken. Failed
the bulb held in hand. Failed each motion

of civility. I lost concentration. An empty
glass. Expectation lingers as a loose

floorboard. The weather will not turn. What
I have lost.

———————

In the movement of my arm a line opens.
As an unused window there is no grace. Tell me

if this hurts. The days are occupied. There are many
motions of human hand; of branch; turnips and carrots

keep well if buried in sand. What I have endured. A dew
turned late frost, weather. Tell me

what this feels like, if it hurts. When I press. I promised
I wouldn't write. The blood of a cut line. The cool glass.

Glacial. A fine eye line. Railing. One. Come
close. This will change. You say I would look. Left
like this late light I will never be a mother. A blue

wall. A making of space. Containers. A thin shell,
waist rising. Off the hook. Scot-free. The kids
thrown out. Gladiolas. A stone

smoothed over. The art you can touch. Flannel. The warm
handle of a car door. Or, a quarter cup of rice. The calories
in tea. Fireweed. The coast on which an arbutus peels.

———————————

The process of not having remembered differs greatly from that
of forgetting: there is no record to misplace. Of light or of light

filtered. What is necessity. Today a slow sequence. A pale cheek
to pale tile. Today green. White. White. White. Green. In slips,
lists. By rote. Today I slept. A movie slips. What is real, what is

hallucinated. The motion of a line opening. What I must look like. Today
I took it easy, which differs from accepting there is nothing to be done.

II.

For three inches, I turned the knife in your neck. I watched
with the word covet. For forty-five days, I missed your hair.

In a borrowed apartment I held this contentment. You gagged
as a slit shell. Your eyes opened as the blue wing of a jay, as
yawn. My tongue in your ear listened to your throat

sing. Those weren't scabs you fingered; but you always did sail
clean on through. For your olives and dry cleaning. For your happiness
I opened as an unused window, without grace and wailing.

———————————

We have no curtains. On the twenty-seventh floor,
I roll my knuckles along your jaw. I was once
inelegant. You knew what you taught. A red vase
with modern arrangement. The view. Desipramine,
lithium carbonate. I don't know if I'm polite. I have lost
perspective. The labels are scratched off; your eyes
are closed. I'm sure there are trees. That there is wind
and that the wind goes through leaves.

Next to your shin I'm hairless. Take the edge off; blue
as a steel beam. Bear down. Friday: mace and crocus,
carnelian, cooking. My leg opens cold
as a prayer. I'm largely contorted; I am largely
wrong. You've tied my feet. But you never did
hear a word I said. This is not determination.

Hepatica, my lips blue-eyed grass. Sonata.
I used to sleep unaided. Four weeks
and a day. Neisseria, your breath crawls.

This is the harbor where I rig your happiness. One thing
into another: you cover my mouth; I play dead. The sheet breathes
and I do not. For twenty-eight days, I pierce an artery; I wring

your joy. While you're up, I wring your joy. With faint
obligation, I wring your joy. As a rope hangs silent
and without forgiveness, with ease, I wring your joy.

For twenty-eight days get your hands dirty. Near the shore,
tear the flesh from a wild bird. Carve soapstone. Walk thrice
where thieves are hanged. Iron your own shirt.

———————————

for feet distorted
for needle
for thrust flesh
for strife, dove-bone
for river-eel, a sword
for bronze discord
for the third dove
for void flesh is silent
for soapstone diligent and
for pure

will flee that place, hold
for

Sarah Lang

One thing I eat becomes another. The
calories; the spores on the wall weren't our
fault. I commissioned a painting. Eye like a jay
hops not unlike your thought. Your shawl
of an arm. I don't blame you. The bonsai
were half-off. In the heat, you confused plastic
with the fruit of any grunted labor; blood
with the juice of an orange.

———————

My back opens on what you demanded. I part
as though this were not difficult. A headlight
circles. We ate dinner after nine. You read

and read fragments aloud; but you never did
hear a word I said. This is the space we agreed
to want. Your hand around my spine; what

I have wrung. The food is now cold. As nerve
from nerve ending, my lips separate. You are certain
I am laughing.

I am making soup. I make bread. I hold a red bowl. I study

scalded. I hold. I gasp. I sit in front of a cake. I tell a story

three times. I offer a dessert fork in exchange for a blind eye.

———————

As a neck bears a hand there was a lawn
or children instead of scars. All woods
and balsam, all thure and camphor, all
run down. My word run down. My word
firmer than your sleep. My word
as the weight of grace holds. As the weight
of grace under. As the weight of resignation.

will flee that place
and hold, punctured
will flee that gasping

Sarah Lang

III.

In a city of glass the airport is no different. Lines open like a voice
amplified without guilt. So we have designed possibility; the morning
I call spring; this tree; everything o but through glass, everything

in warm gasps. We ate with eyes that moved as things do; the future
moves, light moves. From clock to watch, hands move. And to

mouths. Trees like a door left open for air: alveoli without treason and
such scent. Good-bye, in our two languages. In our two languages, the light
warmed this morning I would have called, without hesitation, spring.

———————

As water fills a glass, I am tired. Of course,
there are limits, light; you thought I was
light come through pear-slice, glass; a red

bowl. In the kitchen I collect your shed
scraps. I move without grace, with gum
and glue, I move on hunches, all for you

who call me out. Where did I go? The movement
behind each window. Argon for heat. An opal
for remembrance, for the ability and for risk.

When your skin a callus birch. When we calculate
well. There is no art but skin; no art but
comfort. A warm couch. Clean, there is no art;

your skin is clay shining. I have repainted this wall
three times. When you were carved. When you were
saved. When I knew your neck salted taste.

I would like to say you felt like a couch.
I do not mean felt as in touch. In a taxi
your skin shined; when it is hard to go back.

———————————

Mountain Ash. I can name the plants. The wasp
around a drink. Your arm tracked and thin. I
squint. The phone does not ring. You are wrong,

all. There is a small dog. I look through a window
at your retreating figure. An empty chest-cavity,
an outpouring of color. Your death is sickness

without nurses. In a pale room, I turn back; I look
through a dull mirror. I held a human heart is somewhat
true. Held, in a room of glass, open for movement.

The flight path of swallows, snowfall, is as your wrist
in the red in the lining of a coat. Think of skin as a runway

in dusk. In a room with a shallow closet; the clothes hang
on an angle. On a pale, stretched ward, as a body

you were impossible. If I could draw a line around that
time; here as elsewhere, light is as a principal dancer: superior

and surgical. I would like to know
what it meant. I would like to know like the taste

of rhubarb in pie. But names run together: I will dress
in the dark. I will have left. I will have nothing.

———————

Admittedly, there are ends. I no longer wanted; there are ways
to sign season, home; a body is not tender. I knew change; no,

things grow where they will. To what use? You mimed
movement with the skill of one who has moved. A snail

without shell bruises and bruises easily. Our house is thin,
flat flesh. I never could have swallowed all expectations,

or yours. You were the first instance. Where fall
flames; that is flowers; your bones, like the trees

are a new season. A chest blooms with demands;
a body is erstwhile in its delicate, radiant finery.

On Sarah Lang

THAT FIRST THERE is a rhythmical movement, a bolt of lyric, pause, tightening, a tentative feeling-forward and sharp contraction. As you might try to stroke the lovely and alien face of a light sleeper. "I move without grace, with gum / and glue, I move on hunches," Lang writes.

That first there is that orchestration of rhythm and its implicative meanings: irresolution, attentiveness, mensuration. Quick keen pricks of language "like quills," as another bard observes, "upon the fretful porpentine."

I would say that the rhythms themselves articulately express the emotional complexity of the poems.

And the words, also like quills, pierce the normative frames of their contexts. *I* and *you*, objects and events, the personal and the scientific shed their discretion to collaborate in the development of an epistemology in which observation, rationality, and affectual experience are irrevocably intertwined. "What I must look like" (to myself) leads to how "I would look beautiful pregnant" (to you). But between those two phrases and points of view, *the world itself* tries on pregnancy: "a red glass bowl" suggests the womb. "A spoon" offers the shape of a full belly.

What is most obvious about a line such as "My tongue in your ear listened to your throat" is the synesthesia aroused by erotic penetration. The more disturbing association, reinforced throughout Lang's poems, is the connection between the amative and the allopathic. "My tongue" listens like a doctor to "your throat." The taste of methamphetamines contaminates the body that is broken in the pact between lovers. Elsewhere, the poet invokes other tonics: oatmeal for itching, onion for insects, prayer.

But each remedy generates a new symptom, and the speaker remains uncured. Her insistence that "I'm largely asexual" doesn't extricate her from an ardent relationship in which she continually finds herself opening (eyes and "I opened"). And when Lang writes "my leg opens," using the singular case, the sexual is once again displaced by the surgical implication.

Sarah Lang

Throughout Lang's poems, the erotic is revealed to be not only a lover's discourse, but a discourse between outside and inside the body. When, in a later image, the speaker, vigilant and vulnerable, observes that "My back opens ... ," what she encounters, at once horrific and eerily intimate, is "Your hand around my spine."

—Forrest Gander

Six Poems
Justin Lacour

—Chosen by Peter Gizzi

FIELD RECORDINGS

Before the cupidity, we were a secret,
just wallflowers among the epidemics.
Then surveillance came via the herons,
who flex helixes over the orphanage.
We were hunters then,
never able to vanish again.
You were concealed in a dust mound.
You chose the bluest set of wings for yourself.

*

I heard you grew up in a hotel room,
that while you slept, quills tall as children
grew on your back each night,
but fell off like petals in the morning.
I come from good immigrant stock myself,
live in one of the more radical complexes
notorious for blood feuds and clotheslines.
But on Saturdays, it was like all of Mitteleurope
spilled out to play stickball in my street.
We tossed pie tins till it was too dark to see
by the light of our novelty-sized cigars.
Trains brought condiments from distant bazaars.
I picked up scrimshaw.

*

Back then, quilts were more animated.
You could look into the squares and see
Back East bootleggers cat-o'-nine-tailed,
the demimonde potbellied in the red-light district.
We caught the dim signal of hobnobbers
bloodshot in the polis,
ready to stomp out a twilight code,
lying about the weather and the distance
between us.
So much of our information came that way.
We learned from the example set by Swedish girls
chewing sap outside the church doors.
They wanted to turn so willowy,
until they could disappear behind pepper trees.

*

The roadhouse crew broke their lantern jaws
just to fit in here. They found Greek Revivals,
learned what trees the angels hid in
by dissecting phosphorous apples.
Farmers' daughters promised to horseplay for us,
if we could only spear their hearts out of the vinegar wells.
Aristocrats carried scrolls and teeth up their sleeves.
Temperance ladies offered to fatten us for hairshirts,
sew our eyes shut with the dark hairs of their breasts.

*

Coat of arms could dictate lots of things.
Sleds left to build cabarets on the frontier.
They collected chanteuses in specimen bottles,
believed their torch songs would bring cherry blossoms.
We never heard their voices, but on their kimonos,
night bugs spelled out the old lyrics
"Would you like to spend a weekend in Havana?
I will turn your money green."
Standards only the moths remembered.

*

I don't want to waste time with these nervous years.
I traveled up and down the country, wearing out my clothes.
But the egg found on my doorstep
only grew more blue and smoking.
It was still the spring of our experiments:
criminals flailed in battery jars
to light our main street.
We could walk safely then, arm in arm,
confident traipsing through the muddy boulevards
to the exposition.
There, eagles are intricately posed into colossi.
They graced the bronzed head of every banquet table,
though they could barely wait to knock off,
burlesque near the church bells.

*

I had to stop here, set up shop.
I am a factotum in this mill town,
busy wrapping caterpillars into mummies
for your pockets.
During the panic, you played your squeeze box,
drifting on a keelboat from port to port.
On shore, you slow-danced with one eye
on the harvest.
This is two decades after your lover
was gobbled by the asylum pit.
Out of loyalty, I still lower a canary
through his bars every day,
to see if he's regained his senses.

*

The fish wrapper told me how
the senator swelled lighter than air.
His sulky retinue tugged at his coattails,
but it was a harmless explosion.
"He was without love, even amongst
his native handlers. . . ."
Steamboats left to be trailblazers,
and found the crossroads tar and feathered.

95

Justin Lacour

But in our tents, magic lanterns shined photographs
that could stop this moving world.
How soon we accepted the silver counterpoint
of lamps hung in trees when liberty called.
Boys will smoke the devil's hay, tie wasps' nests
to their fishing lines; their anger is a gift.
Down at the grotto, a moon hangs by razor wire.
The lead actress holds a codex to a water ballet
that keeps changing its allegiance.
Primitive aircraft are bursting from barns.
This is not our home, so we follow the roar.
We can build a night around that sound,
and be swallowed by its dynamite heart.

*

Evicted from the Rooming House Primeval;
buffaloed and shanghaied.
So long since a real romance crawled
out of its matchbox for me.
Sixteen stone in my heyday, I'm whittled
to bantamweight feeding these swine,
who can only dream of a lottery of sawmills.
And this bar is an excellent cover,
but nothing like sipping red liquor
from your crucible.
I've had enough. Me and my "chauffeur"
are getting out of here.
There's time to sweat off these pinstripes.
I'm going to find you beyond these barbwire altars.
After the spikes and electricity,
you are waiting to turn into a lake.
I was always devoted to you.
What's left of you can still be a song.

*

This song comes from the top floor of the hotel.
This song believes in attrition. This is a jealous song.
You are the beard for this adventure.
You grew a second doughface, where your fingers used to be.

96

It could turn the whole green slope to the sepia tone
we knew, when we sang chestnuts, mimicked your growl.
You on my radio is also a country.
You are so light, I can pick you up by your tassels.
Whoever hates his life can build a nest in its gears.

TRUNCATED BLUES LETTER

Dear Boss,

Things have gone from bad to worse
for the man known as weakest link
in the Living Manger. His charley horses
will be the stuff of legend, one day.

But for now, the village is still buzzing.
We're investigating the friendlies
of the stained-glass cartel.
We're a practical people. People of the earth.
To combat geese, we brought in swans,
then the bats (you see where this is going),

but who am I to complain if the rain
falls the wrong way, or not at all?

I am enjoying an entry-level position
biting the tips off aristocrats' cigars
in the country club rotunda,
where catastrophes are meeting
the prerequisites of only the more
avant-garde operettas.

Though this is no impediment yet,
to the run of the land.
Just something I wanted to call
to your attention.

Justin Lacour

MR. GRAVITY'S BLUE HOLIDAY: SONNETS

Over here, it is still the 1-900 hour,
for insomniacs and the exorcees of tenement steps,
where the humidity curls your hair and the canals
aerate a previous night's Courvoisier buzz, as garbage scows
haul off the refuse of the same old hungers
we promised to give up. I am greatly concerned.
The burglars have discovered stilts finally.
They worship in the air, waiting at unlocked windows.

In such a night, I want my obsessions to be more proactive.
There is something I should tell you,
but I contain sentences that could black my eye.

There may be a fireball explosion later,
one of those great pyrotechnic displays of affection,
that we talk about and want so much.

If the Old Gang hadn't said "best party ever,"
I'd be upset over losing my favorite tooth.
Dom Perignon and your heel broke the glass.
Overture to another fracas. The racket
of a klezmer stomp through the old hotel.

I'm in the mood to make pronouncements
for the weekend. To say there are sophisticated
naiads pushing a toy piano down the elevator shaft;
to say this isn't even a hotel, only pajama tops
parading around the jewels in your ears.

At 6 A.M., that martini in your hand
is my favorite thing you've worn. The sun
is beginning to burn my tuxedo.
I have not been home in a long time.

There was a small disaster with the marching band:
Someone's pet was trapped, somehow inside the red drum,
but the parade goers tried to remain polite to us.
Your posture was all the rage that summer,
and earned you celebrity status on the first float.
I existed in a purely ceremonial capacity,
never straying far from the snackbar.
You said this was the simulacrum of a Good Time,
but it would've been the Golden Age of Block Parties,
except the thing in the drum, rattling against the skins.
It was a small part of the music. It was in the guts of the song
that caused the crowd to doff their hats, and weep.

It was so embarrassing. If you hadn't been there,
I don't know how I would have told you.

My stepladder's attuned to the window diorama:
I believe this pillow fight will become something else
entirely: a feathery explosion on the sheets.

The night suddenly wants tiny handcuffs.

You've been gone all day at the aquacade,
descriptions of your sequins came down secondhand.
I cried, but not literally.

I think there is something about the old men fishing
in the country club's water hazard I'll never
understand. I think there is something about the mule-
faced boy rummaging through the garbage
at the stripper colony that has everything to do
with feathers and tiny handcuffs.

This will be the first verse of my country & western song.

Justin Lacour

Just to say: your Cotillion was truly bitchin':
your pink gloves, the broken trellis, our glockenspiel tarantella.
We woke up eighteen hours later, in the doorway of the wrong city.
My white shoes were gone and the streets seemed empty.

Even the iceberg was just our nostalgia for water.

The Renaissance had finally come this weekend,
and the B&Bs were striving to catch up. After dark now,
the local diner becomes a nightclub with a diner theme.

And maybe, if we sit underneath the power lines tonight,
we can see your pink gloves again in the electron collisions,
they are quite silly, with their rhinestone eyes, I am a fan.

In the next world, everyone will be wearing them,
and we'll finally take our gin in soft top hats.

We were waiting out the flood in the tree house.
I had been stockpiling private property.
You were reading "The Other Life of Antarctic Fowl"
in translation. I could not tell you the racetrack
was floating away. After several bourbon & champagnes,
we thought the shutters could control the windows
(it would be nice to watch the Goths jogging again,
after midnight), and the clock tower was radioing
the dollhouse with constant updates, since the inhabitants,
all crinoline and china, kept bringing in new people:
letting them up little staircases to attic rooms.
You hid a smile. You had a faux dimple covering
a real dimple. "It's amazing. It's like they have their own
little business, and no one's disturbed them yet."

If you should suddenly become a swashbuckler
and carve a wren from this stately convertible,
how else to remember, but remain forever astonished.
Even now our ticker tape may prove oracular,
but no one will read the janitor's report.

You said there is a great variety of weather today,
and this trolley runs all the way to the seashore
for the Nights of Absinthe & Lawn Darts,
where the nicotine stains become more flamboyant:
yours showboats on the veranda; it burns up
to your shoulder, orange flight, dusky wings.

We can celebrate tonight under the Welder's Valentine,
its blue-flamed girders are impressive,
like your heart, but more serrated.

These powerful kites are helping with our striptease:
we tied them to our clothes with tiny clear knots,
and now the strings are lifting jackets over the meadow.

We had left the festival early; the Second Band
was a cover band of the First Band, and the children
were all scared by their newfangled cannonade.
I was chairman of the pratfall safari.
My crew found a few hesitant trapdoors.
Even the captured mishap just cooled its heels.

You came disguised as a German holiday,
did a firecracker cartwheel over the hoop of fire.
I was rather struck. And when the sky is full
of kites, when our sweaters and shirts dangle overhead,
I will close my eyes, and call you daredevil.

SHOWBIZ IN WINTER

Plankfoot's would've surely closed,
if not for the tiny mermaid in the terrarium
behind the bar. Her daily feeding drew a crowd
from the pool hall, as she talked suggestively
of her dressing room, hinting at the poor condition
of her tiara.

Outside it was still an election year:
the aerials dripped a ganglion of ice.
By now, the guerrillas have secured the Laundromat,
the Muzak shall be terribly altered.

Each night, she climbs on her sun rock,
asking me to confess childhood sins
or improvise possible tattooing procedures.

There is a large line forming behind me.
She clucks her tongue,
and insists the ankle chain is purely ornamental.

COMMEMORATIVE PLATES

(i)

In this plate,
polished organs are hidden in caverns,
just beyond the borders of this frame.
I used to watch you at the keys for hours;
I learned to play by laying my hands
on top of yours.
Our songs were kept out of sight;
our bygones are forgotten
till celebrated into mystery.
In this plate, I'm the one stroking
a half-mad Appaloosa.
Your sandals are perched on the catamaran.
You're trading winks for rum,

102

waving distractedly as the sails plump with wind.
Why am I painting you this picture
when you're so obviously here?

(ii)

You were too busy running up and down
those pylons to see yourself cloaked
by a host of jackdaws. If you're hoping
for some paint-by-numbers school of memory
to lead you back, you'll find your map room full.
You'd have to go back
and do your traipsing all over again
to really notice paladins noshing in the hedge maze.
In the same spirit, the inspirations for popular myths
are surfacing from the flotsam
lewder than originally composed, reclining
in the motel lot, a bit light-headed.
"All this rushing just to get here and hang out?
All I want is a tribute for my early work
captured in an intricately molded pompadour
that I can carry with me as I go."

(iii)

Well your headdress *was* burning.
But there was also something growing in its plumes.
Its squawks made the peasants kick off their clogs
and hustle downhill. "It has the heart of a bird.
See how deliberately it struggles to break away
though you've prepared a fiery tropics for its home."
This was never your intention, but it became your duty
to carry it up the pines at dusk, promising,
"Soon we'll have a cherry red sky to cozy up to,"
as its cries mixed with the fire crackle.
"The only way to remember this sound
is to keep climbing to a higher branch each night,
long after it is gone."

Justin Lacour

ALONG THE MOJO WIRE

Long in the contested city,

we were making speculations
eclipsing the original owners.

In photographs, your turban unravels,
twisting through the nubile rustics,

that people a pavilion
occulted by the present time.

The moon had a different name then.

It fell under the aegis of Hard Times.
We were in mourning,

building a pyre for local color.
Children were learning a trade.

Drifters marked the houses,
started showing up at inappropriate hours.

Harlots had the great cheekbones,
but you were pale on the water,

the topless one in puddles eating
starfruit, gathering the machetes.

But that was a different climate.
We were of one mind,

dined on huckleberry grunts,
knew the secret to smoking pencil shavings.

But is this really what we wandered
the sewers for?

Look, the stables are clean,
but somehow the neighborhood's worse.

Justin Lacour

Folks here can be so "public"
with their affections,

while some of us go on dusting
toupees in dad's barbershop

(I'm not attached myself,
so I draw a lot of weirdos).

My brother-in-law's *enfant terrible* of the freight yard,
his romance concealed in the switches.

Like Vikings burning their ships,
we both left here with good intentions.

The sedan ferried us to the next intaglio.
We drove to the president's manse.

He was nicknamed "the Little Magician,"
led us through the Aroostook War

and the Panic we weathered,
but never fathomed. Return was impossible.

Not since my prep-school days
had I heard such infernal jingles.

The Harp was miraculous,
but ruled with an iron fist.

She was the Shimmy Queen of the Bs
till ruined by sound.

Life's like that sometimes.

Some days you can stay in pajamas,
taunt lizards on the vine.

Others are percussive as Indonesian
seedpods, complicated by custom.

105

Justin Lacour

Still, I love those old two reelers,
how they grow more silver in the gloam.

In such ways the hunters became
the hunted, you might say.

It must be intimidating having your face
on such a well-known cake.

I own all your own records.

I wanted to meet you in the capital.
Your tour bus passed in the fog.

Things weren't so cut-and-dry,
but we could be friendly for appearances.

Over time, our nails grew long and deadly.

The City kept inflating, but our conversation
salvaged the heydays.

The brains behind the waterfront
were calling shots from umbrella stands.

They dug down to the scratches,
to the center of white suits and fireworks.

For a C-note, you could get a sleeping dictionary
to purr beneath the sheets.

The phenomenon of the Living mural
worked its tentacles and razors,

tried to cut meat pies from our pupils.

The black forest kept us apart for some time.
I could hear you on the other side,

and all the moths in your lungs
begging to become powder.

This noise kept us working through
several depressions and a midlife crisis.

I wanted to be born
to a backwoods conglomerate,

fresh with memories of the hatcheck girl,
but that was not our time.

All too late we noticed the crack
in the phonograph;

those conspirators' shadows
were gone from our lives.

Bony children boarded water lilies
floated across the lake.

Their pure slaves hurried after,
waded up to their top hats.

Tonight the morphine finally sluices to my heart.
Someone carved a hole for it to drip.

And so the sun sets on all the pink motels.

Up in the cold trees, you were tempting
out the static.

Justin Lacour

On Justin Lacour

JUSTIN LACOUR COMES from New Orleans and writes like an angel. I almost said urchin, maybe a street angel. I think he's twenty-five or so and went to school in Houston and Amherst and now lives in Brooklyn. But make no mistake: he is a son of the South, as the saying goes. His regionalism manifests itself in his poems atmospherically. He understands the night and its ablutions, that it softens as it tightens late toward morning in the land of magnolia and trashed Dixie cups. There is also a patina here from the weird old America in his diction, which is a cross between Walt Whitman and Herbert Asbury, Son House and William S. Burroughs, all lit, as he says, "by the light of our novelty-sized cigars." The authenticity of this sound might come from "the Golden Age of Block Parties," or from the feared and fabled territory of rumor itself—"His charley horses will be the stuff of legend, one day"—but mostly it is a direct report of a voice recording a phantasmagorical afterimage "where the nicotine stains become more flamboyant" and "the local diner becomes a nightclub with a diner theme." There is menace sewn into the lining of these poems as they read power and perform their carnivalesque mixture of the sacred and profane. But they are capable of wistfulness, too, imagining "Standards only the moths remembered." He's incorrigibly good, and his honestly enchanting poems are built to last.

—*Peter Gizzi*

108

Seventeen Poems
Michelle Robinson

—Chosen by Jorie Graham

FROM THIS MISERABLE MUTINEER A STUTTER,
FOR WHEN WE ARE READING DOSTOEVSKY IN CAVES

How can I describe to you the sadness of my precision?
I am Brendan, owner of dictionaries,

Whose intoxicating contents leveled me with one blow.

In Stockton, a fellow looked at me. We threw down right
there, behind a Mexican grocery store.
I pummeled him until the grease poured from my fingers.

Ah fuck it all sometimes!
I thought truth would speak from that thing that is
physical. I am wrong.
I want it on my grave:
                    I am wrong.

Whose product follows me, that ghost.
The scuffling sounds of dusty sneakers and sheets flapping. His constant
     clumsiness!
["Don't leave me now. I can't get through this night without you."]

I pummeled him until the grease poured from my fingers. My—

(Has it been a hoax?

The man on Belton Street selling poetry. The man who laid hands on him.
The sandwich board for Johnny's Luncheonette.
And Damrosch, that quick-witted kitten, who will make me laugh anon!)

Michelle Robinson

My fellows!

How can I persuade you of the imprecision of my sadness?
I have forgotten to take this body off

Whose letter ends, "I don't know what to write.
I don't know what you want to read. Not this."

———————

THIS MAY OR MAY NOT BECOME A PERMANENT POSITION

This may or may not become a permanent position.

That was striking to this goon's feeble mind.

When the grammar hung itself from the rafters
they trussed me up like a chicken cordon bleu
and poured chemical insults into my body.

I was the scapegoat, the poor fish tank rustling
the wires and glass that braced my neck.
                    The creaks and screws
that carried me to the table. The fantastic whispers.

In some absent or some other terrain could I have purchased
this exorcism?

This glum November something I am trying to figure
myself into this world, its drab and marvelous bits, its secret
schedules.

All the strangeness and the beauty have been parceled into objects.

Don't misunderstand. It was the most cynical year of our era
and anything would have been better than to have been asked
to find something beautiful.

———————

Michelle Robinson

KEITH

His name is Nick. He is the guy at Vicki's housewarming party
who tells me how to make cocaine in my bathtub.
He looks like this guy on the cover of *The Snarkout Boys
and the Avocado of Death* (in the book he is Walter Galt
and his father is a sausage manufacturer). In this poem he is
the guy who leaves a note in my pocket.

There is a note in my pocket.

I feel like I'm shuffling through this, the fatness of it.
Let me explain:
      Here is when Nick leaves the note in my pocket.
      The note says Nick—the guy from Vicki's housewarming party.
      Call me.
The note means this:
Nick was the name Nick gave when the name Nick
gave was a variable assignment for Nick.

Here there is a break in the pattern;
After this I will refer to Nick as Keith only.

                      "Play out the play" (II.iv.490)

Last night I slept with a belt around my neck.

I say to Keith, "Nick, you must have spilled
Something on your shirt." Keith says, "This is not beer.
I just don't bathe." Keith smells like beer.
Keith talks like something beautiful.

We are eating red Jell-O. There is not a note
in my pocket.

The next day I'm walking down the street Vicki says
who did you sleep with last night I say this guy named
Shakespeare.

———

Michelle Robinson

"Could I be her chauffeur without learning fearful things?"
Orpheus

The devil takes the trouble to learn how to speak
our language, and the sea—the sea is no longer
itself, after this; it doesn't give the "no" of "yes and no,"

It is the sound of a man who knows he is going
to die soon.

"I'D LIKE TO TAKE LEAVE OF THESE THINGS, AND TRY
THE HARNESS AGAIN. IT WOULDN'T BE DIFFICULT."

The first sheet, properly arranged, turns the body into a ghost.

When I grew
to inhabit that skin, it was corroded with slim lines of a deep color:
the flowers from that kimono etched into the flesh: a tag
attesting to its former owner.

The second sheet. The sensation is of a space that cradles you.

A sheet, obsessively rendering its surface.

What heaviness is netted in this cloth,
heaviness not much swayed by wind.

Chandler would have someone say, "How can you talk
like that before breakfast?" Or "You might as well rend
your garments," which is my own invention, but in
his manner, I suppose.

Nothing to do but give your old self the slip.

A sheet: Your head is in a pail of water.

A sheet: You slap out your cigarette if you think someone is coming.

A sheet: Because you won't say anything, I will tell you everything.

———

112

"We couldn't say to you we are not like that at all, we couldn't answer back.
Darling, don't you see you are inventing us?"

The Comedians

Everything beyond Florida Ave. is below sea level, some of it is woefully
below sea level, so that if you walk up the 13th St. Hill you hear hydraulics
plugging away to keep water out.

> "Where we are there's no way to reconcile
the dead and the dead."

We'd fetch them from any gully the frame of a man throwed down.
We'd stick a wrench in the neck, crease it, get in one piece the mug
turned ugly by death's blow, score it with acid, and climb that 13th St. Hill,
where a doc would press putty into the sockets with his thumbs, touch
the bone in search of some physical glitch, touch this
magnificently crafted vessel for its volume, figure the sense
of the cranium by the number of seeds that could be crammed
into its hold. That was no way, Or that was the filthiest way,
with our bare hands: get them to work for us to tell the story
we wanted told.

> "Darling, I've lost my head."
> Says the skull to the doctor—No,
> no (*soothingly*), it's just that the light in the entryway has fused.

"I shall fear not the dark but what's in it."

Here the wind off the river turns the earth too soft for cleats, and later
drives that dirt into grit so sharp it cuts skin.

> "Without my body, I'll have some trouble
> settling down. I'll tell my spirit to go off
> into a corner—you won't have it. They tell me
> I'll grow up, a classroom will pry itself open,
> admit me, will bait my throat with words,
> will call on me (*soon*) for the type of assistance
> only I can provide."

113

Michelle Robinson

THIS PASSENGER IS ONE OF THREE CONSPIRATORS

I'm in a five-by-seven block in a block of five by sevens.

My first take was in the numbers at high stakes.

When a mark threw a fit, clutching my knees, I'd speak:
"Let the fool live, just to punish him."

I've baked blades into cookies. I've baked bread
into bread. I've rolled doughnuts in dentist-quality cocaine.
Pumped them full of liquid ecstasy.
Joe, that meat-headed smuggler, stole my heart.

He was an eighteen-karat sissy. He pulled that trigger
and his face turned to gravy.

Gravy! Dad shopped himself around and ended up in a ditch.
Mom threw down two pair against a flush
and lost my hand. I swear the deck was stacked.

Tomorrow is my wedding day.

Machiavel! Upstart! I spit on his good Kentucky bourbon.
I hear he ripped off Carbury's for a cool million.

When I was fifteen and waiting for the pigs
to come, I heard the whistle of the ice cream
man, someone was selling something as I sat
at the kitchen table, and when I put my head
on that table I heard a voice. . . .

CURRENCY

In the same way it is possible to believe
in the imaginary, we are thinking about each other
as if we are thinking about ourselves.

That matter should exhibit this behavior:
    My father is a blank and not a blank.
    I am a blank and not a blank.

So I ask him about it this morning and he says, "Bring it up in group."

"I cannot tell half of what I saw."

Should this suffer us to join together.
The things that hinge me to you—
We fret, and fret, and we are not altogether unhappy.

If there is a verb that means
unanchored and yet still, it would go here.

        "I cannot tell half of what I saw."
        "We wanted to know if we were good out there."

When we are here
                At once the sense of weightlessness and of slowness

this unexpected depth.

Is there room to enter side by side?

_____

Michelle Robinson

PEPPER

When I am vigilant vigilant remembering the uncensored lines
of you, the stark creases in your hands
not unlike an intermission from madness, greasy and sublime,

yet everything I say is a trembling non sequitur

when you are so anxious for the end of the second act
and the beginning of the third

when I would cross my lover for a Hershey's bar
and you, loathsome, are intensely more rich, more sweet
but reticent, so if I am that source of inexhaustible yes
then yes is a dirty word

you want to scrape all the humor from this wound
and leave only frailty

ABERRATION

Despite untempered idealism and a large bank account,
he could not live in peace with inanimate objects.
Unpremeditated love centrifuged the savant,

unleashed the coarse beast of adult cinema, the convict
of breeding. The fucking idiot—he hated the emotions that keep vertebrate
animals alert. Guilt unhinged the subject,

left a gelatinous mass on the snow, an ex-celibate
seeking self-asphyxia. It would take six men to move him
to a cot of noxious-smelling pine, now a candidate

for capricious stone engravings and ingenuous explanations—
Now I find it is neither easy to be clever
nor clever to be easy. Some god-awful misquotation:

This: an epigraph that cannot be recovered.
This passenger, who mocks his own departure.

116

Michelle Robinson

CLOTHES FOR THE BODY THAT EXPANDS

In his dreams, it is always the other people who are naked.

The curtains in his room give the appearance of a mirror.

A man on the street smokes an unsharpened pencil.

"If I can make it to the end of the street
with my eyes closed, tell me everything

will be OK." This shirt is worn
by an eccentric male character. Max is different,

he does not find the love of others disgusting.
Not Jen, terrible, sweet, she liked to give her hand

up the ass. We are told this is the way things are done
on Wall St. Max seemed to think Jen smelled funny

of course he's right but who's pegging him? I know
he is thinking about this, and possibly small things,

like the man who walked by a stroller outside the T and went
back down to wave at whatever it was that was inside.

Or else, the way things mean less cinematically,
mean even less than before. The shirt—

No guest, however obstreperous, is ever asked to leave.

"So perhaps I am only pitiable, or more likely absurd,
like the boy I heard of who was allergic to grass

       The way my thoughts and her body dovetailed.

       The way I am neither invented nor made by hand.

       The way I am modifying.

———————

Michelle Robinson

"Now I know less and less about who I am or who anybody else is. This river reminds me of another river."
The American Friend

"You have played many jokes on me!" This stiff lug
took off to the traffic light and there affixed himself
so that he dangled like a pendant.

MUCH WAS LOST AND GAINED EN ROUTE

This man is something like a spy.
His eyes tilt closed like a doll's when he leans back.

He has a perforated plastic box and a bottle of fruit juice that splashed
on someone's subscription.

The apple he holds is half cored, half fleshy.

In the underground bus station some hand has scrawled
on the light casings and on the benches, "This is not an exit."

There is a deep bell barely audible down here.

"You don't know me. We have murdered a man together. We are friends."

River of gratitude, River of unthinking, River of cold stones,
In a shooting gallery, a man makes a paper target flutter.

———————

WHEN SMITHSON LOOKED INTO THE SALT LAKE
WHAT HE SAW

When Smithson looked into the Salt Lake what he saw
was not the thing itself but the possibility
of the thing: what had in its approach the possible
consequence of stepping off the land, and into the water
and for which he would be made fun of by name:
clown, you irrelevant, shit-eater, Rob—not
Rauschenberg who erased de Kooning's drawing, nor
Mitchum who could not see the picture, could only see
the frame, nor Stoppard, nor Shakespeare, no sucker
of stones was Smithson, no rocket scientist, whose roughly
carted rock trucked out to the rim of the lake a makeshift
anachronism: sediment, and grew steadily into land
because he did not *faire un trou* but a rotary, a gift and

what will be sweet to remember: swirling into the Salt Lake
he, who could have said, "Take this!" one miserable rock,
who could have said, "Here is something

beautiful for you," who said, who could barely say,
"Someone turned on a faucet inside me"
when he and the world became acquainted,
and thus succeeded in maintaining its mysterious
and wonderful affections, his hand dipping
into the water, occasionally, after the sediment
he was not certain was underneath in the same way he was not
certain the water would not rise about him, and it did: I did not
know for a long time generosity was rare,
or if the world is not eminently just and fair it is
sufficiently so, don't blame me, Smithson,
you were duly exiled: in the film: you run along
the Spiral Jetty, the helicopter cranes
above you, and reaching the end of the curving land
you rest briefly, dizzy and gratified, and start back, you,
who could do nothing: having skirted your way
along the scaffold could do nothing but run back
but I will explain:

THERE BEING TRANSFER

In spite of his recent insomnia, we have had very few complaints from the man whose arm is fastened to the wall of glass behind him; and if his body has been stretched into the position it is now, well, he has hardly anyone to blame for it but himself.

The apparatus was fashioned by Alexander Calder, and is without affectation; the right arm spindles up above the body and into a steel vice, which cuffs, if I may use the expression, the arm to the glass.

The grip draws attention to his five fingers. He is otherwise quite unaccomplished; I've often noticed this.

Someone, perhaps you, drew his attention to the fact of the glass. "We are always two!" he whispered urgently.

Could it be that his voice is still there? His left arm has grown brittle from disuse, and appears to unravel from the shoulder. His hair is limp like wheat, and dust has wrought its way into his collar and cuffs. The tweed a bit brusque, perhaps, but it is of course possible that he has not always had this brutishness about him.

He hides his indifference less and less. Did I say

the difficulty of sleep

"I have ink all over my body"

———————

Michelle Robinson

" 'Take it easy,' says the Red Man. 'Aw, drop dead,' says the White Man. You
see? There's your conflict. But the real conflict is between the White Man and
the prairie."

Leaven of Malice

We bought a coat hook, a two-pronged plate, and pinned it to the wall,
snug to where the doorjamb freed the wall. It was an arched metal rod
like a piece of taffy an assembly line had pulled, torquing it
with a dull spark, and flattening the end into a raindrop, spatulate,
like a miniature shoe horn. In the plate two holes were punctured,
and we fit into the holes two screws that thread it to their margins,
and ground the screws into the pilot holes that the drill bit made,
twice, so that the walls seemed to offer auscultations, suddenly
proffering a crooked finger, and another finger, the shape the hand takes
not having offered but having flung something: a curveball, a bowling ball,
the wrist wrenched to its extremity and the thrust, not like that usual
profligate, nor in the liberal dispensation of that hallowed signifier: Mother,
but the hand that coaxes a bow across a viol, as in Rosenmüller's Sonata 7a.
Though with its prongs no music, so when we pinned it to the wall,
inducing entrance, that he may take off his hat, or his coat
or anyhow another hook to a man should he want to hang something
who enters here, the wall was transformed, dangling our garments
like jowls, or perhaps our assembly nearer now to finished than we first
    believed: Men

    tugged two sheets of plaster over to a corner and built that corner: Men

    slammed two planes together, each shoving the other upright: You Men

    are the first models from which others are copied.

———

121

Michelle Robinson

HE COULD HAVE WRAPPED HIS EYES
AND THROWN THEM AWAY

And there were fire stairs, collapsible ribs slippery
with the rains' residue, dripping like Cerberus's jaws,
spilling open and zigzagging downward like a handyman's
measuring stick, tracing the figure of a upended seismograph and interrupted,
at regular intervals, by a gentle terrace. So that we could be evacuated
real quick!—like the tug on a zipper's pull that spills out its dull
gray ammunition—And the metal frame was lodged to our residence,
declining unvaryingly; each viaduct neatly welded, each flight a sling
sprung up on the side of the building, each edge an engine
turned scallop, cleanly beveled and embossed with robust
crisscrosses whose surface presence suggested a single
efficient mechanism, each ladder heavier than anodized aluminum
and configured such that it appeared to have bolted
itself into itself, the spaces so flush, so cleanly fabricated
that the metal seemed to frame the air it made visible,
like the grappling with Reimann sums that makes matter
over what exists beneath a curved line, rather than above it.

Prometheus, that bird-feeder, never knew this! nor did the bitch
that gave birth to him, a woman "cheap" in the vernacular,
who could have, scouring his face with spit and her thumb,
told him, "Be satisfied! with this: man, a bridge to the earth,
a mountain route stripped of its decametrical mile markers"—
Would he have hankered for atomic power—a gift to which we were
providentially entitled (rather than our enemies), for a short while?

One time you wanted to follow a fire truck,
and took an omnibus train into the country, where
you found one, gliding down the highway in the night
and got closer and closer to it, until your body
shook with the heaving engine you screamed:
"Look at me! Look at me! Look at me!"

122

THE NARRATOR DISMEMBERED THE CORPSE
AND HID THE PARTS IN 3 SECTIONS

You don't have to believe this. But I have no choice.
I live in the back of an elevator, for Christ's sake!
All day mimeographing the words, limbing the dull
things about, filing them chronologically, smuggling my self
for crumbs. Why shouldn't I say things? I think if I explain,
but friendly-like: because I've failed to become the thing,
You are sniffing around, playing the argot, swimming
the witch. Perfidy! By this self, this corner,
sleeve to my soul, this body, I warn you, we will meet.

But I've got another problem on my hands, this body
what confessed, "We didn't believe in the Bible
because God said to, we believed in God,
because the Bible said to." I didn't know
what to do! I clocked him, on account of him saying We—
that was the piece that delivered the sentence.
What can I do with the body? Look, my hands
are up, but you couldn't have otherwise expected me to be
still. Stale fucking cog! He was just another party,
waiting to be left. But you and I, we're riding together. He
didn't even know. He just happened to guess right.

123

Michelle Robinson

THERE BEING TRANSFER

In spite of his recent insomnia, we have had very few complaints from the man whose arm is fastened to the wall of glass behind him.

If his body has been stretched into the position it is now, he has hardly anyone to blame for it but himself.

The apparatus was fashioned by Alexander Calder, and is without affectation.

The right arm spindles up above the body and into a steel vice, which cuffs the arm to the glass.

The grip draws attention to his five fingers.

He is otherwise quite unaccomplished, I've often noticed this.

Someone, perhaps you, drew his attention to the fact of the glass.

Michelle Robinson

MICHELLE ROBINSON'S WORLD is one where belief and person-hood—as a sensation and as a preliminary construct for moral action—both consolidate each other and collide. In response to my question regarding the tone of these remarkable poems, these strange conflations of spiritual rectitude, judgment, self-accusation, and humor, she has written (regarding her person as well as her book, or vision, as a whole):

"I wouldn't like to say its conclusions are dour; I think these poems try to be humming and industrious; their characters pine and attack and dwell interminably on issues that are rarely repaired, only clarified. I hope, most, that they don't sound like a series of imper-sonations in favor solely of wit, but that people, in the poems, like O'Hara's 'Personism—A Manifesto,' make the poems examples of his type of abstractions. So, in short, they discuss the way that peo-ple think about themselves and the way they treat each other—social interactions and rules and what they mean about the way we think about ourselves. I like William Bronk, including his essays; I like George Oppen and John Cassavetes and Agatha Christie and Raymond Chandler. The poems use the cinema, the physical, and mystery (books) as an analogy for the world within reach and the world of everyday; some of them are preoccupied with what preci-sion 'sounds like': the explanation that more satisfyingly explains the state of affairs, even if its terminology is inaccurate, that is fun-damentally my own understanding of religion, anyhow, at least in America.

"I am almost twenty-five years old, judgmental, and soon to be a graduate of the Harvard Divinity School (M.T.S.). In the fall I am going to begin a Ph.D. in American Studies at Boston University. As an undergraduate I attended Harvard and graduated magna cum laude from the English Department; my thesis was on a number of things, primarily Edward Albee's *Listening* and *Counting the Ways,* Beckett's *First Love,* the sculpture of Robert Morris and Piero Manzoni, and David Mamet's one-act *A Life with No Joy in It,* which I reveal purely because I can't think of things singularly. I'm easily distracted. More lately I've written about Lenny Bruce and Charlie Chaplin, T. S. Eliot, and Andrei Tarkovsky. My father is African American, my mother is half Burmese, half Sri Lankan, my sister is married to a gentleman from Finland, and they live with two cats in Seattle. I live in Cambridge, at least for a while longer."

I cannot imagine I could say anything more pertinent to introduce these poems.

—Jorie Graham

Thirteen Poems
Eve Grubin
—Chosen by Fanny Howe

SANITY

Sanity, vowels, and wet hands.
Colors and wild knowledge breathing
at the center of flesh.

Sanity knows a body enters another body as a dream
enters the next dream.

Knows about sorrow's orb, an odor
carried in a net.

A voice pours from the waters:
in the burnt hour slight the father's words,
brush them away—flies circling a summer face.

Across the surface of the earth
hurt lies lustrous.

A GATE WE MIGHT ENTER

The greatest crisis contains a seed.

The seed is a door. Every day

the key clicks
and taps just above, just below the keyhole.

*

The greatest love is anterior. Open the door.

Shards in a man's gestures over the newspaper in the late
restaurant. His fingernails and high forehead and the growing

triangular space made by his uplifting
arm and rounded belly

*

A drug is instilled in every crisis.
The drug emits
seeds as when a poppy unwraps in a windy field.

The seed is a door. Every day
our hands push against the knotted wood.

PRAYER-MOUTH, NEW YORK CITY

When I wake: a tumbling

like stones in a dryer. I pick myself up,
stare into the colors
of my room, drenched in dreams I can't remember
or don't want to.

Smoke across the river.
In the river. In windows.
(In people?)

Did what happened
happen?

Waking into the buckling,
the electric animals sobbing in pipes,
in the marl and shale under the tremulous city.

MORNING PRAYER

It's not the prayer. It's the preparation for prayer.

Less the body than voice, breath, gaze.

It's not faith, it's faltering, yearning.

Less happiness than the laws.
It's not survival.

It's the battle, desire and modesty, the name. Near.
Not near; awe.

Clothing on the body. Distinguishing between night and
day-wake.

Not ambition, silence. Not silence; family.
No, it's husband, wife. Not
your partner; self.

Not *in* peace; *toward* peace.

Less the individual than the group. It's a single human life.

Less the prayer than the story. Less the story than
the story underneath the story.

Not kindness; un-hatred. Kindness.

Not the Nazi, but the Angel of Death.

Not nature, but history. Not region,
but time. Not human; gender. It's human.

Less asking than gratitude. Less grieving than
praise. It's grieving and praise.

Not sex, but two souls. Not ashes;
the body. Less the body than dust.

Trampling, gold song. Pining, scent, shelter. It's not
the preparation for prayer. It's the morning.

Eve Grubin

JERUSALEM

Unmoving on the edge
of Israel, on the edge of Palestine,

everything an edge: his hand,
my hair, the night, my crying like a child
in his lap. *I am so hungry.*

All edges touching. His hand smoothing
my hair. Words against night, Palestine brushing

Israel. My childhood
flanks the present the way
a country flanks another country,

it had its time, and it was done.
Why is it bleeding
into this car?

AFTERWARD, EVE'S MIND

The creature's close voice invited, full
as a swollen leaf:
"Is it true
you must not eat the food from *any* tree?"

With his glaring tongue he pushed
me against warm bark: "See,
you didn't die."

*

This ache in my belly is like the ache
when the white juice ran down my neck. Only now I am like a snake.
All stomach.

*

I can't remember
what this tingling brush between my legs is for.
I used to know. And the purpose
of these breasts, of this
tongue, this palm.
I had something to do with.
Now I want.

*

Once we thought: *blessed.*
Today it's just: *luck.*

Eve Grubin

MARRIAGE DREAM

No picket fence, no jeweled ring or graceful
kitchen. Just me standing on the blond floorboards

in my dry tulle nightgown. Wind lifted
the curtains just barely. Intermittent radio sounds

sprinkling through the window gave
depth to the quiet.

As the silence widened
flowers unlocked thick hearts, powdery faces reaching,

fireworks released,
each color a thumbprint expanding,

contracting, powder festooned
the floor with its reds and blues, spoors across a yellow dome.

A smile broke, hallowed, calm; not a laugh, but a grin, noiseless.
My legs becoming the legs

of Ovid's birds, tightening, thinning,
the nightgown's hem around my ankles raised tenderly

with the curtains. Urgent radio voices collected themselves,
invisible silver slivers pointed through my chest and hair.

No umbrage, no tiredness or fear.
A man in the next room is dreaming in a chair.

Eve Grubin

GAP

First the original pain.
Unremembered by the girl it was still

precise in her body.

Then came the second pain,
the father who turned away.

A gap formed between inner
and outer.

The girl's dream
sought to close the gap:
the father's eyes
are open behind round glasses, listening
to her daylight.

Back in the outer
the gap became larger, the father
continued to be the father,
and there was the first pain
and the second.

133

Eve Grubin

THE UNKNOWING

When I tell
some look at me, their eyes widen,
they back away, smile
and nod, backing away

or some come close wanting
to hear more, and they step in
and stare the way the man
approaches pornography, his eyes dilate,
his hands are numb, nothing
can stop him now from his movement
toward a body he will never come
to know.

MY FATHER'S WORDS

When my father said it
the room tilted

and our bodies tipped
left on the angle with sloping floors and walls,

his words forming a single
sob blossoming above my tongue, rose
as my arms stretched out

as if for balance,
my hands touching his shirt in a gesture

to push him from the room, the hair
sprouting from his chest beneath
his cotton shirt made the touch softer; seduced

by an image of himself as gentle my father
looked surprised when

the sounds coming out of his mouth stopped.
Everything outside

—car alarms, voices in the courtyard—
silent. Just me and my father locked

in the infinite
tilted quiet of the room, his curse and my sob

suspended above our heads: grotesque
stars on a moonless night.

SANITY ARRIVES

Sanity arrives.
Looks you in the eye, unblinking,

lips parted, neck veiled
with water-beads evaporating.

*

Sanity's architecture is supple, the scaffolding
shoulders the weight

as a bridge's frame is built to bend
in a muscular wind.

*

When the mother
holds a wrestling child,

she should grip the child close to stop

a fall; still

she allows
a looseness in her limbs.

"THOUGH I DON'T SEE YOU"

Spaces between cricket sounds   Between
fireflies   flashlight

Between the bomb and the screams

In the broken ground   In a tangle of roots

In books   The hair piled on Isabel Archer's head
wrinkles of Gatsby's small palm
cracks in Huck's raft when he decided
he would go to hell

Something invisible in the body
and in the poem   Unspoken
untasted   unsmelled

The day's silences
After someone stops laughing or the moment

previous to laughter's beginning   Before
the waiter moves his lips   When the pigeon's
wing is about to lift
not when the destination is known   just before knowledge

Before pain started   and when
the pain began
after the nails entered   during

137

Eve Grubin

COMFORT

The rabbi asked *But what is "comfort"*

Is it ". . . a full life"

*

A sitting house on a thicket
of brownish snow

Winter people

Snow   often bridal

today
funeral   plaintive

*

But what is comfort
Is it ". . . completed potential"

*

Faces floating through hallway
bedroom   kitchen   The rabbi   his black torn
shirt   sitting on kitchen tiles

Is it ". . . still alive in memory"

*

Even when my father was in the coma
there was life there   I tell you   life
was happening

I still had a father

*

138

A sitting house on a thicket
of brownish snow

Winter people

Snow   often bridal

Eve Grubin

THE INSANITY (INCOMPREHENSIBILITY) of existence is pressed between three silences, the beginning the end and the overhang of now.

Thinking about silence takes place in a silence that the thought disturbs. Sanity is already threatened.
Insanity is noisy, while sanity is associated with silence.
Likewise an unnamed secret, one that causes distress and shame about one's own being, produces an interior instability. It shakes the foundations of silence where it lives.

The slightest perturbation of silence corresponds to a disturbance of one's reconciliation with one's self. One stretches out of silence through speech toward contact with world and mother, father . . . who might ensure a deeper calm by a tender receiving of one's embrace, or might on the other hand stiffen.

A rejection by another person causes someone to shrink back toward the silence where the instability is a secret. This secret corresponds to prayer, in that the turning to it is a turning to more of what it (the silence) already is, a vault of deepest concealment.

Prayer is thought directed back beyond the attribute of silence, away from matter, deeper into thought, so deep that thought dissolves. Prayer interrupts the repetitive churn of mental chatter and breaks the compass by pointing it backward.

A poem as a prayer represents an effort to direct one's thought toward silence, even as one is straining to call out. It is a contradictory move, but not impossible, to reconcile.

A poet who is after nothing less than this reconciliation between silence and manifestation, or who is after a nondualist apprehension of reality, has her work cut out for her. The quest may lead her outside of literature finally.

If she wants her poetry to draw her to the "effulgence of everlasting light" and "an image of God's goodness" as "that which cannot be shaken," each word must be both fresh and precious. As it is.

—Fanny Howe

140

Severance Songs
Joshua Corey

—Chosen by Michael Palmer

Against *das Todeswort* I purple, I purpose: as pupil's
wart (your donkey your darling) I brag:
enrosed by refraction in your eyes' hover,
existing, complexion sicklied o'er with a pale cast,
lonely, disappeared, all too often charting
my own canker simply to manifest, to force
my own bulb, Eureka City my bray. Hee-
hawed the lantern of dark thought lifted,
dappling white walls and pirate windows,
some alphabet to watch over me, the wink-
ingly blue sky of my taskmaster's iris, steeled
a word for homey security, flied machine
on the wall, a prayer for surveillance (ass
that I am), for one stroke of my ears.

141

Joshua Corey

Wrung from you the crystalline solution arising
like the water vapor stacking itself into mesas
over these eastern hills. The sky has shrunk,
and the pillars of fire have pancaked
into clouds we can't follow. Hardness fools structure
into imitation, initiation into the illusion
of girders in the honeycomb. Can't you see
how sweet can support sweet? What tang
doesn't part you, your unyieldment,
your castellaned face, rigid, while the tear
builds underground? We are Jews (*ah, Carl*),
we will never be safe, you must cross me
with your arms so that blood beats within,
so that our eyes might open to their film of song.

                              *

Sun breaks sixty and the tattering blooms appear,
human and graceless. Heads down, eyes up, churning
muddy children and long boys, the lawgivers.
Beauty depends on concept, spring shrieks, Araby.
We brought our wintry candles unto the maw,
we stilled our voices, let sleeping language lie.
True and town'd together in our black array of masks,
behind each sun darkly downed, its breath that stirs the branches.
Concept relies on fire from elementary, empty hands.
Shake them and the head, the nod for no that goes unheard.
O vigilance, o you kid, o the desert above our heads,
o mirror of the poem cathecting gleams from shattered glass.
What comes to candlepower's ours. Grotesquely mothering sand.
Saltwhite moon by night that brings a scream into our vision.

The sea that smells of another baffles
and batters me. There a white shirt blazing under a blazer.
There a summer dress aswirl in April sun. Agents of air
lift and tease our habits, disclosing mass in form.
A door slams and the wind stops. Entirely local our sense of sea:
mist on the Adirondacks, barley burning on the Plains,
fog crouching among the rockpoints of Big Sur.
The sense of forest within the breast, in the nostril:
earth and fir, a little light
scattered on bleach-blue needles.
Luxe, et calme, her vixen face, body, *volupté*
sensible of clothes, the manmade lover
of man's disobedience, ripe at the tip, the tongue—
the fruit speaking me, afraid, in a world metallic with our garments.

*

I'm hip to coelacanth, to refinding the spines
that were never really lost. The bloom is off again,
on again the oil wells. History: its "comportment"?
Its circulatory system? Its bald mechanics
abstract us from our distraction, distract us from our abstraction.
Its "dialectical images"? Its all-surrendering swoon.
Pace the present's televisual fires, remember:
digital means by hand. Its too easy AWACs?
Its hard-to-sustain homecoming? Again with the island
abstaining its ill wind. The tropical sky was . . .
The Mediterranean . . . All-volunteer hermeneut, I'm a-tumble.
Sustained by a crawl, vicious weather balloon.
The Missouri . . . breaks. . . . The rag ladder has started.
Heavy on my head the home inflammable's my own.

Joshua Corey

A tax on what's true: *echt libris*.
It's getting harder to ignore these propositions:
the contradictions photographed from space
and assembled lovingly yet haphazardly
in the family albums of the horsemen.
Fleeced, fleered, fuddled with drink,
folded in a newspaper boat bound for Yemen.
What's that to do with our valley, its ripenings,
its coffee beans bequeathed by indigenous cultures?
Fingers of sand wave at an oil slick. Heaven invites us
to fill our pipes, while earthly combustion
raises pleasurable plumes. Oh that lawgiver of mine,
what's he done? Ssh, a king's coin has landed on edge
and its blood mills shall fund our sovereignty.

*

Soon I am confronted by a powerful youth.
He is camel-colored, biceptic, a bear-hugger.
A terrible busload of boys is arriving
in the chocolate chips. You were mine
they say are mine to be mined caterwauling the wall.
Upside-down in his iris the Watts Towers rise.
Packed his suitcase, packed heat. To go.
Bedside fury, a terrible bustle at sleep.
That is all Turandot, all memory, head and torso striking
and sinking in a pool of lamentable oils.
All hands at hand, are mute replicas required?
Seeming? Humorous fluids inside and out
the body that flints some fire, denied and beside
the point of entry, swank blamery, bulleted.

144

We are suffering home suffering home our red gates
splayed at random through the occupied city,
old folks at home passing our beloved lungs through smoke,
suffering oxygen divided from nitrogen which goes home
into the soil heaped at the mouths of the red gates
standing open straddling the boulevard arranging air,
turning the ones who enter into gods the ones entered into women
who must suffer to claim the names we've left for them
in bulldozed homes. Human bondage bears out bombs,
bombs embraced our suffering bombs pierced through the tongue
for a poignant pleasure red milk flows through red gates,
red sky thronging above arches and below arches
made into the interior of a plastic envelope bulked suffering,
this is our task to be the wall between and among at home.

*

Numinous grit and ash flew down in a wind
to pepper my skin, sticky now with ascriptions
or a meaningful plurality of incommensurate creeds—
varieties of cross, crescent, and star to maroon in pine tops
on a summer's night. Small page in my pageboy,
flask-bearer drunk on his drunk lord's battlements
from which sober hands pour oil on troubling warriors
whose religious experience can be summed
in a wink and nod. Smoke gets in my eyes, blinking
blooming glory which is changed on colored guitars:
chin music. Cellophane crinkles yellowly, yellowness,
some material in the air. Blank cooked book
in a hairdo, stared blond, I possess some prudery
for the senses, preserving interest in corporate signs.

Joshua Corey

Truth is inimical to the city: this is taught.
The reality of one shows the unreality of the other.
Or the point of manufacture from which it takes flight:
polis falling in flames, *aletheia* blotting the sun.
Unexploded teeth sown in a farmer's field
shall be the meeting place of barbarism and nobility.
Meanwhile the hilltop spires and aspires: breath
fills eccentric sails and wind tears at our blindfolds.
Grip and release a brick, form white bread
into pills. The initiate staggers between the lines
where truth hides from human bondage. And I?
To choose a theory of the hands is no easy thing:
it's listening with the eye or closing ears to a stench.
What the city renders possible, what making has unmade.

*

Domination backs out of all this sheen,
peered and aerial from prosperity's mouth—
a matter of books drown'd. Liquorish the lips
dipped in gold to take the curse off them, and
plonk what's flanked by our inland sea. Wine
stretches it out, that extensive thing, my sense
of elastics in the core of our connection. You
read this to get drunk, to fill crevices in relation,
as I write to be less alone. How to do it?
Most things are made of air or we don't care
much about them, yet it's untrue that every vacuum
yearns to be filled by anthropomorphizing thought.
This is just a record of the human that skips
and the heads that the toe trips lightly.

146

Then Corydon put down his flute and said, "Sincerity,
How thou hast ravish'd me! These fields and rockless hills
Where I and my poor art graze, lent by fortune
Of Caesar's favor, how compacted and free I feel
While my fellows must make the road! Gone for soldiers
While you and I, lamb, pipe it here. Richly served,
Poorly serving grace of guns, the lie direct, official whims—
Like unto the gods who call, 'Corydon, thy airs seem sweet,
So what is rank with us, if you'll pardon the pun, gets hidden;
That greed is gone that has no social smell; our thanks
For thy libidinal song!' Yet something pricks me
Beyond prick—these self-regarding sheep requite me not,
But graze apace this hair of foreign graves. Still, there's luck—"
He spoke, and again struck up his pose of potent reeds.

*

There's a poverty that discerns our ends, rough-
hew them how we will. Defiled at the mouth
coming and going, I stand for what falls in me
at the site of your golden claim. That field
grown monstrous, adorned with feeding two-
headed calves, their flanks pinked by rusting
leaves of grass, bellowing at the horny, two-
toned moon: now that's a nature to run with.
How your hungers have swelled till they're stanched
by starkness. The prank of "irregardless"
aside, I'm fasting without even dirtiness to drink,
bitten once and once again by your topsy-turvy
economics. What we've grown for food shall be left
to stand to rot; likewise, the easements of "if."

Joshua Corey

Bussed like any lover regarding of his skin
I bore down. Say it before the candelabra'd
wintry window, through which starkness makes up
a signifier resting on white distinction.
Why that black-and-blue gesture amid this riot?
What happens to the picture we were not made
to make? The theory of achievement means work:
to find an algorithm from inside mortal eyes.
So the horizontal falls off the wagon again,
so the vertical makes drinking deep possible.
Braced like any other against natural shocks
I bore a basket of goodies midway through
life's wood: grandma some boy's been birching.
Red rubbed the wrong way my belly slick with fur.

*

Pain of the door with a foot in it: meanwhile
a thin exuberance preens alone in the bedroom.
I am looking for you looking to me, a shabbiness
in shoes. Mind the gap. Our frolic fails.
If I held my left hand behind my ear, thus.
If you stood in the window on one leg, so.
It's a petite rememberer in the bedclothes,
ribbons in the air conditioner's dull stream.
Apply ice, don't walk on it. It's a fury
trapped in an elevator, waiting on alarms.
You miss me. Once I laced my fingers for you
and launched you over the wall; you met me
at the gate. Once is a secret handshake
to pull you by surprise, to take you in.

Thrash metal from a passing car dates
as a means of aggression—sap in blades
answers a human's humid sprawl. So eyes seek
a line of hills where napalm walked. Anniversary
forswears detail in a triptych, foresees
the third as an artificial lake hemmed
by red dams surrounding azure mists
into which civilian legs go scissoring.
A made thing, a view of delving, an ack-ack
trembling the Palestine Hotel. Of the earth,
of this foundry, we hew cold knowledges
by hand. At peace we do piecework, at war
we warehouse for wiser generations
these culpability cantos, weary to put down.

*

It appears, we can't explain. Maybe it
was always here or foretold to our trancing minds—
constellation of dews on a sofa left to die
by the summer side of the road. The war holds
me open, leased sun hung like these drying swords
my ribs. The war disappears in a flashbulb,
photoshopped to option our hottest tears.
Consequential is not consequences. The war
is clear and thus explicable, its hatred sparkles
in hock. Every insect eye's turned inward,
where our food lurks inkishly. The republic
reclining and closely shaved by its licensed
detainee: O, I could a tale unfold whose lightest word
would scald thine eyes young again, would winter them.

To venture or to bend toward a vocabulary
that possesses us. Of doing, of technique,
an ace palmed in a dog's broad paw. And
serially to propagate consequences,
ruffed *lieder* ringing across this faded print
of *Doctor Zhivago*. Themed what was found
to be an entire people's jargon, a way of weighing
fine particles in the out-of-doors, in a strong
story's wind. But ashes are flicked for a prologue.
But a narrative by night across a scarred coffee table
only swells in provided silences. Think of me
fumbling with a heavy lighter, expression
of a spark that finds its fuel hesitatingly.
That smoke in our nostrils binding us to me and you.

*

Yew to me is a literary tree. Stout yeoman,
skirted Rand on Captain Kirk's knee. Believe
me faithful to the bow I play—first string.
Buzzed in the air split by Y—give 'em a volley.
Arrows in surprised knights spells Agincourt.
War of choice. Unarmored and free, I stride.
Beweaponed, bedad am. Viceroy in me
is a tale told, chronicle, history once written.
What was nature, a letter to force fruit
from living wood. To build instruments.
To heat homes. Was it the stem that twanged
the apple in flight, split by a silver head?
And from this a blink to phasers set on stun.
A shirted man. The apple bites the gun.

Fingers predict the wrist, what can swivel,
while themselves are what can sway, beckoning
for another drink or a light, or warding away,
begging for a stay; what finally can stiffen
in the grip of prayer, thumbs conferring
abashed beneath pride of nails polished
or ragged with care—all the while a will
in abeyance calls attention to its rest.
Leftovers taken to heart, taken for flesh,
as is the undesert air before a thunderstorm,
palpably sea, a cousinhood, salt within
a cupbearer, a kneeling page, neck inclined
to make a nape. Bendingness, a grace note
sung for survival, rolled off tongues' oh no.

*

What surrounds us compacts itself with brine:
Broth out of milk made out of sight from sun
Miles out from any eye to drink its wine
Silent on whitecaps won from bright tedium
Shingled with white shafts like colorless hay
Burdening vision with mental synesthesia
Founding a sense of island stunned from play
Forgetting our questions of its parousia.
Where are we from if not already home?
Whose eyes are buried here under the sand?
In the slap of human space stolen from foam
Whelmed senses lose their sneer of cold command.
Nothing beside . . . Birded we are caught as seen,
Wingless from above this heaven of between.

The vision: two suits flapping at the edge of a field.
Screened eyes turned inward—the hand pushing
aside cornstalks bears a wedding ring. A nude
is curled somewhere and an earworm
discovers its gender. Vision or its expectation
makes the nude, whose own eyes are shut
in answer. Scared crows describe an upward,
a position imaginable to look down on this
between the sun and a cloud. Like green corn
the nude is hooded, its genitals recognized
by experts. Like men the suits are blackened
by blocking the way toward light. A dog
scents the whole field from his porch, though blind;
a woman thrusts her hands beneath a window to be clean.

*

To begin again with the film of our lives—
substance worthy of the name—sickly and
full of color, frayed, a cover for our hearts
to beat under, illusion of a transport to depth.
That is, I feel myself and you—we've tribed
by reason of potlatch, your regard thrown on the fire
to shame my eye that stops at walls, at skies.
Meantimes I have just the strength to gesture leftward
at the shape of someone's agony under a filthy tarp.
Stop staring and stand here, for sale like the others,
shuffling unsynched sound. Find having yourself
at least if to be is too much to bear, choose
makeup or shaving to prove your skin a home.
But I took a photo of you admiring the flash.

To be party to it I come invited but unrecognized.
The house was quiet and the earth was unmade.
The reader sits or stands or leans outside
the shower curtain. The world was calm
and the rooms of the house embodied by lights
streaming past the windows past a watcher on the lawn.
No one knows me here, the outstretched fingers recede
like serifs in the downfaced book. The earth heaved,
worlding, and the house skated downhill.
The outside gets recognized and is faithfully excluded
from our interior, though loving in every detail.
The house was raucous and the world asleep,
newborn and trusting the blood on its skin.
Unknown and from the book I step out reading its gift.

*

Evidently not more sonnets and not force experiment.
The view from the treetop requires me a tail.
Why joking? Why lowing? Why any animal budding
from the bipedal pivot of a borrowed strut?
Lie down on a breast and get up with the milkman—
with cave pigments, claws, sap standing alive-o.
Cocky muscles insist on each frame's human bed,
testing universals. So I feed intransitively.
And you who offer me your tongue to say this with,
a narrative to take off road—will you wive
me too with your secrets of affect? Come come
wickedly unto me—that's under, that's direction.
A line of pines, a branch of nerve to perch on,
discovering lips to kiss but not with which to speak.

Joshua Corey

ON JOSHUA COREY

READING IN "SEVERANCE SONGS" as the Zukofsky centennial approaches, I am reminded of the lines from "A"—12:

> As the hummingbird
> Can fly backwards
> Also forwards—
> How else could it keep going?
> Speech moved to sing . . .

These songs shuttle between a past and a future, cast adrift or severed from a violent, ashen present into a necessary *untimeliness*, as Edward Said might have phrased it. Citations abound—Shakespearean, biblical—less as neomodernist instruction than as eruption from the logomass, echoic contributions to the extended, fractured cri de coeur. No unitary subject in sight, he do the voices, beginning with the jackass poet's bray, ah Bottom. Angel of History with pointy ears, history as a dust storm or a dung heap of malevolent fools and endless war. What then of the sonnet, repository of desire and enemy of time? It is, as ever, that form by which we reimagine subjectivity to confront altered circumstances, and to assess "the shipwreck of the singular" in the maelstrom of the many.

In periods of tumult, Joseph Brodsky reminds us, baroque form resurfaces. Self and other call from shifting, destabilized positions. The phantasmagoric dissolves the boundary between waking and dream. Representational immediacy is reconfigured, and a vertiginous poetic surplus becomes evident, shoring against *das Todeswort*, against the "televisual fires." Exilic, nomadic, quixotic song?

The stable horizon has disappeared, replaced by zones of conflagration, ashen skies, ahistorical concoctions projected onto the *polis* and into the consciousness, before which history itself "swoons." And the poem is a skipping record of the effort "to be less alone," "to find an algorithm from inside mortal eyes." Yet the song itself is implicated, as is each citizen, in the mendacity and the war against meaning, since there is no "outside." Even homeless, even speaking against, the poet is part and parcel of the decaying body, sojourner in the Palestine Hotel. So, then, these "culpability cantos," "sung for survival." Standing neither here nor there, but elsewhere, neither now nor then but in a rift, senses stunned, "speech moved to sing / to echo the stranger" ("A"—12 again). Even in severance there is a bond.

—*Michael Palmer*

154

Tenían Sed
Tammy Gomez
—Chosen by Sandra Cisneros

MEXICANO ANTONIO

Mexicano
Antonio tugged on his crampons
and proceeded up the laney Laney
my tall gringa friend
so blonde and elevated
dancing tight revolutions
while the pool ball vaqueros squeezed out another side pocket hit
in tight-fitting leather jackets and crusty nightclub shoes
and i refuted the wind-ups (boys)
swooping at me like earnest wine porters
or Tampico-bound Canada geese
begging their unanswerable questions.
¿Quieres Bailar? ¿Tienes Esposo?
Until i said yes, i said nothing . . .
synthesized banda brass tunes
worked up our chakras as it
wore down my resistance to

high speed circle dancing
until at last i chose a
chose a partner,
we danced in awkward flow, he
squeezed my hand so soft
to his heart
to his memory
of something that i could never be
of something lost and catalog wear
his western shirt so thick and rough,
he: well-cleaned and dry

me: dry-cleaned and wry
december.
underivative daguerreotypes are men like him,
and i am digital camera
quicksnap, crusted-over sepia sentiments. all i
wisht was cumbia merengue footwork
and to be early weekend tipsy, amused
at the
Mexicana mae west,
78 and skin-tight
dressed with perfect ruby nails and
a well-tested smile,
endlessly wondering
do you like the drink? strong. strong.
no quiero bailar
no quiero bailar
yes, i like the men.
but no dance, not tonight.

—*About Friday night at Recuerdos de Kansas cantina, Fort Worth, Texas*

IN LAREDO

In Laredo
order a mariachi and get a taco
everybody's on late
i'm on time, makes me look good?
makes me feel like a noodge.
mesquite y palos de palma
por aquí, por alla
"hunting not allowed" on TAMIU campus.
las figuras de tu familia are on the back window
of your car—go figure
bumper stickers announce cuates, a dog, a cat,
and the smallest of birds.
someone "became" Chicana and i argue that she merely
"recognized" what she'd always been.
call yourself what you like. what makes me cringe more:
girl, lady, broad, ho, chick, woman? Latina, Hispanic,

Chicana, Tejana? A personal choice can change
over the various stages of one's life. Yesterday, I was
chaparra, but today the Johnny Carino's (Country Italian) waiter
keeps calling me sweetie. i drink in 3 languages, sip awesome
Belgian beer @ Espuma's. Good German beer & jazz @ OPEN.
Door policy: Let in the Catholic schoolgirls in their short plaid skirts
and tan strong legs. Handbags and hairdos for everybody.
Even the boys like to shop on Saturdays. Parejas,
parejas. The Latinas muy FEMINA FEMININA here. Paty touches up her
polish work with WHITE OUT. Toxic toes. Toxic toes.

—*After trip to Laredo, early April 2003*

I WANT A TRADITION

I want a tradition with feathers
i want a sky with antelope

all i get: winged clouds
in tornado waters

and summer sandía with canteloupe.

UNTITLED

Street
Trade project

South Koga Headquarters

seven xpectations
nueva flirt ass

in peace theft

sliding (into) second
over

157

Tammy Gomez

young
beau

youth league
dance
no diamond soul premiere

—*From utter global clutter series—Bay Area postcard cut up April 4, 2003*

TEDÍO COMO SIEMPRE

Tedío como siempre:
No, I won't eat your goddamn beans.
The manteca is lard, too heavy in the box
more heavy in the heart
on the shelf
white star symbola crayola thick.

Texture in the mouth, accenting mama's tamales,
Salvadoreños,
Tex-Mexicanos, y todos los demás.
Todos con masa.

Whatever—lo que sea.
Don't talk to Pablo,
ya se mea adulterous, alcoholic, demented
demoted he can't ask for his job back,
pero sí, ya 'sta gritando, all pedo, full-throated.

And I won't touch him, call his bluff
porque even though compartimos sangre
I keep distance, separada,
a smile's enough.

Tedío, ya es tarde, and no,
I don't care,
I won't eat your goddamn beans.

158

Tammy Gomez

¿CUANDO VAMOS A LLEGAR?

Cuando vamos a llegar
the nopal whispers nothing
glistening only shine
from ever lasting light of sun

cuando vamos a entregar esa cosa
que se llama libertad
we seeking freedom
in the dusty sands of this country
we dream of freedom
a project we encounter
the small feet and larger hands
are outdone by the
largest hopes of heart
the beating pulse of strong
and dreamy men

¡vamonos pa' america!
dijeron
los veinte-seis yesterday,
today, in half an hour
another group
p'al norte!
three in the river
2 by rail
10 strapped to undercarriages of cars
8 walking walking
tenían sed
tenían sed

una thirst pa' las cositas
not luxuries
but basics
essentials of life
work
hard work
hard work for little pay
hard work for no respect
a walk walk walk to a timeclock

159

a march through desert heat to a check-cashing center
that deducts 10 percent
a crawl under barbed wire to stand on street corners
daily hustle
day labor
morning labor
afternoon labor
evening labor
night labor
every day a labor day

marchando hasta el cheque
apenas alcanzando aguas nuevas
aguas duras
hard hostile
unfriendly
unfree

SUCH SCENE SORROW

Tonight, i perched at the railing on the
summer terrace
hoping to breathe bigger as i looked at the sunset sky
clouds puffed pink with fury
white fluffy, edged w/ rose and lengthening toward
        the night, i haven't quite seen such mad
        sadness, for this reason, since 1991, Santa Fe

        i am flat on my back
        simply breathing
        but somewhere inside
        there's a foot tapping

tonight's clouds, unfolded bedsheets
snap against the line
pushing for
pushing against
cloud clothespin let go

.she dropped down
it went, she threw
tossed cloth doll
sweat hands unclenched
stuffed animal, empty fist
open eyes, cry doll
wet fall, scene sorrow
(such scene sorrow)

DHARMA PANTOUM III

When i met Trungpa it was via book
i prevailed to place new rungs upon my ladder
i released the inner storms that shook
my clinging ways that had merely made me sadder

i prevailed to place new rungs upon my ladder
after watching monks mandala-build by hand
my clinging ways that had merely made me sadder
became dispersed at last like tiny grains of sand

after watching monks mandala-build by hand
the steamed Tibetan momos we were eating
became dispersed at last like tiny grains of sand
another way to see how things in life are fleeting

the steamed Tibetan momos we were eating
were cooked by someone who only had one hand
another way to see how things in life are fleeting
with calmer mind i suffer but also smile and understand

Tammy Gomez

ARCHITECTURE, FORGIVENESS ARCHITECTURE

I trumpet a sallow life
span of a few post-tv blinks
when water glasses sparkle in
emptiness and disrupt the line
of sight. drinks are for optimists,
when the cup is half empty, but
the dry lip of self-concern wants
its full 15 minutes. who am i to
deprive that sullen mouth, bewitched
and perplexed in mocking parallel
distant chirps of stuck auto alarms
and dwindling midnight freight hauls.

fondly, i bespeak this moaning and nod
out the empty cameras, spun dead-ends of
Kodachrome and wanna-be piñata styrofoam.

i am thoracic inlet destroyed and perfect
posture betrayed, trailing my vanished hopes
with the reluctance of short-lived firefly lights.
somewhere a swimmer beckons, if only to summon a
handiwipe, if only to manifest an eventual shrug,
in disappointment, in giving up. wonder why my

porch grins gray, questions about the smooth placid
stone? if i had to denote & deny forgiveness
architecture, then you would be crying too.

ON WATCHING DYLAN SO CLOSELY HELD

Such longing
in perpetuity
i have been alone
my fingers older
and my heart is
hospital
all i know is
the capacity of
the chest
the breaths of my
lungs
the lunge of my love
within the cage
all bones harden
and bleach to dust
i forgot how thin
my life is
how forgotten the trust

watching you again
is love all over
you snapped a string
and we somehow
thought to applaud
in pause i examine
your head tilts
you smile
a glance at drummer
you even look at me
i think i know what
you are thinking
but i must be kidding
myself
must be childless myself
i ran too

Tammy Gomez

HONEST GIRL

Honest girl away walk	looks at floor	remembers walk
try pensive push up glance	into head	notice dust
swallow gum white stuff	get stuck	white clouds
explain explain listen up	countertop	fold dollar
swallow breath loud pause	sink boy	drop eyes
walk slow nothing there	try thirsty	nothing there
honest girl countertop	stab song countertop	points away
shock reply walk away	want a bag	start a fire
jousting mouth a word	thirsty more a word	regret a word
fix my mouth get along	get a song get along	smile new teeth
six days pass forgive	see his face forgive	consider bridge
swallow breath honest girl	chest expands	honest girl

—*After frustrating customer experience w/ Starbucks kid*

164

CLUTTER IS UTTER GLOBAL [EXCERPTS]

EXCERPT 1

The best things are. Stonesaw liked best that her stack of Abe novels was a mere two inches from her bottle of Gerolsteiner natural mineral water. German next to Japanese, allies.

And across the room, more Japanese. Sony fought it out against the two Sharps—one a boombox and the other a minidisc recorder. Bellowing sound things. But the Sonys collaborated in strategy to do a multimedia attack—one a hi-8 camcorder and the other a stereo cassette recorder. Not enough batteries in the house, the war was silent.

She sipped, Stonesaw brought the Gerolsteiner to her lips. An eclectica saliva pulse. Underneath her tongue, madness. It dissolved like a homeopathic home run. And she felt nationalistic.

Still, the Chinese umbrella and the Italian "Dust Snapper" predicted forthcoming disease and fascism, with McDonald red-and-yellow certainty. Scarlet fever, pallid skin? Grimacing legislator, cheeks puffed with fury. Impulsive ship captain, flesh gripped with scurvy. Stonesaw shrugged with Dengue Denial. (Meanwhile, face-masked tourists argued about how to hold a cigarette in their mouths in the glass-walled Bangkok airport smoking cabinets.)

You stay, you must leave. You can stay, but no, you there, quarantined. How funny we fuck up.

No, I don't want to paste anything here.

EXCERPT 2

Clutter is utter global. I want to gloat about that. Stonesaw looks on, not actually disapproving, but tending toward indifference. She picks up the U.S.-made crinkle paper and her contorted face matches. Matches it. Every object a reflection of her flesh. The stuff of mirrors. The stuff is more mirrors. She looks at everything and neglects to punish behind cabinet doors.

Tammy Gomez

Populates the residence. Pompous, I told you.

The last thing I'll say: No Red Sambos. Color-blind my world. Luisa
kind of said that. But Louisa, she lived it. (Neither of these women
know Stonesaw at this time.)

Regrettable.
(But think about food, it'll be all right.)

ON TAMMY GOMEZ

I MET TAMMY GOMEZ by word of mouth first. Somebody I trusted in Austin told me she was good, but with a name like Tammy Gomez I didn't know what to think. Somebody said she played with a band. Maybe her name was part of the act?

But then I heard her perform at a poetry fest. She performed with a bunch of musicians, something I usually don't like, but I liked her. She was tiny and spunky and full of wit and intelligence and passion about things that mattered in the world, not the usual whining and self-indulgence of most of the performance poets I heard. Her poems were funny and witty, as well as generous and concerned about social issues, and I didn't mind that the boys in the band were making a lot of noise so that I couldn't hear the music she was making with her words.

Later, when I got to know Tammy, I would find her generosity and commitment to community meant she would return to her hometown, Fort Worth, a place full of dead ends for artists and people of color. But the city is changing. Poets are part of the renaissance, and Tammy is nudging conservative north Texas into the new millennium. It thrills me to see the work she is doing here in the hard country, by word of mouth and by word of word.

—Sandra Cisneros

Seven Poems
Michael Ives
—Chosen by Robert Kelly

THE NEOLITHIC REVOLUTION

While you weren't in bed again I thought about
the future of philosophy, specifically why
the coaster sets were dishwasher safe, which formed
a starting point for further analysis:
viz. that some nugatory Wankl engine
is a little too busy averaging the preset abundance
beyond recognition, and in valleys
of the modular sectional a frontier opens
where the cone placement for the driving test
constellates a destiny accumulating in boxes
along the basement hallways of moods
that bow to no master.

Toward a resurgent and pesky inquisition
the Being of being drifts, drunk on the liquor
of knowing itself to be a liquor only it can drink,
which waters the vegetation in its path
going down before it whispering pleas
and the interpolated "Mingya!"
Soon, rogue dithers of neuronal passion,
verbal stems suggestive of a "funk" aspect,
wheeled transport, nostalgia for the third
and second millennia B.C., the living room
as cognate with the jaws of a macaque, wine,
all suggest that "events" as we know them
have taken on lives of their own, as if to say to us,
"Look, Mom, no hands!" while they contrive themselves
out of the refrigerator boxes and wheat paste
we momently throw into the space in front of us,

Michael Ives

which always fills right up to, but strangely
never over, a brim established each morning
when food flakes sprinkled from a domesticated heaven
across the unroiled surface yield to us our continents.

There's a virgin forest several flakes west
where the history of a world we forsook
on our first date writes itself in a trail of animal scat.
No shit—sensitive pellets scrabbling themselves
into words like a Claymation Toynbee
tumble over each other, just as we do,
in a race to the end of the sentence.
For the turd that plays the period wins a kingdom.
Then the helicopter lifts off the consulate roof
and a refugee who grabs onto its landing skids
has no idea he allegorically recapitulates
the formation of the first amino acids *(must explain
earlier in poem)*, effectively putting something
into perspective that didn't want to be
during my evening commute home
along the canyon between us. This month
it winds its way among crags and steeps
and features many varieties of thornéd scrub.
Plus, as a bonus, a perilous corridor
dotted by enchained hologram martyrs to earlier fulfillment
will elicit a strangled pity full of leather and berry tones.
You'll want to tell all your friends about it.

AND TO EXPLAIN THE
ACHIEVEMENT OF CONSCIOUSNESS

he had brought out a length of velvet suspended on a drying wicker
and began to address it as "poor James." "*What, what say you,
James, do speak up.*" "By moving one's finger north along poor
James here, north meaning up and out, out there . . . look, do you
see—" and he pointed with great intensity toward some constellation of fiery bodies of his own devising.

169

"My motive in bringing forth poor James? Well I can assure you, I have no intentions of inflicting another damnable golem on the world. They're all the rage, it would seem . . . I have it in mind, in fact, to prove that the world itself is a golem, *the* golem. There can only at all times be one and only one golem. In truth, I thought it might be *me*, until the blessed accession of our poor James convinced me of the *golemite condition of this world—*," and his mechanical genius but a length of fabric, with a nap that trended southward.

"Of course there's no use in explaining oneself, using numbers to account for numbers, that sort of incestuous calculation, you know, bumbershoots and all that, hip-hip, as they used to say, but it is the tissue of that very failure, that singular incapacity to explain oneself—as well to oneself as to another—that brings us round to poor James here, for that failure is the very *consciousness*, you see, breaking forward out of an inertial morass of, oh, how do you say . . . of involuntary preoccupations: cleaning the animal, keeping it warm and whole, or whole-ish at least—'the figure in the carpet,' as someone once remarked—his name escapes me at the moment."

Until the commencement of this earnest demonstration, his dinner guest's every movement, as he described them later, had seemed of the unambiguous "Please, help yourself" variety, but upon his bringing out poor James she ceased paying him any attention, and left abruptly, before the meniscus of her brandy had even yet resolved to the horizontal. Several of his friends at the club, upon hearing of these misadventures, and in possession of some prior knowledge concerning the woman in question, made jokes to the effect that it would never be discovered, the precise location of her genitalia, velvet golem or no, that her legendary clitoris lay stashed away in some Khyber Pass of affective remoteness she was apt to inflict in extra measure on one as gone-and-the-Lord-Chestnut-be-damned as he . . . and his ridiculous "poor James." "Ponder the possibility that perhaps she meant, 'By all means, save yourself,'" one of them suggested. "She plays in a string quartet," another observed. "Good night! How much louder must the warning siren sound?" a third expostulated from across the table. "Read the pattern in your little carpet, old man!"

Oh, but he smarted at this last gibe, for it had been uttered with no consideration for his protégé, upon whom—draped there along the wicker beside him steadfast and quiet for the length of their first luncheon together—he had trained his dearest hopes.

HEGEL UNPLUGGED

—For Ann Lauterbach

The trawlers powering out of the color square
    were once clay. Hidden
        in their resemblance to prophetic interiors
flashing now and again to the surface, they recur
        through the image of an equation
            pulling into its chalk
somewhere remote from me yet more intimate than dust,
        to map one shadow as it darkens another
become the caesium clock of this soft wreckage
        floating without effort.

How much labor to unearth the buried week
    measured in years or in the periodic slippage
        among coordinated belts
        that gives rise to those years,
        descending by visible echoes through the golden bowel
        of everything else: rust grain through pumpkin flower,
            steel premise through translucent carousels of sleep,
        until only an indolent bit of else remain,
solitary else-wen on the face of nowhere—

and the water passions that feed its Cleopatra,
    wild horses to them who would domesticate it,
        collect into a death mist
which both invades and becomes the airspace
        by my drawing enough blood from it
            that it trends toward a breathable transparency.

The mind succumbs then to this soft reckoning
    of intermediate deaths like a young shoot in wind
        whose stem, a cord of wounds in small fractions

171

breaking along its length, straitens into a pliancy
   against the proofs of storms, near where the soft
      auditory bones merge with vector passions
         into a heavily voweled traffic
      lucid with slow thefts of time
         and genial curvatures toward no certainty—

or else several certainties, whole generations of them, wondering through my life
      whether our quibble-blue globe
   lodged in its mild rotational medusa
      is really the cyclone of meaning it wants to be,
         to which irresistible misunderstanding
      I owe this mâché of concepts
         coming apart in my hands.

INSOMNIAC THEATER

For having, hours before, chewed to ribbons
the single extant papyrus scroll that explained
why day and night are one, the Count of the Nocturnal Largesses
has leashed the stupid Beagle Puppy of Day
to the fender of his immaculate, vintage Continental.
The Puppy's clumsy, enthusiastic saltations and barking
at the Count's return from a thruway rest stop
betray its ignorance of what is to come:
that the Count of the Nocturnal Largesses
shall leave Stupid Beagle Puppy of Day tied to fender
and drive the remaining miles to a private Niagara Falls
of unwanted wakefulness for another night of gambling
and rough, hydrocoital naughty.

Night has something to prove, which it does
as ruthlessly as a logician from the Vienna Circle.
Its middle premises, in the form of hours,
throw a vaguely Eastern European facade
over the day's small triumphs that remind one
of cold directorates, in which a business is carried out
in ways as terrifying as these facades are antiseptic and featureless.

And yet, at the door of night, again and again,
I stupidly expect to step into the Honeymoon Suite,
press my face into plush towels,
unwrap the complimentary mint chocolate square on the pillow,
let its ooze run to either side of my tongue, *lento*,
while absently tightening the foil wrapper around my index,
a prelude of delicacies to come. . . . But in an instant
I'm standing under the same naked lightbulb
in the same puddle of water next to the rubber sheets
and battery cables—arranged like a Chardin still life
reworked by Chaim Soutine with his eyelids pinned back.

These intercostal hours between two a.m. and first light
play my diurnal confidence as if it were a concertina.
With its recently flayed skin and muscle lying beneath it in ribboned folds
suggestive of gentle lapping wavelets on a shimmerlingly defiled beach
just west of the sinking tanker, the ribcage of my sleep,
propped in the corner of the bedroom
according to some grotesque feng shui secession complex,
flaunts its indignation as if it had signed a nonaggression pact
with the light of a mercury vapor lamp
reflected off the slickness of exposed organs.
They pump with the mollusklike foolishness
of wet, sessile creatures attempting an orgiastic rite
meant for a very different kind of animal.

FIVE PLONNETS†

Before, nothing but the imposition
of untrammeled sound.
Soon after, sight. And
only then, as a barrier to the audible,
an offering of hands, modeled
on the eyelid, as the eyelid
was modeled after sleep, that antique jetty
lowered against the tide
of the sensual incursion.

173

Michael Ives

Yet how clumsy, stopping the ears
with one's hands, how Rube Goldberg,
putting one's hands over anything, trying
to cover anything.

*

And incidentally, should anything you encounter herein
appear to harmonize
even with the inaudible plainsong
that unites those outer islands of resolve
you know as your teeth, it could only be
on account of the addled Rhadamanthys
who sitteth at the right hand of our every expectation,
growing deaf having mistaken
the two rapidly intersecting gyres of our unexamined drives
for ear trumpets, the better to hear
an ashlike sediment of dead angels
slowly fill the distance between our houses.

Appearance, the eluctability of it, this was the first gift.

*

(From breath to memory)

To hear the world inhale
note the likeness of one thing to another

and any contrast of things
to feel its cool exhalation
against your forehead

but the difference of identical things
is its lungs.

Time makes a hovel in the plump date where crosslegged it struggles,
forcing a horizon from the arrogant predicates of motion.

Michael Ives

Under the burden of this endless work
memory's caryatids twist,
wringing a twilight of stone
out of remembered breath.

*

This group of words, rather than prostrate to you,
and despite not knowing the truth of its own bondage,
jiggles the effective center of your awareness
away from any intimation of refuge.

So, starting now, no primary substance to speak of,
only the brash, centrifugal exemption
from having to mean anything,
fretted with shockfronts of kisses, soft bites
at the dimples and lees of bruised mouths
plumped out against the softer against.

And under it all, a convexity, a belly, not yours but as gently curved,
swelling when it wants, receding as it needs—this hour forever held
in the suspension of all succeeding hours.

*

That the last breath is the truest flower,
will awaken soon, always
soon, out of its analogue to sleep
from which sleep lathes the still truer analogue: a hero's journey
up between two legs of the treacherous stalking mind
who has beaten flat with clumsy vigilance,
patrolled ceaselessly the wastes of sighs and screams and laughter.
But soon the last breath shall shake free its accumulated muck, burst up
triumphant, its seedcase break within you
and a liberated festival of nerves
shoot like fissures in a windshield
across the vast, sudden, and final countenance of this life, rippling with
        scenes of godbirth
and unendurable ecstasy.

---

†Note: A plonnet is a thirteen-line sonnet with wandering (i.e., planetlike) tendencies.

175

Michael Ives

GONG DROPS

I have been raised to think of my fate as a stranger encountered on a train who happens to be reading the same book as I, *this* book in fact, which writes itself by being read on a train by two strangers unaware of something of tremendous importance that must remain hidden for the sake of *that* importance, the hiddenness of which is exactly *this* importance.

Your memory, my memory, their memory—behind the *unchanging* word lies the truth of subjective experience, from which vantage it would appear that *we* are being experienced, that in Lockean terms *we* are mere secondary qualities, though as to the sensorium to which one can attribute us, that must remain unknown . . . an unknown adventure in the life of the partially known.

The self betrays itself so predictably and with such fine rigor, one would think that by now it had made an illuminated manuscript leaf of the "Kick me" sign taped to its back.

Inversions of the parabolistic: the toxic garden of Dr. Rappaccini, the toxicity of the Edenic, for that matter. Horticulturate the false positive and what have you unwittingly mundanitized?

Many mistake childhood for the "regency" period of an individual life, when they should look to middle age for signs of a vacated throne.

Somehow the world was painted over with statements, and now the world is lost. A thing covered over with statements, even a thing as immense as a world, simply will not be found. It is neither a matter of disproving the existence of large, ungainly totalities, nor of putting a halt to the unconsidered use of names for such totalities, but neither do considered worlds entertain grudges such that they might refuse to show themselves merely to spite the worldly ambitions of one person. And if you should try to search out an agent responsible for all of these assertions, this offending graffiti, what you will find in the end is only more assertions, these words for instance, which are every bit as much yours as someone else's. Why do you suppose they have remained hidden from you all this time, so far inside a *terra incognita* that they might as well have been furled up within a single hair on the head of someone worlds away? Yet the scroll tucked inside the hair is identical to the person lost in a world covered with his own statements . . . or someone else's. As I say, it makes no difference. One person's center is only another center's person. But that is to speak only of centers. And persons. What else is there? I'll tell you. But don't paint it. Stop painting.

I spend so much time getting what I want, there's no time left to do anything.

A metallurgist learns more by apprenticing to a weaver than the gold would like.

The insipidity of contemporary culture is profitably understood as a constant in a set of equations that describe public life in terms of profit and loss.

Perihelion in the orbit of the concept. Aphelion in the orbit of the object of the concept. Murk of gray matter between.

What we want is a better theory of equivalence, or better, an interfusion of theories, those of the grotesque and the equivalent. To hold a mirror up to the self, to take in unflinchingly the supreme hideousness—not of the self, but of the luxury to contemplate self, which gave rise to self.

The paean of Parmenides: just one more vulgar extraction from the impeccable (in-peckable) round. *The corpse eventually robs its own grave.*

Animal bipes implume, Plato called the grammatical species—a two-legged animal without feathers. The meaning of the designation captures less of our "truth" than its suggestively tripartite form:

every two positive attributions require a negative one, as an ersatz regulative function in the absence of a regulating reality. Thus does language furnish us with wings—by telling us we have none. As for a more explicitly descriptive label, *animal quadrupes adrogans* should suffice, for with the disappearance of open spaces unmolested by ownership and "development," we withdraw farther and farther into the civilized pasturage of our words, which, by their oddly refractive properties, though they give us the appearance that we walk erect, have so successfully upended the theater of our endeavors as to reduce us to the cleverest but most presumptuous, and teeteringly perpendicularized, of ruminants. Presumptuous? Yes, because while we preen and luxuriate and make a Trimalchio's Feast out of even the most inconsequential desire, the vast number of cognitive stomachs through which the tiniest grain of providential humility must pass to reach our consciousness guarantees we will have swallowed the deadly thorn long before we know we have. Then again, at the time that the virgin continuum first suffered its anatomization into parts of speech, no one, neither vegetable nor animal nor god nor world, could conceive of so bizarre and destructive an innovation as self-consciousness, which then lay as far distant in the trackless, unspatialized future as our delivery from the ills and perils of self-consciousness seems to us now, lost as we are in the labyrinthine, suburban sprawl of that same future.

The invention of the circle: such particularly fine notions as *life* will not be deterred from the creation of confections, for the sweet promise of a heaven they can no more deny themselves than water an unobstructed declivity to the level sea and, with serious hands, place their delicious glazed *summa* teetering on a spicule infinitely slender—and us all around in a ring to catch it when it falls.

The plague victim's mephitic breath, like all volcanic exhalations, is accompanied by a lava flow of unnaturally vivid tongue.

Touched, generate; retouched, regenerate; unretouched, unregenerate; reunretouched, reunregenerate; unreunretouched, etc. The maintenance of norms *re*quires constant *re*qualification. *Re*member to pencil in the *re*bellion.

Political animal: what sight loves, sound rejects as touch. What touch can tolerate, smell will drop. It breaks into indistinguishable flavors. Shelter made of an emptiness: is *this* the comfort?

Eternity: or parasitical vine growing proximately along persons, though root and apical structures may extend from the basilary number fetish into a heavens complex respectively, and which often requires surgical adjustment through various cauteries of wonder and/or awe receptors.

Pictures form effortlessly in the mind because the mind is void of pictures.

Shut off from your awareness because they innerve your awareness. . . .

To stare at an object until it's nothing but a congeries of colored patches, to repeat a word until all of its signifying force is drained away, to reduce the great mass of organic response to axiomatic notions, to Platonize, to drag race with death. . . .

The martyrs of a hidden echo as good as plead for their own destruction.

The sacred moment waltzes lambward into self-slaughter. Being: a ritual scarification practiced among intoxicated premises.

Hives of activity are only the scrambled signal of uncertified indolence.

Mother: the four-star generals that defecate shrapnel and cormorants, they too were once boys, and this dark mindless ice once water, these hands, this face in ribbons, the passivities turned to starvation—all that once fed on your sweet blood and breath.

Michael Ives

If words were actually to rise to the expected level of fidelity with those circumstances to which they refer, we would never be able to find our way home.

Milk flows from rents in the cloth of privation.

Again, our average distance from the ground, from all stimulus, as determining the texture of our experience—We're far enough away from everything for desire to have enjoyed the luxuries of a remote empire unmolested by invasion, a perverse enclave of exotic architectures and milk-fed fauna, isolated in the mountains it has discharged around itself, not as an intentional means of defense, but just midden heaps of negations left over from the furious, coiled industry of its formation. Or better, it is from these steeps, these unnamed wastes and wilds, that we deduce the unobservable, exquisite center, our nougat, our *civitas dei.*

Weather represents the most distant yet still articulated interface between motivation and purposelessness; thus, it was the first god.

Time was once conceivable as the aspect and mood of the god verb: a durative tone, the texture of the feeling of movement through a resistant medium. Time has long since been conceivable as the god of *our* aspects and moods: a mercantile tone, the texture of the value of movement through a monetary medium.

Me I could do without. You, however—you remain indispensable . . . then again, only to me. I speak of a you less specific than an actual companion, less generalized than a concept of personhood. Everyone "has" a you and a me—not by choice, not a you according to the me's dictates, yet a me forged in the glow of you. Nor will we find that centrifuge in the form of a stronger verb than "has" that could separate out into possessor and possessed these thoroughly confused elements; a more vivid word would only constrain the easy transmissibility that allows us to represent ourselves in such impersonal and—more to the point—convenient terms. The government of personal pronouns goes to great lengths to maintain a bland, unremarkable surface of signification, an Eisenhower-like rectitude and

180

sleepy competence, but beware the debilitary-pronominal complex that lurks beneath these expediencies, providing and denying certitudes according as one's faith in stable identities wanes and waxes. Thus the tides of our lunacy, governed by little words.

Now means its own brave demolition more than I have ever meant me.

A doctrine concerning the Buoyant Heart has been set adrift in a cask of blood—a bit of itself to eat each day, a quantity of blood to wash itself down, and a rhythm to mark the autophagy, dotted with the trembling sources of unacknowledged hungers. Admonitions that nothing be spared to keep afloat this doctrine of the heart's necessary buoyancy circulate like a sentinel lymph among the letters of the docrine. And hollowing out the vowels of these warnings: a cargo of chained hands, clawing their way toward a relative utopia, where hope is measured in units of chain, where the unhoped-for word cannot be forgotten, nor the unspoken hope forgiven.

The master of any rite is forbidden to witness it. By rite we mean any form of verification. We mean all perception. By a blindness of rites, we mean.

Geological survey: since it has not suffered the fatal *ecstasis* of voluntary movement, as horizonless as it is still, the mineral memory exults through dense systems of modular recollection latticed along arrogant, motiveless integrities, and urged by gracious easements in the closed earth, gives up an occasional (soon to be prostituted) gleam to this peculiar layer of awareness the "laughing animal" chose to inhabit soon after the dove returned to the ark with its legs shackled through a hole in its beak.

Dolphins and tuna: the vagaries of living threaten our way of life. A passing mood has established its own state flower and bird, each hour is busy carving a motto into its forearm, every individual breath must stand on line to register its serial number as an indemnity against the waves of deniers that beat individual things into a submission of indistinctness, against which the deniers themselves are

Michael Ives

helpless, caught as they are in their own mood, the same seine of hours and breaths.

I have taken up the task of being the last thing hereabout and feel the great distance between us holding out in front of me the awareness that very soon I am to be alone. It was not among my intentions, whenever I last had them out, to be the only one left, but I cannot be sure of this. I am so busy guarding my intentions whenever I air them, that I never have a chance either to count or examine them with the least scrutiny. For all I know, many of my intentions might not even belong to me. They could as well have been the possession of another who had them out and I saw a few that I liked and understood them as belonging to me. In fact, some of them may even have sub-intentions all their own. Perhaps several intentions are busy inside me, building my awareness of them, exactly the way I keep busy out here, guarding them, wondering if they're mine, wishing I knew them better. Perhaps it is my intentions who wish for me to be the last thing. That way I will have no reason to go on guarding them. I will finally have the freedom, the luxury, to scrutinize my intentions, perhaps even mother them a little. But by then, they will already have run away.

And in precious torrents of a Creole only half-understood, each passing instant dies equivocating as to who is passing whom, while we lie awake at night unable to sleep, wishing the roots of it all were really the roots of it all.

Each passing day crystalizes into a memory, and every grain of memory fills in an originary Nile, whose inundation once watered our serene, faultless beginning. One's navel is his Valley of Kings.

Into the lake of the mouth, one syllable at a time, I followed a retrograde umbilicus hand over hand back to my thoracic Eurydice.

Michael Ives

PORTRAIT IN THE NEW GRIEF

First you've got *words*, the most
  primitive assault on thought imaginable, that is
after *sentences*, and the wholesale rape
  by *predication* of every last nuance
of original feeling. Then you've got
  the inexorable herniation of pronouns
into empty space causing all these insufferable
  personalities to form. You've got
the forced agglutination of once independent
  memories into a single omnivorous worm, and
a really barbaric disinterest in *mind*
  driving people straight into *mind's* duplicitous arms.
You've got untold numbers of midbody
  extrusions trying to domesticate the *utopia*
of knowledge instead of the reverse
  and getting nowhere a little too quickly, plus
all these oblique *purification rites*
  where single persons break into married couples
and begin to beat each other with earth-
shattering *linguistic concepts* that double
as heavy truncheons. As if that weren't enough,
  there are all of these pre-enjoyed
wedge issues, all this walking *forward*
  by moving *sideways*, and moving *sideways*
by extolling Cézanne and Ellington
  as against Ingres and Basie, and of course
the innumerable efforts to box in a growing
  realization that we're really just the passing moods
of machines and silicate brainstems. Add
  to this the well-funded, age-old campaign
to make cost-effective the practice of excoriating
  tomorrow with an expensive gravel rubdown
of leveraged *anxiety*, and in the end
  what have you got but the same old ruinous *beauty*
of a man dressed in garbage bags asleep
  in a box outside the stock exchange.

183

Michael Ives

ON MICHAEL IVES

THE MOTORIC ENERGY of his inspections is what first caught me: not just the energy—metabolism is general in the animal kingdom— but that the urgency of breath and its deeper, darker sources were being used to inspect—to investigate.

He notices and connects. The brilliance of music is around these texts of his, the general sense of music (the vertical moving forward horizontally, the complexity of harmony simplified into forward melody) yes, but also his specific engagements with the practice of that art.

Ives has the haunted urgency of the autodidact—which in modern America usually means someone whose undergraduate degree serves only as an irritant, no sign of accomplishment but a goad to handle the unknown, and more (sometimes) compelling than the unknown, to embrace the known that is scorned, the textus rejectus of the centuries as well as as-yet unwelcomed innovations in arts and thinking.

And his work has a curious privacy, a man keeping his mind alive in the silences around him, a privacy in which anything can be tried out, try anything once. This is the privacy that is shared by two kinds of people, the savvy loner and the performer onstage, and Ives has been both of those people.

Reading his work makes me think of many things, but most of all it makes me aware of what seems to be, though I don't know that he has announced it as such, the project of his poetics. I take it to be the healing of the parting of the ways that set in, after Modernism, in the long but all too intermittent story of the Conversation poem. Horace, Dryden, Coleridge, Pound's Mauberly—but then a fork: one lane leading to the late masterworks of W. C. Williams and (say) middle Rexroth's skinny and intelligent discourses, one street to- ward the urbane daytime dramaturgy of O'Hara, Schuyler, Ashbery. I feel in all Ives's learned and almost theological searching nonethe- less a nostalgia for the feeling world of Auden, the glistening every- day beauty of the New York School. Societal speculation is the way shy men handle the social.

With Ives's work, I find myself both in familiar territory (the word- learned elucubrations of Moore and Pound, along with the fevered associational midnight logic of Clark Coolidge), but also somewhere I have not walked before. This busy, none too neighborly man is actually trying to make sense of all this stuff. His is not just lyrical

Michael Ives

bravado out of bebop and the OED—he's after something. And his almost remorseless quest for connectivity, *not* association, is what makes his work so striking to me. He writes with an accuracy that glories in words that are so specific that he can say a whole lot very fast—he writes "the inexorable herniation of pronouns," five words that say what I would need to write an essay to get at. Of the texts gathered here (meant to be a sampling of his ways and means of working), the poem called "Portrait in the New Grief" seems clearly to define his process of taking notice, of how he registers the world around him, as well as his compassionate goal.

—*Robert Kelly*

Seven Poems
Genya Turovskaya
—Chosen by Ann Lauterbach

TEMPUS EVERSIONIS

unfinished
symphonies
        over the well edge
        (inverted
tower)

when the whole village came to watch
the armies walking upright

    on the steps of the monastery

              an interior quality

the lens of compassion
like a begging bowl

      we were there too

      rocking over the book   beards
brushing against

the floating filament of temporary
vowels

———

instead of brute force
there is a delay: formalities   stopovers
on the gauge-thin line

186

Genya Turovskaya

the rail will end
and spill

to quantify the losses   name all names

                              we can start

with the names of trees   insect life   the orchestra
of indigenous birds

        that sang to us Mein Schatz

———————

removed from geography   the nonevent   the human
silhouette impressed in an embankment of mud

land mass torn free of the continent

                            it was a house
                            pulled by the ebb tide
            into the gulf stream   its lights
            still on beyond the skyline
                            of the metropolis

seen from a great distance

it could have been a pleasure ship
                            the list of passengers
            suspended
between hemispheres   waving
                  streamers

Genya Turovskaya

inside the closed library

physics and the transmigration of souls
through a keyhole   a light trail   victory arch
relentless dust
rope bridge
          over that primitive landscape

we could start with
we could live with

no rank
no memory   no one lived

a gradual citizen

          just
                              your voice again lagging
                              in the din of the underpass

were the cooling ponds
          to contain the course
          of the searchlight's stroke

                    _____

or the hands erased from the clock

the clock from the wall

the wall from the house

the house from the field

the field from the landscape
in the transient fact of dusk

188

it is metallurgy
        aluminum

the cicadas stirring in the trees

        in counterpoint

against doubt
a moment of faith cannot reconcile
    the heart and its nonsense

        to have said all   in quiet
                                         astonishment

            come back

            theories have broken down
            radiance

        its sound in the causeways

            the Chinese
        string instruments
        whose names were just
            as beautiful

THE BRIDE

    bone-wood cradle   she replaces I   in the slant light's slight
hand   the die rattles in its cup   like croup in moist lungs   catarrh
                    game of craps
informal pronoun you   are dear to me as luck   fortuna   rack and wheel

Genya Turovskaya

          spade   saturnine
indelicate vocabularies guttural   angels   caught in the centrifuge
of the divine act   turning   the leaves gold in leave-
taking   and fall   as led

          one degree   in time of
      separation   (already I have forgotten
      which)   one
degree more or less   this oh this   now   changes breeze
    blown reconfigured trees   the icon painter peels
         metal's counterfeit   eyelids
        in intimate   alloy gilded dome

remained as   relic reliquary   and every end is reached   where
           the source of that red
      unraveled   the stair moves here   to there
      and also   the opposite is true
      we   as we were   is true
  withdrew the word   for such futility   trompe l'oeil

    as the reluctant I   bride   dithered at the entrance
    the floating bridegroom's   wavered   gossamer
bent down   spittled the breast hart in the bright duration's
    bleating   houses   be filled with
    owls   the lyric   he is   I and I
           she

FIVE WINTERS TO VLADIVOSTOK

> *. . . the night lacking darkness but brightened by no light.*
> — Maurice Blanchot

FIRST WINTER

he is lowered into the streets
of his childhood as into
a well

the arcade echoes with the gait
of angry emperors

the boy thinks himself a bell
bell tones

the clang
and clamor

conscripted

sent eastward

out to sea

encephalitis
was vocation in viral form

what is called
a calling

the poet's
prose

thickened in the valves and chambers
of a submarine

he spent his childhood
at extreme ends of the empire's
dictionary

transgressed against
the birch trees

broke ice

with his throat
singing

SECOND WINTER
(NO GRASS IN THAT FIELD OF GRASS BUT LOVE)

every morning he would wake
before dawn
to watch her bicycle
past him
toward
the flaming house

she would at that
very moment of proximity

prevent him

from the fragmented ordeal of speech

he touched the skin
of the passive voice

absorbed the seepage of ink
with its gauze

sepia
as the tea stain

centerless circle

the circumference of his mouth
irreparable

the gaping hole where words
    alight

and die

THIRD WINTER
(MEET ME AT FINLAND STATION)
the body reached its border

his own body
    arbitrary
is a gift

once it has been given

    thinned

by turpentine to no-color

he cannot discern right
    from left
    down from up

what is above his feet

        below his head

    is it snow
the salt plain
    or
      a page

abroad his body grows
heavy
    as a ship

shoaled in the frozen harbor

Genya Turovskaya

because he is of *there*

of *that* illogical element

rather than of another

the woman's
voice saying I want

to prolong your life

FOURTH WINTER
(THE ICE OF LAKE LADOGA)
but the equilibrium
in the inner ear
suggests that he is
still

without movement

tooth marks on the stubbed pencil

a signature
orphaned of its hand

vapor
rises from the swamplands

the throat spasms

the bottle emptied

the sarcoma cut away

he stands knee-deep in the snow
declining
comment

his arm extended
    expectant
      as a falconer's wrist

as the encroaching light disrupts
the teary film
on the eye of the statue

FIFTH WINTER
(EARTH HEAVEN EARTH)
what dies when seen or what
    on seeing
dies

    he said

out of lack the voice
    comes

parallel to speech

hunger
    in the curled fist

ache in the groin

to breathe finally
    is the minimal act

drifting off to sleep his mouth invents

    the verb

to reconcile oneself with the inevitable

    what follows
behind the floats
    of the victory parade

the noise of the spectators' receding
in the newsreel's hum

his tongue gropes for his teeth
inside his mouth

for her

teeth in the absence of his own

he thinks
do we love
those most

who have long forgotten

us in white nets of inertia

the dulled relief on the sarcophagus

are these gates of ivory
gates of horn

BENIGN ARCHITECTURE

1.

He turns to the diorama's benign architecture, builds cathedrals out
of Popsicle sticks and tongue depressors, huts for the peasants, sheds
for the domesticated animals. But the plague is slowly moving down-
river toward the moat and the drawbridge, toward the market stalls
and the *kunstkamera* and his miniature city is burning with the
anticipation of fever.

2.

The airplane monitor reads rising temperatures, terminal velocities.
Upon arrival there will be a telephone booth, the smell of an apothe-
cary, ether, and women waiting, if not eagerly then at least with
some faint sense of the thread remaining intact. He has remained
intact. He asks them: are you still alive? Do your hands still move
beneath the rubble? I am so tentative with desire; your hands do not
move beneath the rubble.

3.

To return to the point of origin he will resurrect himself as a hairless
sphere. What can be reproduced from memory will find its form in
the source, the pocked asphalt, salt-traced, and the traffic of souls
over the boulevards: stone, bronze. The horses flanking the bridge
twist into perpetual submission. The palaces of culture, the palisades
he sees with the eyes of a tourist carried by the dishwater throng.
The metro's mechanized voice announces, stand clear the sky is
closing.

4.

Turned on its side the milk factory gives off a sweet stench. The
boiler room attendant adjusts the valves and the gauges, reads the
thermometers, a book on Euclidean geometry. Every door is like
every other door, every point in the world touches another point as
a map is folded into the breast pocket of the old overcoat. What he
doesn't see is the woman stumbling through the day-old snow, banging on all the black doors marked with a white x, looking for him in
the room with the steam valves and the dingy curtained-off couch,
late for their rendezvous.

5.

Inside the café across the street he drinks a cup of tea to pass the time
and taps his foot under the table to last year's radio anthem, an aging
pop star singing take me with you in a girlish voice. He thinks that
he has shrunk in size, an effigy of himself, like the full-grown Christ
sitting on the Virgin's lap.

Genya Turovskaya

THE INEVITABLE

Like a somnambulist approaching the refrigerator the swimmer
swims out of the spectator's eye to that line in the sea where he
cannot be seen from shore. It is the way of the animal finding its
way home. He swims into the event horizon from which there
is no swimming forward as there is no swimming back.

We have paled without fluorescence as bottom feeders
in that imperturbable depth where mutation
can be mistaken for an act of genius or defiance. What changed.
What straits have narrowed, what genius is the sea's but mutability.
And theirs the face in a ¾ view, the face en face, the bodies raised
upon the swell and then cut down.

Not the diver but the diver's clothes. Not the body but the flippers
aqualung precision instruments. Not the sea but its Hs and O.

Not the sea but its particular gesturing of graphite azure slate.
Not the affair but the affair's discretion. Not the lust but the slate
of the face.

Not the diver but incidental swimmers air drying on the rocks.
Not the proposition but the sudden change in the air. Not the
swimmers but their humid fluctuating shapes.

Not the sun but the baroque excess of sun. Not the proposition
but the lust before erasure of its singular intent. Not the discretion
but the unverifiable act.

Not the affair but its concession to the sea.
Not the body but the bodies on the rocks.

(ELEGY)

You lived astounding things as breathing
air and in the shallows under water faced
the shore as shovels face away in hesitation
from the grave you left the sea behind you saw
in the mirror the back of your head and it was shaved
bereft of clouds the sky was the simplest blue
dogs whined outside the window it was night
and also day or day-for-night clouds moved
across the page and through your voice
and in your mind it must have rained it rained
as tunelessly the singers sang the widows
danced their husbands out of sleep and sons
grew beards and stooped over their books
while elsewhere Ithaca was glittering intact

IRREGULAR SYMMETRIES

1. HAVING LOOKED INTO HIS LOVER'S EYES
HE THOUGHT HE CAUGHT A GLIMPSE OF THE WIFELY GAZE

he writes *martial variations*   erratum: *marital*

the misplaced *i* incidental
to the erasure of the other

rogue body

annulled into silence
coiling and uncoiling

the broken spring
mechanism of the white

night things pinned to the clothesline

he steps outside
"for a pack of cigarettes" and contemplates

Genya Turovskaya

the beauty of the pay phone

the *i*

a loose term of endearment

2. HE BUILDS A TERRARIUM FOR HIS DESPONDENT SNAKES
the snakes he names Maria Dolorosa and Maria Lachrimosa

he had considered Moses and Aaron (the sex indeterminate)

but decided that he preferred the company
of dismal women

and the milk curdles
eats like rust into his teeth

the belfry peals its sinister monotony

long before his train is due to leave
he checks the tables for his own arrival time

and disembarks and climbs aboard again

3. NEITHER HIS WIFE NOR HIS LOVER SEEMS TO NOTICE
    ANYTHING OUT OF THE ORDINARY
the sun obstructs the diminutive of sun

eclipse pauses flight

birds fall from the sky and (this
is difficult for him to say) break

the fugue structures of his heart

irradiated on X-ray film

Genya Turovskaya

halved (in him)

as an atom
of daily bread

4. ALONE AMONG WOMEN

he thinks that he has lifted the wrong
veil
it had all been reduced

to the simple gestures

the way the eyes were cast
by the old masters or the animal

sound of the gulls circling amid the debris
of the empire

the telephone booth pockmarked by the elements
as the only constant

but it remained
consistent

he lifted the veil or the veil fell away

he tossed a coin or a coin was tossed
and one man left
while another man stayed

they drove south to the sea
then west to the sea

then north to the sea
then swam

Genya Turovskaya

5. HE BUILDS THE SPARE, THE NECESSARY HOUSE
and nothing grips like this hybrid logic

he knows it is easier to bring a sentence
to its conclusion than it is to breathe

to breathe is Herculean

what does it matter what he does

what does it matter what he does
away with

there were two churches
two peaked houses

one leaned to the right the other
to the left

ANCHORAGE

dragging over portals, portages, the time of wandering
is winter, the emissaries are sailors on the sea, are tramps
on dry land

———————

we came first, inverted as a momentary merger of light
and dark,
the most immaculate luster becoming us
in the haze: rain had set in
                our clothes were gone

Genya Turovskaya

all of this is real
   it came down, the felled
quarterback, the inarticulate
empire approximating cataclysm, timber

———————

whose boat is this? the foghorn and the quay

but we are still at sea, we climbed into the rocking
boat again, the things that we could not afford
to remember in the vernacular

                 sun
             sinking backward into the world's
             light industry, Eros in idle hands

———————

according to the script
it was the day's end when the first sky thickens and the second
   sky upends
   the roots of trees
when walking in the arbor someone's cell phone rings the tune
of "Auld Lang Syne"
the careless scraping of the iron gate

———————

destabilizing the air, in order to achieve a perfect quiet,
exponentially expand the orchestra

further afield, outside the conference halls
       frenetic times of claims, counterclaims

to see the way ahead toward true signatures, luminous things:
       a tailor's dummy, field of daffodils,

203

to permit trespass through the membrane of the duel's
white glove

for the second
to show the third where the first lay dying
and died

---

in any case it was a futile exercise: the world or its dark horse

it came slowly
that pain doesn't hurt, the blows rained down

---

but the white swells of the mind
remained as harbor lights of temporary cities
                    we made it out of the fog: a figure
swimming to shore with a bag
of winter oranges

lights tinkled around its body
and its eyes

On Genya Turovskaya

A DECADE AGO, Genya Turovskaya, while still an undergraduate, joined my graduate poetry workshop at City College; she was, I recall, attentive to the point of muteness, which she broke from time to time with questions and comments of remarkable acuity. Her poems were unfledged, but showed, in their grasp of prosody and their urge toward complexity, unmistakable signs of a real gift. In the intervening years, she has become not only an accomplished translator from Russian (her first language), specifically of the work of the celebrated poet Arkady Dragomoschenko, but a poet of startling freshness and command.

This past summer, she received a master's degree from the Milton Avery Graduate School of the Arts at Bard College. Her thesis collection is called, simply, "Taking Place" (this selection of poems were all included in it). The title is indicative of her verbal economy: things that take place are events; *place*, on its own, a sign of geographical bearing and physical presence. Within this dynamic construction of event and locale her poems unfold, in Guy Davenport's apt phrase, *a geography of the mind.*

How does a lyric poem think? Through which resources of mind does the poem come into being? Now, of course, the contested lyric must have a certain heightened awareness, spun forth from a vulnerable, mutable agency in which the poet, mobile as this or that pronoun, stripped of identifying attributes, might find multiple perspectives. This necessary flexibility of voice, neither coercive nor arbitrary, is one of the signal traits of Turovskaya's work.

But what gives this work true distinction is, I think, a subtle suspension between the extremity of two iconic cultural/historical moments: the hegemonic hyperbole of late capitalist America and a Russia struggling to find bearings within the ruptured and disorienting conditions of postcommunism. In her work, frames of intimacy and history become fluid constructions, imbued with materials that originate somewhere between personal observation and cultural memory, drawn as much from the immediacy of present particulars as by the almost invisible constraints of cultural markers:

> he spent his childhood
>> at extreme ends of the empire's
> dictionary

205

Genya Turovskaya

> He thinks that he has shrunk in size, an effigy of himself, like
> the full-grown Christ sitting on the Virgin's lap.

Turovskaya's poems resonate within the intricacies of this dual linguistic, geographical and historical heritage. They seem to hover above the incidents to which they refer, but are in themselves concrete, never vague. This is due to the clarity and precision of diction, and the pacing of the lineation. They have neither the murky strains of recollection nor the exaggerations of dream; they do not indulge in self-conscious *angst* about the inadequacies of form. Narrative elements retain the tonal intimacy and immediacy of *telling*, but the range of inclusion, the agile swerves into and away from specific setting, belie any simplistic notion of witnessing. In "Five Winters to Vladivostok," for instance, locale is dis/placed while a narrative motion pushes forward; a rupture of temporal and spatial coordinates that collapse into a nearness, a musical conviction, that gives many of her poems their special character.

> he stands knee-deep in the snow
> declining
>   comment
>
> his arm extended
>   expectant
>   as a falconer's wrist
>
> as the encroaching light disrupts
> the teary film
> on the eye of the statue

In Turovskaya's poems, each line carries an obligation to make something happen—Pound's dictum ("use no word . . .") revised and extended from word to line. There are surprising shifts in texture and pitch. Incidents accrue toward revelation, revelation is thwarted by incident.

> whose boat is this? the foghorn and the quay
>
> but we are still at sea, we climbed into the rocking
> boat again, the things that we could not afford
> to remember in the vernacular
>
>   sun
>   sinking backward into the world's
>   light industry, Eros in idle hands

206

Genya Turovskaya

Genya Turovskaya's work, its surface shimmering with an almost vertiginous attention to the pulse of the mind as it listens to the heart, pivots and comes to rest exactly where the mystery of language touches down on the mystery of life. Much pleasure for her readers ensues.

—*Ann Lauterbach*

Stone Animals
Kelly Link

HENRY ASKED A QUESTION. He was joking.

"As a matter of fact," the real estate agent snapped, "it is."

It was not a question she had expected to be asked. She gave Henry a goofy, appeasing smile and yanked at the hem of the skirt of her pink linen suit, which seemed as if it might, at any moment, go rolling up her knees like a window shade. She was younger than Henry, and sold houses that she couldn't afford to buy.

"It's reflected in the asking price, of course," she said. "Like you said."

Henry stared at her. She blushed.

"I've never seen anything," she said. "But there are stories. Not stories that I know. I just know there are stories. If you believe that sort of thing."

"I don't," Henry said. When he looked over to see if Catherine had heard, she had her head up the tiled fireplace, as if she were trying it on, to see whether it fit. Catherine was six months pregnant. Nothing fit her except for Henry's baseball caps, his sweatpants, his T-shirts. But she liked the fireplace.

Carleton was running up and down the staircase, slapping his heels down hard, keeping his head down and his hands folded around the banister. Carleton was serious about how he played. Tilly sat on the landing, reading a book, legs poking out through the railings. Whenever Carleton ran past, he thumped her on the head, but Tilly never said a word. Carleton would be sorry later, and never even know why.

Catherine took her head out of the fireplace. "Guys," she said. "Carleton, Tilly. Slow down a minute and tell me what you think. Think King Spanky will be OK out here?"

"King Spanky is a cat, Mom," Tilly said. "Maybe we should get a dog, you know, to help protect us." She could tell by looking at her mother that they were going to move. She didn't know how she felt about this, except she had plans for the yard. A yard like that needed a dog.

Kelly Link

"I don't like big dogs," said Carleton, six years old and small for his age. "I don't like this staircase. It's too big."

"Carleton," Henry said. "Come here. I need a hug."

Carleton came down the stairs. He lay down on his stomach on the floor and rolled, noisily, floppily, slowly, over to where Henry stood with the real estate agent. He curled like a dead snake around Henry's ankles. "I don't like those dogs outside," he said.

"I know it looks like we're out in the middle of nothing, but if you go down through the backyard, cut through that stand of trees, there's this little path. It takes you straight down to the train station. Ten-minute bike ride," the agent said. Nobody ever remembered her name, which was why she had to wear too-tight skirts. She was, as it happened, writing a romance novel, and she spent a lot of time making up pseudonyms, just in case she ever finished it. Ophelia Pink. Matilde Hightower. LaLa Treeble. Or maybe she'd write gothics. Ghost stories. But not about people like these. "Another ten minutes on that path and you're in town."

"What dogs, Carleton?" Henry said.

"I think they're lions, Carleton," said Catherine. "You mean the stone ones beside the door? Just like the lions at the library. You love those lions, Carleton. Patience and Fortitude?"

"I've always thought they were rabbits," the real estate agent said. "You know, because of the ears. They have big ears." She flopped her hands and then tugged at her skirt, which would not stay down. "I think they're pretty valuable. The guy who built the house had a gallery in New York. He knew a lot of sculptors."

Henry was struck by that. He didn't think he knew a single sculptor.

"I don't like the rabbits," Carleton said. "I don't like the staircase. I don't like this room. It's too big. I don't like *her*."

"Carleton," Henry said. He smiled at the real estate agent.

"I don't like the house," Carleton said, clinging to Henry's ankles. "I don't like houses. I don't want to live in a house."

"Then we'll build you a tepee out on the lawn," Catherine said. She sat on the stairs beside Tilly, who shifted her weight, almost imperceptibly, toward Catherine. Catherine sat as still as possible. Tilly was in fourth grade and difficult in a way that girls weren't supposed to be. Mostly she refused to be cuddled or babied. But she sat there, leaning on Catherine's arm, emanating saintly fragrances: peacefulness, placidness, goodness. *I want this house*, Catherine said, moving her lips like a silent-movie heroine, to Henry, so that

209

neither Carleton nor the agent, who had bent over to inspect a piece of dust on the floor, could see. "You can live in your tepee, and we'll invite you to come over for lunch. You like lunch, don't you? Peanut butter sandwiches?"

"I don't," Carleton said and sobbed once.

But they bought the house anyway. The real estate agent got her commission. Tilly rubbed the waxy stone ears of the rabbits on the way out, pretending that they already belonged to her. They were as tall as she was, but that wouldn't always be true. Carleton had a peanut butter sandwich.

The rabbits sat on either side of the front door. Two stone animals sitting on cracked, mossy haunches. They were shapeless, lumpish, patient in a way that seemed not worn down, but perhaps never really finished in the first place. There was something about them that reminded Henry of Stonehenge. Catherine thought of topiary shapes, *The Velveteen Rabbit*, soldiers who stand guard in front of palaces and never even twitch their noses. Maybe they could be donated to a museum. Or broken up with jackhammers. They didn't suit the house at all.

"So what's the house like?" said Henry's boss. She was carefully stretching rubber bands around her rubber-band ball. By now the rubber-band ball was so big she had to get special extra-large rubber bands from the art department. She claimed it helped her think. She had tried knitting for a while, but it turned out that knitting was too utilitarian, too feminine. Making an enormous ball out of rubber bands struck the right note. It was something a man might do.

It took up half of her desk. Under the fluorescent office lights it had a peeled red liveliness. You almost expected it to shoot forward and out the door. The larger it got, the more it looked like some kind of eyeless, hairless, legless animal. Maybe a dog. A Carleton-sized dog, Henry thought, although not a Carleton-sized rubber-band ball.

Catherine joked sometimes about using the carleton as a measure of unit.

"Big," Henry said. "Haunted."

"Really?" his boss said. "So's this rubber band." She aimed a rubber band at Henry and shot him in the elbow. This was meant to suggest that she and Henry were good friends, and just goofing

210

around, the way good friends did. But what it really meant was that she was angry at him. "Don't leave me," she said.

"I'm only two hours away." Henry put up his hand to ward off rubber bands. "Quit it. We talk on the phone, we use e-mail. I come back to town when you need me in the office."

"You're sure this is a good idea?" his boss said. She fixed her reptilian, watery gaze on him. She had problematical tear ducts. Though she could have had a minor surgical procedure to fix this, she'd chosen not to. It was a tactical advantage, the way it spooked people.

It didn't really matter that Henry remained immune to rubber bands and crocodile tears. She had backup strategies. She thought about which would be most effective while Henry pitched his stupid idea all over again.

Henry had the movers' phone number in his pocket, like a talisman. He wanted to take it out, wave it at the Crocodile, say, Look at this! Instead he said, "For nine years, we've lived in an apartment next door to a building that smells like urine. Like someone built an entire building out of bricks made of compressed red pee. Someone spit on Catherine in the street last week. This old Russian lady in a fur coat. A kid rang our doorbell the other day and tried to sell us gas masks. Door-to-door gas-mask salesman. Catherine bought one. When she told me about it she burst into tears. She said she couldn't figure out if she was feeling guilty because she'd bought a gas mask, or if it was because she hadn't bought enough for everyone."

"Good Chinese food," his boss said. "Good movies. Good bookstores. Good dry cleaners. Good conversation."

"Tree houses," Henry said. "I had a tree house when I was a kid."

"You were never a kid," his boss said.

"Three bathrooms. Crown moldings. We can't even see our nearest neighbor's house. I get up in the morning, have coffee, put Carleton and Tilly on the bus, and go to work in my pajamas."

"What about Catherine?" The Crocodile put her head down on her rubber-band ball. Possibly this was a gesture of defeat.

"There was that thing. Catherine's whole department is leaving. Like rats deserting a sinking ship. Anyway, Catherine needs a change. And so do I," Henry said. "We've got another kid on the way. We're going to garden. Catherine'll teach ESL, find a book group, write her book. Teach the kids how to play bridge. You've got to start them early."

He picked a rubber band off the floor and offered it to his boss. "You should come out and visit some weekend."

Kelly Link

"I never go upstate," the Crocodile said. She held onto her rubber-band ball. "Too many ghosts."

"Are you going to miss this? Living here?" Catherine said. She couldn't stand the way her stomach poked out. She couldn't see past it. She held up her left foot to make sure it was still there, and pulled the sheet off Henry.

"I love the house," Henry said.

"Me too," Catherine said. She was biting her fingernails. Henry could hear her teeth going click, click. Now she had both feet up in the air. She wiggled them around. Hello, feet.

"What are you doing?"

She put them down again. On the street outside, cars came and went, pushing smears of light along the ceiling, slow and fast at the same time. The baby was wriggling around inside her, kicking out with both feet like it was swimming across the English Channel, the Pacific. Kicking all the way to China. "Did you buy that story about the former owners moving to France?"

"I don't believe in France," Henry said. *"Je ne crois pas en France."*

"Neither do I," Catherine said. "Henry?"

"What?"

"Do you love the house?"

"I love the house."

"I love it more than you do," Catherine said, although Henry hated it when she said things like that. "What do you love best?"

"That room in the front," Henry said. "With the windows. Our bedroom. Those weird rabbit statues."

"Me too," Catherine said, although she didn't. "I love those rabbits."

Then she said, "Do you ever worry about Carleton and Tilly?"

"What do you mean?" Henry said. He looked at the alarm clock: it was 4 A.M. "Why are we awake right now?"

"Sometimes I worry that I love one of them better," Catherine said. "Like I might love Tilly better. Because she used to wet the bed. Because she's always so angry. Or Carleton, because he was so sick when he was little."

"I love them both the same," Henry said.

He didn't even know he was lying. Catherine knew, though. She knew he was lying, and she knew he didn't even know it. Most of the

212

time she thought that it was OK. As long as he thought he loved them both the same, and acted as if he did, that was good enough.

"Well, do you ever worry that you love them more than me?" she said. "Or that I love them more than I love you?"

"Do you?" Henry said.

"Of course," Catherine said. "I have to. It's my job."

She found the gas mask in a box of wineglasses, and also six recent issues of the *New Yorker*, which she still might get a chance to read someday. She put the gas mask under the sink and the *New Yorkers* in the sink. Why not? It was her sink. She could put anything she wanted into it. She took the magazines out again and put them into the refrigerator, just for fun.

Henry came into the kitchen, holding silver candlesticks and a stuffed armadillo, which someone had made into a purse. It had a shoulder strap made out of its own skin. You opened its mouth and put things inside it, lipstick and subway tokens. It had pink gimlet eyes and smelled strongly of vinegar. It belonged to Tilly, although how it had come into her possession was unclear. Tilly claimed she'd won it at school in a contest involving doughnuts. Catherine thought it more likely Tilly had either stolen it or (slightly preferable) found it in someone's trash. Now Tilly kept her most valuable belongings inside the purse, to keep them safe from Carleton, who was covetous of the previous things—because they were small, and because they belonged to Tilly—but afraid of the armadillo.

"I've already told her she can't take it to school for at least the first two weeks. Then we'll see." She took the purse from Henry and put it under the sink with the gas mask.

"What are they doing?" Henry said. Framed in the kitchen window, Carleton and Tilly hunched over the lawn. They had a pair of scissors and a notebook and a stapler.

"They're collecting grass." Catherine took dishes out of a box, put the bubble wrap aside for Tilly to stomp, and stowed the dishes in a cabinet. The baby kicked like it knew all about bubble wrap. "Whoa, Fireplace," she said. "We don't have a dancing license in there."

Henry put out his hand, rapped on Catherine's stomach. *Knock, knock.* It was Tilly's joke. Catherine would say, "Who's there?" and Tilly would say, Candlestick's here. Fat Man's here. Box. Hammer. Milkshake. Clarinet. Mousetrap. Fiddlestick. Tilly had a whole list of names for the baby. The real estate agent would have approved.

213

"Where's King Spanky?" Henry said.

"Under our bed," Catherine said. "He's up in the box frame."

"Have we unpacked the alarm clock?" Henry said.

"Poor King Spanky," Catherine said. "Nobody to love except an alarm clock. Come upstairs and let's see if we can shake him out of the bed. I've got a present for you."

The present was in a U-Haul box exactly like all the other boxes in the bedroom, except that Catherine had written HENRY'S PRESENT on it instead of LARGE FRONT BEDROOM. Inside the box were Styrofoam peanuts and then a smaller box from Takashimaya. The Takashimaya box was fastened with a silver ribbon. The tissue paper inside was dull gold, and inside the tissue paper was a green silk robe with orange sleeves and heraldic animals in orange and gold thread.

"Lions," Henry said.

"Rabbits," Catherine said.

"I didn't get you anything," Henry said.

Catherine smiled nobly. She liked giving presents better than getting presents. She'd never told Henry, because it seemed to her that it must be selfish in some way she'd never bothered to figure out. Catherine was grateful to be married to Henry, who accepted all presents as his due; who looked good in the clothes she bought him; who was vain, in an easygoing way, about his good looks. Buying clothes for Henry was especially satisfying now, while she was pregnant and couldn't buy them for herself.

She said, "If you don't like it, then I'll keep it. Look at you, look at those sleeves. You look like the emperor of Japan."

They had already colonized the bedroom, making it full of things that belonged to them. There was Catherine's mirror on the wall, and their mahogany wardrobe, their first real piece of furniture, a wedding present from Catherine's great-aunt. There was their serviceable queen-size bed with King Spanky lodged up inside it, and there was Henry, spinning his arms in the wide orange sleeves, like an embroidered windmill. Henry could see all of these things in the mirror, and behind him, their lawn and Tilly and Carleton, stapling grass into their notebook. He saw all of these things and he found them good. But he couldn't see Catherine. When he turned around, she stood in the doorway, frowning at him. She had the alarm clock in her hand.

"Look at you," she said again. It worried her, the way something, someone, *Henry*, could suddenly look like a place she'd never been before. The alarm began to ring and King Spanky came out from under the bed, trotting over to Catherine. She bent over, awkwardly—ungraceful, ungainly, so clumsy, so fucking awkward; being pregnant was like wearing a fucking suitcase strapped across your middle—put the alarm clock down on the ground, and King Spanky hunkered down in front of it, his nose against the ringing glass face.

And that made her laugh again. Henry loved Catherine's laugh. Downstairs, their children slammed a door open, ran through the house, carrying scissors, both Catherine and Henry knew, and slammed another door open and were outside again, leaving behind the smell of grass. There was a store in New York where you could buy a perfume that smelled like that.

Catherine and Carleton and Tilly came back from the grocery store with a tire, a rope to hang it from, and a box of pancake mix for dinner. Henry was online, looking at a JPEG of a rubber-band ball. There was a message, too. The Crocodile needed him to come into the office. It would be just a few days. Someone was setting fires and there was no one smart enough to see how to put them out except for him. They were his accounts. He had to come in and save them. She knew Catherine and Henry's apartment hadn't sold; she'd checked with their listing agent. So surely it wouldn't be impossible, not impossible, only inconvenient.

He went downstairs to tell Catherine. "That *witch*," she said, and then bit her lip. "She called the listing agent? I'm sorry. We talked about this. Never mind. Just give me a moment."

Catherine inhaled. Exhaled. Inhaled. If she were Carleton she would hold her breath until her face turned red and Henry agreed to stay home, but then again, it never worked for Carleton. "We ran into our new neighbors in the grocery store. She's about the same age as me. Liz and Marcus. One kid, older, a girl, um, I think her name was Alison, maybe from a first marriage—potential babysitter, which is really good news. Liz is a lawyer. Gorgeous. Reads Oprah books. He likes to cook."

"So do I," Henry said.

"You're better looking," Catherine said. "So do you have to go back tonight, or can you take the train in the morning?"

"The morning is fine," Henry said, wanting to seem agreeable.

Carleton appeared in the kitchen, his arms pinned around King Spanky's middle. The cat's front legs stuck straight out, as if Carleton were dowsing. King Spanky's eyes were closed. His whiskers

twitched Morse code. "What are you wearing?" Carleton said.
"My new uniform," Henry said. "I wear it to work."
"Where do you work?" Carleton said, testing.
"I work at home," Henry said. Catherine snorted.
"He looks like the king of rabbits, doesn't he? The emperor of Rabbitaly," she said, no longer sounding particularly pleased about this.
"He looks like a princess," Carleton said, now pointing King Spanky at Henry like a gun.
"Where's your grass collection?" Henry said. "Can I see it?"
"No," Carleton said. He put King Spanky on the floor, and the cat slunk out of the kitchen, heading for the staircase, the bedroom, the safety of the bedsprings, the beloved alarm clock, the beloved. The beloved may be treacherous, greasy-headed, and given to evil habits, or else it can be a man in his late forties who works too much, or it can be an alarm clock.
"After dinner," Henry said, trying again, "we could go out and find a tree for your tire swing."
"No," Carleton said regretfully. He lingered in the kitchen, hoping to be asked a question to which he could say yes.
"Where's your sister?" Henry said.
"Watching television," Carleton said. "I don't like the television here."
"It's too big," Henry said, but Catherine didn't laugh.

Henry dreams he is the king of the real estate agents. Henry loves his job. He tries to sell a house to a young couple with twitchy noses and big dark eyes. Why does he always dream that he's trying to sell things?
The couple stare at him nervously. He leans toward them as if he's going to whisper something in their silly, expectant ears. It's a secret he's never told anyone before. It's a secret he didn't even know that he knew. "Let's stop fooling," he says. "You can't afford to buy this house. You don't have any money. You're rabbits."

"Where do you work?" Carleton said in the morning when Henry called from Grand Central.
"I work at home," Henry said. "Home where we live now, where you are. Eventually. Just not today. Are you getting ready for school?"

Carleton put the phone down. Henry could hear him saying something to Catherine. "He says he's not nervous about school," she said. "He's a brave kid."

"I kissed you this morning," Henry said, "but you didn't wake up. There were all these rabbits on the lawn. They were huge. King Spanky–sized. They were just sitting there like they were waiting for the sun to come up. It was funny, like some kind of art installation. But it was kind of creepy, too. Think they'd been there all night?"

"Rabbits? Can they have rabies? I saw them this morning when I got up," Catherine said. "Carleton didn't want to brush his teeth this morning. He says something's wrong with his toothbrush."

"Maybe he dropped it in the toilet, and he doesn't want to tell you," Henry said.

"Maybe you could buy a new toothbrush and bring it home," Catherine said. "He doesn't want one from the drugstore here. He wants one from New York."

"Where's Tilly?" Henry said.

"She says she's trying to figure out what's wrong with Carleton's toothbrush. She's still in the bathroom," Catherine said.

"Can I talk to her for a second?" Henry said.

"Tell her she needs to get dressed and eat her Cheerios," Catherine said. "After I drive them to school, Liz is coming over for coffee. Then we're going to go out for lunch. I'm not unpacking another box until you get home. Here's Tilly."

"Hi," Tilly said. She sounded as if she was asking a question.

Tilly never liked talking to people on the telephone. How were you supposed to know if they were really who they said they were? And even if they were who they claimed to be, they didn't know whether you were who you said you were. You could be someone else. They might give away information about you, and not even know it. There were no protocols. No precautions.

She said, "Did you brush your teeth this morning?"

"Good morning, Tilly," her father (if it was her father) said. "My toothbrush was fine. Perfectly normal."

"That's good," Tilly said. "I let Carleton use mine."

"That was very generous," Henry said.

"No problem," Tilly said. Sharing things with Carleton wasn't like having to share things with other people. It wasn't really like sharing things at all. Carleton belonged to her, like the toothbrush. "Mom says that when we get home today, we can draw on the walls in our

217

rooms if we want to, while we decide what color we want to paint them."

"Sounds like fun," Henry said. "Can I draw on them, too?"

"Maybe," Tilly said. She had already said too much. "Gotta go. Gotta eat breakfast."

"Don't be worried about school," Henry said.

"I'm not worried about school," Tilly said.

"I love you," Henry said.

"I'm real concerned about this toothbrush," Tilly said.

He only closed his eyes for a minute. Just for a minute. When he woke up, it was dark and he didn't know where he was. He stood up and went over to the door, almost tripping over something. It sailed away from him in an exuberant, rollicking sweep.

According to the clock on his desk, it was 4 A.M. Why was it always 4 A.M.? There were four messages on his cell phone, all from Catherine.

He went online and checked train schedules. Then he sent Catherine a fast e-mail.

Fell asleep @ midnight? Mssed trains. Awake now, going to keep on working. Pttng out fires. Take the train home early afternoon? Still lv me?

Before he went back to work, he kicked the rubber-band ball back down the hall toward the Crocodile's door.

Catherine called him at 8:45.

"I'm sorry," Henry said.

"I bet you are," Catherine said.

"I can't find my razor. I think the Crocodile had some kind of tantrum and tossed my stuff."

"Carleton will love that," Catherine said. "Maybe you should sneak in the house and shave before dinner. He had a hard day at school yesterday."

"Maybe I should grow a beard," Henry said. "He can't be afraid of everything all the time. Tell me about the first day of school."

218

"We'll talk about it later," Catherine said. "Liz just drove up. I'm going to be her guest at the gym. Just make it home for dinner."

At 6 P.M. Henry e-mailed Catherine again. "Srry. Accidentally startd avalanche while puttng out fires. Wait up for me? How ws second day of school?" She didn't write him back. He called and no one picked up the phone. She didn't call.

He took the last train home. By the time they reached the station, he was the only one left in his car. He unchained his bicycle and rode it home in the dark. Rabbits pelted across the footpath in front of his bike. There were rabbits foraging on his lawn. They froze as he dismounted and pushed the bicycle across the grass. The lawn was rumpled; the bike went up and down over invisible depressions that he supposed were rabbit holes. There were two short, fat men standing in the dark on either side of the front door, waiting for him, but when he came closer, he remembered that they were stone rabbits. "Knock, knock," he said.

The real rabbits on the lawn tipped their ears at him. The stone rabbits waited for the punch line, but they were just stone rabbits. They had nothing better to do.

The front door wasn't locked. He walked through the downstairs rooms, putting his hands on the backs and tops of furniture. In the kitchen, cut-down boxes leaned in stacks against the wall, waiting to be recycled or remade into cardboard houses and spaceships and tunnels for Carleton and Tilly.

Catherine had unpacked Carleton's room. Night-lights in the shapes of bears and geese and cats were plugged into every floor outlet. There were little low-watt table lamps as well—hippo, robot, gorilla, pirate ship. Everything was soaked in a tender, peaceable light, translating Carleton's room into something more than a bedroom: something luminous, numinous, a cartoony midnight church of sleep.

Tilly was sleeping in the other bed.

Tilly would never admit that she sleepwalked, the same way that she would never admit that she sometimes still wet the bed. But she refused to make friends. Making friends would have meant spending the night in strange houses. Tomorrow morning she would insist that Henry or Catherine must have carried her from her room, put her to bed in Carleton's room for reasons of their own.

Henry knelt down between the two beds and kissed Carleton on

219

the forehead. He kissed Tilly, smoothed her hair. How could he not love Tilly better? He'd known her longer. She was so brave, so angry.

On the walls of Carleton's bedroom, Henry's children had drawn a house. A cat nearly as big as the house. There was a crown on the cat's head. Trees or flowers with pairs of leaves that pointed straight up, still bigger, and a stick figure on a stick bicycle, riding past the trees. When he looked closer, he thought that maybe the trees were actually rabbits. The wall smelled like Froot Loops. Someone had written HENRY IS A RAT FINK! HA HA! He recognized his wife's handwriting.

"Scented markers," Catherine said. She stood in the door, holding a pillow against her stomach. "I was sleeping downstairs on the sofa. You walked right past and didn't see me."

"The front door was unlocked," Henry said.

"Liz says nobody ever locks their doors out here," Catherine said. "Are you coming to bed, or were you just stopping by to see how we were?"

"I have to go back in tomorrow," Henry said. He pulled a toothbrush out of his pocket and showed it to her. "There's a box of Krispy Kreme doughnuts on the kitchen counter."

"Delete the doughnuts," Catherine said. "I'm not that easy." She took a step toward him and accidentally kicked King Spanky. The cat yowled. Carleton woke up. He said, "Who's there? Who's there?"

"It's me," Henry said. He knelt beside Carleton's bed in the light of the Winnie-the-Pooh lamp. "I brought you a new toothbrush."

Carleton whimpered.

"What's wrong, spaceman?" Henry said. "It's just a toothbrush." He leaned toward Carleton and Carleton scooted back. He began to scream.

In the other bed, Tilly was dreaming about rabbits. When she'd come home from school, she and Carleton had seen rabbits, sitting on the lawn as if they had kept watch over the house all the time that Tilly had been gone. In her dream they were still there. She dreamed she was creeping up on them. They opened their mouths, wide enough to reach inside like she was some kind of rabbit dentist, and so she did. She put her hand around something small and cold and hard. Maybe it was a ring, a diamond ring. Or a. Or. It was a. She couldn't wait to show Carleton. Her arm was inside the rabbit all the way to her shoulder. Someone put their hand around her wrist and yanked. Somewhere her mother was talking. She said—

"It's the beard."

Catherine couldn't decide whether to laugh or cry or scream like Carleton. That would surprise Carleton, if she started screaming, too. "Shoo! Shoo, Henry—go shave and come back as quick as you can, or else he'll never go back to sleep."

"Carleton, honey," she was saying as Henry left the room, "it's your dad. It's not Santa Claus. It's not the big bad wolf. It's your dad. Your dad just forgot. Why don't you tell me a story? Or do you want to go watch your daddy shave?"

Catherine's hot water bottle was draped over the tub. Towels were heaped on the floor. Henry's things had been put away behind the mirror. It made him feel tired, thinking of all the other things that still had to be put away. He washed his hands, then looked at the bar of soap. It didn't feel right. He put it back on the sink, bent over and sniffed it and then tore off a piece of toilet paper, used the toilet paper to pick up the soap. He threw it in the trash and unwrapped a new bar of soap. There was nothing wrong with the new soap. There was nothing wrong with the old soap either. He was just tired. He washed his hands and lathered up his face, shaved off his beard, and watched the little bristles of hair wash down the sink. When he went to show Carleton his brand-new face, Catherine was curled up in bed beside Carleton. They were both asleep. They were still asleep when he left the house at five-thirty the next morning.

"Where are you?" Catherine said.

"I'm on my way home. I'm on the train." The train was still in the station. They would be leaving any minute. They had been leaving any minute for the last hour or so, and before that, they had had to get off the train twice, and then back on again. They had been assured there was nothing to worry about. There was no bomb threat. There was no bomb. The delay was only temporary. The people on the train looked at each other, trying to seem as if they were not looking. Everyone had their cell phones out.

"The rabbits are out on the lawn again," Catherine said. "There must be at least fifty or sixty. I've never counted rabbits before. Tilly keeps trying to go outside to make friends with them, but as soon as she's outside, they all go bouncing away like beach balls. I talked to a lawn specialist today. He says we need to do something about it, which is what Liz was saying. Rabbits can be a big problem out here. They've probably got tunnels and warrens all through the yard. It could be a problem. Like living on top of a sinkhole. But Tilly is never going to forgive us. She knows something's up. She says she doesn't want a dog anymore. It would scare away the rabbits. Do you think we should get a dog?"

"So what do they do? Put out poison? Dig up the yard?" Henry said. The man in the seat in front of him got up. He took his bags out of the luggage rack and left the train. Everyone watched him go, pretending they were not.

"He was telling me they have these devices, kind of like ultrasound equipment. They plot out the tunnels, close them up, and then gas the rabbits. It sounds gruesome," Catherine said. "And this kid, this baby has been kicking the daylights out of me. All day long it's kick, kick, jump, kick, like some kind of martial artist. He's going to be an angry kid, Henry. Just like his sister. Her sister. Or maybe I'm going to give birth to rabbits."

"As long as they have your eyes and my chin," Henry said.

"I've gotta go," Catherine said. "I have to pee again. All day long it's the kid jumping, me peeing, Tilly getting her heart broken because she can't make friends with the rabbits, me worrying because she doesn't want to make friends with other kids, just with rabbits, Carleton asking if today he has to go to school, does he have to go to school tomorrow, why am I making him go to school when everybody there is bigger than him, why is my stomach so big and fat, why does his teacher tell him to act like a big boy? Henry, why are we doing this again? Why am I pregnant? And where are you? Why aren't you here? What about our deal? Don't you want to be here?"

"I'm sorry," Henry said. "I'll talk to the Crocodile. We'll work something out."

"I thought you wanted this, too, Henry. Don't you?"

"Of course," Henry said. "Of course I want this."

"I've gotta go," Catherine said again. "Liz is bringing some women over. We're finally starting that book club. We're going to read *Fight Club*. Her stepdaughter, Alison, is going to look after Tilly and Carleton for me. I've already talked to Tilly. She promises she won't bite or hit or make Alison cry."

"What's the trade? A few hours of bonus TV?"

"No," Catherine said. "Something's up with the TV."

"What's wrong with the TV?"

"I don't know," Catherine said. "It's working fine. But the kids won't go near it. Isn't that great? It's the same thing as the toothbrush. You'll see when you get home. I mean, it's not just the kids. I was watching the news earlier, and then I had to turn it off. It wasn't the news. It was the TV."

"So it's the downstairs bathroom and the coffee maker and Carleton's toothbrush and now the TV?"

"There's some other stuff as well, since this morning. Your office, apparently. Everything in it—your desk, your bookshelves, your chair, even the paper clips."

"That's probably a good thing, right? I mean, that way they'll stay out of there."

"I guess," Catherine said. "The thing is, I went and stood in there for a while and it gave me the creeps, too. So now I can't pick up e-mail. And I had to throw out more soap. And King Spanky doesn't love the alarm clock anymore. He won't come out from under the bed when I set it off."

"The alarm clock, too?"

"It does sound different," Catherine said. "Just a little bit different. Or maybe I'm insane. This morning, Carleton told me that he knew where our house was. He said we were living in a secret part of Central Park. He said he recognizes the trees. He thinks that if he walks down that little path, he'll get mugged. I've really got to go, Henry, or I'm going to wet my pants, and I don't have time to change again before everyone gets here."

"I love you," Henry said.

"Then why aren't you here?" Catherine said victoriously. She hung up and ran down the hallway toward the downstairs bathroom. But when she got there, she turned around. She went racing up the stairs, pulling down her pants as she went, and barely got to the master bedroom bathroom in time. All day long she'd gone up and down the stairs, feeling extremely silly. There was nothing wrong with the downstairs bathroom. It was just the fixtures. When you flushed the toilet or ran water in the sink. She didn't like the sound the water made.

Several times now, Henry had come home and found Catherine painting rooms, which was a problem. The problem was that Henry kept going away. If he didn't keep going away, he wouldn't have to keep coming home. That was Catherine's point. Henry's point was that Catherine wasn't supposed to be painting rooms while she was pregnant. Pregnant women were supposed to stay away from paint fumes.

Catherine had solved this problem by wearing the gas mask while she painted. She had known the gas mask would come in handy. She told Henry she promised to stop painting as soon as he started working at home, which was the plan. Meanwhile, she couldn't decide on colors. She and Carleton and Tilly spent hours looking at paint strips with colors that had names like Sangria, Peat Bog, Tulip, Tantrum, Planetarium, Galactica, Tea Leaf, Egg Yolk, Tinker Toy, Gauguin, Susan, Envy, Aztec, Utopia, Wax Apple, Rice Bowl, Cry Baby, Fat Lip, Green Banana, Trampoline, Fingernail. It was a wonderful way to spend time. They went off to school, and when they got home, the living room would be Harp Seal instead of Full Moon. They'd spend some time with that color, getting to know it, ignoring the television, which was haunted (haunted wasn't the right word, of course, but Catherine couldn't think what the right word was), and then a couple of days later, Catherine would go buy some more primer and start again. Carleton and Tilly loved this. They begged her to repaint their bedrooms. She did.

She wished she could eat paint. Whenever she opened a can of paint, her mouth filled with saliva. When she'd been pregnant with Carleton, she hadn't been able to eat anything except olives and hearts of palm and dry toast. When she'd been pregnant with Tilly, she'd eaten dirt once in Central Park. Tilly thought they should name the baby after a paint color—Chalk, or Dilly Dilly, or Keelhauled. Lapis Lazulily. Knock, Knock.

Catherine kept meaning to ask Henry to take the television and put it in the garage. Nobody ever watched it now. They'd had to stop using the microwave as well, and a colander, some of the flatware, and she was keeping an eye on the toaster. She had a premonition, or an intuition. It didn't feel wrong, not yet, but she had a feeling about it. There was a gorgeous pair of earrings that Henry had given her—how was it possible to be spooked by a pair of diamond earrings?—and yet. Carleton wouldn't play with his Lincoln Logs, and so they were going to the Salvation Army, and Tilly's armadillo purse had disappeared. Tilly hadn't said anything about it, and Catherine hadn't wanted to ask.

Sometimes, if Henry wasn't coming home, Catherine painted after Carleton and Tilly went to bed. Sometimes Tilly would walk into the room where Catherine was working, Tilly's eyes closed, her mouth open, a tourist-somnambulist. She'd stand there with her head cocked toward Catherine. If Catherine spoke to her, she didn't answer, and if Catherine took her hand, she would follow Catherine back to her own bed and lie down again. But sometimes Catherine let Tilly stand there and keep her company. Tilly was never so attentive, so *present*, when she was awake. Eventually she would turn and leave the room and Catherine would listen to her climb back up the stairs. Then Catherine would be alone again.

Catherine dreams about colors. It turns out her marriage was the same color she had just painted the foyer. Velveteen Fade. Leonard Felter, who had had an ongoing affair with two of his graduate students, several adjuncts, two tenured faculty members, brought down Catherine's entire department, and saved Catherine's marriage, would make a good lipstick or nail polish. Peach Nooky. There's the Crocodile, a particularly bilious Eau de Vil, a color that tastes bad when you say it. Her mother, who had always been disappointed by Catherine's choices, turned out to have been a beautiful, rich, deep chocolate. Why hadn't Catherine ever seen that before? Too late, too late. It made her want to cry.

Liz and she are drinking paint, thick and pale as cream. "Have some more paint," Catherine says. "Do you want sugar?"

"Yes, lots," Liz says. "What color are you going to paint the rabbits?"

Catherine passes her the sugar. She hasn't even thought about the rabbits, except which rabbits does Liz mean, the stone rabbits or the real rabbits? How do you make them hold still?

"I got something for you," Liz says. She's got Tilly's armadillo purse. It's full of paint strips. Catherine's mouth fills with water.

Henry dreams he has an appointment with the exterminator. "You've got to take care of this," he says. "We have two small children. These things could be rabid. They might carry plague."

"See what I can do," the exterminator says, sounding glum. He stands next to Henry. He's an odd-looking, twitchy guy. He has big ears. They contemplate the skyscrapers that poke out of the grass like obelisks. The lawn is teeming with skyscrapers. "Never seen anything like this before. Never wanted to see anything like this. But if you want my opinion, it's the house that's the real problem—"

"Never mind about my wife," Henry says. He squats down beside a knee-high art deco skyscraper, and peers into a window. A little man looks back at him and shakes his fists, screaming something obscene. Henry flicks a finger at the window, almost hard enough to break it. He feels hot all over. He's never felt this angry before in his life, not even when Catherine told him that she'd accidentally slept with Leonard Felter. The little bastard is going to regret what he just said, whatever it was. He lifts his foot.

The exterminator says, "I wouldn't do that if I were you. You have to dig them up, get the roots. Otherwise, they just grow back. Like your house. Which is really just the tip of the iceberg lettuce, so to speak. You've probably got seventy, eighty stories underground. You gone down on the elevator yet? Talked to the people living down there? It's your house, and you're just going to let them live there rent-free? Mess with your things like that?"

"What?" Henry says, and then he hears helicopters, fighter planes the size of hummingbirds. "Is this really necessary?" he says to the exterminator.

The exterminator nods. "You have to catch them off guard."

"Maybe we're being hasty," Henry says. He has to yell to be heard above the noise of the tiny, tinny, furious planes. "Maybe we can settle this peacefully."

"Hemree," the interrogator says, shaking his head. "You called me in because I'm the expert, and you knew you needed help."

Henry wants to say, "You're saying my name wrong." But he doesn't want to hurt the undertaker's feelings.

The alligator keeps on talking. "Listen up, Hemreeee, and shut up about negotiations and such, because if we don't take care of this right away, it may be too late. This isn't about home ownership, or lawn care, Hemreeeeee, this is war. The lives of your children are at stake. The happiness of your family. Be brave. Be strong. Just hang on to your rabbit and fire when you see delight in their eyes."

He woke up. "Catherine," he whispered. "Are you awake? I was having this dream."

Catherine laughed. "That's the phone, Liz," she said. "It's probably Henry, saying he'll be late."

"Catherine," Henry said. "Who are you talking to?"

"Are you mad at me, Henry?" Catherine said. "Is that why you won't come home?"

"I'm right here," Henry said.

"You take your rabbits and your crocodiles and get out of here," Catherine said. "And then come straight home again."

She sat up in bed and pointed her finger. "I am sick and tired of being spied on by rabbits!"

When Henry looked, something stood beside the bed, rocking back and forth on its heels. He fumbled for the light, got it on, and saw Tilly, her mouth open, her eyes closed. She looked larger than she ever did when she was awake. "It's just Tilly," he said to Catherine, but Catherine lay back down again. She put her pillow over her head. When he picked Tilly up, to carry her back to bed, she was warm and sweaty, her heart racing as if she had been running through all the rooms of the house.

He walked through the house. He rapped on walls, testing. He put his ear against the floor. No elevator. No secret rooms, no hidden passageways.

There wasn't even a basement.

Tilly has divided the yard in half. Carleton is not allowed in her half, unless she gives permission.

From the bottom of her half of the yard, where the trees run beside the driveway, Tilly can barely see the house. She's decided to name the yard Matilda's Rabbit Kingdom. Tilly loves naming things. When the new baby is born, her mother has promised that she can help pick out the real names, although there will only be two real names, a first one and a middle. Tilly doesn't understand why there can only be two. *Oishii* means delicious in Japanese. That would make a good name, either for the baby or for the yard, because of the grass. She knows the yard isn't as big as Central Park, but it's just as good, even if there aren't any pagodas or castles or carriages or people on roller skates. There's plenty of grass. There are hundreds of rabbits. They live in an enormous underground city, maybe a city just like New York. Maybe her dad can stop working in New York, and come work under the lawn instead. She could help him, go to work with him. She could be a biologist, like Jane Goodall, and go and live underground with the rabbits. Last year her ambition had been to go and live secretly in the Metropolitan Museum of Art, but someone has already done that, even if it's only in a book. Tilly feels sorry for Carleton. Everything he ever does, she'll have already been there. She'll already have done that.

Tilly has left her armadillo purse sticking out of a rabbit hole. First she made the hole bigger, then she packed the dirt back in around the armadillo so that only the shiny, peeled snout poked out. Carleton digs it out again with his stick. Maybe Tilly meant him to find it. Maybe it was a present for the rabbits, except what is it doing here, in his half of the yard? When he lived in the apartment, he was afraid of the armadillo purse, but there are better things to be afraid of out here. But be careful, Carleton. Might as well be careful. The armadillo purse says don't touch me. So he doesn't. He uses his stick to pry open the snap mouth, dumps out Tilly's most valuable things, and with his stick pushes them one by one down the hole. Then he puts his ear to the rabbit hole so that he can hear the rabbits say thank you. Saying thank you is polite. But the rabbits say nothing. They're holding their breath, waiting for him to go away. Carleton waits, too. Tilly's armadillo, empty and smelly and haunted, makes his eyes water.

Someone comes up and stands behind him. "I didn't do it," he says. "They fell."

But when he turns around, it's the girl who lives next door. Alison. The sun is behind her and makes her shine. He squints. "You can come over to my house if you want to," she says. "Your mom says. She's going to pay me fifteen bucks an hour, which is way too much. Are your parents really rich or something? What's that?"

"It's Tilly's," he says. "But I don't think she wants it anymore."

She picks up Tilly's armadillo. "Pretty cool," she says. "Maybe I'll keep it for her."

Deep underground, the rabbits stamp their feet in rage.

Catherine loves the house. She loves her new life. She's never understood people who get stuck, become unhappy, can't change, adapt. So she's out of a job. So what? She'll find something else to do. So Henry can't leave his job yet, won't leave his job yet. So the house is haunted. That's OK. They'll work through it. She buys some books on gardening. She plants a rose bush and a climbing vine in a pot. Tilly helps. The rabbits eat off all the leaves. They bite through the vine.

"Shit," Catherine says, when she sees what they've done. She shakes her fists at the rabbits on the lawn. The rabbits flick their ears at her. They're laughing, she knows it. She's too big to chase after them.

*

"Henry, wake up. Wake up."

"I'm awake," he said, and then he was. Catherine was crying. Noisy, wet, ugly sobs. He put his hand out and touched her face. Her nose was running.

"Stop crying," he said. "I'm awake. Why are you crying?"

"Because you weren't here," she said. "And then I woke up and you were here, but when I wake up tomorrow morning you'll be gone again. I miss you. Don't you miss me?"

"I'm sorry," he said. "I'm sorry I'm not here. I'm here now. Come here."

"No," she said. She stopped crying, but her nose still leaked. "And now the dishwasher is haunted. We have to get a new dishwasher before I have this baby. You can't have a baby and not have a dishwasher. And you have to live here with us. Because I'm going to need some help this time. Remember Carleton, how fucking hard that was."

"He was one cranky baby," Henry said. When Carleton was three months old, Henry had realized that they'd misunderstood something. Babies weren't babies, they were land mines, bear traps, wasp nests. They were a noise, which was sometimes even not a noise, but merely a listening for a noise; they were a damp, chalky smell; they were the heaving, jerky, sticky manifestation of not-sleep. Once Henry had stood and watched Carleton in his crib, sleeping peacefully. He had not done what he wanted to do. He had not bent over and yelled in Carleton's ear. Henry still hadn't forgiven Carleton, not yet, not entirely, not for making him feel that way.

"Why do you have to love your job so much?" Catherine said.

"I don't know," Henry said. "I don't love it."

"Don't lie to me," Catherine said.

"I love you better," Henry said. He does, he does, he does love Catherine better. He's already made that decision. But she isn't even listening.

"Remember when Carleton was little and you would get up in the morning and go to work and leave me all alone with them?" Catherine poked him in the side. "I used to hate you. You'd come home with takeout, and I'd forget I hated you, but then I'd remember again, and I'd hate you even more because it was so easy for you to trick me, to make things OK again, just because for an hour I could sit in the bathtub and eat Chinese food and wash my hair."

"You used to carry an extra shirt with you, when you went out," Henry said. He put his hand down inside her T-shirt, on her fat, full

229

breast. "In case you leaked."

"You can't touch that breast," Catherine said. "It's haunted." She blew her nose on the sheets.

Catherine's friend Lucy owns an online boutique, Nice Clothes for Fat People. There's a woman in Tarrytown who knits stretchy, sexy argyle sweaters exclusively for NCFP, and Lucy has an appointment with her. She wants to stop off and see Catherine afterward, before she has to drive back to the city again. Catherine gives her directions, and then begins to clean house, feeling out of sorts. She's not sure she wants to see Lucy right now. Carleton has always been afraid of Lucy, which is embarrassing. And Catherine doesn't want to talk about Henry. She doesn't want to explain about the downstairs bathroom. She had planned to spend the day painting the wood trim in the dining room, but now she'll have to wait.

The doorbell rings, but when Catherine goes to answer it, no one is there. Later on, after Tilly and Carleton have come home, it rings again, but no one is there. It rings and rings, as if Lucy is standing outside, pressing the bell over and over again. Finally Catherine pulls out the wire. She tries calling Lucy's cell phone, but can't get through. Then Henry calls. He says that he's going to be late.

Liz opens the front door, yells, "Hello, anyone home?! You've got to see your rabbits, there must be thousands of them. Catherine, is something wrong with your doorbell?"

Henry's bike, so far, was OK. He wondered what they'd do if the Toyota suddenly became haunted. Would Catherine want to sell it? Would resale value be affected? The car and Catherine and the kids were gone when he got home, so he put on a pair of work gloves and went through the house with a cardboard box, collecting all the things that felt haunted. A hairbrush in Tilly's room, an old pair of Catherine's tennis shoes. A pair of Catherine's underwear that he found at the foot of the bed. When he picked them up he felt a sudden shock of longing for Catherine, like he'd been hit by some kind of spooky lightning. It hit him in the pit of the stomach, like a cramp. He dropped the underwear in the box.

The silk kimono from Takashimaya. Two of Carleton's nightlights. He opened the door to his office, put the box inside. All the hair on his arms stood up. He closed the door.

Then he went downstairs and cleaned paintbrushes. If the paintbrushes were becoming haunted, if Catherine was throwing them out and buying new ones, she wasn't saying. Maybe he should check the Visa bill. How much were they spending on paint anyway?

Catherine came into the kitchen and gave him a hug. "I'm glad you're home," she said. He pressed his nose into her neck and inhaled. "I left the car running—I've got to pee. Would you go pick up the kids for me?"

"Where are they?" Henry said.

"They're over at Liz's. Alison is babysitting them. Do you have money on you?"

"You mean I'll meet some neighbors?"

"Wow, sure," Catherine said. "If you think you're ready. Are you ready? Do you know where they live?"

"They're our neighbors, right?"

"Take a left out of the driveway, go about a quarter of a mile, and they're the red house with all the trees in front."

But when he drove up to the red house and went and rang the doorbell, no one answered. He heard a child come running down a flight of stairs and then stop and stand in front of the door. "Carleton? Alison?" he said. "Excuse me, this is Catherine's husband, Henry. Carleton and Tilly's dad." The whispering stopped. He waited for a bit. When he crouched down and lifted the flap of the mail slot, he thought he saw someone's feet, the hem of a coat, something furry? A dog? Someone standing very still, just to the right of the door? Carleton, playing games. "I see you," he said, and wiggled his fingers through the mail slot. Then he thought maybe it wasn't Carleton after all. He got up quickly and went back to the car. He drove into town and bought more soap.

Tilly was standing in the driveway when he got home, her hands on her hips. "Hi, Dad," she said. "I'm looking for King Spanky. He got outside. Look what Alison found."

She held out a tiny toy bow strung with what looked like dental floss, an arrow the size of a needle.

"Be careful with that," Henry said. "It looks sharp. Archery Barbie, right? So did you guys have a good time with Alison?"

"Alison's OK," Tilly said. She belched. "'Scuse me. I don't feel very good."

"What's wrong?" Henry said.

"My stomach is funny," Tilly said. She looked up at him, frowned, and then vomited all over his shirt, his pants.

"Tilly!" he said. He yanked off his shirt, used a sleeve to wipe her mouth. The vomit was foamy and green.

"It tastes horrible," she said. She sounded surprised. "Why does it always taste so bad when you throw up?"

"So that you won't go around doing it for fun," he said. "Are you going to do it again?"

"I don't think so," she said, making a face.

"Then I'm going to go wash up and change clothes. What were you eating, anyway?"

"Grass," Tilly said.

"Well, no wonder," Henry said. "I thought you were smarter than that, Tilly. Don't do that anymore."

"I wasn't planning to," Tilly said. She spit in the grass.

When Henry opened the front door, he could hear Catherine talking in the kitchen. "The funny thing is," she said, "none of it was true. It was just made up, just like something Carleton would do. Just to get attention."

"Dad," Carleton said. He was jumping up and down on one foot. "Want to hear a song?"

"I was looking for you," Henry said. "Did Alison bring you home? Do you need to go to the bathroom?"

"Why aren't you wearing any clothes?" Carleton said.

Someone in the kitchen laughed, as if they had heard this.

"I had an accident," Henry said, whispering. "But you're right, Carleton, I should go change." He took a shower, rinsed and wrung out his shirt, put on clean clothes, but by the time he got downstairs, Catherine and Carleton and Tilly were eating Cheerios for dinner. They were using paper bowls, plastic spoons, as if it was a picnic. "Liz was here, and Alison, but they were going to a movie," Catherine said. "They said they'd meet you some other day. It was awful—when they came in the door, King Spanky went rushing outside. He's been watching the rabbits all day. If he catches one, Tilly is going to be so upset."

"Tilly's been eating grass," Henry said.

Tilly rolled her eyes. As if.

"Not again!" Catherine said. "Tilly, real people don't eat grass. Oh, look, fantastic, there's King Spanky. Who let him in? What's he got in his mouth?"

King Spanky sits with his back to them. He coughs and something drops to the floor, maybe a frog, or a baby rabbit. It goes scrabbling across the floor, half-leaping, dragging one leg. King Spanky just sits there, watching as it disappears under the sofa. Carleton freaks out. Tilly is shouting, "Bad King Spanky! Bad cat!" When Henry and Catherine push the sofa back, it's too late, there's just King Spanky and a little blob of sticky blood on the floor.

Catherine would like to write a novel. She'd like to write a novel with no children in it. The problem with novels with children in them is that bad things will happen either to the children or else to the parents. She wants to write something funny, something romantic.

It isn't very comfortable to sit down now that she's so big. She's started writing on the walls. She writes in pencil. She names her characters after paint colors. She imagines them leading beautiful, happy, useful lives. No haunted toasters. No mothers no children no crocodiles no photocopy machines no Leonard Felters. She writes for two or three hours, and then she paints the walls again before anyone gets home. That's always the best part.

"I need you next weekend," the Crocodile said. Her rubber-band ball sat on the floor beside her desk. She had her feet up on it, in an attempt to show it who was boss. The rubber-band ball was getting too big for its britches. Someone was going to have to teach it a lesson, send it a memo.

She looked tired. Henry said, "You don't need me."

"I do," the Crocodile said, yawning. "I *do*. The clients want to take you out to dinner at the Four Seasons when they come in to town. They want to go see musicals with you. *Rent. Phantom of the Lion Cabaret*. They want to go to Coney Island with you and eat hot dogs. They want to go out to trendy bars and clubs and pick up strippers and publicists and performance artists. They want to talk about poetry, philosophy, sports, politics, their lousy relationships with their fathers. They want to ask you for advice about their love lives. They want you to come to the weddings of their children and make toasts. You're indispensable, honey. I hope you know that."

"Catherine and I are having some problems with rabbits," Henry said. The rabbits were easier to explain than the other thing. "They've taken over the yard. Things are a little crazy."

"I don't know anything about rabbits," the Crocodile said, digging her pointy heels into the flesh of the rubber-band ball until she could feel the red rubber blood come running out. She pinned Henry with her beautiful, watery eyes.

"Henry." She said his name so quietly that he had to lean forward to hear what she was saying.

She said, "You have the best of both worlds. A wife and children who adore you, a beautiful house in the country, a secure job at a company that depends on you, a boss who appreciates your talents, clients who think you're the shit. You *are* the shit, Henry, and the thing is, you're probably thinking that no one deserves to have all this. You think you have to make a choice. You think you have to give up something. But you don't have to give up anything, Henry, and anyone who tells you otherwise is a fucking rabbit. Don't listen to them. You can have it all. You *deserve* to have it all. You love your job. Do you love your job?"

"I love my job," Henry says. The Crocodile smiles at him tearily. It's true. He loves his job.

When Henry came home, it must have been after midnight, because he never got home before midnight. He found Catherine standing on a ladder in the kitchen, one foot resting on the sink. She was wearing her gas mask, a black cotton sports bra, and a pair of black sweatpants rolled down so far that he could see she wasn't wearing any underwear. Her stomach stuck out so far she had to hold her arms at a funny angle to run the roller up and down the wall in front of her. Up and down in a *V*. Then fill the *V* in. She had painted the kitchen ceiling a shade of purple so dark it almost looked black. Midnight Eggplant.

Catherine had recently begun buying paints from a specialty catalog. All the colors were named after famous books—*Madame Bovary, Forever Amber, Fahrenheit 451, Tin Drum, A Curtain of Green, 20,000 Leagues Under the Sea.* She was painting the walls *Catch-22*, a novel she'd taught over and over again to undergraduates. It had gone over pretty well. The paint color was nice, too. She couldn't decide if she missed teaching. The thing about teaching and having children was that you always ended up treating your children like undergraduates and your undergraduates like children. There was a particular tone of voice. She'd even used it on Henry a few times, just to see if it worked.

All the cabinets were fenced around with masking tape, like a crime scene. The room stank of new paint.

Catherine took off the gas mask and said, "Tilly picked it out. What do you think?" Her hands were on her hips. Her stomach poked out at Henry. The gas mask had left a ring of white and red around her eyes and chin.

Henry said, "How was the dinner party?"

"We had fettuccine. Liz and Marcus stayed and helped me do the dishes."

("Is something wrong with your dishwasher?" "No. I mean, yes. We're getting a new one.")

She had had a feeling. It had been a feeling like déjà vu, or being drunk, or falling in love. Like teaching. She had imagined an audience of rabbits out on the lawn, watching her dinner party. A classroom of rabbits, watching a documentary. Rabbit television. Her skin had felt electric.

"So she's a lawyer?" Henry said.

"You haven't even met them yet," Catherine said, suddenly feeling possessive. "But I like them. I really, really like them. They wanted to know all about us. You. I think they think that either we're having marriage problems or that you're imaginary. Finally I took Liz upstairs and showed her your stuff in the closet. I pulled out the wedding album and showed them photos."

"Maybe we could invite them over on Sunday? For a cookout?" Henry said.

"They're away next weekend," Catherine said. "They're going up to the mountains on Friday. They have a house up there. They've invited us. To come along."

"I can't," Henry said. "I have to take care of some clients next weekend. Some big shots. We're having some cash-flow problems. Besides, are you allowed to go away? Did you check with your doctor—what's his name again, Dr. Marks?"

"You mean, did I get my permission slip signed?" Catherine said. Henry put his hand on her leg and held on. "Dr. Marks said I'm shipshape. That was his exact word. Or maybe he said tip-top. It was something alliterative."

"Well, I guess you ought to go then," Henry said. He rested his head against her stomach. She let him. He looked so tired. "Before Golf Cart shows up. Or what is Tilly calling the baby now?"

"She's around here somewhere," Catherine said. "I keep putting her back in her bed and she keeps getting out again. Maybe she's looking for you."

"Did you get my e-mail?" Henry said. He was listening to

Catherine's stomach. He wasn't going to stop touching her unless she told him to.

"You know I can't check e-mail on your computer anymore," Catherine said.

"This is so stupid," Henry said. "This house isn't haunted. There isn't any such thing as a haunted house."

"It isn't the house," Catherine said. "It's the stuff we brought with us. Except for the downstairs bathroom, and that might just be a draft, or an electrical problem. The house is fine. I love the house."

"Our stuff is fine," Henry said. "I love our stuff."

"If you really think our stuff is fine," Catherine said, "then why did you buy a new alarm clock? Why do you keep throwing out the soap?"

"It's the move," Henry said. "It was a hard move."

"King Spanky hasn't eaten his food in three days," Catherine said. "At first I thought it was the food, and I bought new food and he came down and ate it and I realized it wasn't the food, it was King Spanky. I couldn't sleep all night, knowing he was up under the bed. Poor spooky guy. I don't know what to do. Take him to the vet? What do I say? Excuse me, but I think my cat is haunted? Anyway, I can't get him out of the bed. Not even with the old alarm clock, the haunted one."

"I'll try," Henry said. "Let me try and see if I can get him out." But he didn't move. Catherine tugged at a piece of his hair and he put up his hand. She gave him her roller. He popped off the cylinder and bagged it and put it in the freezer, which was full of paintbrushes and other rollers. He helped Catherine down from the ladder. "I wish you would stop painting."

"I can't," she said. "It has to be perfect. If I can just get it right, then everything will go back to normal and stop being haunted and the rabbits won't tunnel under the house and make it fall down, and you'll come home and stay home, and our neighbors will finally get to meet you and they'll like you and you'll like them, and Carleton will stop being afraid of everything, and Tilly will fall asleep in her own bed, and stay there, and—"

"Hey," Henry said. "It's all going to work out. It's all good. I really like this color."

"I don't know," Catherine said. She yawned. "You don't think it looks too old-fashioned?"

They went upstairs and Catherine took a bath while Henry tried to coax King Spanky out of the bed. But King Spanky wouldn't come out. When Henry got down on his hands and knees and stuck the flashlight under the bed, he could see King Spanky's eyes, his tail hanging down from the box frame.

Out on the lawn the rabbits were perfectly still. Then they sprang up in the air, turning and dropping and landing and then freezing again. Catherine stood at the window of the bathroom, toweling her hair. She turned the bathroom light off, so that she could see them better. The moonlight picked out their shining eyes, the moon-colored fur, each hair tipped in paint. They were playing some rabbit game like leapfrog. Or they were dancing the quadrille. Fighting a rabbit war. Did rabbits fight wars? Catherine didn't know. They ran at each other and then turned and darted back, jumping and crouching and rising up on their back legs. A pair of rabbits took off in tandem, like racehorses, sailing through the air and over a long curled shape in the grass. Then back over again. She put her face against the window. It was Tilly, stretched out against the grass, Tilly's legs and feet bare and white.

"Tilly," she said, and ran out of the bathroom, wearing only the towel around her hair.

"What is it?" Henry said as Catherine darted past him and down the stairs. He ran after her, and by the time she had opened the front door, was kneeling beside Tilly, the wet grass tickling her thighs and her belly, Henry was there, too, and he picked up Tilly and carried her back into the house. They wrapped her in a blanket and put her in her bed and because neither of them wanted to sleep in the bed where King Spanky was hiding, they lay down on the sofa in the family room, curled up against each other. When they woke up in the morning, Tilly was asleep in a ball at their feet.

For a minute or two last year, Catherine thought she had it figured out. She was married to a man whose specialty was solving problems, salvaging bad situations. If she did something dramatic enough, if she fucked up badly enough, it would save her marriage. And it did, except that once the problem was solved and the marriage was saved and the baby was conceived and the house was bought, then Henry went back to work.

She stands at the window in the bedroom and looks out at all the trees. For a minute she imagines that Carleton is right, and they are living in Central Park and Fifth Avenue is just right over there.

237

Henry's office is just a few blocks away. All those rabbits are just tourists.

Henry wakes up in the middle of the night. There are people downstairs. He can hear women talking, laughing, and he realizes Catherine's book club must have come over. He gets out of bed. It's dark. What time is it anyway? But the alarm clock is haunted again. He unplugs it. As he comes down the stairs, a voice says, "Well, will you look at that!" and then, "Right under his nose the whole time!"

Henry walks through the house, turning on lights. Tilly stands in the middle of the kitchen. "May I ask who's calling?" she says. She's got Henry's cell phone tucked between her shoulder and her face. She's holding it upside down. Her eyes are open, but she's asleep.

"Who are you talking to?" Henry says.

"The rabbits," Tilly says. She tilts her head, listening. Then she laughs. "Call back later," she says. "He doesn't want to talk to you. Yeah. OK." She hands Henry his phone. "They said it's no one you know."

"Are you awake?" Henry says.

"Yes," Tilly says, still asleep. He carries her back upstairs. He makes a bed out of pillows in the hall closet and lays her down across them. He tucks a blanket around her. If she refuses to wake up in the same bed that she goes to sleep in, then maybe they should make it a game. If you can't beat them, join them.

Catherine hadn't had an affair with Leonard Felter. She hadn't even slept with him. She had just said she had, because she was so mad at Henry. She could have slept with Leonard Felter. The opportunity had been there. And he had been magical somehow: the only member of the department who could make the photocopier make copies, and he was nice to all of the secretaries. Too nice, as it turned out. And then, when it turned out that Leonard Felter had been fucking everyone, Catherine had felt she couldn't take it back. So she and Henry had gone to therapy together. Henry had taken some time off work. They'd taken the kids to Disney World. They'd gotten pregnant. She'd been remorseful for something she hadn't done. Henry had forgiven her. Really, she'd saved their marriage. But it had been the sort of thing you could only do once.

If someone had to save the marriage a second time, it would have to be Henry.

Henry went looking for King Spanky. They were going to see the vet: he had the cat cage in the car, but no King Spanky. It was early afternoon, and the rabbits were out on the lawn. Up above, a bird hung, motionless, on a hook of air. Henry craned his head, looking up. It was a big bird, a hawk maybe? It circled, once, twice, again, and then dropped like a stone toward the rabbits. The rabbits didn't move. There was something about the way they waited, as if this was all a game. The bird cut through the air, folded like a knife, and then it jerked, tumbled, fell, the wings loose. The bird smashed into the grass and feathers flew up. The rabbits moved closer, as if investigating.

Henry went to see for himself. The rabbits scattered, and the lawn was empty. No rabbits, no bird. But there, down in the trees, beside the bike path, Henry saw something move. King Spanky swung his tail angrily, slunk into the woods.

When Henry came out of the woods, the rabbits were back guarding the lawn again and Catherine was calling his name. "Where were you?" she said. She was wearing her gas mask around her neck, and there was a smear of paint on her arm. Whiskey Horse. She'd been painting the linen closet.

"King Spanky took off," Henry said. "I couldn't catch him. I saw the weirdest thing—this bird was going after the rabbits, and then it fell—"

"Marcus came by," Catherine said. Her cheeks were flushed. He knew that if he touched her, her skin would be hot. "He stopped by to see if you wanted to go play golf."

"Who wants to play golf?" Henry said. "I want to go upstairs with you. Where are the kids?"

"Alison took them in to town, to see a movie," Catherine said. "I'm going to pick them up at three."

Henry lifted the gas mask off her neck, fitted it around her face. He unbuttoned her shirt, undid the clasp of her bra. "Better take this off," he said. "Better take all your clothes off. I think they're haunted."

"You know what would make a great paint color? Can't believe no one has done this yet. Yellow Sticky. What about King Spanky?" Catherine said. She sounded like Darth Vader, maybe on purpose,

239

and Henry thought it was sexy: Darth Vader, pregnant, with his child. She put her hand against his chest and shoved. Not too hard, but harder than she meant to. It turned out that painting had given her some serious muscle. That will be a good thing when she has another kid to haul around.

"Yellow Sticky. That's great. Forget King Spanky," Henry said. "He's great."

Catherine was painting Tilly's room Lavender Fist. It was going to be a surprise. But when Tilly saw it, she burst into tears. "Why can't you just leave it alone?" she said. "I liked it the way it was."

"I thought you liked purple," Catherine said, astounded. She took off her gas mask.

"I hate purple," Tilly said. "And I hate you. You're so fat. Even Carleton thinks so."

"Tilly!" Catherine said. She laughed. "I'm pregnant, remember?"

"That's what you think," Tilly said. She ran out of the room and across the hall. There were crashing noises, the sounds of things breaking.

"Tilly!" Catherine said.

Tilly stood in the middle of Carleton's room. All around her lay broken night-lights, lamps, broken lightbulbs. The carpet was dusted in glass. Tilly's feet were bare and Catherine looked down, realized that she wasn't wearing shoes either. "Don't move, Tilly," she said.

"They were haunted," Tilly said and began to cry.

"So how come your dad's never home?" Alison said.

"I don't know," Carleton said. "Guess what? Tilly broke all my night-lights."

"Yeah," Alison said. "You must be pretty mad."

"No, it's good that she did," Carleton said, explaining. "They were haunted. Tilly didn't want me to be afraid."

"But aren't you afraid of the dark?" Alison said.

"Tilly said I shouldn't be," Carleton said. "She said the rabbits stay awake all night, that they make sure everything is OK, even when it's dark. Tilly slept outside once, and the rabbits protected her."

"So you're going to stay with us this weekend," Alison said.

"Yes," Carleton said.

"But your dad isn't coming," Alison said.

"No," Carleton said. "I don't know."

"Want to go higher?" Alison said. She pushed the swing and sent him soaring.

When Henry puts his hand against the wall in the living room, it gives a little, as if the wall is pregnant. The paint under the paint is wet. He walks around the house, running his hands along the walls. Catherine has been painting a mural in the foyer. She's painted trees and trees and trees. Golden trees with brown leaves and green leaves and red leaves, and reddish trees with purple leaves and yellow leaves and pink leaves. She's even painted some leaves on the wooden floor, as if the trees are dropping them. "Catherine," he says. "You have got to stop painting the damn walls. The rooms are getting smaller."

Nobody says anything back. Catherine and Tilly and Carleton aren't home. It's the first time Henry has spent the night alone in his house. He can't sleep. There's no television to watch. Henry throws out all of Catherine's paintbrushes. But when Catherine gets home, she'll just buy new ones.

He sleeps on the couch, and during the night someone comes and stands and watches him sleep. Tilly. Then he wakes up and remembers that Tilly isn't there.

The rabbits watch the house all night long. It's their job.

Tilly is talking to the rabbits. It's cold outside, and she's lost her gloves. "What's your name?" she says. "Oh, you beauty. You beauty." She's on her hands and knees. Carleton watches from his side of the yard.

"Can I come over?" he says. "Can I please come over?"

Tilly ignores him. She gets down on her hands and knees, moving even closer to the rabbits. There are three, one of them almost close enough to touch. If she moves her hand slowly, maybe she can grab one by the ears. Maybe she can catch one and train it to live inside. They need a pet rabbit. King Spanky is haunted. He spends most of his time outside. Her parents keep their bedroom door shut so that King Spanky can't get in.

"Good rabbit," Tilly says. "Just stay still. Stay still."

The rabbits flick their ears. Carleton begins to sing a song Alison has taught them, a skipping song. Carleton is such a girl. Tilly puts

241

out her hand. There's something tangled around the rabbit's neck, like a piece of string or a leash. She wiggles closer, holding out her hand. She stares and stares and can hardly believe her eyes. There's a person, a little man, sitting behind the rabbit's ears, holding on to the rabbit's fur and the piece of knotted string with one hand. His other hand is cocked back, like he's going to throw something. He's looking right at her—his hand flies forward and something hits her hand. She pulls her hand back, astounded. "Hey!" she says, and she falls over on her side and watches the rabbits go springing away. "Hey, you! Come back!"

"What?" Carleton yells. He's frantic. "What are you doing? Why won't you let me come over?"

She closes her eyes, just for a second. Shut up, Carleton. Just shut up. Her hand is throbbing and she lies down, holds her hand up to her face. Shut. Up.

Wake up. Wake *up*. When she wakes up, Carleton is sitting beside her. "What are you doing on my side?" she says and he shrugs.

"What are you doing?" he says. He rocks back and forth on his knees. "Why did you fall over?"

"None of your business," she says. She can't remember what she was doing. Everything looks funny. Especially Carleton. "What's wrong with you?"

"Nothing's wrong with me," Carleton says, but something is wrong. She studies his face and begins to feel sick, as if she's been eating grass. Those sneaky rabbits! They've been distracting her, and now, while she wasn't paying attention, Carleton's become haunted.

"Oh yes it is," Tilly says, forgetting to be afraid, forgetting her hand hurts, getting angry instead. She's not the one to blame. This is her mother's fault, her father's fault, and it's Carleton's fault, too. How could he have let this happen? "You just don't know it's wrong. I'm going to tell Mom."

Haunted Carleton is still a Carleton who can be bossed around. "Don't tell," he begs.

Tilly pretends to think about this, although she's already made up her mind. Because what can she say? Either her mother will notice that something's wrong or else she won't. Better to wait and see. "Just stay away from me," she tells Carleton. "You give me the creeps."

Carleton begins to cry, but Tilly is firm. He turns around, walks slowly back to his half of the yard, still crying. For the rest of the afternoon, he sits beneath the azalea bush at the edge of his side of the yard, and cries. It gives Tilly the creeps. Her hand throbs where something has stung it. The rabbits are all hiding underground. King Spanky has gone hunting.

"What's up with Carleton?" Henry said, coming downstairs. He couldn't stop yawning. It wasn't that he was tired, although he was tired. He hadn't given Carleton a good-night kiss, just in case it turned out he was coming down with a cold. He didn't want Carleton to catch it. But it looked like Carleton, too, was already coming down with something.

Catherine shrugged. Paint samples were balanced across her stomach like she'd been playing solitaire. All weekend long, away from the house, she'd thought about repainting Henry's office. She'd never painted a haunted room before. Maybe if you mixed the paint with a little bit of holy water? She wasn't sure: what was holy water anyway? Could you buy it? "Tilly's being mean to him," she said. "I wish they would make some friends out here. He keeps talking about the new baby, about how he'll take care of it. He says it can sleep in his room. I've been trying to explain babies to him, about how all they do is sleep and eat and cry."

"And get bigger," Henry said.

"That, too," Catherine said. "So did he go to sleep OK?"

"Eventually," Henry said. "He's just acting really weird."

"How is that different from usual?" Catherine said. She yawned. "Is Tilly finished with her homework?"

"I don't know," Henry said. "You know, just weird. Different weird. Maybe he's going through a weird spell. Tilly wanted me to help her with her math, but I couldn't get it to come out right. So what's up with my office?"

"I cleared it out," Catherine said. "Alison and Liz came over and helped. I told them we were going to redecorate. Why is it that we're the only ones who notice everything is fucking haunted around here?"

"So where'd you put my stuff?" Henry said. "What's up?"

"You're not working here now," Catherine pointed out. She didn't sound angry, just tired. "Besides, it's all haunted, right? So I took your computer in to the shop, so they could have a look at it. I don't know, maybe they can unhaunt it."

"Well," Henry said. "OK. Is that what you told them? It's haunted?"

243

"Don't be ridiculous," Catherine said. She discarded a paint strip. Too lemony. "So I heard about the bomb scare on the radio."

"Yeah," Henry said. "The subways were full of kids with crew cuts and machine guns. And they evacuated our building for about an hour. We all went and stood outside, holding onto our laptops like idiots, just in case. The Crocodile carried out her rubber-band ball, which must weigh about thirty pounds. It kind of freaked people out, even the firemen. I thought the bomb squad was going to blow it up. So tell me about your weekend."

"Tell me about yours," Catherine said.

"You know," Henry said. "Those clients are assholes. But they don't know they're assholes, so it's kind of OK. You just have to feel sorry for them. They don't get it. You have to explain how to have fun, and then they get anxious, so they drink a lot and so you have to drink, too. Even the Crocodile got drunk. She did this weird wriggly dance to a Pete Seeger song. So what's their place like?"

"It's nice," Catherine said. "You know, really nice."

"So you had a good weekend? Carleton and Tilly had a good time?"

"It was really nice," Catherine said. "No, really, it was great. I had a fucking great time. So you're sure you can make it home for dinner on Thursday."

It wasn't a question.

"Carleton looks like he might be coming down with something," Henry said. "Here. Do you think I feel hot? Or is it cold in here?"

Catherine said, "You're fine. It's going to be Liz and Marcus and some of the women from the book group and their husbands, and what's her name, the real estate agent. I invited her, too. Did you know she's written a book? I was going to do that! I'm getting the new dishwasher tomorrow. No more paper plates. And the lawn-care specialist is coming on Monday to take care of the rabbits. I thought I'd drop off King Spanky at the vet, take Tilly and Carleton back to the city, stay with Lucy for two or three days—did you know she tried to find this place and got lost? She's supposed to come up for dinner, too—just in case the poison doesn't go away right away, you know, or in case we end up with piles of dead rabbits on the lawn. Your job is to make sure there are no dead rabbits when I bring Tilly and Carleton back."

"I guess I can do that," Henry said.

"You'd better," Catherine said. She stood up, with some difficulty, and came and leaned over his chair. Her stomach bumped into his shoulder. Her breath was hot. Her hands were full of strips of color. "Sometimes I wish that instead of working for the Crocodile, you were having an affair with her. I mean, that way you'd come home when you're supposed to. You wouldn't want me to be suspicious."

"I don't have any time to have affairs," Henry said. He sounded put out. Maybe he was thinking about Leonard Felter. Or maybe he was picturing the Crocodile naked. The Crocodile wearing stretchy red rubber sex gear. Catherine imagined telling Henry the truth about Leonard Felter. I didn't have an affair. Did not. Is that a problem?

"That's exactly what I mean," Catherine said. "You'd better be here for dinner. You live here, Henry. You're my husband. I want you to meet our friends. I want you to be here when I have this baby. I want you to fix what's wrong with the downstairs bathroom. I want you to talk to Tilly. She's having a rough time. She won't talk to me about it."

"Tilly's fine," Henry said. "We had a long talk tonight. She said she's sorry she broke all of Carleton's night-lights. I like the trees, by the way. You're not going to paint over them, are you?"

"I had all this leftover paint," Catherine said. "I was getting tired of just painting with the rollers. I wanted to do something fancier."

"You could paint some trees in my office, when you paint my office."

"Maybe," Catherine said. "Ooof, this baby won't stop kicking me." She lay down on the floor in front of Henry, and lifted her feet into his lap. "Rub my feet. I've still got so much fucking paint. But once your office is done, I'm done with the painting. Tilly told me to stop it or else. She keeps hiding my gas mask. Will you be here for dinner?"

"I'll be here for dinner," Henry said, rubbing her feet. He really meant it. He was thinking about the exterminator, about rabbit corpses scattered all across the lawn, like a war zone. Poor rabbits. What a mess.

After they went to see the therapist, after they went to Disney World and came home again, Henry said to Catherine, "I don't want to talk about it anymore. I don't want to talk about it ever again. Can we not talk about it?"

"Talk about what?" Catherine said. But she had almost been sorry. It had been so much work. She'd had to invent so many details that eventually it began to seem as if she hadn't made it up after all. It was too strange, too confusing, to pretend it had never happened, when, after all, it *had* never happened.

Catherine is dressing for dinner. When she looks in the mirror, she's as big as a cruise ship. A water tower. She doesn't look like herself at all. The baby kicks her right under the ribs.

"Stop that," she says. She's sure the baby is going to be a girl. Tilly won't be pleased. Tilly has been extra good all day. She helped make the salad. She set the table. She put on a nice dress.

Tilly is hiding from Carleton under a table in the foyer. If Carleton finds her, Tilly will scream. Carleton is haunted, and nobody has noticed. Nobody cares except Tilly. Tilly says names for the baby, under her breath. Dollop. Shampool. Custard. Knock, Knock. The rabbits are out on the lawn, and King Spanky has gotten into the bed again, and he won't come out, not for a million haunted alarm clocks.

Her mother has painted trees all along the wall under the staircase. They don't look like real trees. They aren't real colors. It doesn't look like Central Park at all. In among the trees, her mother has painted a little door. It isn't a real door, except that when Tilly goes over to look at it, it is real. There's a doorknob, and when Tilly turns it, the door opens. Underneath the stairs, there's another set of stairs, little dirt stairs, going down. On the third stair, there's a rabbit sitting there, looking up at Tilly. It hops down, one step, and then another. Then another.

"Rumpelstiltskin!" Tilly says to the rabbit. "Lipstick!"

Catherine goes to the closet to get out Henry's pink shirt. What's the name of that real estate agent? Why can't she ever remember? She lays the shirt on the bed and then stands there for a moment, stunned. It's too much. The pink shirt is haunted. She pulls out all of Henry's suits, his shirts, his ties. All haunted. Every fucking thing is haunted. Even the fucking shoes. When she pulls out the drawers, socks, underwear, handkerchiefs, everything, it's all spoiled. All haunted. Henry doesn't have a thing to wear. She goes downstairs, gets trash bags, and goes back upstairs again. She begins to dump clothes into the trash bags.

She can see Carleton framed in the bedroom window. He's chasing the rabbits with a stick. She hoists open the window, leans out, yells, "Stay away from those fucking rabbits, Carleton! Do you hear me?"

She doesn't recognize her own voice.

Tilly is running around downstairs somewhere. She's yelling, too, but her voice gets farther and farther away, fainter and fainter. She's yelling, "Hairbrush! Zeppelin! Torpedo! Marmalade!"

The doorbell rings.

The Crocodile started laughing. "OK, Henry. Calm down."

He fired off another rubber band. "I mean it," he said. "I'm late. I'll be late. She's going to kill me."

"Tell her it's my fault," the Crocodile said. "So they started dinner without you. Big deal."

"I tried calling," Henry said. "Nobody answered." He had an idea that the phone was haunted now. That's why Catherine wasn't answering. They'd have to get a new phone. Maybe the lawn specialist would know a house specialist. Maybe somebody could do something about this. "I should go home," he said. "I should go home right now." But he didn't get up. "I think we've gotten ourselves into a mess, me and Catherine. I don't think things are good right now."

"Tell someone who cares," the Crocodile suggested. She wiped at her eyes. "Get out of here. Go catch your train. Have a great weekend. See you on Monday."

So Henry goes home, he has to go home, but of course he's late, it's too late. The train is haunted. The closer they get to his station, the more haunted the train gets. None of the other passengers seem to notice. It makes Henry sick to his stomach. And, of course, his bike turns out to be haunted, too. It's too much. He can't ride it home. He leaves it at the station and he walks home in the dark, down the bike path. Something follows him home. Maybe it's King Spanky.

Here's the yard, and here's his house. He loves his house, how it's all lit up. You can see right through the windows, you can see the living room, which Catherine has painted Ghost Crab. The trim is Rat Fink. Catherine has worked so hard. The driveway is full of cars, and inside, people are eating dinner. They're admiring Catherine's trees. They haven't waited for him, and that's fine. His neighbors: he loves his neighbors. He's going to love them as soon as he meets them. His wife is going to have a baby any day now. His daughter will stop walking in her sleep. His son isn't haunted. The moon shines down and paints the world a color he's never seen before. Oh, Catherine, wait till you see this. Shining lawn, shining rabbits, shining world. The rabbits are out on the lawn. They've been waiting for him, all this time, they've been waiting. Here's his rabbit, his very own rabbit. Who needs a bike? He sits on his rabbit, legs pressed against the warm, silky, shining flanks, one hand holding on to the rabbit's fur, the knotted string around its neck. He has something in his other hand, and when he looks, he sees it's a spear. All around him, the others are sitting on their rabbits, waiting patiently, quietly. They've been waiting for a long time, but the waiting is almost over. In a little while, the dinner party will be over and the war will begin.

From How I Escaped My Certain Fate
J. W. McCormack

MY MOTHER'S METAPHORS HAD, in the time I had been away, taken on a tendency toward the eerily surgical. I was tying her knotted umbilical cord into more lumps and bows, she said; I was a tumor, albeit a benign one; a blocked artery, though my own anesthetic. A whole passive/aggressive biology worked up over my refusal to take back my room. I told her I had my own parthenogenesis to attend to, but my attempt to speak her language was, I think, a failure.

I knew that at least some of it was true: I was leaving her all alone in her upstairs room, with nothing to do but listen to old Sarah Vaughan records and mouth the words. So if I cannot entirely refute this claim, then at least let me stress that I really did make frequent trips to the old house on Woodpecker Drive, staying with her for hours on end, usually right up to the point that the conversation turned to the question of my reinstating myself within my former sanctuary. Let's see, why did I refuse exactly? Was it perhaps the unwelcome prospect of what I would become if I loafed away the afternoons in the mediocre glow of the goddamn television or the thought of so many fitful sleep-turns taken in the night, when the squirrels clawed their way back and forth through hollow walls? Certainly I was less than thrilled to think I'd soon be sipping wine at house parties and playing pick-up-sticks with middle-aged hippies. Horrors! Ah, but see how nimbly I dodge the much more significant question of my father's absence, pushing it to the very bottom of the paragraph in point of fact.

Sitting with my mother in those dreary afternoons where summer breezes failed to materialize beyond the stone subdivision marker for lack of trees to blow through, I'd feel his not-being filling up the rooms, an icy lacuna I could not forget even long enough to wonder where he had gone or why. And since my last little trip, I had learned the value of containing certain fruitless speculations as to whether he had, say, been abducted by aliens or pirates, right down to the more reality-soaked suppositions that he'd turned into one of his roles in a bout of profound marital exhaustion (a performer who

249

threw everything into the ritualistic immersion of drama, he'd often seemed on the verge of losing Ian Blake altogether) or run off with an attractive understudy.

So I lived, that summer, in my transitional abode: a third-story apartment on Gay Street overlooking an industrial park. I slept on a mattress whose comfort must be ranked *character building*, positioned at an angle in the center of a labyrinthine ring of postage boxes. Across the room, up on wooden panels, was a television with its screen cracked wide open as if shattered by some massive internal eruption. This was a relic rescued in the first week of my residence from among the wasted odds and ends below. Within it I'd set a collection of candles, now melted to the wick and spewing forth from the cracked glass a waxen film coating the wires and inner skeleton of that ruined altar.

Years ago I had gleaned not only entertainment but a wisdom encompassing all walks of life before the benevolent glare of a different TV set, extracting the hidden lessons from soap operas and situation comedies and carefully applying these to my own life. In time, it was given to me that the codes that made up my seemingly inconsequential day-to-day activity could be broken merely by tuning in daily to my favorite show, *The Bomber Brothers*. After repeated viewing of each masterful episode I realized that that inexhaustible trio of ball-breaking special detectives was a perfect facsimile of my own little circle. The two-fisted Detective Breakerage with his cool demeanor of nonchalance and fierce loyalty to the United States of America (despite his secret knowledge of certain covert missions carried out in the bowels of Antarctica, for which knowledge he'd been dishonorably discharged) was none other than my constant companion Jasper Foez. And as for that eccentric loose cannon Mr. Boxx, whose ingenious inventions supplied the brothers with an inexhaustible catalogue of clever gadgets guaranteed to pluck them from certain death at the hands of assorted international criminals and genetically enhanced super thieves? Why, who but Paul Valentine could be the brains behind so many plots and astonishing acts of technological derring-do? Finally there was Sarge, whose own uncertainty regarding his lover (the double agent Sofia Bloom, whose infidelity was ingeniously mirrored by her conflicting governmental ties) belied his ability to wield the brothers as one indomitable unit, tied together by his Holmes-like grasp of cause and effect, not to mention his beloved twin pistols, Firefly and Tico. I myself owned no such pistols, but I understood that they, like the unlikely adventures depicted in each nightly installment, were a metaphor for certain of my own adolescent tribulations whose meaning could be deciphered by me alone.

Now time had erased the show from the airwaves and I had been away long enough that I barely cared. I told myself that perhaps agency had returned to my own secular universe and were I to seek an understanding that transcended the imperfect noise of Exville, it would grow from within me and not from televised serials. Still, I had not forgotten the valuable lessons of the Brothers and employed my faithful Meridian with as much razor-sharp accuracy as Firefly and Tico in the callused hands of Sarge, wielded against the deadly shock troops of the Invisible Empire.

The apartment was not unlivable, only beset by the unhappy specter of permanent transition. It was the not being able to find everything I wanted, or needed, that set me on edge. Mostly I had halves of things meant to come in pairs: toothpaste but no toothbrush; shoes but only one forlorn sock; bread but nothing to put on it to make it more than precisely halfway edible. The visions I'd seen that night by the river's side, and Dotty, who had brought me to them, each demanded immediate interpretation, but thanks to my apartment's characteristic disarray, I came back to the solace of a warm shower only to spend an hour trying to assemble a complete change of clothes before I finally surrendered to the incomplete. I remained dripping and shivering well into the night, thinking of rivers and faraway lights.

I wasn't the least bit sleepy, so I leafed through a few books on witchcraft, borrowed indefinitely from a girl I hadn't seen in years. Instead of finding anything pertaining to the sort of thing I'd seen across the river, I managed to upset the happily dormant memory of Genevieve—the witch I'd dated as a twiggy adolescent trying marijuana for the first time and devouring sci-fi and horror stories, stuff like H. P. Lovecraft, anything that used words like "eldritch"— lifting her smell (you could bottle it and call it Rosewood Clove, an eldritch incarnadine smell of thin vegetable sophistication and burnt-out autumn) from every page, tracing her imprint in the drawings of middle-aged, occasionally horned, hippies with flower-shaped nipples. Then, in a stroke of even worse luck, I happened upon a letter she'd written me after we'd split, stuck in between a chart of the phases of the moon and a chapter called "Elements and Elementals":

251

J. W. McCormack

> Christopher Blake, you are a deceitful person. If I had the
> means and if I thought for a minute that you were *worth it*, I
> would pay an airplane pilot to write CHRISTOPHER BLAKE
> IS A DECEITFUL PERSON WITH CREEPY EYEBROWS on
> a big banner and fly it across the sky. I would pay mosquitoes
> to give you diseases. I would train snakes to bite you. I am
> currently casting a number of hexes, which I hope will suc-
> ceed in leaving you with a shriveled useless husk of an
> inseminator, a service for which womankind as a whole
> ought to rise and thank me. I sincerely think you would ben-
> efit from having the living shit beaten out of you by someone
> larger and with a better grip on reality than you, *which
> means everyone!* Your obsessive—

Which is all I read of it, though it went on for another couple of
pages in more or less the same merrily opened vein. Why had I held
on to this of all things? There had been relationships that had left me
more deeply altered and thoroughly scarred than the one I'd had with
Genevieve; she'd been deactivated from the Meridian for four years
and I'd reasonably thought I'd exorcised her lurking ghost from our
once-shared catalogue of secret places, purged myself of our library
of in-jokes tearlessly. I put the books away, having succeeded only in
conjuring a latent lonely spark I'd thought I'd managed to forget.
Now I looked to the Meridian.

The Meridian beckoned from behind a pair of curtains that parted
to either side to reveal that magnificent device of which I was archi-
tect and sole Operator. I could never tire of its shape, that loving six-
layered spiral that encompassed the wall, built against a plastic back-
drop that looked (at least to my admittedly biased sensibility) like
marble. The Meridian was a sort of wheel of little things picked up
and remembered—preserved and intersecting elements—to create
that which to the eyes of those uninitiated in the mysteries of the
Meridian would have resembled a wall-sized web strung with little
ornaments not unlike the squirming bodies of insectile captives.
Six elements composed my Meridian: shells, feathers, petals (these
were the three inner circles) and then matches, candy wrappers, and
fortune-cookie fortunes, each ring wider than the one before. This
being Tennessee, shells became after a while hard to discover with
any kind of consistency, so I'd turned to rocks about halfway
through. This was the only regard in which the Meridian was blem-
ished. The Activated seemed to smile at me, symbolized sibyls,
markers upon the structured history of my secret world.

Was it perhaps the thrill of beholding the partly permeated

mystery, the cosmic flowchart that passed through eye and brain to take on that meaning of which I alone was custodian? Was this the source of my secret joy, or was it only the natural thrill of the creator, Michelangelo stepping back and receiving grateful judgment from the eyes of David, mutually freed of each other at last? Only one other had ever trespassed upon the Meridian—a different Meridian from a different time—and so quickly had I leapt up to disguise it that I could not know whether he had felt the same stirring of a fantastic verge in his breast. There were touches of all things in the Meridian, and the Activated took on some of the gravity of figures from myth, enchanted by a relational energy and infused with the angelic fates of the graphically elect. Often I had wished I could forget how to read the Meridian and look on it with newborn eyes purely as a thing of beauty unburdened by momentous meaning personalized and set into a pocket universe there on my humble wall. And who could guess that a wall could be such a thing, such an overwhelming map of life? Jasper Foez's falling out with Paul Valentine turned into Castor and Pollux, Jacob and Esau, Jasper recast in the role of an amorous Cuchulain perched to rescue Dot from the clutches of Victor, Victor himself having passed through the Meridian many times and in many different roles, like so many before. There were people I barely knew among the Activated as well as those whose intimate hopes and dreams I knew well enough that their case histories filled nine to ten pages.

Seven years ago, when I'd first built the Meridian, I had not understood the importance of representation and had used the files themselves as markers on the face of my creation. This made it into a mockery of its future glory, a hodgepodge of names and dates, reticulate with information that obscured entirely the sinuous beauty of that piecemeal pinwheel, that altar to significance, my precious *weltanschauung*. I had since become meticulous in keeping a case history separate from the Meridian—in a chest to its right—each page constantly updated and correspondent to a piece of meandering paper or some similar trinket: a dark-eyed Gypsy cut from a *National Geographic*, a quote lifted from some work of inalienable genius, a faded photograph, a playing card, anything. All were located somewhere in the Meridian, in a location of perpetual flux. Jasper got a lizard, for example, and its cheap rubber feet had traversed almost every inch of the Meridian, from Shells to Fortunes. After the night's adventure at the river, I had several changes to carry out. Jasper's lizard currently occupied Matches, the fourth circle, where he would

253

stay, but rotated up toward the position in Wrappers, where I hung my new daisy chain for Dotty.

Oh, Dotty, I barely saw you in the porch light, your skin stretched too thin, growing wan behind black curls, and already I know you. Not like a lover, but like one who has really seen you. I hold in my fifth circle your tenuous connection to yourself, I pay tribute to your stems as they wrap one around the other, knots so tight that life no longer flows through them, and I place your hollow flowers on my wall, noting your resistance to the changing seasons.

I entered her into my dossiers, taking care to list everyone I knew she knew, the things that brought her luck, the things I'd guessed at, and the things that returned to me. Later I would set aside some time to learn her horoscope, the numeric meaning of her unfortunate name, analyzing the quotient for Cabalistic significance. I would try to know her as an intimately secret benefactor, as I transformed her from incompleteness to mimeographed Activation, the translucent border of life and fiction where both are bred. I would, you might say, envelop her.

It was one of the unfortunate side effects of the Meridian that I was perhaps uncomfortably aware of the subtle shifts in relationship (I mean the word in its true sense) and it had been an unusually long time since any of the Activated had entered beyond the fourth circle. Mostly, they orbited around each other, chased to the outer strands of the same circles—Jasper and Paul hot on each other's heels like Orion and his Scorpion. But every story that the Meridian told need not be so large; there were a million smaller stories like the one unfolding between Dot and Jasper; and every one of the Activated would occupy several roles (as specified in their files) through the magic of relation. The first of the Meridian's many lessons: there is a hero for any persuasion.

Horizontal movement on the Meridian was relational. But to cross from one circle to another was to deviate in your degree of personal truth (not my truth—*this* was my truth). To go from Wrappers to Matches, for example, was to come a whole level closer to becoming who you were supposed to be. On the other hand, you might drift away, lose sight of your goals and specific drives (again outlined in my files), and find yourself hurtling headlong toward the dreaded sixth circle. Of course I almost never encountered ones or twos, but I dreamed of meeting such enlightened individuals. I knew that they must exist, since I had allowed for them.

The dominion of my peculiar lifeline, you understand, was strictly limited to the observational, the world of phenomena. The same need that led me to transform reality in this way dictated also that I keep all its imperfection and limitations intact. I pieced together the Meridian with as much rigor and scientific accord as the Aztecs their doomsday calendar. As Operator, I was sworn to reflect the world of my friends and acquaintances as I saw it, as an ever-changing cosmos contained (to paraphrase one who might have been Operator in his own time) in a nutshell of infinite space, albeit with implication toward a fractal galaxy of psychic correspondences and myth. But it did happen from time to time that the Meridian would seem to prefigure some new development, seeming to predict the future. I didn't have the smallest suspicion that this was actually the case, you understand, any more than I believed that in the stars were writ the predilections of future love affairs and promotions. I had grown accustomed to the returning, used to the future's familiar fall into the past. But I still searched out the Meridian for some structural instability that had perhaps affected my point of view unduly, only to come to the happy conclusion that my little system was so perfect that I occasionally knew the raw circumstances so well that I could prefigure their consequences.

As Operator, I would never dream of interfering in that swell of activity that the Meridian was built to mirror and so I never revealed my knowledge of the shape of things, though I believed I had nevertheless accumulated some small reputation as having a keen sense of where they would go, which relationships would last and which would prove explosive. I could hardly help it, so thoroughly were my ledgers filled. I had strengths and weaknesses all observed as my limited powers allowed, circles of influence checked and rechecked, and, best of all, a tally of every common trait. I knew which markers would gravitate toward others, which of the Activated would be prone to rotate as change took a hold, and which would stay put, content to remain within a single circle. This was the real payoff, you see: getting to lovingly put together those stories only to watch them play out on the casual theater, and I the man behind the curtain, the watching watchmaker, fitting the circuits into place on a metaphoric mainframe. I stress again that I didn't interfere—I didn't have to. Mine was simply to record. Yes, this I lived for. It was with a much heavier assumption of responsibility that I observed the reverse, to be the unfortunate witness of destructive tendencies pronounced and watch someone revolve toward calamity as feuds grew and the Activated grew divided.

But I missed the days when some three dozen players would dance upon my marmoreal stage, glittering with existence upon my portable wheel of fortune. There were all too many who were Deactivated, whose signifiers lay uncollected, gathering dust atop their untended files. I'd been out of the circuit for too long and where I'd been they had disallowed my meritorious Meridian. I had found shorthand Meridians, microscopic microcosms that scarcely had any interior life at all and that failed to really interest me in the end. And certainly all fell away before the thing itself. But now I was back. My father had his stage, somewhere, and my mother had hers, in the scratched vinyl whispers of her upstairs room, and I had mine, here, which was nowhere. And a silent joy sang through me as I imagined all the things I would be privy to, the details waiting in the wings, waiting to be Activated.

New Hope for the Dead
John Sayles

Characters:

PHARAOH
CANDACE

(PHARAOH, *a man in his thirties, works steadily at troweling popcorn from an enormous bin into dozens and dozens of cardboard vending cartons scattered around him. He sings unevenly to himself—*)

PHARAOH. Oh the sexual drive of the camel
Is much stronger than anyone thinks
Consider the very first camel
Who attempted to bugger the Sphinx

But the Sphinx's sexual organs
Were clogged by the sands of the Nile
Which explains the hump on the camel
And the Sphinx's inscrutable smile

(PHARAOH *continues his work.* CANDACE, *a tall woman in hot pants and a silky top, comes limping on, carrying a pair of spike-heeled shoes. She doesn't see* PHARAOH *at first, preoccupied with the pain in her swollen ankle.*)

CANDACE. *(Angry.)* Oh God. Oh God. Oh damn you. This is it. This is the lowest, this is it. You really hit bottom with this one, Candy, you really done it this time. Oh God. Ground zero. The absolute pits.

PHARAOH. Hello.

(CANDACE *jumps, startled, putting weight on her bad ankle and screaming in pain—*)

John Sayles

CANDACE. Aaaaaah!

(*She falls down, clutching the ankle—*)

Don't you touch me! You stay away from me! Goddamn pervert, sneaking around in the dark down here—

PHARAOH. Hello.

CANDACE. Oh God. On top of everything else I got the Phantom of the Arena here—who are you? What are you doing down here?

PHARAOH. This is where I labor.

CANDACE. Look, if you're some kind of a creep, I just don't have the time. I gotta tell you that right off.

PHARAOH. This is where I labor. You hurt your foot.

CANDACE. Sherlock Holmes. I broke my fucking ankle on the fucking stairs! Would you back off a little, please? See that wall over there? Why don't you just go stand over by that wall and let me suffer in peace, all right?

PHARAOH. That must hurt.

CANDACE. Dr. Kildare. Oh God. This is the bottom, Candy. Look at this—elephant ankle. I'm in a cellar with elephant ankle and some asshole lurking in the dark who says it must hurt. (*Notices.*) And there's popcorn all over the place.

PHARAOH. It's mine.

CANDACE. I'll never touch the stuff again.

(CANDACE *struggles to her feet and tries a few lurching steps—*)

Look at this. I can't walk. First they tell me I can't act, then I can't sing, then I can't dance, now I can't fucking walk. Nice. Very nice.

PHARAOH. (*Holds out his hand.*) My name's Pharaoh.

CANDACE. Ask me if I'm interested.

PHARAOH. If you want some popcorn, take it from the bin, not the boxes.

CANDACE. Look, Farrell—

258

PHARAOH. Pha-*raoh.*

CANDACE. How do you spell that?

PHARAOH. I can't spell.

CANDACE. Figures. You don't have any ice down here, do you?

PHARAOH. Just popcorn. What's your name?

CANDACE. Candace. I wonder if it's broken. You think it looks broken? Never mind, what would you know, can't even spell.

PHARAOH. Candace like Candy?

CANDACE. Candace like Candace. I am not now nor have I ever been a Candy. You got that?

PHARAOH. I'm Pharaoh like Land of the Pharaohs. The guys upstairs named me.

CANDACE. The guys upstairs got a name for everybody. I wonder if they've got ice.

PHARAOH. I don't know. I've never been up there.

CANDACE. You're a pretty fishy character, you know that?

PHARAOH. I'm an idiot savant.

CANDACE. The first part I believe—what's a savant?

PHARAOH. I know things.

CANDACE. Name one. Name one thing you know.

PHARAOH. Amenophis the Fourth was not a handsome man but he refused to have his portraits idealized.

    (A pause—)

CANDACE. What's that supposed to be?

PHARAOH. Something about Egypt. I'm an Egyptologist.

CANDACE. *Oh.*

PHARAOH. Someone who knows all about ancient Egypt is an Egyptologist.

CANDACE. That's wonderful. You know what I am? I'm an ass-holeologist. I know all about assholes. I could write a history of

259

assholes. *Assholes I Have Known. Assholes Through the Ages.* I know how to recognize them, where to find them, their habits, their speech and customs—and I hate to tell you this, Farrell, but you got all the telltale signs.

(*She limps around a bit more—*)

So cut the crap. Who are you and what do you really do?

PHARAOH. I box.

CANDACE. Joe Louis. You box my ass. The guys upstairs *box.* And none of 'em are white guys—black guys, Puerto Ricans, Costa Ricans, Jamaicaricans, you name it—no white guys. Hasn't been a white guy who boxed since the Irish moved to Jersey.

PHARAOH. (*Adamant.*) I box. The guys upstairs vend. I box and they vend. I don't see them anymore but I know that's what they do with it.

CANDACE. What are you talking about?

PHARAOH. The *pop*corn. I box it and they vend it. The guys upstairs. Only they give me too much shit so I leave before they come down.

CANDACE. That's what you do? Popcorn boxer? You get paid for *that?*

PHARAOH. I used to. There was a man and he said he had a job for me and I didn't have one then and he'd give me five dollars. Then I stopped seeing him. But there kept being popcorn and I'd box it and go away and when I'd come back there would be more. There's always more popcorn.

CANDACE. You do this for free?

PHARAOH. Everybody needs a job.

CANDACE. God give me the strength to get out of here.

(CANDACE *starts limping around again—*)

PHARAOH. Why do you wear those little shorts?

CANDACE. Hot pants. What, you were born down here or something, you never seen hot pants?

PHARAOH. Why do you wear them?

CANDACE. You *are* an idiot.

PHARAOH. Why do you wear them?

CANDACE. *(Pissed.)* I wear 'em so the guys upstairs can whoop an' holler and tell me what they're keepin' in their jeans for me! I wear 'em so they got something to conjure up when they go to the john! *(Yells.)* Hey sweet*hot! Show* me dat thang!

PHARAOH. Oh.

CANDACE. I wear them so the asshole who got me this stupid job can feel like he owns me and so I can break my fucking ankle running to hide from him so he can't tell me to put out or get out and end up talking to some moron who shovels popcorn for fucking free under the fucking arena!

PHARAOH. Oh.

(A pause.)

(Timidly.) What's your job?

CANDACE. Two guys, two non-Caucasian guys, beat the crap out of each other in a ring for three minutes. Then a bell rings and I stand up and hold a piece of cardboard with the round number written on it and walk around the ring like this—

(She demonstrates, holding an imaginary card, smiling with all her teeth, hobbling to four corners—)

—while the guys upstairs look at my ass and whistle in four different languages. Oh God. Look at this. I can't go on like this. This is it, God, rock bottom—

PHARAOH. I've never heard of that job.

CANDACE. AT LEAST I GET PAID FOR IT!

(CANDACE sits on the ground holding her head. PHARAOH watches a moment, then goes back to the popcorn.)

(Wearily.) I wasn't always a card girl.

PHARAOH. Is that what they call your job?

CANDACE. You can't even spell—shut up and listen!

(A pause. She gets her mood back.)

I was gonna be an artist, you know? I didn't know what kind, in what *field* exactly, but I had this burning desire. I was willing to do the work. I'm *still* willing to do the work, damn it. I was gonna be an artist and make something or be somebody that would last forever.

PHARAOH. I think I can help you.

CANDACE. (*Brandishing a shoe.*) You know what kind of damage a heel like this could inflict? Puncture wounds you wouldn't believe. Box your popcorn and keep your mouth shut.

(PHARAOH *goes back to work.*)

Everything I tried, there was always an asshole between me and success. Every goddamn time. I came here sixteen—no—seventeen years ago. Jesus. I won't say where from but it was highly agrarian. People dreamed about owning backhoes. They knew the names of fertilizers. (*She looks to* PHARAOH.) Farmers. First I was going to be an actress.

PHARAOH. I've heard of that job.

CANDACE. I answered an ad in the trades and I got the first part I auditioned for. "Woman, twenties, tall, athletic, auburn hair." I dyed my hair in the morning, auditioned in the afternoon. I was so excited. It was a guy named Phil and a girl who had answered for "Woman, twenties, blonde, heavy legs," and me and Raoul, who was the actor-director-playwright. Raoul said we'd be creating a theater piece by cutting to the bone of our souls and building on the debris of all the inhibitions we were going to lose. He was so artistic, I could hardly stand it.

PHARAOH. I've never seen a play. I don't think I have.

CANDACE. It was very—very *phy*sical. But I figured it must be what real acting was. Raoul would touch me certain places and we'd mime certain acts of passion together and it made me very uncomfortable. But Raoul said we were coming close to a breakthrough.

PHARAOH. Mostly I've seen a lot of funerals.

CANDACE. The girl with the thick legs was even dumber than I was. We rehearsed in Phil's living room. Phil and Raoul were best friends. We'd rehearse every evening, with me and Raoul working as partners on the floor and Phil and Thick Legs on the couch.

After a month and a half I still didn't feel very comfortable, so one day I'm sitting on top of Raoul in rehearsal and I say, "Raoul, I know we're artists and all but I don't know what's going to happen when it comes time for a performance." And Raoul looks at me and he says, "What do you mean? This *is* the performance."

PHARAOH. I've been to a *lot* of funerals.

CANDACE. Now and then I look in the trades and see Raoul's ad for replacements and understudies. They keep replacing the cast but that show is still running. Seventeen years—it's like *The Fantasticks.*

PHARAOH. Do they vend popcorn there?

CANDACE. Raoul was my first asshole. God I wanted to be an actress. I tried so *hard.* I auditioned for everything, I took classes, had new head shots made every month, worked on my instrument—

PHARAOH. The god Atum, one of the Creators, formed himself from Nothing out of his own will.

CANDACE. What?

PHARAOH. Then he created other gods by mating with himself.

CANDACE. Listen, Farrell, if you can't spell I figure you can't read. If you can't read how'd you learn all this stuff?

PHARAOH. I don't know. Maybe somebody told me. Or maybe not. Whenever I hear something about Egypt it's like something I already knew a long, long time ago, like something I forgot and then I just remembered it.

CANDACE. You remember ancient Egypt?

PHARAOH. Like I was there.

CANDACE. Did they have theater back then? Plays?

PHARAOH. I remember funerals. I remember religious ceremonies—

CANDACE. I mean, were there actresses?

(*She starts to limp around again—*)

Let's say I'm this ancient Egyptian, right? And I—

PHARAOH. You wouldn't be.

263

John Sayles

CANDACE. Huh?

PHARAOH. Too tall. We didn't have women as tall as you. Too tall.

CANDACE. That's what the casting directors used to say.

PHARAOH. I'm sorry.

CANDACE. They said that, too. Look, the reason I'm asking is I've got this theory that it's not my fault. I'm just in the wrong *time* is all. I mean, maybe back in ancient Egypt I would have been their greatest actress—

PHARAOH. *(Shakes his head.)* Too tall.

CANDACE. Twerp. You haven't even seen my work.

PHARAOH. We had magic back then. Mostly the priests were in charge of that.

CANDACE. My second acting job was as a magician's assistant. Same outfit as this, only with spangles. The Amazing Elmo.

PHARAOH. They could change sticks into serpents and serpents into sticks.

CANDACE. I actually lived with that asshole. You wanna know his one big joke? You wanna know the joke I ran into every single night after the show for the whole time I was with him?

PHARAOH. I don't know any jokes. I know some riddles.

CANDACE. *(Demonstrates.)* Here—pull your pockets out so they hang down—that's it—now you start to unzip your fly and you say to me—"Hey, little girl, you wanna see an elephant?"

(A pause.)

Great joke, huh?

(Another pause.)

These are the ears, see, and when you pull your thing out, it's supposed to look like—oh never mind.

PHARAOH. Can I zip my fly now?

CANDACE. Suit yourself.

(CANDACE limps some more.)

264

When I split from Elmo I decided to be a singer. I moved in with my voice teacher. He said he admired my lungs.

PHARAOH. We had singing. At funerals, we sang.

CANDACE. He used to have me stick my arm down his throat. All the way up to my elbow. Really gross. He learned how to loosen his throat muscles from a sword swallower. He started as a tenor, then he learned that trick and turned into a basso profundo.

PHARAOH. We had swords.

CANDACE. Sticking my arm down was bad enough. Then he tried to make *me* learn how to do it.

PHARAOH. To lower your voice?

CANDACE. No.

PHARAOH. Why then?

CANDACE. He had his reasons. Asshole. [*She limps.*] I bet you had *that* back in ancient Egypt, too.

PHARAOH. What?

CANDACE. Skip it. After he told me he liked my lungs but my diaphragm was never gonna make it I went into my dancing phase. I got involved with an asshole dancer who played a shepherd in the Christmas show at Radio City.

PHARAOH. We had shepherds.

CANDACE. [*Pissed.*] You were pretty well equipped back there in ancient Egypt, weren't you? Is there anything you didn't have?

PHARAOH. Popcorn.

CANDACE. I was a pretty good tap dancer. I was a *very* good tap dancer. Only this was before all the revivals. I was born too late. Or too early. I could have been Ann Miller. I was willing to do the work.

PHARAOH. Who is Ann Miller?

CANDACE. He's never heard of Ann Miller. How 'bout Ginger Rogers? Isadora Duncan? Twyla Tharp?

John Sayles

(PHARAOH *looks at her blankly.*)

Salome? Little Egypt?

PHARAOH. Sorry.

CANDACE. I have a thing about famous people. I think I was meant to be one of them.

PHARAOH. I remember seeing Moses. Is he still famous?

CANDACE. Moses like in *The Greatest Story Ever Told?*

PHARAOH. He was a troublemaker.

CANDACE. But people remember him, he left something. To this very day people are breaking the commandments he laid down. I'd give anything to be remembered like that.

PHARAOH. I think I can help you.

CANDACE. I've always wanted to have people know who I am. And when I go I want them to mourn my passing. Weeping in the streets. Like Valentino. Or James Dean or John Lennon. Even if it's just a big send-off that gets you famous. Like that girl who was murdered at the Met. She was just another cello player and now she's famous. Whatsername.

PHARAOH. I think I can help you.

CANDACE. I think famous people have an immortality the rest of us can't hope for. They live forever in the minds of men.

PHARAOH. I know I can help you.

CANDACE. Don't be an idiot, you can't even spell.

PHARAOH. Is Ann Miller immortal?

CANDACE. (*Looks at him, sits.*) Oh Christ.

(*She looks at her ankle mournfully.*)

I'll never tap dance again.

PHARAOH. What's tap dancing?

CANDACE. I was born at the wrong time. I wonder if tap dancing will ever come back?

PHARAOH. Once a year the Nile would flood its banks, then recede, leaving silt for the farmers to plant in.

CANDACE. I read where they can freeze people for ages. "New Hope for the Dead." It was an article in *Reader's Digest*. Mostly it's for people with diseases that don't have cures yet, but it could be something else. You wake up just the same age as when you were frozen. I could put a sign on my vault—DO NOT THAW TILL TAP DANCING COMES BACK.

PHARAOH. We'd pull the brain out of the skull with a hook. Out through the nose. That went in one jar.

CANDACE. Might be a pretty long wait.

PHARAOH. Then we'd cut out the viscera—lungs, heart, liver, kidneys, stomach—each would go in a separate jar.

CANDACE. Pretty hard to practice, too.

PHARAOH. Then we'd replace the blood with pickling fluid before we wrapped the body. The fluid smelled like asparagus. I remember.

CANDACE. Gross. That's really disgusting, you know that? This freezing thing, they leave you in one piece. You keep your figure, everything. I heard that Walt Disney had it done.

PHARAOH. I've heard that name.

CANDACE. He died before his time.

PHARAOH. Is he immortal, too?

CANDACE. He was a visionary. You think your pyramids are something, you should see some of the things he built. He invented all these animals—

PHARAOH. Ra, the sun god, was born of the Great Cackler.

CANDACE. *What?*

PHARAOH. The celestial goose who broke the silence of the universe. It laid the cosmic egg and when it hatched there was Ra.

CANDACE. You're making this up.

PHARAOH. Some versions say it was a white crane and not a goose.

CANDACE. Walt Disney never had a goose. He had a lot of mice and some dogs and a little baby deer and one duck who was very important, but never a goose. Leave it to the ancient Egyptians to base something on a goose.

PHARAOH. Was he one of the Creators?

CANDACE. *(With emotion.)* You bet your ass he was. And if he hadn't died before his time we wouldn't be living in New York Scumbag City, we'd be living in Disneyworld. A community of the future. He was a visionary. He was planning model communities and he liked tall women who were willing to do the work and if he hadn't died we'd be riding *monorails* without graffiti all over them and we wouldn't be stepping over the muscatel-for-lunch-bunch sprawled out all over the sidewalks and we wouldn't be living with rats and pigeons and cockaroaches!

PHARAOH. We'd have mice and ducks instead?

CANDACE. WE WOULDN'T HAVE A LOT OF DUMB GEESE RUNNING AROUND LAYING COSMIC FUCKING EGGS, I CAN TELL YOU THAT!

PHARAOH. And now he's immortal?

CANDACE. He's on ice. Waiting for them to come up with a cure for his death, so he can oversee his Land and his World and clean the rest of this mess up.

PHARAOH. Osiris was a great ruler who was killed by his brother Set. Set chopped him into pieces and scattered them all over the world, but his mother Isis found all the pieces and put them together in a mummy. Now he rules the Underworld.

CANDACE. You know what my worst nightmare is? It's not even for me, it's for Walt Disney. I dream that they find a cure and they thaw him out, and he wakes up, just like in "Sleeping Beauty," only everything has gone to shit. I mean in Disneyland. It's a slum. They're strip-mining on the Matterhorn and the Jungle Safari is all overgrown with the river all clogged with poisonous chemicals. There's derelicts drinking Night Train Express on Tom Sawyer's Island and there's perverts in the Haunted House waiting to flash you when you come around a corner on one of those little cars. The rides are all massage parlors now—in the dream I'm working in one of them, dressed up like Alice in Wonderland. Mr. Disney

268

takes one look and crawls back into his vault.

PHARAOH. In ancient Egypt, at first only the Pharaoh claimed immortality. As years went by, other nobles began to say they could have an afterlife, too, and by the time of the New Kingdom some members of the middle class were having themselves mummified at death and placed in elaborate tombs.

CANDACE. I just want a little recognition, that's all.

PHARAOH. The Pharaohs thought the more colossal the monuments they left were, the better their chances of being accepted into the afterlife.

CANDACE. I suppose you worked on the pyramids?

PHARAOH. Look at these hands.

CANDACE. It must have been hot.

PHARAOH. Not once you started working on the interior. The Pharaoh's closest servants and his engineers and his workers were supposed to be sealed in the tomb with his body to help his soul on its journey to see Osiris. It was a great honor.

CANDACE. I bet it was.

PHARAOH. Sometimes we'd build secret escape routes while we worked on the interior.

CANDACE. That's terrible.

PHARAOH. The mosquitoes were the worst part. We'd have to hide in the bulrushes for weeks till the excitement of the burial died down.

CANDACE. That's terrible. That pisses me off.

PHARAOH. Then you'd run into people who knew you. "I thought you were sealed up with Ramses," they'd say. "Oh no, there wasn't enough room for us all."

CANDACE. I think that really stinks! You were supposed to be his devoted servants! You were supposed to believe in the afterlife!

PHARAOH. You think we'd have built so many monuments if we were sure about it?

CANDACE. I hate it when people crap out on their promises. My whole life has been one asshole after another crapping out on his promises. I mean, weren't you supposed to go along with your master and serve him in the afterlife? Wasn't that some consolation?

PHARAOH. They only said that to get you in the tomb.

CANDACE. So do you or don't you believe in all that stuff?

PHARAOH. Without it life was so hard. Sand, heat, disease, hard work. And then you'd look at something like the tomb that Ramses the Second built for Nefertari—

CANDACE. That was his wife?

PHARAOH. And his daughter.

CANDACE. You're kidding. Didn't they have a taboo or something?

PHARAOH. Most pharaohs were married to and had children by their mother or their sisters or their daughters.

CANDACE. That's disgusting.

PHARAOH. Incest was preferred among the royalty—

CANDACE. They're disgusting people. Ancient, disgusting people.

PHARAOH. It kept the bloodline pure.

CANDACE. No wonder you're an idiot. You know what that kind of business does to your gene pools? I bet they started young, too, little ancient Egyptian brothers and sisters playing I'll-show-you-mine-if-you'll-show-me-yours down by the Nile. No wonder the civilization didn't last.

PHARAOH. It lasted over two thousand years. How long has this one been around?

CANDACE. Did they put a man on the moon? Huh? Two thousand years of rock piles and incest—I'm sorry, I'm not impressed.

(PHARAOH *shrugs and goes back to work.*)

PHARAOH. You had to be there.

(CANDACE *mimes walking the sign around again. Her limp is worse.*)

CANDACE. Damn it!

270

Damn it, I need the money, too. Sometimes I think I should have just gotten off that bus seventeen years ago, pulled my pants down, spread my legs, and laid down under a big sign that said WELCOME, ASSHOLES! I mean, I've always been willing to do the work. But you have to have talent, too, say the assholes. Talent. If I had done that, given them all a crack at it right off the bat, maybe I would have been able to get somewhere. It wouldn't have taken long—they never hung around much after they made their break-through. Right there in the Port Authority bus terminal—"Get it while it's fresh and then leave me alone for the next seventeen years."

I think this might be it, though. I can't even walk across a fight ring and shake my snatch at a bunch of beer guzzlers. This is where I throw in the towel. Seventeen years—I might as well have stayed out in the soybean fields and let them plow me under. Just another little lump on the Great Plains. I never even came close. No Rise and Fall of Candy, just the same old shit from the minute I stepped off that Greyhound with my suitcase full of movie magazines. My *land*lord doesn't even know my name.

PHARAOH. I can help you.

CANDACE. I would have been so nice if I got to be famous. This isn't the real me you're seeing here. If I was famous and fell down in here with you I'd be nice and sweet and take an interest in all your bullshit about Egypt and then I'd have a photographer come down and take a picture of us together in the popcorn. "To Farrell, with love from Candace."

PHARAOH. I can help you.

CANDACE. I never asked for much. Just to be given a chance to show what I was worth. Instead I get seventeen years of assholes and people telling me I was too tall or too old or too late or tap dancing had gone away.

PHARAOH. I can help you.

CANDACE. I'm beyond help. I'm a fucking nothing and that's the way it's gonna stay.

PHARAOH. I've got wraps.

CANDACE. Wraps?

John Sayles

PHARAOH. The guys upstairs left some down here. They said they wrap their hands.

CANDACE. Yeah, before they fight. So what?

PHARAOH. I could wrap your ankle. Maybe you could walk.

CANDACE. If I didn't need the money—OK. But no funny business.

(PHARAOH *smiles and comes up with a roll of elastic bandages from among the popcorn boxes—*)

Should I sit?

PHARAOH. No, that's fine.

(CANDACE *balances herself as best she can as* PHARAOH *goes to work with the bandage—*)

CANDACE. Don't do it too tight.

PHARAOH. I know how to wrap.

CANDACE. You know it's not really the fame that hurts the most. It's worse than that. I fall in love with assholes. Time and again. Me, the world's leading expert, believing all their crap.

PHARAOH. Flex your toes.

CANDACE. I fall in love and the fame isn't so important. It's like whatever asshole I'm with becomes Time—like Time and Space, right? And as long as he loves me I'm famous forever. That's all I need. Isn't that fucking pitiful? Farrell, you may have met a bigger idiot than you are. Every time I do the work, I give it everything I've got. Did you have love in ancient Egypt? I mean, let's face it, you were a pretty morbid bunch.

PHARAOH. I don't remember.

CANDACE. When you give everything you've got to somebody and then you end up getting smacked in the face with it—I don't know. You lose something, some part of you. Like your friend there who got chopped up—there's a piece of me on East Tenth Street, a piece of me in the Village, odds and ends on the Upper West Side—

PHARAOH. Now relax your foot. Let it hang.

CANDACE. I think being famous might make up for it. I'm not sure, though. I always figured that all the famous people knew each

272

other automatically. Like you get a key and you open a door and there they all are. Living and dead.

(PHARAOH *is wrapping her legs together now*—)

PHARAOH. We'd bury our dead in the West. That was where the sun disappeared every night. We'd row the body across the Nile and place it in a tomb where the family would leave food and water for the soul on its journey. The soul had wings like a hawk.

CANDACE. Living and dead. "We've been waiting for you," they say. "What took you so long?" "I had some trouble with assholes." "Oh," they say, "we don't have any of *them* in here."

PHARAOH. The soul had wings like a hawk. It had to fly across the Great Nowhere to reach the Hall of Judgment, where Anubis, the jackal-headed god, would lead it to Osiris, King of the Underworld.

CANDACE. And then you go in and things fall into place. All these people are there who you've worshipped from afar, they're right there and it's like they know you already and they *like* you already 'cause you under*stand*, right, you understand what it's like to be one of them.

PHARAOH. The soul would declare its innocence before Osiris, while Thoth, the ibis-headed god, recorded its words. Then the heart of the deceased was put on one side of the scale and Mayet, goddess of truth, was put on the other.

CANDACE. I'll look around and there'll be some guy, somebody famous, and he'll be the one who's supposed to fall in love with me. And it's guaranteed he won't mess me over 'cause he knows he'd get booted out and nobody who's ever made it there could bear that.

PHARAOH. If the heart didn't balance, Ammut the Devourer, half crocodile and half lion, stood waiting to put an end to the soul forever.

CANDACE. And the people—the people—there's Jimmy Stewart and President Kennedy and Judy Garland and all of the rock and roll people who took overdoses or choked on something or crashed in airplanes and there's Elvis and Thelma Ritter and Baryshnikov and Jesus Christ is there but only as a celebrity—he's not laying any big religious trip on anybody. There's the real Wild Bill Hickok standing with the guy who played him on TV and there's Liz and Dick and Janet and Tony and Cher and Sonny and they're all talking about getting back together again.

PHARAOH. But if the scale balanced, Mayet would dress the soul in the green feathers of truth and lead it once again to Osiris, who would grant the gift of eternal life.

(PHARAOH *has wrapped* CANDACE *mummy-fashion almost up to her neck.*)

CANDACE. And this guy comes and I'm not sure of his name but he's good-looking and he's famous and he never lies to me and he says, "Hi. You've done the work, Candace, it wasn't all for nothing. We've been watching you and we want you to know that everything has its reward. Let me show you where you'll be living." So we go through this gate and it's like all of a sudden everything is in color and the air we're breathing is like sweet water and your skin turns the exact shade you've always wanted it to be and there's singing in the air like warm hands holding you and I see it and it's beautiful, it's so beautiful, it's like Heaven, it's like—it's like Disneyland.

(PHARAOH *wraps her mouth and face over and lays her down gently—*)

PHARAOH. And they take you through a gate and you're above ground again and it's beautiful, it's gold, it's the Nile, giver of life, snaking away from you as the sun is rising, catching the water just perfectly to shine a glorious river of gold.

(PHARAOH *looks at the mummy for a moment, then, as the lights fade, begins to sing as he goes back to his popcorn.*)

Blues fell down on Memphis
Blues fell down like morning rain
Blues fell on the Delta
Blues been drivin' me insane
My baby crossed that river
Won't see her face round here again

The Gateway
T. M. McNally

BEAT, THEY SAY in the screenplay trade—not to indicate violence, or the plausibility of victory, or defeat. When we say beat we mean instead *the passage of time.*
A moment, say. Preferably one meant to be felt, like life.

I was in Paris, staying at a hotel behind the Cathedral St. Sulpice, when I was visited by an old girlfriend. I was sitting naked on the bed, a white cotton spread, fresh from the bath because earlier that morning I had been caught in the rain. There was rain falling in the courtyard filled with flowers. My wife, Phoebe, was out shopping for a new Parisian hat for our three-year-old daughter. She wanted me to buy a new suit.
We're in Paris, she said. Buy yourself a suit.
On the way to the Arc de Triomphe, Phoebe had discovered a designer she took instantly a shine to. On the way back to our hotel we stopped again and she purchased three new dresses and was, my guess, feeling slightly spendthrift. In the small, polished store I held Isolde on my hip and watched my wife through the slightly parted fabric of the changing room slip her body into one dress, and then another; I watched her pull back her hair only to let it alight upon her long, pale neck. Fabulous, said the woman who ran the boutique, standing beside me, lifting her chin and watching my wife. The woman turned to me and said, in that oddly intimate moment, You have a beautiful family, and then the woman reached for my daughter to brush aside a lock of her hair. Then my wife stepped out of the dressing room in this midthigh silk dress, the color of a robin's egg, or the St. Louis sky in spring. The dress had spaghetti straps and a row of buttons running from the center of my wife's chest, down across her navel to the hemline, and I thought, This is the woman with whom I have made it all the way to Paris.
There was also a raw silk shawl, which covered her bare shoulders. We had a daughter now, Isolde. We had a house on San Bonita in

275

St. Louis with a Stickley-influenced banister and a seventy-year-old oak staircase—original stained-glass windows, a slate roof over our heads. The person whom you marry, it changes your life.

And the person whom you do not marry?

Earlier, while Phoebe and Isolde went shopping for a hat, I had sat in the rainy mist in a park across from Notre Dame. I was sitting there, smoking a Gauloise, when I realized a hundred feet off to my left there was a pair of lovers on a bench, beneath a handsome tree, which protected them from the drizzling rain. The woman had her raincoat spread about her boyfriend's hips, straddling him in the rain, and I could hear them laughing, because they must have been in love. I picked myself up, moved to another bench, and then it really began to rain and I gave in to the weather and walked back to the hotel. On the way back, I stopped in at the Cathedral St. Sulpice to light a candle for my father, who had recently died, and to give thanks—I don't know to whom—for the fact of my wife and daughter.

Back in my room, I ordered hot chocolate and took a bath. I opened the window to smoke a cigarette, and sat on the bed, listening to the rain, and turned on CNN, World Edition, and there she was— Amanda Cunningham Amachi. The girl I met in college. The girl I lived with in California while writing screenplays. The girl who gave me lice. The girl who after telling me she was pregnant then proceeded to have an abortion, without telling me, and prevented me from becoming a father sooner than I ever should have. The girl who told me, after I decided to give up on Hollywood, Oh God, Thomas. I always knew you were a failure.

I met Ed Zwick once. The director? But that's another story.

My wife had lived in Paris for a year and a half after she finished college—painting pictures—while I was pitching scripts in L.A. My thinking was I'd sell out to Hollywood in order later to write haunting novels about the human condition. When that fell apart, I started writing nonunion scripts for children's television at nine hundred dollars a whack. To get by, I had to sell two a month, which meant I actually had to write five. If you know anything about Hollywood, then you know that children's television is the scut work of the industry, and if you have children, then you may have seen one or two of my episodes, like "Dildar and the Laser of Doom." Lots of Kung Fu and galactic monsters and neon outfits with invasive special effects. The week I finally realized I should be ashamed, I returned alone to St. Louis—the place of my birth, the very gateway to the West. The French, they discovered St. Louis. By 1904 it had become one of the most industrial and economically driven cities of the world.

Amanda Cunningham Amachi—I'd known her before the Amachi became appended—was living in a small town north of Dubuque, Iowa. She was an Associate Director of Economic Development. She had gained weight and, having married my former roommate from college, Dan Amachi, had now brought forth into this world two children. He was, last I'd heard, Regional Sales Manager for Briggs and Stratton—the engine on your lawnmower. Apparently, the small town in which they had settled had missed out on the economic boom of the nineties, its downtown having been decimated by the encroaching Wal-Marts and Home Depots, and Amanda Cunningham Amachi, as Associate Director of Economic Development for the City Council of Three Falls, had been called upon by CNN to serve as an expert witness.

First I left Hollywood, land of the movie house, and then I went home, and now I sell people houses and make dreams come true. I sell houses in the suburbs of Kirkwood and Webster Groves and, if a client really has any dough, Clayton. I generally don't sell the city, because the city is destroyed, we actually have abandoned skyscrapers, and you can buy a house in St. Louis on your credit card, but I do sell a lot of houses and I have a lot of people now who sell houses for me. I'll show you a house in University City if I know you don't have any kids, same with the Central West End, but if you do have kids, and unless I know you are prepared to give up your lease payments on your SUV and instead spend your money on private schools, then I know you aren't going to buy a house there, because I'm the guy who also listens to your concerns about The Schools. I'm the guy who explains to first-time buyers the meaning of points and listens patiently while you talk yourself into spending more than you thought you could possibly afford in spite of your lease payments on that SUV. I'm the guy who, along with another at Saint Louis University, started a housing program for refugees across the world. And before that, I was also the guy who used to teach Advanced Screenwriting for Hollywood as a Part-Time Professional at a local university that fancies itself as being its own World Headquarters. Honest, that's what the sign says, complete with a picture of the world.

T. M. McNally

After I failed big in Hollywood, I got in my old car and drove across the country. Once I hit the city limits, I went directly to the arch. I put my hand upon the sleek and silver curve of it and the world went right on by. A couple hundred years ago, the French, they wanted to make some discoveries, which is what travel always permits, so they came to America. When I went to Paris, I flirted with a woman with whom my wife would select three dresses. The woman wore stylish eyeglasses, and when the French arrived in what would eventually become New Orleans, they wandered up the Mississippi River to Laclede's Landing and built the once-magnificent city of St. Louis. They built the city into which I was born and took their fill.

On Art Hill, in Forest Park, there is a magnificent statue of Mr. St. Louis, overlooking the park, which is designed to resemble those in Paris. When I was a kid, we used to steal his sword.

As Sean Connery says to Julia Ormond, Marry the king, Guinevere. But love the man.

Years ago, when my wife was in Paris, she was twenty-two and living in the Seventh Arrondissement. Her boyfriend back in the states, Future Rock Star, was sleeping with a woman who also had a crush on Phoebe and who would later become an editorial lieutenant of a magazine empire. My wife did not know Claire was sleeping with Future Rock Star. She thought they were having coffee in Boston. I know because she was writing to him at that very same moment that I was standing in St. Louis with my hand on the tender curve of the Gateway Arch. All of this is true.

When you visit, Phoebe wrote, *we'll make love in the Luxembourg Gardens.*

There was a boy, Jean Claude, who lived in the flat across the hall. Jean Claude was beautiful and shy, and on one fine spring day when Phoebe's toilet backed up, he opened the door for her at her knock.

Yes? said Jean Claude.

My toilet backed up, Phoebe said. May I use yours?

She was giddy with the excuse to step inside his living room, which was filled with books. The terror of living in a beautiful place like Paris is that you are always lonely, no matter how many people you might sleep with. What you want is someone to hold your hand. What you want is somebody to look into your eyes and explain that the ache and absolute apprehension you feel inside your heart is normal. Life is bitter. Life is sweet. Let's talk, then we'll fuck.

278

T. M. McNally

The landlord charged my wife several thousand francs for breaking the toilet. It was one of those space-saving European metal things that always cause the room to smell like piss. My wife, she stepped into Jean Claude's bathroom, and then she washed her hands, which were stained with paint and smelled faintly of turpentine, and then her face. She thought, I am in Paris in a French boy's bathroom. There were condoms on the sink. She stepped out of the bathroom, water on her cheeks, as if she had been crying, and Jean Claude handed her a glass of wine. His eyeglasses were slightly smudged and the hair on his wrist was fine and pale. He handed her a glass of red wine and said, Phoebe?

Yes, she said, her heart lifting.

He raised a finger into the air and touched the mole on the edge of her mouth. Phoebe, he said. That means Moon, no?

Yes, Phoebe said. She began to unbutton her blouse, which was covered with paint, then hesitated. Catching his eye, she began again, and said, Want to see?

Jean Claude kissed her hands. From the feel of things, he had an enormous penis. They could hear Rosalia, another tenant, across the hall. Apparently Rosalia had lost her keys. Phoebe ripped open her jeans, and then his. She kicked off her shoes. Additionally, this was Phoebe's first uncircumcised penis, which amazed her, the way it emerged so keenly from the flesh that held it. Paris was a boy, too, she thought. Paris was the boy who stole Helen of Troy and, in turn, started the entire Trojan War. She slipped the condom on Jean Claude tenderly.

It was a tight fit. For a while he hurt inside of her, but after a while the hurt turned to a kind of sweet and rueful pleasure. When she was three, she had seen her father naked, once, though she no longer remembered it. A man has a son, the world pivots on its axis; but when a man has a daughter, a little girl like my own, even the axis turns. It turns on the very center of your heart. Then the condom split. That night, returning to her flat, the smell of sex in her hair, which reminded her of freshly mown grass, Phoebe wrote to her boyfriend, Future Rock Star, who was at that moment having an argument with a future editorial lieutenant. For the second time that evening, Phoebe removed her jeans, and then her underwear and socks, while I went to my father's house and sat in the kitchen, drinking a beer, and explained to him my decision to give up on Hollywood. Everybody has to eat, I said, making excuses for what I'd done. I don't remember what he said, but I do remember my father

279

T. M. McNally

pouring himself a beer and nodding sympathetically, taking his time, not wanting to raise a head. And years later, sitting naked in my hotel room behind the Cathedral St. Sulpice, before the open window that looked out onto a courtyard filled with flowers, I watched Phoebe sit at her small table in her small flat. I watched her cross her legs and take out a tablet of purple paper on which to write her boyfriend back in the states a love letter. I watched the ink from her pen, following the direction of her mind, her tongue, and her breath.

I've met the sweetest boy, she wrote. *He works for the telephone company part-time and studies philosophy.* She wrote, *Give Claire my love.*

She wrote, *Watch out for the groupies.*

She used a lot of Xs and Os—*kisses & hugs.* She kissed the paper, her lips tasting the faintest trace of the tree from which it once came, and the bitter scent of ink, and then she went to bed and dreamed of home, which was far away, all the way across the Atlantic. She fell asleep along the way at sea.

Ron Shelton, too. I met him once, and he was kind and polite, and he insisted I send him something, but I never did. I liked leaving L.A. with an open invitation like that.

Meet me for coffee? said the woman, slipping me a piece of paper, on which she had written her telephone number and the name of a café. Phoebe and Isolde were outside, on the Parisian sidewalk, looking for puddles. The woman had fine hair parted in the center and a silk blouse through which I could see the fabric of her lingerie. I signed the credit card receipt, and slid it back across the counter, and then her wedding-ringed hand fell onto mine, and I said, I've never been to Paris.

It's lovely in the spring, said the woman. I do not live far from here.

She stepped back, and laughed, and glanced at a co-worker, equally chic, stepping through the curtains. The woman before me with the rich perfume wiped her mouth with the back of her hand and said, Five o'clock? I will show you some sites.

This is not the kind of thing that often happens to single men, or rather it does, but only on the late-night cable with all the rented furniture. Like crack cocaine and unfettered capitalism, like wars of aggression, it's the kind of thing that destroys a home, which is what you dream of most when you do not have one. Home ownership. It's why we privilege the industry with our tax laws and it's why we

280

have ancillary industries with patriotic names to furnish them—
Ethan Allen, Martha Stewart. It's why, after you fail at one career,
you can always take up selling houses. When you walk inside somebody's house, you can tell how much they read. You get instantly a
feel for their sex life by the size of the television in the bedroom and
the pictures on the walls, the pillows on the bed and the color of the
sheets. Is there a copy of the *Kama Sutra* on the nightstand? In
the kitchen, you can spot instantly who knows how to cook. My
father, who died three weeks before my seventh anniversary, used to
say he liked Amanda Cunningham Amachi because, as he put it, she
was corn-fed.

Though I was in Paris, sitting in a park in the rain beside a pair of
lovers, smoking a Gauloise across from Notre Dame, I had been feeling sad. There were boughs protecting the lovers from the rain. My
father was a great thinker. The Colossus, his colleagues called him.
My father, who worked with seeds, invented a process that led various industries to develop agricultural forms of genetic engineering.
In the pictures I have of myself in my youth, you can see I am my
father's son. I am my father's son *sans* the colossal intellect.

Earlier that day, in our perfect hotel, I'd had breakfast—a bowlful
of coffee, chocolate croissants—beneath a glass canopy, and Michelle,
the waitress and chambermaid and sometimes desk clerk, cooed
over Isolde and brought her apricots. While Phoebe read her share of
the *Herald Tribune*, I read a story about genetic engineering. The
French agricultural community was very upset about it. One leader,
Mr. French Leader of the Free Farms, was quoted as saying, These
huge tomatoes. It is so American. It is an outrage and an invasion
just like Normandy!

My father had been a part of that invasion. He served as a medic,
tying up the various limbs that still might not need to be completely
severed, on the way to liberating Paris. He finished college on the GI
Bill and became a genius, and I know for a fact that my father didn't
want to make fake food: he wanted instead to feed the world. The
starving kids in Ethiopia and El Salvador and China—it's one thing
to make a life, but quite another to feed it. He'd say, Whatever you
do, Thomas, make this world a better place.

I was sad because the world was full of such sweetness and mercy
and light and because I wanted to be at least partially responsible for
some of it. Phoebe says she was a good enough artist to know she
herself never would be, which is why she now runs a gallery. It's her
fate, she'll tell a young artist she wants to show, to help the others.

T. M. McNally

And besides, she *wants* to.

Man, says Aristotle, is desire. The best I can explain is this:

Once upon a time, a boy named Paris desired a pretty girl, and in so doing started a war that became an epic poem and then a city to which I took my wife and our three-year-old daughter to celebrate our seventh anniversary and the fact of our lives together. In the park across from Notre Dame, two lovers were making love, and possibly a baby, in the rain. My old girlfriend was on the television. After she became pregnant, she told me so in the kitchen of our apartment, and I said, This complicates things, but we can work it out, can't we? And then Amanda Cunningham Amachi said she wasn't certain, but that she was very glad I was not upset with her, and she said she also wasn't sure she wanted to spend the rest of her life with me, and then she went to a friend's house for the weekend, just to take a break, she said, during which her friend took her to a clinic where she held Amanda's hand while a doctor in fresh scrubs performed the generally uncomplicated procedure. Meanwhile, there she was on the television in Paris, and a married woman in a tony boutique had slipped to me a piece of paper, asking for a date, which smelled like her rich perfume, having been in contact with her wrist, and now my wife, Phoebe, was shopping for a hat on the Champs Elysées and Isolde, our daughter, was holding her mother's hand. Isolde was holding her mother's hand tightly because she liked the way her mother's wedding ring made a grip for her small fingers. And Henri, the concierge at our perfect hotel, was ringing up his niece because, as he was about to explain, the American couple with the sweet little girl wanted a sitter for tonight to celebrate.

What I love most about the history of the world is the history of the world—yours, mine, a pale woman with a perfumed wrist who slips you a piece of paper across a countertop. And what I love about that stranger is that brief moment of contact, that moment of possibility when, you never know, another world just might be opening up its doors to welcome you inside.

Do you stay? Or do you go?

I love the word *stay*—the action of halting, or a corset stiffened with bones. To fasten. More at *stand*. I love the way my wife's body fills a dress.

All of this is true. Years ago, at a swishy private college in New England, Phoebe did her senior thesis on Sir Thomas Malory's *Morte*

D'Arthur, which is, among other things, the story of King Arthur and Lancelot and Guinevere. And even more years ago, at a slightly less swishy private college in Minnesota, I did the same thing. Given that less than one half of one percent of the entire country has even *read* the *Morte D'Arthur*, it seemed like fate, us bumping into each other like this, in the French Quarter of St. Louis, Soulard, before a row house I had recently renovated and carved into three apartments. I gave Phoebe a break on the rent and installed for her a security system. She was this long-legged, pale girl in sandals and jeans and a tank—dark hair; a long, pale neck; Mediterranean eyes. She had a beauty mark on the corner of her mouth. I warned her to be careful with her sandals, lest she step on an abandoned hypodermic. I asked her if she had seen the arch. I said that to really see the arch, first you had to touch it. I asked her if she'd like to go to the symphony.

Yes, she said.

I mean with me. Would you like to go with me?

Most girls you meet in St. Louis, they want to go to a disco named Oz, across the river to all the legalized vice, so when Phoebe said, Yes, that would be nice, my heart trilled. Then I dated her in courtly fashion for a period of several months. I remember the first time we kissed, on the steps of her apartment, the scent of wine on her breath. I remember her explaining to me that a man she knew at Harvard Business School, Future Internet Billionaire, had asked her to come back to Cambridge and marry him, and I remember her saying, squeezing my hand, I'm not going to, don't worry, and then she stepped inside the door and shut it gently behind her and I listened to her feet climb the stairs I had spent two weeks sanding and then refinishing on my hands and knees. It was a beautiful night, and I returned to my car and drove to my own then house on Lafayette which was kitty-corner to the Abandoned City Hospital. I sat on the porch with my friend, Benjamin, a cop who had been shot two years ago by a fellow officer. The copper and wiring and fixtures had long been stripped out of the Abandoned City Hospital. Benjamin told me stories about how black kids who were shot didn't get CPR. He told me he was thinking of moving to Chicago, or San Francisco, or re-enlisting. I had met Benjamin after being mugged, when he had come over to the hospital to take my report, and then he had taken my screenplay writing course, at World Headquarters University, because as an African-American cop he wanted to set the record straight, but actually he just wanted to meet some girls. Mostly he wrote screenplays about a cop who wrote screenplays who just wanted to meet some girls, and then I quit teaching Advanced Screenplay Writing for Hollywood, because I had no business doing that, and he quit writing screenplays, not having met any girls, and that night Benjamin asked me if I was getting any, meaning the regular thing it means, and then we drank a couple beers and listened to the gunfire in our neighborhood. Earlier that week our neighbor, Christopher, had been shot in the thigh for his wallet, and a week before a retired schoolteacher had been raped in Lafayette Park while taking her morning walk. Beside the Abandoned City Hospital there were drug dealers on the corner making deals. Then Benjamin, being off-duty, called his precinct to request a show of the flag.

My last screenplay for children's television was about a giant crab with lasers that threatened to destroy Civilization as We Know It.

The episode was called "Civilization as We Know It."

I was named after a poet raised in St. Louis who once wrote, In my beginning is my end.

Phoebe was lonely in Paris, writing letters to her boyfriend, who was sleeping with her best friend; she was lonely in Paris and painting nude portraits of Jean Claude. After their initial introduction to each other's physiognomy, during which he had come in her hair, she had asked him to sit for her, on the rooftop of their building, where she often worked. In the background of one picture, she has drawn the silhouette of the Eiffel Tower. Then Jean Claude took a photograph that hangs today in Phoebe's study: she is twenty-two and long-legged, wearing a short skirt, straddling the Eiffel Tower, which appears in the distant background. You cannot see her face, but Phoebe tells me she was happy at the moment.

Jean Claude was flattered. Sometimes he wore Rollerblades and would skate around the rooftop. There was a garden filled with flowers and herbs. Phoebe began sunbathing on the roof, the springtime sun warming her long body, while Jean Claude practiced his saxophone. They would skate together through the streets of Paris. They drank espresso in the cafés. Phoebe wrote her parents and thanked them for providing her with the time of her life, which is what all parents provide—the time of your life. As Patrick Swayze says in *Dirty Dancing* to Baby, placing her hand against his chest, *Thump thump.*

My father died on a Sunday afternoon, in his big car, backing out of the driveway. He had been to church—St. George's—and had come

home for a quick lunch, and had gathered some notebooks in order
to start work on a new project involving pumpkin seeds. After he
had placed the transmission of his car into reverse, the heart attack
struck—the iced pain in the chest, as if he had just swallowed a
snowball; the ache of the bone-cold numbness in his arm, and then
shoulder. He died fairly swiftly, his foot slipping off the brake, per-
mitting the car's idling engine to roll the vehicle back down the
drive, and then left, toward the Dubinkerrs', where he rolled up onto
the front lawn. The grass needed cutting. I had sold the Dubinkerrs
their house two years earlier—a typical U City three story made of
fine St. Louis brick, designed specifically for the faculty and deans at
Washington University. The Dubinkerrs had two Asian girls they
had adopted, and as my father's car rolled up onto their lawn, the
Philosophy Professor, Dr. Dubinkerr, yelled to his little girls to stand
back. Stand back, he yelled, spreading wide his arms by which to
shield them. They had been playing Tea Time with dolls and a china
tea set. The professor ran to my father's car, and pulled him out,
and then he began to perform CPR, his breath spilling into my
father's now deflated chest. He called to his wife, also Professor Dubinkerr, who was presently reading a set of exams on Modern Political Theory—Locke, Hobbes, A Great Big Fish. And then she heard
her husband's cry, and the cry of her daughters, Amber and Kaitlin,
each of whom came running through the house into the kitchen,
screaming.

Mommy, Kaitlin exclaimed. Daddy's kissing Mr. Sellers!

The Scientist, Amber said, nodding. He's on the grass.

The ambulance took forty-five minutes to arrive, because there
had been a gang-related shoot-out on Delmar, two officers down, and
there was a little boy down, too, who died en route having had a
bullet pierce his liver. By the time the ambulance actually arrived to
rescue my father, the one Professor Dubinkerr was putting down her
girls for a nap, and the other was drinking a glass of lemonade to get
the taste of my father's quick lunch—pastrami and Muenster—out of
his mouth. At the funeral, they each wore black, and later the Pro-
fessors Dubinkerr gave to me a signed edition of *On Death and
Dying*, which had been inscribed with best wishes to a woman
named Jean.

I found on my father's desk a letter he had been writing to me. It
was a letter to celebrate my forthcoming seventh anniversary, and he
had beside it three tickets to Paris. He wrote, among other things,
that the best thing I ever did was marry Phoebe.

Take your family to Paris now, he wrote, *and you will be able to return. I regret I never took you there myself. Your loving father, Dad.*
This is what my father thought when he was dying:
God, it hurts.

If the cell is the source of life, as my father used to say, then we are bound to be prisoners of our condition. When I was writing my children's television screenplays, I was always given an assignment—namely, the special-effect footage with the karate kids in masked outfits, fighting the various and mechanized demonic beasts, all of which had been shot in Japan. My job was to take the Child American Actors and the Special Effects and to join them by way of a plot kids could sit through—the brain-candy of death and destruction and doom. One kid, Alexander Jay Pratt, had a mother who thought Young Alexander should be earning more, and so I wrote also the episode that made Alexander Jay Pratt—the kid in green—a Senator for Galactic Peace and sent him through The Great Portal to the Great Galactic Peace Conference in the Sky. A new kid in green was on board the very next episode. It was magic. Better yet, it was non–capital intensive and highly profitable. It was the kind of magic only a tightwad Hollywood producer could ever dream up, and it made my heart ache. There was enough violence in the world without my encouraging four-year-olds to kick each other in the face.
Phoebe was in love, and in Paris, but she was feeling lonely. Meanwhile, her Future Rock Star boyfriend had by now cut an album, and Claire had written to Phoebe an awkward letter in which Claire confessed her deepest longing thus:

> *Remember when we went skinny-dipping in the lake? Remember the way I looked at you, and my chest flushed, and then I ran into the lake? I have become lovers with your lover so that I may become your own. Please,* Claire wrote, *please do not be angry with him. He is a dog, like all men.*
>
> She wrote, *I love you and want you to want me to come to Paris. A rose is a rose—will you be my Alice?—is a rose.*

Phoebe loved flowers—and still does—and she read that letter on the garden terrace, at night, the scent of freesias and lilies and spring-time roses filling up the night. Behind her rose the Eiffel Tower, that mechanized hymn to phallic torture, glowering in the night sky, all rivets and bolts. She thought it odd the way the French felt com-pelled to light it up at night, which struck her as faintly impolite, like shining a flashlight on your lover in the dark. She lit a cigarette, being in Paris, and then she held the letter before her and set it on fire.

You light up my life, she thought, which was once the title of a pop song, as well as a made-for-television movie.

Dust to dust. She brushed the ashes from her fingertips, and lap, and then she wiped her fingertips along the legs of her jeans. She reached for her Evian, and took a drink, and then she set the Evian aside, and went down the spiral staircase to her room, where she poured herself a monstrous glass of wine. Then she poured herself another. Then she grabbed her wallet and her black leather jacket and went out for the night.

She walked to St. Michel, and stopped at a café, and ordered Pernod. There was an American couple nearby, bickering, and then she went to a bar that played salsa music on the stereo and served Jack Daniels in thick-bottomed glasses, and she drank that, neat, one after the other. A boy approached—wispy-bearded, cigarette in hand—and asked her if she'd like to get it on. Hey, Baby, said the boy. He kissed her cheek and nudged himself into her body. She could feel his cock rubbing against her thigh, and then he kissed her again.

In France, to kiss can often be to fuck. *Baiser.* She said, kissing him, Let's dance. She said, taking his hand, I might be a lesbian before you know it.

This caused the boy some excitement. There were two women dancing together, and there was Phoebe, drinking her bourbon, and now the French boy who wanted to get it on. He looked like a biker—black jeans, black leather jacket, just like hers—who did not know how to ride a motorbike. He looked like any other boy who lived in Paris.

He said, *Je m'appelle* Louis, and she said, *Ah oui*, Louis. *Enchan-tée*, Louis. She said, A lesbian does not sleep with the man she loves.

The room was smoky, lit with candles, and Louis was grabbing at her breasts. She thought about going home with him, almost glanc-ingly, but she simply couldn't get that far in her mind. Instead she understood finally what she had always feared most. The thought struck clean as the light of day, or a knife.

I will never be a decent painter, she thought. Fuck it.

To avoid breaking into tears, she went to the bar, and had another fast drink, and then she left. Outside she blinked her eyes into the hysteria of the city lights. She walked along the streets. Once, at Pigalle, she had gone into a dark theater with Jean Claude to see a sex show where a man in charge of special effects had pinched her ass. She had also spent a lot of time at the Louvre. She walked by Napoleon's cannons. She pictured Rodin, sculpting his naked bodies out of marble, and then breathing into them a life of their own, before fucking his sitter, and then having a bottle of wine to celebrate his life's work. Everywhere you went, Paris was full of itself.

By now she was stumbling and weeping, and she discovered along the way that she had lost somewhere her black leather jacket. Eventually she found a cab, and the driver asked her if she needed to go to the hospital, and she said, No, only to my flat. I'm lost.

We are all lost, he said. You want to buy some cocaine? Some ecstasy?

She said, Take me to the Seventh.

On the stairs to her flat, she twice stumbled, and by the time she got there, she wasn't certain whose door she belonged to. She stood in front of her door and thought, If you go in there, you might disappear.

Who am I, she thought. And why?

Paris is an existential city. She had left her keys inside her flat, beside her hot water pot, on the tea bag box. She turned and banged on Jean Claude's room, in case he might be home, though she knew he wouldn't be. To be, she thought, is to do. Then she walked down the hall to Rosalia's room. She banged at the door. There was music, Bryan Ferry, the kind of music one had sex to, and she turned, and Rosalia opened the door, wearing an unbuttoned shirt, a blue denim shirt that belonged to Jean Claude—Phoebe knew because she had worn that very same shirt on like occasions—and Rosalia said, her mouth flushed, Phoebe! and Phoebe put her arms inside of Rosalia's open shirt, onto Rosalia's waist, and kissed her deeply on the mouth to see what it would taste like, which wasn't much different from kissing Jean Claude, or her Future Rock Star Boyfriend back in the states, except maybe for the lack of beard, and then Jean Claude, sitting naked on the futon, beside his sax, said, Phoebe?

Breast to robin-hearted breast. Rosalia stepped back into the room. Phoebe, she said, taking Phoebe's hands with her own. This—this is just friendship. It is—

Though she knew that, now, and never before in her entire life had she ever felt so entirely alone. So profoundly discrete and disconnected. She felt utterly at a loss, a leaf tossed into the self-important Parisian breeze, and then she rushed past Rosalia, and ducked into the bathroom, and vomited.

Later, she rinsed her mouth and took a bath, in the foot of Rosalia's shower, the water pouring down upon her. Jean Claude had found his spare key to her apartment. Bryan Ferry was singing *more than this* and she sat in the foot of the bath rocking.

Then Rosalia loaned her a robe—a hip-length red kimono with Japanese flowers—and took her to her room and put her into bed. She brought Phoebe a glass of water. Then Phoebe, the girl who would become my wife, fell asleep beneath the comforter her mother had sent to her for Christmas. While wrapping the package for her daughter, her mother, back in Rhode Island, had sprayed some of her own perfume on the comforter to make certain Phoebe understood just how deeply she was loved. It smelled like home.

Later that night I was mugged on South Grand by three kids with a chain, to whom I lost my Japanese import car and three of my teeth. Striking me repeatedly, they cracked two of my ribs. And later, much later, I came to realize that the violence in my city merely mimicked the violence of the globe and, more precisely, the terror that resides more or less within the experience of living. That is to say, some have more, others less.

God may be omniscient, but I have never met him. On the seventh day, one story goes, God rested. I think during a moment when God must have blinked, or turned away to sneeze, I think it is then my father must have died—sitting at the wheel of his car, going backward. I think there will never be enough people like my father to feed the multitudes God has so neglected. Sometimes I wonder where he is, my father, and then I understand that he is wherever it is that I happen to think of him. My wife and I named our daughter, Isolde, after our mutual affection for the first novel to be written in the English language, the *Morte D'Arthur* by Sir Thomas Malory. The root of all romance is the story of our lives. Romance, from the French, for *anything written in French,* and as the French will surely tell you—especially if you are an American—that which is novel is not always new. First Phoebe and I decided to make our lives together, and then we decided to make our baby, and then we decided to make love in the sunroom of our house.

This is what I was thinking about in the Luxembourg Gardens, walking along the finely graveled paths with my daughter, Isolde. She was wearing her new purple hat, her dark curly hair swaying in the breeze. She would stop at the puddles and splash in them with her red boots. We were walking by a fountain where children were sailing boats, and Phoebe was back in the hotel, planning our evening. She knew I wanted to eat in one of those restaurants Fitzgerald and Hemingway used to hang out in. She knew I was feeling rueful.

Take Isolde to the park, Phoebe said. Stop thinking so much.

At one place, a man was selling pony rides. Isolde picked out a yellow one, an old pony with a beard, and the man said, No, not him.

Why? said my daughter.

He is old, said the man. He is tired and used up.

She rode another while I sat on a bench and watched my little girl navigate the rhythms of her pony's gait. She rocked in the air and beamed in the sun like a pop song while I tapped my foot and understood I was going to have to decide what to do about that perfumed piece of paper in my pocket. At first I thought a married man does not worry about such decisions unless he is uncertain he wants to be a married man, but then I understood that this was not quite accurate, because what the body longs for is a fact, no different than the fact of an intriguing woman beckoning to you across a city park, and not an idea. A man may desire another's body, but what charges that desire is evidence of that body's spirit—in my case, the tilt of an eyebrow, or the set of her lip. The sound of her voice.

Later, while walking back to our hotel, still in the vast park, Isolde paused to examine a worm. The worm lay stranded on a patch of sand, and Isolde paused, and then she picked him up and delivered him safely to a nearby puddle.

She put together her hands and dusted them off, the way I had taught her. She said, That worm was tired and used up, too. He was old.

Like the pony, I said.

Like Grandpa Sellers, Isolde said. He's dead.

Everywhere you go, my father would say, people are dying. My father taught me that worms were necessary to fertilize the soil of the crops that grew the food we ate. My father used to say a man will sow his seeds, but a good man will do so carefully. Once, when I was a boy, my father while drinking a martini spit out an olive seed into his glass, the seed ringing against the fine glass, and I understood what he had been talking about. A good man always spits his seeds into a glass. I felt my eyes welling up, as they had been doing at the oddest moments whenever my recently dead father's presence was invoked. When my daughter was born, when my father died, I wept.

I said to Isolde, rubbing my eyes, Grandpa Sellers was old, but he's in heaven now, working in a special laboratory full of pumpkin seeds.

When you get old, Isolde said, taking my hand, you won't die. I'll protect you.

And then I scooped her up into my arms and buried my nose in her hair, which smelled like her mother's, like grass and fine soap, and she said, Like when we watch movies.

It is a sad, sweet life that I have, and what I felt, setting my daughter upon my shoulders, was gratitude for the opportunity to have it. I thought, listening to my daughter sing, Thank God Amanda Cunningham Amachi let me go twelve years ago in California.

At the time I hadn't been so certain. I had a graduate degree from one of those How to Be a Haunting Novelist programs, in which I had written seven and a half short stories, and I had by now a dozen screenplay credits for a hideous television program: I was making contacts: people said it was important to do a lot of lunch, and to get an answering machine, but my girlfriend was also sleeping with a Team Associate at The California Pizza Factory, and he was the only person who ever left a message on the new answering machine, and the smog was exacerbating my allergies, and I was also getting tired of pitching scripts about aliens: Aliens in Space, Aliens Spawning at the Wal-Mart, Aliens with Wigs in Colonial America. Everywhere I turned I saw unemployed writers and actors and singers convinced they weren't going to be the ones who remained unemployed. As Jennifer Beals dances to in *Flashdance,* Take your passion and make it happen. Most people I knew wanted to be more important than that which they did, which is the root of all failure, and then one day Amanda Cunningham came home late, smelling all damp and spoiled, and I understood, standing in our crappy overpriced one-bedroom apartment kitchen off a Southern California freeway, that I was no better than anybody else.

Truth is, it was the first time I had failed at anything.

So I said to Amanda Cunningham Amachi, I think I'm going to call it a day and go back home. I said, testing the waters gently, Do you think you might want to come with? To which she said, *Oh God,* et cetera, and then three months later I received a postcard asking me if I'd been scratching much lately, to which I replied by telling her not to worry, it was a common ailment, lice, and that I was certain we must have picked it up mutually at the beach, and three years later I received a phone call telling me she was getting married and I said that's wonderful and she said I miss you and I said give Dan my regards and she said she would and then, that very same day I was walking through the Luxembourg Gardens with my daughter perched upon my shoulders, Amanda Cunningham Amachi had made in my hotel room various remarks about the lack of economic development in the country's heartland.

The French, they have their feelms. And we Americans, we have our popcorn. It's a small neighborhood, what this world has become. The couple I saw in the park, making love in the rain, they weren't a handsome couple. The woman had pox scars on her face, and the man had that worn look of those who work too long outdoors for too little money, but they were in love, at least at that moment, and the sight of them was proof of that and fortified my heart. As for Phoebe, hungover and adequately shamed by the experience of growing up, it was only a matter of time before Claire and Future Rock Star arrived to talk things out, sensibly, which they did, each with several suitcases in tow, though by the time they landed at Charles de Gaulle Phoebe had already returned to Rhode Island, where she spent a month walking on the beach planning her next move. She gathered her wits and took a breath and went to Manhattan and began making various contacts at the proper galleries. Claire works for a fashion magazine now, the kind in which nobody has ever suffered from acne, or pox, and Future Rock Star is on last month's cover of a magazine. Phoebe's mother keeps tabs on this stuff, serving as an independent clipping service, sending us all the various news stories about the people Phoebe used to know.

Even in the dying city of St. Louis, with my wife and our daughter and our now forthcoming son, six months along the way, it is possible to become in the know.

Failure doesn't make for a good pitch: imagine John Nash, mad without the genius. Mel Gibson without all the hardy muscles. Still, I can't help it, my favorite films are those that make my heart ache. It's not the winning I admire; it's the struggle. It's the very beating of my own life's pulse.

Movies may try to capture life, but they do not replicate it. Our lives, for example, do not come supplied with a soundtrack—French horns to trumpet the American experience, catchy pop tunes to illuminate the romantic montage? The clutching of the hands, that paroxysm, at the moment of the celluloid orgasm? The art of the film is the art of illusion: first we see it through the glass of the camera's lens, and then we pay cold cash to see it projected upon the screen. And it's that screen, that silver screen, that puts you in the dark. Which separates you from that which brought you into these reclining seats. In the dark, you cannot rewind. In the dark, you cannot see just how the magic's made. You feel the magic, the director's hand, but you do not see.

After I was mugged by those three kids on South Grand, I became afraid. I became afraid I'd never be able to feel safe or look again in the eye another black kid wearing Nikes. *White fuck,* they called me, taking out my teeth with a chain. But then I went to the dentist, who fixed me—it was only teeth, and my pride, and a car with a hundred thousand miles—and then I began to talk to my neighbors, and to their neighbors, and then I met Phoebe, who reminded me that anything can happen anytime to anyone, and so knowing that, I became braver. What I'm saying is that at any moment in this life you can meet somebody who will change your life.

As Judy Garland says, bless her ardent heart, There is no place like home.

This is how I proposed to my wife:

I took off for the day, a Tuesday, and showed up at her gallery for lunch, and then I drove us to the Gateway Arch. We went underground to the museum, and because it was a Tuesday, and dead winter, we had no crowds to contend with, and so we took the cantilevered elevator to the top of the arch. Once there, you could feel the wind buffeting the entire structure. You could feel the floors bending beneath our weight as we walked across the platform. Then we stood before the small windows, and I said, That's St. Louis. I wanted, you see, to sell her on the city. I pointed out Union Station, which had become a shopping mall at risk, and I pointed out the Botanical Gardens, and I said, pointing, There is Washington University.

I said, Here, look.

I offered her a pair of binoculars, which she took. She held them to her eyes and nudged her hip into my side. I said, Look there, and she said, Where? and I said, pointing, There, to a place where I had tacked a small sign to a tree.

Phoebe, it said. *Will you marry me? Thomas.*

It was the best thing I had ever written—a scene right out of three of my own screenplays; once, I'm told, I almost came close. Still, even with those binoculars Phoebe couldn't read a word of it.

She said, adjusting the focus, What?

And so I translated it for her, and then she said, turning, Yes. I think so.

But I need to make a trip first.

I held my breath. I stood bravely and told myself I did not look disappointed.

I said, OK, I can wait.

And she said, I'll leave tomorrow.

Jesus, I said. I'll drive you? To the airport?

No, she said, taking my arm. I just need to do this.

OK.

We took the ride back down, and located my blue car, and then I dropped her off at her office in the Central West End. I watched the wind catch at her long coat as she walked up the sidewalk alongside Left Bank Books. She pulled open the door to her gallery, turning to smile at me; she brushed the hair from her eyes and stepped inside, and then, the next morning, she called a cab, which arrived in front of her Soulard apartment, which I have since loaned out to a refugee family from Srebrenica. At Lambert International, our airport, she walked beneath a small plane that once belonged to Charles Lindbergh, who was first to fly all the way to Paris. Phoebe walked beneath Lindbergh's small plane on her way to her gate. The wheels of her carry-on kept catching at the plastic molding on the floors. On her own plane, an antiquated 727, Phoebe leaned back into her seat and took a breath. She thought, Every place you go is merely one place along the way to where you're going.

The plane sailed down the runway. The wind, lifting the plane by its very wings, raised it into the air. You can see it, can't you? The plane? It's become the iconic image for our times. At any given moment, there are a quarter million people in the air flying from one destination to another. I thought when Phoebe was sitting back in the plane flying into the sky that she was going off to visit Claire, or Future Rock Star, or maybe The Big Wheel at Internet International. I thought maybe there was somebody else I did not know of—which there would be, dozens of others she may have at one time known and loved, being human.

T. M. McNally

The body does not lie. The first—and the last—thing the body does is take a breath. When I die, I want to be put inside a furnace: I want to go up in flames. The mind may live within our bodies, but our lives are housed within our minds, and this, right now, at this given moment, this is what I'm thinking, stepping inside a cab with my wife beneath the Parisian sky.

It's a warm night. The sky has cleared. When I shut the door, the driver says in his best American, Where to?

I put my arm around my wife and let her provide directions. On the radio, thumping into the sweet insulation of the quiet car, a girl is saying to the music, *I find you very attractive.* The music has a brassy horn thing going on in the distance. Phoebe settles back into the seat, crossing her long legs, and takes my arm. We are feeling bright and sassy, my wife in her new red dress, having dined in a restaurant only the French could possibly devise, and Phoebe says, closing her eyes, and placing my hand beneath the fabric of her dress, Notre Dame.

After disembarking from that flight to Providence, Phoebe went directly to her father and explained that she was prepared to marry a man who sold houses in the dying city of St. Louis. Her father was in the garden, raking leaves, when she arrived; he was wearing brown khakis and a blue sweater full of moth holes. Then he dropped his rake, and took her into his arms, and then they stepped into their fine wooden house through the kitchen, and opened a bottle of wine, and called to her mother who was upstairs making a quilt. Nine months later, the quilt would end up neatly finished across the foot of our bed, and that day, when Phoebe's mother came down the narrow back stairs, her quilting glasses set on her nose, Phoebe told her the news and they sat at the small kitchen table and drank the wine. Then Phoebe called me that night, and asked me to fly out, and on the phone her father asked me lots of questions about where I thought mortgage rates were heading.

When I hung up, the phone rang. Benjamin, telling me he was giving up on the city and reenlisting in the Special Forces. The army was going to give him several grand as a signing bonus and he was going first to take one of those singles cruises in the Bahamas to spend it. No married women on those boats, he said. No college girls. These women have jobs! He asked me if I was getting any, or not, and if I'd list his condo, and later that night I took my father out to dinner. At Dressel's we ran into Clarence Harmon, who would eventually become mayor of St. Louis, and John Goodman, the actor.

295

Everywhere you go, my father said sadly. Everywhere you go people are famous. Bigger than life.

And then I told my father about my plans to marry Phoebe. He liked that news. He walked over to another table, where his friend Leon Strauss was sitting—the developer who saved first the DeBaliviere neighborhood, and then the Fabulous Fox Theatre—and spread the word. Soon everybody was buying me drinks just for getting married, even John Goodman, who bought the house a round, and who as you may or may not know is bigger than life. When things died down, my father returned to our table, and he started talking about things like legacies and grandchildren. After dessert, we discussed then President Bush's decision to go into Somalia, and I remember thinking of Benjamin, M-16 in hand, giving out candy bars to promote democracy, and an equitable distribution of humanitarian aid, and then I told my father about my idea for providing housing to refugees. America was a land of second chances, I explained. It would be good for everybody.

These are empty houses I'm talking about, I said, getting excited. They're going to waste.

St. Louis is good for you, my father said, and we rose and buttoned up our coats and stepped out onto the street. There were panhandlers sitting in the cold, and my father and I gave them our change, and then I walked my father to his car. I walked my increasingly frail father back to his car because even then I feared for his life.

People used to call my father The Colossus; then he died; and eventually, not that far into the future, there will be nobody left alive to remember the things he said and did. But when I was a boy, he explained to me the history of the world. There are seven wonders of the world, he explained, and there are seven seas to be crossed if you are willing to risk that adventure. You measure the days of your weeks by the seven nights during which you sleep, assuming all is right with the world, beneath the roofs with those you love most. Then my father taught me the constellations in the sky— God's house, the very first, our very own. The place my mother must have filled inside his heart, I don't know how my father survived that loss. The grief our lives were made to bear, it astounds me still.

Be small, my father taught me. Like the seed in a field. Like a star in the sky.

*

On the lip of this new millennium, nobody knows just yet where we are going to, but I do know that we are going somewhere. As Obi-Wan Kenobi advises Luke Skywalker, it's important to *use the force*. In our cab, in Paris, the driver grips the wheel with two hands and honks at anybody who comes his way. Eventually, he skids the car into a curb, and across the River Seine, in front of Notre Dame, Phoebe and I exit the cab into the night sky.

Here, I say, taking Phoebe's hand. This way.

We make our way into the park. Inside my pocket is a perfumed piece of paper, which I dip into a birdbath in order to permit the ink to bleed. Sometimes I think there is enough violence in this world to break God's heart, if only he had one, but I've learned to protect myself by loving those I can. The paper dissolves into the color blue, the very color of the sky, and as we make our way beneath the trees into the bower, where we are to be protected by a rooftop of branches and leaves, I breathe in the scent of my wife's perfume. She has placed the perfume behind her ears and along the sides of her throat and between her breasts. The scent blooms off her body like a flower.

I say, I've never done this in public before.

It's only public if people see you, says my wife.

Like a beam of light, I think. Like a candle lit on a dark night, or a lover's kiss. I take off my jacket and spread it across the bench. Phoebe places my hands on her rib cage, then raises them so that I might attend to the buttons on her dress. This way, she says. She undoes my belt and leans me back into the bench and lifts the soft fabric of her dress.

If you disenfranchise the heartland, said Amanda Cunningham Amachi, on CNN, then you disenfranchise the entire population.

I don't know what *disenfranchise* means, but I do know that the heartland is a place within the body and has a constitution all its own. Mostly I think it's the place where my wife's heart beats. It's the place where we raised our daughter into being, and it's the same place where my wife's been leading me ever since we met, all the way to here, right now, to this spot just beneath the sky.

Where to next? Phoebe says, into my ear, her hands on my chest.

In my beginning, wrote somebody else, is my end.

I don't know, I say. A church?

A cathedral, she says. Paradise.

Amen, said Sir Thomas Malory, while writing what would eventually become the story of his life. At the time he had been in prison, and it was dark. Did I tell you that my name is Thomas? Did I tell you that this is the story of my life? That night I could feel my heart beating against my wife's hands. You get your teeth knocked out, it's easy to think it's never happened to anybody else, but it does, and it will continue to, and the only thing you can do to stop it from happening is to look the other way until you die. All of this is true. Sometimes, sometimes while making love to my wife, I think, This is why God made the world. I think God made the species because he likes to watch us fuck. Do you see what I mean? You see two people who love each other, doesn't it make you feel alive? Doesn't it make your heart brim? I'm not talking about an art film or the soft porn on the late-night cable. I'm not talking about peeping over your neighbor's fence. I'm talking about seeing a man or a woman nudge up against another's body. *Oh, Baby,* Amanda Cunningham used to say, fucking madly in the dark. I'm talking about two people taking each other by the hand. And this is how my wife and I made a girl— and now a boy on the way—who looks like us. As my father would explain, sadly, this is how it's done everywhere. That night, my wife's hands were all over me; and mine, her—skimming beneath the fabric of her dress, over the surface of her ribs. I could taste the wine on my wife's hot breath. Sometimes I think God must be lonely, not being able to do something so simple and sweet as that. You can be tender, you can be loving, you can be lonely and stupid-drunk or hot as all getout. You can be crazy with grief, delirious with lust. You can be so dizzy you're carried away—by men with handcuffs, or birds of prey. You can be all these things, I think, because that's what you are made of, and God knows that, but he's not allowed to play, because he's God. Zeus, that was a different story, all those heifers and swans. And then I'll think, taking a breath, maybe looking at my wife's pale neck, or the mole on the lip of her mouth, Stop thinking. I'll think that no man alive knows this kind of fierce love until he finds it. And then I'll think that same man ought to stop thinking and simply feel it—the history of the ages, the origins of the cosmos, the mysteries of his universe—and let himself go.

To oblivion, like the seeds in the grass.

Three Poems
Gustaf Sobin

TRANSPARENT ITINERARIES: 2002/2003

all you'd ever known had been density; all you'd ever
sought: passage.

wherein the body, in pursuit of its lost etiology, would
be seen as nothing more, finally, than expedient.

than conduit.

than a flexed assemblage in the service of its own ex-
tenuation.

grappling as it went for glints, intimations, radiant
insignia.

. . . there, that is, in those
lost landscapes, where
muscle
would serve as little more than sphincter to
image: sheath within which the
be-

loved, perfectly diaphanous,
slumbered.

---

rare mirror that, rather than reflecting, assimilated.

as if absolved.

wasn't that why you'd adopted that obsolescent vocabulary as you had: idiom in which the verb, once, had
managed to shimmy free of its each and every substan-
tive.

and rise, so doing, pulsatile . . .

where, at the extreme outskirts of every such utterance, might have entered, finally, those empty densities.

no, not by anything you'd have said and, in saying,
circumscribed, but—in the nimbleness of a given artic-
ulation—vacated.

scientia bene modulandi: that science, as Censorinus
had called it, of fine tuning.

. . . being locked into
all
that clattering
canebreak, squinted, didn't you, in search of
interstice: *lapsus* in the midst of
textus for winnowing your

words
through.

---

that they might have alighted, thereby, upon that som-
nolent figure, lapping as they did at each of her cher-
ished features.

having assumed—at that remove—the exact same properties as those they'd evoked.

the blown heart, the blown lily's.

—their blessed conflations—

while pretending, all the while, that you'd returned
to the given, the assumed, the linguistically pre-
scribed.

that the breath might have managed to wrest itself
free from the magnitude of such an encounter.

. . . its proffered succulents . . .

that "here" was still here, and world something other
than the fast-fading imprint of something it never
was.

Gustaf Sobin

PRELUDE XI

. . . you, who'd
long since lost track of yourself, wrote for the
indices, didn't
you: the wizened benchmarks at the extreme
edge of those
re-

spiratory landscapes. no, no dahlias, no
marigolds, any longer, came to
relieve that

miasmatic expanse; no way, the
way's
blanched trajectory. there, only the deflected, it

seemed, drew; only the obliterated,
magnetized. in the wake, then, of such
massive
withdrawal, would sleep, but where? would read, but

what? troughed in shadow, had
resonance left, at
least, the sparkling residue of some decimated letter? winnow, then,
what-

ever little remains. yes, sip the slightest
vestigial syllable. that the future—that's forever
earlier—might wedge vibratory
be-
tween tongue and teeth.

Gustaf Sobin

SEPTEMBER
—*For Michel Mayan*

... now that the Swan
has swung southward on its blue
wind-
beaten pedestal, will the syllables, at long

last, harden? the breath, so
doing, catch on its
lost

dictata? the heavens themselves, as a set of
recondite signals, would release the
ruffled, the winged, the
intuitively
dis-

posed. lactiferous, hadn't she, from the deepest
pleats of
her

being, already insinuated, by her
inclination alone, the
Way?

303

Scenes Inside the Ruined Walls

Can Xue

—Translated from Chinese by Karen Gernant and Chen Zeping

"INSIDE THESE RUINED WALLS"—he sketched a circle with his hands—"you'll see pleasant scenery everywhere, even if your eyes are closed. For example, this wall: we don't know when it collapsed, nor do we care, but from inside this crack, we can discover algae. Algae."

He plastered his floppy ear against the crack, but I didn't pay any attention since he did this many times a day.

"Bo, bo, bo," he said. "Bubbles. This marsh is a special one, soft and exceptionally springy. People can walk back and forth on top of it without sinking in. Algae grow densely in the watery depression over there. You must see it, too. Our eyesight is about the same. Listen: bo, bo, bo. Could you ever deny that the sound of bubbles is unique? You've stood up. What are you thinking? Do you think she'll come?"

"Of course she will. The sun is growing older by the day, and my clothes are too thin. If there's frost at night, I really don't know what it will be like. I've never experienced this before."

I turned my eyes toward the distant sun. Since we'd come here, the sun had changed into a frosty, symbolic spheroid. Its surface still looked brilliantly dazzling, but bathing in its light, we didn't feel the slightest warmth. All we could do was wear more clothes to conserve our body heat. At night, we couldn't expose any parts of our bodies to the air because of the ever-present danger of frostbite. To protect ourselves from the nighttime cold, we wore the gloves and face masks that we'd brought from home. I counted the days. We'd endured one summer like this, and it was said that one could also get through the winter. Who said? It didn't matter.

He was always excited like that, chattering about all kinds of scenery. Even though I could see what he had seen, he still talked on and on about it. Day after day and month after month, he talked of these boring topics, sometimes annoying me so much that I couldn't help but suddenly ask him, "Could you please discuss something

304

else?" I asked twice. Each time, he hung his head and pretended he hadn't heard. He didn't say anything for a long time, and so I understood.

Now I realize those bubbles and the marsh are only imaginary scenes. They had conquered my heart with their bright, beautiful, fluctuating colors, but this, after all, happened long ago. At present, the chief problem was the cold. I was wearing all the clothes I'd brought with me, and it wasn't even winter yet.

He didn't give any thought to this problem. He'd heard that it was possible to get through the winter, and it seemed he had no doubt about it. I was rather resentful of the way he recklessly ignored the problem, and sometimes I said that my toes were frostbitten.

"And it isn't even winter yet!" he said in astonishment. With that, he seemed to immediately forget about it. I really don't know where his confidence came from.

Most of the time I stared at the sun. The sun shone every day here. You needed only to look up to see that dazzling ball.

Originally, I had come here with him because the ruined walls interested both of us. We used to arrive here in the morning and go home at night. Later, the two of us felt this was too much trouble, and so we simply stayed here at night, too. This seemed to help us feel at ease. All along, he remained just the way he'd been at first: both day and night, he pressed his ear against the cracks in the wall and mumbled. Whenever I heard his voice, I saw the scenes he described. And so I chatted idly with him from time to time. I always talked about the same things, my words dry as dust—much less interesting than his. I seldom used adjectives.

When we were bored, we talked of her. Of all the people we knew, she was the laziest old woman. We'd known her since we were children, but we hadn't ever talked with her. In the daytime, she slept in her room. Sometimes nothing moved in her room for more than ten hours at a time. When occasionally she went out, she didn't look anyone in the eye. It was as if she was walking along with her eyes closed. Maybe she thought it would consume too much energy to prop open her eyelids and look at people. Anyhow, that's what I thought. Once, as an experiment, and also out of spite, I walked up to her. I wanted to see whether she would bump into me, but she turned away—still without raising her eyelids.

After we decided not to go home at night, we began talking of her. For no reason, both of us felt she would surely pass this way, and perhaps our goal in life became just to wait for her to pass. When the

305

conversation turned to her, I raised a question: "Which one do you think is older—her or the sun?" Of course, the sun was older, he said, but I replied firmly that she was older. And so we had another long argument. My grounds were this: the birthday of the sun could be approximately verified, but she—well, I'd already asked numerous people, and not one could confirm when her birthday was. Even the oldest grandfather among us couldn't say when her birthday was.

Later on, he agreed with me. "So she's sure to pass by. Besides, these last few days the algae have begun to wither a little. Is winter coming? What will winter be like? There's still no change evident in the marsh. And the mosses are really strange—always densely woven. My fantasies are always crammed full of them. Sometimes it makes me feel like weeping."

I don't remember how I got mixed up with someone like him. When we were back home, the two of us both loved to show off. In the summer he painted his whole body dark green, and went around as soundlessly as a fish. I loved to paint my whole body black and look for an inconspicuous corner where I could stand motionless. We managed to get through the endless heat, each in his own way. Everyone knew our strange habits, and called them "showing off." Maybe it was just because we both acted like this for a long time that we came to appreciate each other. More often than not, he would float up to me like a fish, and say, "There's a kind of mosquito that is very affectionate. They've been nurtured by the fertile water of the marsh for a thousand years." And so we began to talk affectionately with each other.

Forgetting almost everything else, we rushed over here. It was a terribly long day, and the distant sun didn't set for a long time. It seemed fresh and sentimental. The sound of wheels rolled in the clear, cloudless sky. Coming from the ruined wall in front of us was the sound of boiling water. Steam was constantly rising from it. He resolved to call the steam "bubbles," and I didn't have any doubt about his choice of words. That day, in the radiance of the setting sun, he vowed that the time would come when he would "penetrate the wall" like an X-ray. When he said this, he was like a human marionette, repeatedly stamping his feet on the pile of broken bricks and waving his hands.

He and I both realized that the warmth between us was diminishing day by day. Now we seldom paid attention to each other. We were both waiting for the turning point—the arrival of the old woman who had never looked us in the eye. During the cold nights, we took shifts, taking turns sleeping. This had one advantage—the long night became a lot shorter. As the weather grew colder, my anxiety gradually deepened. But he wasn't the least bit aware of my anxiety: he lived blindly on in the marsh, talking zealously.

Steeped in worry, I became overcautious. Sometimes an eagle would sweep past in the sky, and its shadow would fall on the wall. My heart would jump and I could scarcely keep from screaming. Every day, I said, "What if there's frost tonight? How will we keep warm without enough clothing?" And there was something else I said every day: "The sun is growing older by the day." Perhaps because I detested its indifference.

Regardless of how much enthusiasm had once bubbled up in my heart, it, too, was now diminishing daily. The two of us had stayed here for only one tiny reason: we hadn't looked before we leaped. We had been too hasty in rushing straight for this spot. Now, although we said we were waiting for the old woman, any normal person could instantly tell what was really going on. In the past, he and I had always been rash in our actions—"obsessed," as others said. For instance, coming here: at that time, I'd gotten excited when he had just vaguely mentioned he "was going to roam around somewhere else," and I'd hustled here along with him. It could have been enthusiasm that made me reluctant to leave, but really that's an exaggeration. As I've said, my enthusiasm was waning daily, because nothing that had excited me existed any longer.

Most recently, because I'd been staring at that radiant sphere too long, I felt my eyeballs gradually beginning to harden. For convenience, I simply turned myself into a sort of plaster model. All of my movements were now stiff and slow, and for a long time I hadn't bent over or turned my head or moved my eyeballs. Noticing the change in me, he laughed and then continued with his own recreation. He became stranger and stranger. Once, he even stuck his head into a crack in the wall, then couldn't pull it out. All he could do was shrink against the side of the wall like a bent nail. Later, I pulled him out with such sudden force that his face was covered with blood. Grinning and pointing at the traces of blood on his face, he said, "If I couldn't become an X-ray, it's not bad to have become a balloon. When my head was stuck in there, beautiful flies were buzzing near me. Their wings were like a rainbow. Actually, it's been a long time since we've seen a real rainbow. It's always this monotonous burning sun and this clear sky. It's disappointing. But, whether you believe it or not, the wings of those flies were far more dazzling than any rainbow we've ever seen. And the tiny black mosquitoes' singing made me weep. For someone like me, who's lived so many years, to be unable to stop putting my head into the wall—you can imagine how enticing all this must be."

One day, because I was cold and afraid, I suggested that we shout in unison. That way, perhaps our voices would reach the outside world, and change our circumstances a little. Not until we were about to shout did we realize that we'd forgotten how: our voices glided, but without volume. There was essentially no way they could reach the outside world. As a result, we were even more afraid, even more cold. So we abandoned the attempt. "We don't have to especially exert ourselves in the attempt," he said. "Just look at this wall. The deep, quiet, narrow paths inside it are as dense as spiderwebs. I've known this for years. Another thing—we have to pretend we're waiting for her, and that gives us a reason for being delayed here. All we do each time is shout briefly. It's not necessary to take this seriously. We have to make every effort, yet the efforts are almost meaningless. As a reminder, I'll ask you once more: are you still waiting for her?"

"Of course. Otherwise, what would I be doing here? Just be here to stare at that ancient, glaring thing all day long? But probably no one will ever pass through here again."

"I like to think of it this way: one day, some people will be coming, and this wall and these broken bricks will be in front of them, but they won't see them. Talking and laughing, they'll go on. There's a touch of conceit in this thought. But I need to think like this."

"When we rushed over here, someone noticed."

"That's exactly right. That person is constantly watching our every movement, so the three of us will surely meet here."

"Do you think we can make it through the winter?"

"I've heard it's no problem. Besides, there's no distinct change of seasons here. I don't think there'll be much difference. It'll just be a little colder than when we first arrived, that's all. Judging from the angle of the sun, there's no change. I'll tell you a secret: in that marsh of mine, the seasons change according to my imagination."

I suggested we set a time for the old woman to pass by, because people always associate unpredictability with bad luck. I settled on a date a month away. Depressed, he nodded. He was now no longer the person I remembered who had painted his whole body dark green. His beard had grown long, and his clothes were in rags. When I mentioned the pigment he'd painted himself with, he laughed, so it was perfectly clear this no longer meant anything to him.

"Before a month has passed, you'll have forgotten your deadline," he said, sulking. "She's too lazy. She'll probably never start out: coming here would be a major decision. I bet she won't come herself, but will send some kid. A kid would likely run fast and be flexible with changing circumstances. Nobody could predict his movements."

We covered our faces each night. Whenever we looked at each other's covered faces, we were terrified. All around, it was too quiet, too cold—to the point that we each hallucinated that the other was harboring murderous intentions. This would go on for ten minutes or more every night. During that time, he and I were both jumpy, and unpredictable scenery appeared before our eyes. It was indescribable—blurry and fluctuating, as if a black rabbit were passing through the wall.

The month was almost over. He had already forgotten my deadline, but I kept counting the days. We were both very clear that this was one and the same. Then I suggested setting a new date: I wanted to make it one year.

"OK," he agreed simply. "I guess the kid will be here soon. Someday when she wakes up, it will suddenly occur to her to send a kid here. It's quite possible."

Recently, the scenery had become rather dull—always the same tableau of a brown sandy beach extending to the distant setting sun. Sometimes the sandy beach changed into rivers, and occasionally an eagle or some geese skimmed by in the sky, casting moving shadows on the ground. He still put his head into the wall, but he seldom mentioned words like "bubbles." Now he always complained of dizziness, because he was empty inside. So he flailed around without a firm foothold. He could have fallen at any time. He said, "I'm like this inside the wall, too. When I'm on those small paths like spiderwebs, I'm always falling. As soon as I stop, I see a person about to stick a large hypodermic needle into my back, saying he has to extract all of my bodily fluids. When he sticks the needle in, it doesn't hurt much, but afterward I'm terribly dizzy."

"Everything can be arranged," I responded with a gesture like a plaster model. "Look at the sun: doesn't it show a more and more leisurely demeanor? I bet she sleeps for longer and longer periods. Very likely she can arrange everything while she's sound asleep. Isn't that the way she is? All we need to do is stick to our usual schedule, and it'll work out. For example, your problem with dizziness: you have to get used to it. There's no other way out. Once you're used to it, the algae will grow all over your head again, and you won't be able to refrain from making the 'bo, bo, bo' sound again. My plaster heart will sometimes be moved by the unhurried demeanor of that thing on the horizon. I predict we'll eventually get used to all this."

I don't remember when we started giving up night-watch duty. Like large rocks, we hunkered at the foot of the wall—motionless, staring into the darkness, forgetting the passage of time and the pain that the cold brought to our flesh. All night long, we were like this— sober and uncommunicative.

Time passed even more quickly. We didn't have a moment to stop and think how it had gone by. In fact, we didn't pay any attention. He was still frequently dizzy, but also obviously much calmer. We still talked of the kid and the old woman. We both knew what that meant. I started making up some extremely dull stories to tell him. I talked of a certain autumn when I had planted a large field of vegetables on a mountain slope. They grew very well. I didn't talk of this for any reason other than that I wanted to spill such words as "autumn" and "vegetables" from my mouth. Such words poured life into my withered body. But after talking of this, my exhilaration didn't last long. Another time, I talked of a large watery depression that had been formed by rainwater accumulating at the entrance to the house. I had moved large rocks from a distant spot and placed them in the watery depression. Were those rocks still there now? I had almost completely forgotten everything from the past. I could only remember these dull, fabricated stories. As he listened to my narrative, his eyeballs kept moving, and from time to time he inserted some irrelevant adjectives into my sentences. He did this with great finesse, as though he was a skilled worker.

"One Sunday evening," I said at random, "there was a downpour. I sat at my desk and spontaneously drew a holly bush."

"Was it a torrential rain?" he asked.

I nodded.

"Three years ago today, the days were growing shorter and shorter. Before we'd even had time to eat lunch, it was dark. But back then," I went on, "I didn't understand. Not until now did I realize that this is connected with the sun."

"It's like the saying 'Time flies like an arrow!'" he said with something like a sigh. "In the past, everyone said I was like a dragonfly; that whenever I felt good, I was forever circling over people's heads! I was so light that even I couldn't believe it. It's as though I'm re- membering this, but is it an incident from the past? To tell you the truth, it's a metaphor I thought up on the spur of the moment. My life now is like a metaphor covering a metaphor, or you could say a metaphor within a metaphor. This second metaphor is concealed inside an even bigger metaphor. As to my adding 'in the past,' well, that's just habit."

One noon, we invented a kind of recreation—running around the ruined wall. We ran and ran, our tattered clothing flying, and our disheveled hair also flying. We were like two ghosts. When we looked at each other's specterlike features, we screamed and ran even faster. Later he told me that it was while we were running that he saw the kid go past. The kid was carrying a small basket. He popped his head into a hole in the wall, then turned, took another small path, and went off.

"While we're running, we'd better not look at each other. It's dangerous. If we just run without stopping," he went on, "it'll be OK. When I looked at you, I felt chilled to the bone. I was scared to death. I know you come from around here. I've emphasized this to myself, but it's useless. I feel that a great disaster is hanging over us. I think you have the same feeling. We mustn't look at each other while we're running."

I agreed but I still couldn't keep from stealthily sizing him up while we were running. His words made sense, but I couldn't control this desire. Once when I was doing this, I noticed a ruthless expression cross his face. He looked like a blood-sucking black bat in hot pursuit of me, and I felt my neck being pecked. I went numb all over, and cold sweat instantly poured out of me.

After we finished running, we stood panting at our starting point, heads hanging down. When I looked up, I suddenly saw again the sun of many years ago. This sun wasn't growing old; it was still calm and unhurried as usual. I told him this, my tone dispirited.

"We're always the first to be done for. It's always like this," he said. "Haven't you figured that out yet? But if we don't leave here, we'll gradually turn into rocks—just like those rocks you placed in the watery depression. This story of yours is exquisite; there's nothing like it. After you arrived here, you fabricated it, as if it was predestined. Your scenery isn't the same—it's another scene. But sometimes it overlaps with my scenes. And sometimes I see your scene from a distance. As soon as I gaze at it, I get dizzy."

I was constantly bothered by the question *Do our voices reach the outside world?*

Finally, I shouted loudly, "Is anyone there?"

Can Xue

It was very quiet in the wilds. The indifferent sun spilled over us. That eternal sphere was far away. My voice rotated like a propeller that had never left its original place. After a while, it faded away.

I saw him going into the wall. His head was flat yet pointed, and he was extremely agile. From inside the deep and quiet small path, I heard indistinct waves of sound—one after another, rising and falling unpredictably.

Harboring a common interest in the ruined walls, he and I had hustled over here, relying only on one old woman to keep up a wisp of a connection with the outside world. Now that connection seemed more and more tenuous, more and more inauthentic. He and I still talked about the old woman, because she was our only thread. We grabbed one end of the thread for all we were worth, and wrapped it around our hands, but it often broke and slipped to the ground. We never figured out the actual state of the other end of the thread, yet we both understood this.

She Forgot
Rick Moody

SHE FORGOT AND SOMETIMES it was a good thing.

She forgot what I brought her and what I fed her for dinner from the tray by her bed.

She forgot the sound of rubber wheels wobbling down a corridor.

She forgot that a certain nurse often carried in the tray, a nurse with a mother of her own, and she forgot that the food was the same every Sunday when I visited. Salisbury steak, peas, mashed potatoes, plastic container of apple juice.

She forgot the fruit cup with the pineapple slices, the green grapes, the cling peaches, and because she forgot the menu she never tired of it.

She forgot dinner as soon as it was removed, if not before, and as soon as I was gone she forgot that I'd visited, which was *not* a good thing, because then she forgot that I'd made the effort. Though she'd forgotten I was related to her, she did recognize that I was not a party to be feared.

She forgot that there was no view out the window but parked cars. She forgot that she might have had a view that was otherwise.

She forgot that nothing in the room belonged to her but dusty

Rick Moody

framed photos, including a picture of me in a tweed suit, from back when I still had hair.

She forgot her hip fracture, which was only a few months ago, she forgot the pain of it. She forgot physical therapy and the nurse who presided there. A large Nordic woman, Claire, whom she disliked.

She forgot that they strapped her in at night, and therefore she was condemned each night to experience anew the straps fitted around her.

She forgot that she wandered, and that this was why she was strapped in, and she forgot that forgetting itself implied wandering, the forgetting of her room, the forgetting of the wing she lived in, the forgetting of the layout of the corridor, the forgetting of the institution. She forgot the terror associated with this forgetting, which was probably greater than the terror of being strapped in.

She forgot weeping in front of the nurses' console after wandering, without any idea about where she was. What room, what place, what state, what period of her life.

She forgot how to protest about being strapped in.

She forgot the whole debate on free will and determinism, and so she didn't mind giving up her will, in all but a very few cases involving things like the television remote control, which she'd forgotten how to operate, but to which she clung desperately.

She forgot about her opposition to the gun lobby, to the last couple of wars, to the Eisenhower administration, the McCarthy hearings, she forgot all these things, and she forgot that she and I disagreed on these things. She forgot Lyndon Baines Johnson. She forgot

314

Richard Milhous Nixon, and other men whose middle names are always included.

She forgot that she was dubious on racial issues, and as a result she forgot to be suspicious of nurses who were a different color from her. She forgot that she was afraid of them, and so she often loved them, even when they were admonishing her.

When she woke in the night, she forgot that it was night, and she forgot what straps were, and that straps were affixed, and so in the middle of the night, when she was often awake, she experienced the straps and the night and the insomnia and the loneliness, and these must have been hard for her, but she also forgot her anxiety, and so she slept.

She forgot about the dawn. Each morning was the first. The sun rising over the cherry trees at the far end of the parking lot. The sparrows in the trees. The sanitation collection engineer, banging around some cans, hydraulically lifting a dumpster so that its refuse tumbled into his truck. How beautiful it must have been, this first dawn of hers, dew on the lawn, a retriever racing up the sidewalk in the distance, the baroque cursing of the sanitation engineers.

She forgot everything that was mundane and everything that was humdrum, and so there was no mundanity. The taste of toothpaste. A cup full of water, light refracted in it.

She forgot that I'd lost my job. I kept telling her. One day, I experimented and told her three times that I'd lost my job. The news became routine. Telling her again and again that I had lost my job diminished the catastrophe for me, if not for her. I changed the specifics of my job the third time, just slightly. She was unable to hear differences in this story, and so each time she worried afresh. If only for an instant.

*

Rick Moody

She forgot the circumstances of all stories before they reached their conclusions, no matter what the stories were. As a result, what she liked about stories was the details. I could use the word *chenille* in a story any time and it would delight her. Cobwebs were also good, though somewhat frightening. Chrome, lilies, maple sugar, blueberries, wood smoke, flannel, baby oil, hot water bottles, whiskey, cigarettes. These pleased her.

She'd forgotten how to respond to good news, though she tried. When I told her I was dating again, she had trouble understanding my meaning. She'd forgotten that I'd once been married. I tried making up good news. I told her I had a daughter, though I did not. She was happy for a minute or two.

Of the books she loved, not a line remained. Herman Wouk. Will and Ariel Durant. James Gould Cozzens. John P. Marquand. She could read sorrow in a face, though. To forget sorrow exists in the face of another person you have to forget what faces mean. The day was not so far off.

She forgot her name, even if the nurses repeated it to her, as one nurse unfailingly did. It was just a courtesy, the employment of her name.

If she remembered something, if some clogged neurotransmitter fired briefly, and the flood of events came back, as sometimes happened, and if she then spoke a complete sentence, *Darling, could you please drive me back to the house,* she nonetheless soon forgot.

She forgot the time they complained to me about lateness of payments. She forgot that I snuck in the service entrance sometimes, just to avoid walking past Accounts Payable. She forgot when we pauperized her so that the state would make the payments instead. She forgot when I asked her to sign things. She forgot her signature, and so she forgot how to be a signatory.

*

316

She forgot anything about my appearance that she disliked.

She forgot darning socks, she forgot mending curtains, she forgot about when I first grew out the crew cuts of my childhood and how upset she was. She forgot the tweed suit she made me wear, she forgot how she so disliked denim, which she called *low class* and *unflattering*.

She forgot the pomegranate. She forgot the persimmon. She forgot the after-dinner mint. She forgot bubblegum, she forgot that she thought women who chewed gum were tramps. She forgot marzipan. She forgot bittersweet chocolate, which she preferred to milk chocolate. She forgot white chocolate, which she preferred to bittersweet chocolate.

The cedar mulch always looked fresh, on the grounds, and the hedges looked newly clipped, and one afternoon I took her out to look, but it was difficult and she was afraid of open spaces, since she had forgotten how to negotiate them.

She forgot the chandelier in the dining room in our house, which she'd bought at an antique store in Vermont in the fifties. She was so proud of that chandelier, which is still in my house, now my wife's house.

She forgot the varieties of light cascading through an old dusty crystal chandelier.

She forgot that she had granddaughters, the children of my brother, who didn't often visit. First she forgot the birthdays of her grandchildren, because they were barely out of diapers, then she forgot how many of them there were, then she believed she had one grandchild who stood in for all grandchildren, then she conflated me with her grandchildren, then she conflated me with her husband, my father, long since dead, and then she began to forget me.

*

She had cousins and children of cousins. Which was which? No more gift buying or feeling guilty about forgetting to buy gifts. No more worrying about whether the kids got gifts of equal value and size. She forgot who was a blonde and who was a redhead, which eyes were hazel and which blue.

Along came a day when it was unavoidable, the conclusion that what she'd really forgotten was time itself. No moment was before or after any other moment. She lived in a sequence of present instances, sundered from origins and destinies, and please note that in many precincts this is considered a wise and brave way to live.

Once, we happened to watch on television a montage sequence in black and white where the pages flew from a desk calendar. She paid no attention.

What she had *not* forgotten was how to see and hear and taste, as these apparently required little or no memory. So she was a seeing and hearing and tasting entity. Also a waste producer.

She forgot every day that she was a waste producer, and I think she was always shocked when she needed to be helped with this, but she never got over her sense of decorum, which, it would seem, is not part of character, but is housed somewhere lower down.

Since she forgot her children and grandchildren, it follows that she forgot reproduction. What a relief. She forgot the rhythm method, she forgot condoms, she forgot the advent of the birth control pill. She forgot the foams and sponges, she forgot the Morning After Pill, which she'd denounced as an abomination before God only five or six years ago. She forgot abstinence and birth control, she forgot that there was fornication, lovemaking, copulation, human sexuality. She forgot the missionary position, she forgot there was anything else besides.

318

Rick Moody

*

She forgot whatever lovemaking she might have done; she forgot, no doubt, kissing some boy in a waving field of wheat back in the teens or twenties, before she was courting my father. She was blameless and immaculate.

She seemed to remember pleasure when a hand was pressed against her forehead. Was she capable of a delight in being touched? Or had she forgotten that too? I always took her hand in mine, and in this way I tested the remembering or forgetting of hands. I warmed her hands. I looked closely. Her hands seemed like marble now, as if forgetting had rigidification as a physical by-product.

I took her hand in mine and she remembered, in her skin, that there was something nice about having one's hand held. She remembered that whenever her hand was held, whether the holder was man, woman, adult, or child, there was some glorious feeling attendant thereupon, and she remembered this, or perhaps she just felt that it was glorious, in her skin. She forgot where she had learned this novelty of hand-holding, but her hands remembered.

She forgot labor, she forgot the breaking of water, she forgot the agony of labor before anesthesia. She forgot the anxiety of giving birth to a boy during the Depression. She forgot the doctor who came round to the house with his bag of opiates and his unsterilized tools.

She forgot blood everywhere, she forgot the slime and horror of delivery, she forgot her husband, out back, smoking incessantly. She forgot the placenta, which was a blue like few blues she had seen.

She forgot the smell of childbirth, she forgot the child wailing at the smack on its behind. She forgot pregnancy and how much she hated her husband during pregnancy.

*

319

Rick Moody

She forgot that she outlived him by thirty years.

She forgot the Jazz Age, she forgot the origins of jazz, if she had ever known them, she forgot the big band period, she forgot the smooth jazz favorites that they played in the hall by the nurses' console. The residents didn't like the loud stuff, though they had forgotten why.

She forgot thorns. She forgot weeds. She forgot poison ivy and poison oak. She forgot gardening. She forgot that she had often knelt in fresh soil and tried to help rosebushes in bad shape. She forgot transplanting.

She forgot all storms and all threatening weather, and this I know because two weeks ago I was there when a thunderstorm passed through the neighborhood. A look of stunned incomprehension swept across her face.

She forgot the playground near my house. She forgot the stone arch on the way to the playground. She forgot the path that led to the stone arch that led to the playground, she forgot that way a swing arcs out when you put a kid in it.

She forgot that she was not a child herself.

She forgot space. Did I mention this already? She forgot the ability to understand a space beyond what was immediately visible. She forgot that there was a hall outside her room, and when she was in the hall, she forgot that she had a room. And if she had forgotten *both* space and time, what exactly could she have remembered?

She forgot that I asked her to tell me what was beyond the door into the hall, and she forgot that she couldn't answer. She forgot all that lay beyond what she could see: a television set, a number of framed photographs of me, my father, my brother, and his children. A spider plant. A stuffed bear that I brought one day since she was not allowed to have any pets.

She forgot that a window was not an easel painting. She forgot that the door was not some kind of ornament, and that beyond the hospital was a road, and that along the road was a mall and a country club and post office.

She forgot that she had once intended to leave. She forgot that this was home and no other home had existed, nor had ever existed, as far as she knew.

She forgot the seasons. She forgot the delicious part of spring that cries out that summer is coming. She forgot lilacs and Scottish broom, magnolia season. She forgot the smell of fresh popcorn. She forgot all varieties of pie. At one time, she lectured me about how mince pie had to contain venison, and now she had forgotten all pies.

She ate apple cobbler without complaint, or perhaps she simply forgot to complain.

She forgot that she was a forgetter. She forgot that I was coming in the door again, and that I had brought a jar of honey that I had bought in a foreign land.

She forgot that I needed to leave soon, so that I could come back again. If I went out to talk to the nurses when I returned it was an entirely new visit.

She forgot that this was to be another evening spent with an almost entirely forgotten person, dimly recognized but mostly forgotten, a person in the process of being forgotten, who walked through the door from somewhere, though from where was forgotten. Again

321

there would be the language of his recounting. There would be this person, speaking these words, and his questions were entirely new or incompletely forgotten.

She forgot that I too lived in a dread of forgetting, because of her forgetting. And so I tested myself, with these stories. Did I forget parts of the stories I told her when I came to visit? Or did I tell the stories the same way? Did I forget and begin to invent, and did I do these things out of compassion, because forgetting begs to be forgotten?

Would I too forget? I asked. Could I simply be, as she was, a forgetter, rather than an anguished rememberer, in the beginning of growing old? And then I asked other such questions, going into the steamer trunk of memory. Remembering and forgetting, in the stories I told her, her life and mine.

She forgot, and sometimes it was a good thing. And sometimes not.

Forbidden City
Tova Reich

WHEN THE GOBI DESERT came to Beijing on the first day of the lunar month, Reb Pesach Tikkun-Olam Salzman, known throughout China as the Tzaddik of Sin for his celebrated deeds of righteousness, told his girls to get up and put on their masks—they would grab this opportunity for an outing to the Forbidden City to sing morning prayers. True, the sands of the wasteland had been advancing toward the capital for years now, borne in on savage winds meeting weaker and weaker resistance as the Bosses set about taking down all non-essential barriers standing in the path of expansion and progress. Reb Tikkun-Olam, by the way, was in full agreement with the Bosses on this policy, as he found himself to be on almost every other issue. "Who needs trees anyhow?" Reb Tikkun-Olam would say. "Did you ever hear of a normal human being having a vision sitting up in a tree? But in the desert—ah, that's another story entirely. There's no such thing as too much desert."

In fact, he and the Bosses were partners, collaborators in the most constructive sense of the word; quietly and behind the scenes they did business together, especially in matters pertaining to acquiring and disposing of the girls. Like the assembly of seventy-one sages in ancient Israel they were, Reb Tikkun-Olam liked to say of the Bosses, perplexing the official with whom he might be haggling concerning final arrangements re one of the girls—"Like the Sanhedrin of old," Reb Tikkun-Olam would make a stab at clarifying, "you know, the *Sin*-hedrin, so to speak," he would add with a throwaway laugh like a shrug. The fact that *Sin* was Hebrew for China was a sly message Reb Tikkun-Olam took benign delight in communicating, particularly to an agent of the Bosses who was trying to squeeze every last cent out of him on a deal involving the girls, and whose English was good enough to get the point without taking undue offense. As for the girls themselves, one of their selling points was that they all knew English; it was a prerequisite for an American market. They were bilingual in comprehension even if they could not speak at all by the time he was finished with them. The language

323

germ was carefully implanted; he guaranteed this in writing.

In the mornings, wrapped in his prayer shawl and bound in his phylacteries, with his girls—those who were able to stand on their own two feet lined up in order behind a bamboo screen—he led them in the Benedictions and intoned his gratitude to the Lord, For not having made me a woman. He gave them the choice of two positives instead of that one negative—either the traditional feminine substitution, For having made me according to his will, or alternatively, an original neuter variant of his own spawning, For having made me *Sin-i*—that's how much Reb Tikkun-Olam respected the Chinese. No question, Reb Tikkun-Olam had a deep and abiding regard for the Chinese—deep and abiding, he would reiterate. The Chinese were, in his personal opinion, a mutant form of Jew—hardworking, high IQs, possessing a genetic gift for mathematics, business, music, with a specialty in string instruments, and so on, clumping right there with the Jews along the superior tail of the bell, and, of course, also like the Jews, they were a minimum of five thousand years old and long-suffering. The main difference, Reb Tikkun-Olam liked to say, was that there were a whole lot of them, whereas, on the other hand, not so many of us. Despite God's promise to Abraham, Reb Tikkun-Olam commented, it was they, and not us, who were so multitudinous that they could not be counted—like the sands of the Gobi now coming to bury Beijing. With his girls, at least this situation of the disparity in numbers was something that the Tzaddik of Sin, in his own small way, was doing his part to correct.

Why Reb Tikkun-Olam was inspired on this day of all days to treat his girls to a field trip was that the sand was pouring down so thickly, like a cascading drapery of bone scrim behind which nothing but flailing shadows was visible, that it created, in his estimation, an ideal environment in terms of protecting his girls from prying eyes, sparing them from unwanted attention. Not only they but everyone without exception would be wearing a mask that day, his girls would not stand out, and, also, of course, there was the sensitive issue of modesty. Reb Tikkun-Olam stressed modesty; it was a subject about which he was known to be ultrastrict. Even within the walls of their rooms in their small dwelling in the narrow, winding *hutong* in the heart of Beijing, Reb Tikkun-Olam required that his girls be fully covered at all times. Only their small pale hands showed from the wrists fanning out. Every strand of silken black hair, plus the dark orifices and tender, pendulous flesh of the ears, was concealed under a blue cotton kerchief, though indoors, for health considerations and to ease problems related to breathing and speech, and also, of course, for taking in essential nutrients, Reb Tikkun-Olam permitted the girls to be without the mask that straddled the bump of the nose, the moistness of the nostrils, and, most importantly, the red wound of the mouth, which, in Reb Tikkun-Olam's opinion, was a far more intimate zone than, let us say, the hair, although, according to traditional classifications, the hair ranked third in the levels of female nakedness after, first, the frank nakedness of the body from the neck down and second, the nakedness of the woman's voice, whereas for some unfathomable reason, the mouth itself from which the voice emanated did not rank at all—an omission that never failed to set Reb Tikkun-Olam's head shaking back and forth in bemusement, it was so manifestly naive.

However, needless to say, if the girls ventured out into the *hutong* courtyard for even one second to fulfill some purpose or other, they were obliged to put on their masks, no exemptions granted. But this happened very seldom, after all, as there was plenty to keep them pleasantly occupied right inside the house at all times, what with the sands of the Gobi Desert penetrating day after day through the cracks in the walls or even through the door and windows if, from lack of consideration, some guilty party failed to seal them shut promptly. Just a few spoons and cups, maybe a sieve or a funnel or a colander, perhaps a small pot or pan—that was all that was required to keep the girls busy indoors. For hours they would squat there on the floor, their feet tucked compactly under their haunches, playing within their own four cubits in perfect contentment, constructing imaginary cities of pavilions and palaces and pathways in their own private sandbox.

The one charged with the task of sweeping up the sand into piles and carrying out other assorted housekeeping chores, plus tending and supervising the girls, not to mention performing such services for Reb Tikkun-Olam himself as picking the grains of sand out of the crevices and creases, folds and furrows of his soft, large body, was Dolly, the name instantly bestowed upon her by Reb Tikkun-Olam's youngest daughter just a short while before his wife, Frumie, declared that she couldn't take it anymore and headed straight back to her parents' house in Brooklyn with all eight of their kids. Until it had been her peculiar fate to land in Beijing, the rebbetzin Frumie Salzman had known absolutely nothing from the Chinese except the laundries on Bedford Avenue where she used to bring her husband's white shirts for heavy starch, and twice a year, around the Yom

Kippur and Passover holidays, his long white *kittel*. Even the restaurants meant zero to her, she never noticed them at all on the streets at home since they had no connection whatsoever to her life, some wise guy once told her that they didn't mix meat with milk in there, which was the lame excuse, she figured, for why a certain category of so-called Jews considered it a commandment of their faith to eat Chinese at least once a week—but she herself was strictly kosher, super glatt, what are you talking about? And chopsticks? Don't even get me started on chopsticks, Frumie cried. What was China to her? Dishes—five-piece place settings displayed in a blond-veneered breakfront next to the sterling and cut crystal—that's all she ever needed or wanted to know about China, anything else was more information than she could bear, thank you very much. Oh, why were they ever shipped off to be Judaism's emissaries in such a strange land, an assignment to the opposite end of the earth to which she used to pretend to dig in the dirt as a little girl but never truly hoped to arrive there, it was like another planet, with only a handful of local Jewish remnants in any halfway recognizable shape or form targeted for outreach, but no matter how much you knocked yourself out to draw them back into the fold, it was hopeless, they were already such a lost cause, it was a total waste of energy, and other than these miserable specimens, nothing but Jewish tourists passing through, flatulent tourists on packages to whom she in her wig and her husband in his sidecurls and beard were an in-joke, familiar freaks, a couple of snapped curiosities in a roll, or for the more nostalgic among them, a comforting taste of home, like the Jewish McDonald's. China was exile, China was punishment. What had she done to deserve it? By the waters of Babylon there we sat and also we wept as we remembered Zion. What in the world was China doing alongside Mount Sinai?

It was because the child resembled a tiny porcelain doll that the name had stuck when Reb Tikkun-Olam brought Dolly home that day, more than ten years earlier. He had found her sitting solitary, absolutely alone, absolutely still and expressionless like a baby Buddha on a torn and filthy straw mat with a tin can for coins stinking of fish placed beside her and flies swarming around her head on Wangfujing Street in front of a department store. "Just what we needed," Frumie said as the entire family gathered around and Reb Tikkun-Olam peeled off her soiled rags to confirm their assumption with regard to the gender; the Chinese, they knew very well, even the most desperate, did not just leave their precious only boys lying around in the street like stray dogs for any pervert to pick up. The girl lay totally unresisting as they closed in to inspect her, her eyes frozen, never letting out the faintest cry. Reb Tikkun-Olam used the occasion to instruct his children in the lesson that the first piece of information sought out about a human being, at the moment of birth, is derived from a swift glance to the private parts; it is in that direction that the eyes of all present automatically turn and this is the first news that is reported before any other, this is the screaming headline. And afterward, too, Reb Tikkun-Olam taught, what is always noted and registered first when you meet a new person, imperceptibly, whether you realize it or not, before any other business is commenced, is the sex, gleaned from the visible secondary characteristics, you tick off a little box inside your brain—male or female or other or whatever—so you will know how to proceed, which was another reason, Reb Tikkun-Olam pointed out, always to be on guard to practice the strictures of modesty—defensively, like a shield, like a suit of armor to protect you against the intrusiveness of such scrutiny.

Dolly was maybe between one and three years old, they estimated, when Reb Tikkun-Olam found her and carried her home under his arm like the baby lamb from the market that Father bought; it was impossible to know her age exactly, she was so small, yet fully formed, with the defined shape and gravity of a resigned mortal. She was strangely passive and robotic for a child, which at first led Reb Tikkun-Olam to conjecture that she might have been massively drugged before being set out there in the street to beg for the family, but when she continued to maintain that odd impenetrable composure, and, moreover, practically every single one of the many girls he had processed since that time over the subsequent years also demonstrated some variation of a similar blankness, Reb Tikkun-Olam decided that this must simply be how it was—this was an ethnic type, there was no point in arguing with nature, perhaps God in his wisdom created them that way for a very good purpose, innately obedient and submissive for survival reasons; a definite market value could be set on such qualities, especially for a woman. For his part, he, the Tzaddik of Sin, would receive them as they were; he would not seek to change them, he would love them unconditionally, he would sanctify his energies to labor in their behalf.

When Reb Tikkun-Olam announced that he believed that the child had been sent to him by God to show him his mission on earth, Frumie registered silently that this was it; the time had come to call her mother and start packing. It was also around then that he declared he would no longer answer to the name Pesach, given to him by his father to mark his arrival on Passover eve, his exemplary mother taking only the necessary time off from the strenuous preparations for the holiday to give birth to him—it all went very quickly, he was her fourteenth child—smoothing her housecoat and getting up to resume her work in time to roast the shank bone and grate the bitter herbs. Henceforth, he advised Frumie, he would be known as Tikkun-Olam, to denote his kabbalistic mandate to repair the shattered vessels of this world.

It had not escaped Frumie's notice that her husband had become progressively weirder and weirder, in her opinion, as the years accumulated in this upside-down place China. For example, instead of dressing like a normal person, in a black kaftan with a tasseled rope belt to separate the lower carnal section of his body from the upper spiritual part, and a fringed garment as a reminder that he belonged to the One Above, a black hat on weekdays in all seasons over his velvet yarmulke, and a sleek fur *streimel* on the Sabbath, he now decked himself out bizarrely in a long embroidered turquoise silk Chinese robe, loose drawstring pants that required pulling down to do all his business, cotton shoes like a mourner, and on his head a black satin skullcap with a ridiculous pom-pom. He looked like a Confucius with sidecurls; it was understandably very embarrassing to introduce him on those rare occasions when friends or family took the trouble to trek around the globe to visit. And even more upsetting, something she was too ashamed to confide to another soul, even to her own mother, was the period of time during which he would not stop badgering her to organize a Rosh Chodesh prayer group exclusively for women. It was her responsibility as his helpmeet to undertake this project, he insisted; he was envisioning a women's celebration to welcome in the new moon at the head of each month through ritual that harnessed the natural female lunar energy, he said, with chants and dances, and an altar and candles and incense and a vessel to collect the cyclic blood.

But the last straw for Frumie came when he informed her that although all the other discarded girls he would be rescuing as part of his mission to repair the world would be for the purpose of finding them good Jewish homes and adoptive Jewish parents from among the increasing numbers of older overeducated infertile Jewish couples of America with dual incomes who could afford the fees, thereby, as a side benefit of saving the children, also drawing from the demographic plenitude and genetic variation of the Chinese to correct the population shortage and chronic inbreeding among the Jews, throwing in as a bonus for the customer's convenience the extra service of personally converting the girls in advance through ritual-bath immersion, like prekoshered chickens, already salted and soaked—this particular girl, this Dolly, his first, he would keep, not for his own sake, God forbid, but for hers, for Frumie's sake, to raise Dolly to serve as his *pilegesh* when she came of age so that he would no longer have to bother Frumie with his needs even during the periods when she was not ritually impure, when she was technically available to him albeit suffering from a terrible migraine. Though the revered medieval scholar and physician Maimonides had decreed that a concubine is permissible only to a king, other rabbinical authorities have argued that to preserve peace in the household between husband and wife, and to offset the masculine tendency to fool around either with oneself or with others if not satisfactorily serviced, an appreciative *pilegesh* was indeed a practical solution that, in the end, did not really hurt anyone. Never mind the Old Testament account of the *pilegesh* from Gibeah, handed over to the gang to be molested, and then butchered and hacked up into twelve parcels and sent special delivery to each of the tribes of Israel as a cautionary message regarding property rights. That happened very long ago, in the wild east of the Judges; it was ancient history, it was no longer relevant. These, on the other hand, were modern times, Reb Tikkun-Olam pointed out, enlightened times, and China was the country of the future—China was the cutting edge.

Pushing with his troop of girls through the heavy gauze of the swirling sand to the Forbidden City, Reb Tikkun-Olam was thinking, This must be it, the approaching day that is neither day nor night, as the prophet had foreseen. Ungraspable apocalyptic shades were thrashing in the miasma in front of them as their little procession lunged ahead. Lashing blindly with weapons choked with grit, a phalanx of guards posted by the Bosses sought in vain to seize the lone Falun Dafa practitioner in defiant slow motion, taunting them behind the screen of raining sand in the vast desert that had once been Tianammen Square. Reb Tikkun-Olam trudged behind his girls through this end-of-the-world landscape, clutching the tail of the rope that tethered them all in one line. Instead of a mask, his capacious white prayer shawl with the licorice black stripes and the neck

ornamentation of silver and gold embroidery was drawn across the
lower portion of his face and hooded over the phylactery box on his
head—like a Bedouin in a sandstorm, he pictured himself, Salzman
of Arabia.

Dolly, too, at the head of the line, with her end of the rope looped
around her wrist, was also excused from wearing a mask. This was
because her slight form, showing only the barest, though unmistakable, swellings of budding womanhood, was shrouded from the top
of her head to the tips of her toes in a stale bedsheet that they had
fashioned like a burka, the perfect garment for what turned out, after
all, to be a classical Islamic climate—Reb Tikkun-Olam could only
marvel at the way practical and spiritual imperatives merged in the
costumes of evolving cultures. Over the narrow rectangular opening
cut out for her eyes, thick tinted glasses in black plastic frames were
perched, which they obtained free of charge through the good offices
of the Bosses, and renewed annually as her eyesight progressively
deteriorated. A short while after he had carried Dolly home, and
Frumie absconded with the kids, it became clear that the explanation for the hours during which the girl would lie mute, curled up
under the table with eyes stubbornly shut, was not attributable to
incipient brattiness or plain ingratitude, say, or to infantile depression, as some visiting American woman magazine reader had insinuated, but, rather, was actually due to a concrete problem—the child
had difficulty seeing and had simply given up trying.

It was then that Reb Tikkun-Olam was struck with his second revelation regarding his new mission: not only would he rescue the
Chinese girl babies dumped out by families who would accept nothing less than a boy for the one-child-per strictly mandated by the
Bosses to stanch the population glut, but his niche would be placing
for adoption the problem cases—seconds, irregulars, damaged goods,
so to speak—Specials, as Reb Tikkun-Olam labeled them to shop-
pers, because, first of all, they were "special" in the euphemistic
sense, and secondly, he could also offer them at a special price, a nice
discount, cut-rate, cheap, relatively speaking—ultimately making up
the difference in volume. And to his gratification, in his targeted U.S.
markets, from Cambridge, Massachusetts, to New York City's Upper
West Side, for example, prospective clients responded overwhelm-
ingly, leaping with ferocious energy and resourcefulness to claim
these markdowns. Not only did they perversely prefer girls, Reb
Tikkun-Olam was stunned to discover, and not only did they favor
Chinese girls who would inevitably be italicized among all those

Semitic types in the Byzantine world of girlhood intrigue, but astonishingly, counterintuitively, they prized the added challenges, as they called them, the bonus disabilities, physical and/or mental, that came with Reb Tikkun-Olam's particular stock, which would be overcome by their professional competence and their mastery of detail and their genius for follow-up, their lists and schedules, their contacts and connections; they never doubted their powers for a minute. There was no joke that God could possibly perpetrate through his infinite and grotesque variations on a theme that could faze them; Reb Tikkun-Olam was awed and humbled. In spite of all the evidence to the contrary, they believed with a full faith that they were in control.

The three infants, to take a case in point, that Dolly in her ghostly robe was now carrying in the soft hammocklike sling across her almost but not quite flat chest, would be snatched up by these customers within the year—Reb Tikkun-Olam had absolutely no worries on that score; the profit margin would be satisfactory, there were no anticipated problems with overstock or remainders. They had been delivered just the previous week by the Bosses, deposited at dawn in a suitcase at their doorstep in the *hutong*. When he opened the suitcase he actually found five girl babies packed inside, but two, not surprisingly, had already spoiled, and had to be picked out, like moldy strawberries at the bottom of the basket, and set out by the side of the road to be collected for recycling. Of the three that remained, now being borne by Dolly in her improvised baby tote, like fledgling doves to the Forbidden City, one's feet were crippled maybe from botched binding, the second had a dark port-wine stain on her cheek in a shape that resembled a cartoon dragon, and while the third had no obvious defect or deformity, Reb Tikkun-Olam never questioned for a moment that there was something wrong with her—the Bosses never made a mistake in these early-detection matters, probably it was some kind of mental issue, a self-esteem problem, maybe, or a suicidal tendency, not yet discernible to the naked eye but diagnosed by wise men who placed three fingers on the pulse and consulted the charts.

As usual, all of the girls were called Lily. When he first started in business, he would give each one her own individual name, giving himself a headache at the same time as he struggled to come up with something perfect and unique to match the pictured face in the catalogue and the Web site blurbs. But what was the point of going to all that trouble, after all? The fact was, you could hardly tell them

331

apart anyway. And should he need to summon or refer to one of them, it didn't really matter in the end which one it was; any one of them would do just as well as another. Besides, as soon as the deal was finalized and ownership transferred, a personalized name would be bestowed by the adoptive family upon its new daughter— Shoshana-Bracha Mei-Ling Srulovich-Seltzer, or another such equally creative effort; the name pool was open and available and free for anyone to dip into. In the meantime, for the sake of efficiency, instead of names, prospective customers could refer to the desired item by noting the catalogue number within the lily logo underneath the mug shot. The Lilys that Dolly was transporting in her pouch through the Gobi wind and sand that morning were numbers five ninety-four through six. Five Lilys, Lily number five hundred and eleven through five fifteen, were plodding in a row behind her along the extended rope, which was noosed around each of their waists in turn and culminated in Reb Tikkun-Olam's fist.

These five, as it happened, were proving to be an extremely difficult lot to place; Reb Tikkun-Olam would definitely incur a severe loss due to them especially when you factored in the maintenance expenses and overhead costs for well over the year that they had already been with him. What rendered them almost unmarketable as a product, so to speak, was that, in addition to other problems, they were afflicted with the one drawback that even Reb Tikkun-Olam's usual clientele, with all their managerial expertise and enthusiasm, could do nothing to overcome—namely, their age. They were appealingly miniature, true, but nevertheless there was no getting around the fact that they were already well past the optimal age for adoption, like expired merchandise in a grocery case, which, in the end, could only be tossed out. Reb Tikkun-Olam suspected that three of them at least might even already be in the two-digit range, from which, once entered in a lifetime, there is, except in the rarest of cases, no exit. They had been deposited on his doorstep in a plastic dumpster marked Guangdong Province Hospital, huddling on a bed of blood- and pus-stained bandages and other assorted medical waste. It was essentially for the sake of these overage five that all of them were struggling that morning to part the heavy curtains of sand and make their way to pray in the Forbidden City, which Reb Tikkun-Olam regarded as a holy place, especially for women, by virtue of its sediments of concentrated unrecorded ancient female suffering, both inflicted and endured. Hearing their prayers from this sacred site, perhaps the Master of the Universe would look upon these foundlings with kindness and arrange suitable homes for them at last, as he has been known to occasionally turn a mischievous prankster's eye upon some ill-favored woman as she prayed for a husband—nothing fancy, just any old husband, please God—and grant her wish. They were dressed in faded blue Mao suits too large for them, these five Lily rejects, and blue cotton kerchiefs wound tightly around their lowered heads. Naturally, in strict adherence to the rules, they all wore their masks.

Bringing up the rear of his file of girls, Reb Tikkun-Olam responded to the automatic bow of the ticket collector at the entrance gate to the Forbidden City with a jaunty salute of his own patent, taking care to give no sign whatsoever that could in any way be interpreted as bowing in return. A Jew bows down only to the One Above, for this gentile's information; for that principle alone the throats of centuries of martyrs had been cut. Despite the custom of the land, not even with the slightest dip of the head would Reb Tikkun-Olam allow himself to betray his holy ancestors—the Chinese, even these atheist officials, appreciated a man who respected his ancestors—and certainly he would never execute any facsimile of the prostration and the banging of the brow on the stones that was the throbbing pulse within the walls and moats of this compound in imperial days; he could feel the vibration of the head pounding rising up still from the tortured ground. By prior arrangement with the Bosses, the ticket collector waved them through, compliments of the house—the least you could expect, really, when you considered the percentage cut that Reb Tikkun-Olam was obliged to fork over for the Bosses' cooperation on every single deal he closed involving the girls. The little smirk on the ticket collector's face at the spectacle of this oversized alien gone native wrapped in some kind of white horse blanket with a black leather cube strapped to his head, and his menagerie of harnessed girls in tow, blindered and muzzled, was a fact of life that Reb Tikkun-Olam had grown immunized to over the years in Beijing. On the one hand, it was an insult and condescension he might coldly ignore, as no doubt was warranted, but on the other hand, it was important to be on friendly terms with the locals, and especially with the officials linked to the Bosses, so in man-to-man code to suck in this ticket collector, Reb Tikkun-Olam gave a rough yank to his end of the rein as he drove his team through the Gate of Supreme Harmony, tipping his line of girls precariously backward in the stinging sand, and with his free arm lashing in the Gobi wind, he mimicked the rise and fall of a whip's arc.

The point was to get his girls as efficiently as possible past the great public ceremonial spaces with their wooden palaces and halls in glossy reds and golds—the aesthetic prototype, in Reb Tikkun-Olam's mind, for Chinese restaurants in malls across America, a genre of establishment that, to be perfectly honest, he had entered only once in his lifetime in a bathroom emergency and was nearly wiped out by essence of pork. He hustled his girls forward through the sand-streaked atmosphere, past dogged tourists persevering in the face of mounting panic as the relentlessly falling grit stuffed up every hole in their equipment, past the sand-plugged bronze incense burners and great water urns that eunuch slaves kept filled day and night to prevent the place from burning to the ground.

Wherever Reb Tikkun-Olam turned, peasants were invading the palaces, even as the sand was burying them. Cutting his way through the masses, he steered his charges toward the private inner court-yards of the gynaeceum at the northern end of the complex. Maybe they would hold their prayer service in the Hall of Forgotten Favorites, he was thinking, that might be appropriate, but he had not yet made a final decision. Because setting aside all of the evidence pressing in upon them from every corner, of idol worship, of de-bauchery, of extravagance, of intrigue, what was this place after all but a retirement home for used concubines? And all things consid-ered, it was not such a bad deal for some nice Mongol debutante from a decent family, Reb Tikkun-Olam reflected—a lifetime pension, including room and board and a whole array of perks within the con-fines of this five-star estate for what might amount in the end to less than a single night's work if you weren't overly ambitious—express delivery, gift-wrapped in a black cloak, over the spongy shoulder of a royal eunuch, off-loaded on the floor at the foot of the dynastic bed, bathed and perfumed and depilated and stripped naked as a security precaution against the concealed dagger you might plunge into the heart of the Son of Heaven. Was one night's work too much to expect in exchange for guaranteed tenure in this exclusive domain, with all of its comforts and luxuries, Reb Tikkun-Olam asked himself as he pushed ahead in the spectral landscape toward the Imperial Garden.

Through the veils of sand he could barely make out the slumped backs of his leftover girls straining along the rope emanating from him like his own entrails unraveling. Searching for the fading vision of Dolly at the head of the line, his eyes were guided downward along her body, coming to rest at a startling burst of crimson stain radiating through the haze from her pale robe where it tented out ever so subtly. So it has come to her at last, Reb Tikkun-Olam took in—a significant moment, a milestone, a life-cycle event, her initiation into the sisterhood of the lunar flow. He understood that she might now be too drained to walk all the way home after their service though naturally she would never raise her voice to utter a word of complaint; he might have to carry her, though, along with the spared newborns in her sack, as he had carried her on the day he had found her when she was also unclean. And then, once they were home, once she had removed her street garment and taken off her glasses, it would be his duty to strike her, draw a symbolic drop of blood from her lip perhaps, yes, he would be obliged to slap her on the face—an old custom at the onset of womanhood, mysterious, unexplainable, but for those reasons alone, all the more necessary. And Dolly had no mother to do it for her, poor child.

The lustful mothers of China, the dragon ladies, Dowager Empress Cixi and Madame Mao, liked to do something nice for themselves on the first day of the lunar month, taking a well-deserved break from their post behind the bamboo screen from where they painstakingly fed the words into the mouth of the enthroned Son of Heaven and the Chairman giving audience on the other side, and accompanied by a sisterhood of concubines whom they had handpicked to nourish the male energy, personally rating each beauty contestant for a discreet Adam's apple and smooth lips and regular teeth and pink tongue and sweet breath and plump uvula, they were borne on palanquins by fat eunuchs through the Imperial Garden of the Forbidden City up the fourteen meters along winding pathways to the top of the Hill of Accumulated Refinement for the empowering refreshment and relaxation of enjoying the view. The view, Reb Tikkun-Olam noted, as far as the eye could see, was sand blowing, flying, twisting wildly on agitated currents of air. The civilizing divisions between heaven and earth laid down during the first days of creation bringing order to the world had vanished entirely. The spirit of the Gobi was churning over the face of the waters.

Reb Tikkun-Olam, now at the head of the line, jerked the rope urgently, dragging his girls up the hill into the shelter of the pavilion at the top. Sand was falling all over China. The Forbidden City below, and everything that lay beyond, was returning to dust. From the viewing pavilion at the top of the Hill of Accumulated Refinement they could see nothing, emptiness and void, nor could they be seen in turn. It would be safe now for his five girls yoked along the rope to lower their masks. When they opened their mouths for prayer, their raw harelips and cleft palates would not offend. The shredded sounds coiling upward from their mouths, rising in lamentation, would not violate the strictures of modesty as he was the only male present to hear their naked voices—and he was like a father to them. Their naked voices would be covered by the voice of the Lord making the desert convulse.

Reb Tikkun-Olam removed his phylacteries in anticipation of the extra service, a poor substitute for the fiery sacrifices of the first of the month on the altars of the holy temple, destroyed for our sins. It was essential that they block out all earthly distractions, focus inward spiritually, concentrate intensely. Maybe then God would incline favorably toward them and be pacified at last. Maybe he would bend to accept their prayers in lieu of the new moon burnt offerings—the young lambs, unblemished.

Nine Yelps from the Eisteddfod of Idiots
M. T. Anderson

I.

A MAN ONCE WOKE and found he had disappeared, goes the old fable. *There was nothing to see. For a time, he regarded his hands, because otherwise the white was terrible.*

After a while, he got to his feet and walked.

There was no horizon. There were no sights. He could not rule out the idea that this was the bottom side of a traditional continent.

He walked in what might have been a line.

He still could recall things from before, from the time of plenitude: geese beside the highway; the scent of the pharmacy; his mother in a plastic chair, teetering on the edge of the stairs; the kite unused in the basement, hung beside the pegboard. But he was filled more with a wonder at objects' serene absence, or his, than with any longing for them materially to return.

You have told me this fable, facing away, perched richly on a stool, engaged in some house project with wood and a gouge. You have built things while the story is spoken. I sit in my corner and do not argue.

He wandered through the white.

When there was nothing more to establish, he stopped, paunch cocked, and craned his neck.

He wanted to go back to the place where he had awakened. He rubbed his heel upon the white. There was some disappointment that he had not left a mark or keyhole at the spot where he had first arrived. He looked about his body for tokens or furnishings. As ornament, there were only the hairs, which seemed perilously thin. Against the white, they were slim; their slim was hideous: placed upon the ground, a hair diminished, and seemed to speak of universal maw.

He padded back. He did not know if he had found the spot. He rested where it might have been.

After a time, the last meal he had eaten in the world of objects stirred within him. He looked for a place that would not be tainted. His knees were turned inward. He paced one way and then the other. He would not meet even the blankness at eye level. He snapped lightly with his fingers, a shuffling, soft-shoe rhythm.

When he could not button himself up any longer, he gave himself over; he crouched and released the stool. It was independent. It was a feature in the blank terrain.

This, he thought. This could be a henge, a dolmen.

He paced away from it, looked back upon it, and named it A.

By dividing it and transporting it with his fingers, he deposited marks in other places. There were two more: which he called B and C.

From each of them, he could see across the half mile or more to the others. He was on a plane. He was delighted with his work.

He would go, in the long solemn silences, from A to C. From C to B. From B to C. He voyaged from one to another, and felt content in his mobility and the promise of geography. He walked between his monuments, his places.

And so the rest of his story may be told in this way:

CAB, BCBACB, BCABCBA, ABABACBC, CBABC, BACBACB, BA.

A
C
B
C
B
A
C
B
A

(And so on.)

II.

Last night, at around 4:50, the fire department drove up to the building. I assumed I had performed some secret wrong. I sat on the bed with my arms across my knees and awaited apprehension. The fire department came into the building. I stood by the window and let the lights revolve across my stomach. The men ran in the front door. A few minutes later, they left.

They could not have put out a fire in that time.

It is my concern that it may be here still, between things, burning slowly.

This place is not ours anymore.

III.

Things and some people vanish every day. After they are gone, they may be referred to as "the evanid."

When I was in Cub Scouts, we had that vanishment badge. We ran through the gorse and listened for things that were gone forever. We jumped through hoops for that damn badge. Top of the list were burnt, dusty, old ceramics, and the previous evening. I barked up my knees on the rocks at Felton's Point. But by three o'clock, I had ten items. Have you seen one of those shirts with snaps on the nipples? I hate to find one of those under a juniper bush, all dirty from having hung there for days with everything else missing. It's like a little horror novel.

In any case, generally: if someone puts something in your hand, don't open your eyes, for God's sake. You play the game, you get the badges.

We learn nothing by these exercises. I got the vanishment badge, but I was not ready for the day fifteen years later when I myself was Taken.

Bam.

It was not so much the cold as my nakedness after the teleportation that startled me.

I was outside the Levines' summer place, but it was winter. I had never seen it like this. The shutters were matted with leaves that had blown there and then stuck. The woods were very full and quiet.

I could not help, darling—darling—but remember our time—by which I mean the screen door yoked with springs; dancing on the porch; eating sandwiches; after six, coated cards and crabgrass wine;

339

M. T. Anderson

cicada husks laid gently upon our coverlet. You brushed them off briskly, joyously, with a hand flat as tea.

Now the snow was complete. The forest was thick with it. Wind blew by the Levines' loose goods, their old milk and aquarium. Seven miles of white pine with all the phones disconnected.

Nothing was in the parentheses of the lake. I tried the door, which had been locked since the lake had frozen. I was up to my shanks in drifts.

Your skin so white, so blank; so though it was cold, and I was in Ontario, evanid, I could not stop caressing the house, or fondling it, or calling it by your name.

IV.

Every night we left out a small box to trap the mammal that lived up in the rafters. Every morning it left its dung right next to the bait.

On that particular morning, we had gotten out your lacrosse cards and were arranging them on the floor. I took more of the stack than you did.

You got tired of my little ways and you sighed and said *had I checked the trap.* So much for great lacrosse legends of the past. Suddenly it was all business.

This is just one example, fig. 9b.

Now that things weren't going your way, oh, no more playtime, there were errands you had to run, oh, some hammering, oh, weren't things uncoiled? Well, it's fine to put your head where your arms should be. That's fine now, "honey," but what will you do when you want to run naked in the car wash, so to speak, when you want to throw things off the quay? Someone could have a little think about that, Squat Pants.

No, I did not complain. I was meek. I said that the mammal had not come down. I kept going with the cards. You had stood up. You were looking down at me.

I flipped my part of the deck. On card after card, there was a picture of tools. Each player was a tool. "This is a whole different series," I said.

You reached down and rubbed my face sadly. "The animal could have come down while we were sitting here," you said.

I said, "It could have gone up while you scolded."

V.

Mood: all the holes in the pinball machine are plugged with wood. My wrists are tired from slapping the flippers. Someone built games out of brick. I am wearing an overcoat with too much cheese in the pockets.

When I'm in this mood, the arcade concierge says, "This way to the concessions. This way to the concessions."

At the arcade, the concessions are cooked in steam, as are our human tongues.

VI.

Seven of them came originally. Seven, and she was the seventh. They came to the house with the board. It was the first time I met her.

Greg insisted on doing everything. That's just like him. I'm talking almost entirely in guffaws now.

She could arch herself in any old damn way. Together, we were like dine-in on Naugahyde chairs. Both the good and the bad. This is something I think about now.

She was perched on the balustrade, flourishing there, and Judith was down the hall. Pots and pans. The rain. You can't beat that.

Singing, like a damsel with a sistrum, singing old songs, singing,

> I shall meet you under the sheepwillow tree
> Where the branches meet with the bole . . .

Seven of them, and her numero seven.

VII.

The woman's daughters said I would have to wait for her to finish vacuuming the curtains before she could read my scat. "Have you left it," they said, "where it lied?" They were doing their social studies on the settee. "Sometimes," they said, "it roll in transit or splay."

I answered, "Girls, I have retained its integrity."

"Swell," said one of the daughters without enthusiasm. They went back to their homework.

I could hear the vacuum in the woman's sin lab.

I held the tray in my hands.

Thinking. *(The gouge in the house; the seven arriving at once; the cards that were neither yours nor mine, but which were shared equally between us; the square you could not lift. Because you could not lift it, I held it dear.)*

"She done, mister. You go in."

I plucked away the saran wrap from my tray. I stepped in.

The old charlatan wore a turban. She took the tray from me, and set it down with the kink in the neck we get when handling swaddled infants.

I told her about you.

She drew ley lines between my stool, which she called my pretty eidolons. Her hand flew over the tray like a gull.

I thought about all these things. *Gouge, cards, nor mine, equally, not lift, dear.*

Finally she asked, "You come in here through the front door?"

I said I had.

"You have the smell," she said, "of a jimmied window man."

"Insults aside," I prompted, "what is your reading of my leavings?"

"Mm-hm. You ever broke an arm?"

"Yes."

"Ever try to hold someone's hand with your arm broke? In twain?"

"No."

"Your lady. Sometimes a weak clutch feel like a caress."

"And sometimes?"

"You don't even have a hand to spare."

VIII.

Gone, the policeman's beat, lagging seconds behind his nightstick.

Gone, the vacuity of doors. The brutality of schoolyard cranks grown tall. The entry of vice-chancellors. And also the grip, once slackened, the lap, once lifted, the sight, once silenced, the bird.

We cannot have the murmur we requested; the gift of jingoism comes easily to some. You may look with your eye through the body up to the knees, but there things get thick. Not even worth it to try the rest.

Now the banks close, and all things follow too closely, one after another. The air cools, the sun withdraws from shop and industry, and in the hobby hut, the little streets for playing little games are crawling with evening commuters.

The city diminishes to half size in the heat; too many things will fit in a row.

You and I never will lick the problem with sidewalks; that they are always laid disjunct. And so we walk, the cracks beneath us, the sky a fissure above.

Singing,

> I shall meet you under the sheepwillow tree
> Where the branches meet with the bole,
> And all that never shall be, shall be,
> With the suckers, the sap, and the soul.

I do not know whether we ever sat in the same room.

IX.

Just Because It Never Happened Doesn't Mean We're Still Alive

Ben Marcus

I WAS FORTUNATE TO FIND a person who would solve my solitude. She would use her hands on my person until it was soothed. She would chop at my husk, then spoon out my sorrow and be its keeper. I located her at a castle. My intention had not been to find her, for I had been busy being lonely with someone else. It was a tangled area of preening people, mostly diaper free, with real feet and hands, and each was traveling alone. You could ask about the weather there, and people would answer you in English.

The great Horace, childhood lover to Homer the Blind, when asked of love and its effects by the town council, who were conducting their Survey of the Mysteries, gathered his robes, stood up, left the auditorium, and never spoke again.

The time was technical summer, a season that had been achieved by nature so many times, so incessantly, that a clotted arrangement of birds created splotches of ink called shadows, and whole days went by without gunfire. Shadows were simply blind spots that everyone shared. Kill holes were called graves, and apologies known as writing were incised in their surface. Rotten bags were called people. Milk was never sprayed from a fire hose at children until they skittered over the pavement like weevils, but the children wore shields of clothing regardless, and the people who guarded them were often trembling.

There was a chance, however remote, that we—among all the others who also famously walked the earth—would not breathe again, however much our mouths looked wet and ready for action. If we pictured ourselves in the future, we were forced to imagine our coffins shifting on a loosely soiled terrain, slipping into their pre-dug holes.

In short, it was necessary to establish a romantic alliance and to publish the results inside each other's bodies. In short, when we referred to our fear as "tomorrow," our only solution was to seek aerial sensations with each other. In short, although we pretended to choose who we would destroy in the name of a relationship, we were instead forced at each other, feigning admiration for the way our bodies lacked fat, hair, and color.

We together conceived of solitude as a math problem, such like the ancients must have encountered when they saw two different suns in the sky: a daytime sun that was hot and burned out the eyes, and an evening sun that was cool, pale, and white. Each would soon have its own name, but for the time being the suns were anonymous, and they careened to a complex logic, and they were frequently misunderstood. People often died of heartbreak because of them. Maps of the dead called snowdrifts gathered in the mountains. An obituary water called rain fell everywhere, and the ancients turned the hammered surface of their faces into it, but still could not feel better.

Questions we did not ask, because Ovid already asked them so well: in what way would commitment to each other differ from a commitment against our own solitude? In what way would our daily compromises, our small shifts against our own nature, build into bulldogs of resentment that we would soon unleash upon each other? In what way would our displays of affection toward each other differ from advertisements of what we most wanted done to ourselves?

A relationship between us—two average-sized people who could not be mistaken for chess pieces, however much our faces looked chiseled and wooden and overnoticed—would be a chance to mutually seek solutions to the dilemma of solitude. Other people, we

345

discovered, had a plus or minus charge, similar to those colored beads called electrons. To be around the minus people was to have one's solitude erased, whereas the plus people seemed only to add to the solitude, which had a limitless growth potential, a way of swelling inside the skin, creating an aroma called disgust. If one of us experienced a deepening solitude in a crowd, a so-called Spanish Moment, we might conclude that a majority of the crowd was plus capacity, so overflowing with their own solitude that they could do nothing but share it with whoever entered their sphere. These people hated mud. They did not wish to be killed.

We were partners in a puzzle then. The difficulty level was 9, or 9.3. There were no clues. We would have to wait until we parted from each other to discover whether we had won or lost. This was incentive enough to overexplore each other's eccentricities, to enter a race toward bored familiarity.

This took place in an area known as the world, where people cannot fly. Cocoons called nightgowns adorn the bodies there. When the cocoons are lifted, an investigation occurs, and the result is often a wetness, a smearing on of fluids. In this country, we breathe into each other's genitals with a periscope called a straw. We blow on them. We make a fan out of notebook paper and wave it over the area, using the age-old excuse that we simply love to read, and what better narrative than the one inscribed upon the genitals of our familiars? We play pipe organ music out of a stereo that looks like an old wooden shoe. Sex is not an event that someone is invited to, however much we sit by the phone anyway, waiting. Oh, there has been so much wetness between the people that streets have been built to collect the runoff.

As Cicero, the great sage, said: and an old shoe is beaten against the pavement. Yes, when the lovers meet, we destitute ones hide in the road and beat our hard old shoes against it.

We met inside the fat clear globules known as air. There was no fudge in the room. Swimming skills were not required. There were no weapons. A pocket-sized emissary named "Joe" introduced us. I did not love myself.

Afraid of the predictability of my attraction, I started a project with her called "I don't like you." It was intercut with other popular projects, such as "I am tired and scared," and "You are so beautiful that I am afraid to have sex with you." Her project revolved around the "Everything's fine" model. She held her cookie up high, and I jumped and touched my cheek to it. Through several mutual misunderstandings, we grew to need each other, a need that could be charted on a calendar. The parchment was signed with an evidence stick. Many children clapped.

It was agreed. She would chop at my husk, and I would begin publishing my name inside her mouth.

Courtship is based on hatred, according to one of the great thinkers, Robert Montgomery, a man who ate a series of meals, belched into a well, and then died. Hatred was a tactic the Phoenicians used when they met an enemy, and it has been the reigning wartime model ever since, however plain, however obvious. She and I, my solitude defeater, were no more enemies than any ancient man and woman bagged in cheap skin and fading hair, yet a battle was afoot, employing weaponry such as indifference and laughter, kissing and ambivalence, rubbing upon each other's bottoms with a bath brush, and waiting to see who would have the honor of starting the first argument. The goal was not to admit that we each suspected a future dependence upon the other. We commenced a theater of attractive indifference in order to seal our obligation to each other. We engaged in a strenuous denial of need. A holiday might one day be made out of this behavior. It would be called "Monday."

It was not illegal to know each other. It was just difficult. We used different cities as launching pads, when cities were linked by layers of chuff called roads and roads were not called devil carpets.

The ancients were so disloyal that they died and never thought of their loved ones again. Homer called dead people "traitors." The greatest loves were simply forgotten, and the bodies of leaders and slaves alike began to melt. The love between two people has never been stored in a vial and sold in a shop, yet sometimes she and I, the two of us, on the threshold of no longer caring for each other, a precipice called the Waking Moment, lay together in the bed shaking at each other's bodies as though we only had water inside us and could be just so easily poured away. We used a wringing technique called a hug, and squeezed at each other with great force, hoping that somewhere on a floor beneath us there was a drain big enough to take the water part of this stranger we had been loving and wash them away, quite far from us, and then further still, until we could only hear the faintest sound, which we might mistake for a river.

Head Arrangements
Gilbert Sorrentino

ONE O'CLOCK JUMP

HE GOT TO THE PARTY late. She was sitting on the floor just inside the entrance to the living room, talking with two other girls. He knew she had to be there with somebody, maybe, yes, Cliff. After a while he danced with her, and soon after they got their coats and left. They could hear Cliff shouting drunkenly from the apartment, I'll kill the bitch! He didn't care what Cliff said or thought. When they got downstairs they saw that it had just begun to snow, and they started walking toward the bar. It was very cold and he gave her his scarf to wear.

[Pale blue organza dress; black slingback pumps; Phil Kronfeld tie of green, black, and white biomorphic figures; Gordon's gin; "You Belong to Me."]

The place was fairly crowded and they knew a lot of people there. They sat at the bar. He said something foolish to her, then put his hand under her skirt, and spread his fingers on her thigh. She didn't say anything, and he waited for her to say stop or to mention Cliff. He knew that they were engaged; she wore a small diamond ring, but he didn't ask about it, he didn't care about it. He moved his hand higher on her thigh and she suddenly leaned forward to kiss him. Jimmy came over and served them two more drinks. He rapped his knuckles on the bar. Good luck! He was half-drunk and so were they.

[White slip with lace edging; black woolen coat with a gray Persian lamb collar and cuffs; sheer honey-colored nylons; "It's All in the Game."]

In the frigid gloom of her back porch they kissed and kissed and groped each other. He pulled her skirt up to her waist and put his

349

hand between her legs and she masturbated him, both of them smiling idiotically at each other in the dark. Why, *Cliff!* she said. He walked back to the bar through lighter snow and saw Cliff with two other men he recognized. Cliff snarled at him and said something, but all he heard was *cunt.* Just like Cliff, the moron. He turned his back and lit a cigarette and Jimmy came over. Hey, sport! You back already? He winked out of his vast drunkenness. Gordon's?

[Wood challis scarf in tan and wine paisley; Philip Morris; Gordon's gin; *bitch;* "Because of You." She didn't invite him in.]

*

It was starting to snow by the time he got to Tony's party. He saw Kenny and Gary, Tony and Donnie and Cliff and Jake, and there were other people from the neighborhood, Ray and Carmine, and some he didn't know. She was sitting on the living-room floor talking to Dolores and Claire; he'd seen her on the street for years but suddenly he saw her. Her name was Anne. She had to be there with somebody, but somebody didn't own her. They danced a few times and at some point a drunk came up to them and said that he was welcome to the bitch. He and Anne left, putting on their coats as they went downstairs, followed by the drunk's shouts. He didn't know who he was, he didn't ask. He didn't care. He stopped her on the landing and kissed her, put his hands inside her coat and felt her warm flesh through the smooth fabric of her dress. They walked out into the snowy night. Your shoes? he said. I'll take them off at the bar. So, good, she wanted to go to the bar, that's what he wanted: booze and laughter, soft lights and sweet music, and you, and you. They'd be two more holiday drunks in out of the cold, to be close, to flirt with love, to pander to amorous clichés and listen to the hot sexual blood lie to them. In the light snow of the city night he heard her clothes rustle, imaged her sweet body inside them.

[Soaked shoes; Buddy Lee off-white wraparound overcoat; very Merry Christmas; pale pink-white lipstick; "Early Autumn."]

The bar was full of happy drunks, befitting the season and the snow and bitter cold. She opened her coat and he looked at her small breasts move beneath her snug bodice. So you don't mind about Norman? she said. Who's Norman? Norman, she said,

Norman, the guy at the party? I never saw him before, he said. He put his hand under her skirt and she looked right at him. Well, she said, you're a fast worker, and she opened her thighs a little. She put her whiskey sour to her mouth. Her mouth. And sipped it. Her lips. He drank his gin and waved to the bartender, Jimmy? *He* thought it was something, thinks it's something, but it's not. He leaned toward her and kissed her and she pushed her body closer to him. His hand was high up on her thigh, burning.

[Music from the back room for dancing, the Sapphire Room, what is the joint coming to? "No Moon at All." Her lips full with desire, the bar filled with cheap and lovely Christmas lights glittering on the lenses of her glasses. She shone in the light, her whole body shone in her pale blue dress in the light, he imagined his tongue into her every crevice.]

In the dark and cruel cold she sat on the porch railing and they made love, her flesh barely exposed because of her coat and dress and slip. The bum was at the bar when he got back there, in a strange distant ecstasy, his delight still upon him. He clapped the snow off his sleeves and shoulders and sat at the bar, taking his gloves off. Whore, the guy said, across the bar. He turned his back and lit a cigarette. Norman. Oh brother, he thinks it's something, the poor bastard. You're a winner, *Norman.*

[Snow drifting from trees in a whispery gossamer dust; her thighs soft and cool as the collar of her coat; "Blue Velvet"; he had her sodden, lacy handkerchief in his pocket and held it tight in his fist; she was in the cloth; why hadn't she invited him in?]

*

She was sitting on the floor talking to some friends when he came into the party from the snow. He saw her immediately and she was as immediately isolated from the others; he knew that he would leave with her before the night was over. She would, over the next five years, carelessly, even blithely, savage him, and, unwittingly, herself. They danced together, she seemed familiar, as someone who had been importantly peripheral to his life. She was with somebody he'd never seen, a giant with a college letter jacket. They paid him no mind and left to walk through feathery, blowing snow to Jimmy's Place, down the same street they'd walk, in the still heat and breathtaking humidity of an August night six years hence, as she told him, almost brightly, that she was leaving him, and she was really sorry, for an ROTC officer in the navy. She was really, really sorry, she was in love. What? he'd say, what? Some altar boy who'd spent his youthful life masturbating to fantasies of someone else's wife? Oh God, she'd say. He gave her his scarf to wear, a soft wool challis in a paisley print of wine and gold. Six years later the *whore* would take it with her when she left to live her comic-strip life—but not for long—with Don Winslow of the navy, the hero with happiness nicely chilled, just waiting for her.

[Pall Malls; blue rustle of her dress; in her mouth the taste of raspberries; "I'm in Love Again"; and again and again; Merry Christmas; celebrate while the celebrating's good; trouble in mind and slingback shoes, soaked.]

He was stupid drunk, so of course it was only right that he put his hands on her breasts and then under her skirt in front of the bartender, who looked away. He didn't care, nor did she, and she bent toward his bar stool so that he could touch her more easily. A bad sign, no doubt, for prior to Don Winslow's true and noble love, many men would touch her, some of them in this very bar, some of them sitting on the stool on which he now sat, thinking himself suavely amorous. He kissed her and her tongue was sweet, sweet with the absolute taste of raspberries. She gave a little grunt and opened her thighs, a bad sign.

["I'm Glad There Is You"; red, green, white, blue, orange Christmas lights, tawdry and beautiful; the next day here already; snow sweeping past the windows of the bar filled with the pleasure of abandon; they sat in the dimmest of lights in the Sapphire Room, blue lights, groping, holding, caressing each other's thrilling bodies.]

Romance in the dark, the dark, enfolded within which he was in her hot, wet body, the strange wetness of her secret parts. Many others would feel these feelings, think these thoughts, and soon enough, soon enough. He knew that he would ask her to marry him, fool that he was, knew that he would be a fool to do so, knew that she would say yes. She was deeply engaged in being fucked, giving herself to the act with sublime concentration, in

---

herself completely. He was somehow certain that part of her profound pleasure lay in that fact that they were on an open porch and might be interrupted, embarrassed at any minute, she loved it. She loved it. Years later, she would fellate a man she'd met on the subway in the back booth of a crowded diner on Utica Avenue, she'd love it. He walked her home. In Jimmy's he saw Letterjacket at the bar, who looked at him threateningly. Go fuck yourself, he did not say. He was possessed of happiness, squandering too much of the precious stuff.

[Her odor on his hands; he was, of course, lost; "Haunted Heart"; in his pocket, her gloves: they belonged to him, they were hers, who belonged to him, so he thought; she'd said that it was too late for him to come in.]

BLUE SEVEN

EARLY SEPTEMBER

Indications of disaster for the approaching marriage were rather clear. To proffer but one of them, the morning of the wedding day: here is the young groom, in his only suit, a midnight blue serge one-button lounge, as they were called in the early fifties, those lost days of innocence and hope, Joe McCarthy and the blacklist, nuclear-arsenal buildups and the Korean War. It is already eighty-seven degrees at ten o'clock in the morning, and the groom is sweating. The air that moves into the windows of his little studio apartment is syrupy, filled with the nauseating stale-garlic smell of the cheap lunch meat that is made in the small factory next door. The sun has the malignant, hazy quality that identifies New York late summers so precisely—maniac weather: nothing will ever come out right, such light says, nothing. Time for a drink. Or two. At the bar, sweating, he wants to flee, somewhere. But things have been said, things have been done, things have been settled. And so the festive day begins with a drunken groom, who will soon be off to find his best friend, his drunken best man.

He made love to his bride five times on the wedding night, and although he duped himself into thinking that this pitiable if not ludicrous feat had to do with his ungovernable desire for her, it was actually—sad word—rooted in the gloomy fact that she had called him by another man's name. And, somehow quite terribly, not while in the mindless raptures of lust, but while she showered after they had got into the stuffy hotel room from their post-wedding party, a story in itself, oh yes indeed, but not one to be told here. "Billy, honey, can I have a washcloth, please?" His name is Greg. So Greg had to prove himself more of a man than the amorous specter, Billy. Five times prove so. And when he gave up, finally, at 5 A.M., his penis was numb; he may have thought, crassly, yes, but sadly, of the sickly pink bolognas carted out of the neighborhood factory. His bride was exhausted, her hair plastered to her forehead, her flesh sticky with sweat and semen, exhausted and dumbfounded by this morose, labored mime of passion that she'd endured. Not at all, no, not at all a fair portent of things to come for their conjugal relations, as they say, despite the banners of virility that fluttered, in enervated metaphor, above the damp, rumpled sheets.

EARLY OCTOBER

Greg's innocence, his naïveté, in the face of the limping, tattered sexual innuendos of this Greenwich Village human flotsam, would make him cringe and despise himself in the roiled years to come, but for the present he was vaguely admiring and surely envious of the shabby liars who regaled him and Patricia with what they thought to be sophisticated conversation and strange, exciting ideas about *life*.

They sat at a round table at the front of the room in a worn-out bar on, let's say, Grove Street. Greg and Patricia had been taken up by three men: a "reporter" of about fifty, wearing a blue polka-dotted tie over a dirty red-and-white-striped shirt, and a tweed jacket with a cigarette burn on one sleeve; another man, equipped for his "poetic" vocation with a greasy gray fedora, a bedraggled, muddy-looking tie, and black fingernails; and a third man, the youngest of the aesthetic trio, a "freelance editor," with pale skin, pale eyes, pale hair and eyelashes, whose lascivious smirk accompanied his fevered, rapt gaze at Patricia, a gaze that made Greg feel as if her clothes were being wished off her, one garment at a time, until she would sit, naked finally, the pale man's toy; most disturbingly, he also felt that she would be his complaisant, pleased, lecherous toy. He felt this, but would not, could not, really, think it. Or dare think it.

How the three men—I apologize for the glum fact that they

354

look like stereotypes—had welcomed them to their rotting Bohemia! And how they talked so glibly and thrillingly of putting finishing touches on stories and plays and poems and novels, of editors and magazines and theater and parties. Creativity virtually leaked from them, a sort of artistic urine, and Greg, he who unloaded freight from trucks, he who stacked shelves with tawdry products, he who packed and shipped and lugged and sweated, he who made forty-four dollars a week and hadn't read a book save for *Studs Lonigan* since high school, Greg was assigned to watch the aesthetes ogle his wife, and to listen to them make sly but filthy suggestions to her through their decaying mouths. *All she has to do is send him home, why not?* Polka-dot tie said something like that, he did, yes, he did, and brown teeth noted, "You can't wear it out, sweetheart, didn't Mommy tell you that?" No, he hadn't actually said that, but what had he said? Greg was appalled and astonished at his persistent image of Patricia naked, her breasts resting on the sticky table, of her laughing along with these corrupt animals; she fingered her nipples voluptuously at their behest. He felt dizzy.

He got her out of the bar, he asserted himself, or pleaded drunkenness, sickness, something: he got her out of there. This may have been accomplished easily because Patricia was a wife of the fifties, but she may well have been unconsciously frightened by the way that Greg was being slowly but absolutely excluded from the night's increasing weirdness. Perhaps, just perhaps, she had smelled the sweet odor of degradation and it unsettled her.

But whatever her qualms, if there were any, she was overtly angry and hurt, and she made it clear that she was humiliated as well. That Greg—Greg!—should insult her, should treat her like a *child* in front of three, ah, three *interesting* men! Professional people who wrote, who knew books and artists and all sorts of interesting things! Who lived in Greenwich Village, not goddamn Brooklyn! Isn't being with people like that better than what we do every weekend? He looked at her. What did they do every weekend and was it so bad, so stupid, that it turned her ugly and petulant? Movies and walks and late breakfasts, reading the Sunday papers, some old friends, sometimes a party, and: and, and, and. Was it *that* boring?

She was, however, shocked out of her sullenness when Greg, on Eighth Street near Broadway, suddenly stopped her and said, distinctly and bitterly, that she was a fool, a fool not to see that those *interesting* men wanted only to humiliate her, to get rid of him and humiliate her, fuck her, for Christ sake! And then laugh about it. You idiot, you idiot, you fool. She said nothing and they walked on in silence.

They never spoke of that evening again, but Greg always remembered how perfectly willing she'd been to stay in that gray, morose bar with those three men; and how willing she might well have been to do what they would have suggested. So he thought and, rightly or wrongly, would always think. Patricia, too, remembered that night, of course, but as one of fun and danger and daring and a kind of uninhibited, provocative joy in what might happen: a night on which freedom had been denied her by this man she had *married.*

So this seamy encounter with what are now known as losers, early in the marriage, served as another sign of what might be called "disturbances" to come. But just *because* it was early in the marriage, the delights and surprises, the inventions and failures of sex, the discoveries both mundane and astonishing of two people living "on top of each other," was the phrase, the sturdy banality of keeping house—all would combine in regulated and heuristic domesticity, so that the lewdly dreamlike night would not be recognized as the venomous catalyst that it surely was. Which does not mean that its slow-acting poison would not have its deadly effect on the marriage. And the effect would be so far removed in time and mood and substance from its cause that the link between them would never be found, would never, for that matter, be suspected.

MID-DECEMBER

A month or two after the Greenwich Village "adventure," Patricia was sleeping with a co-worker, a blondish man who thought of himself as dryly witty, subtly ironic, and sexually sophisticated as well as expert. He was, as you may have surmised, none of these things, but another wandering orphan of the age, playing his pair of deuces with a knowing smile. On the other hand, a very other hand, he wasn't *Greg,* and he did have an MG, of which he took great care: he loved his car, as he said over and again. Thus Patricia was seduced, which does not, perhaps, say too much for her. Well, she was but nineteen, and thought it somehow daring that a man, just a little older than she, could flaunt a car so remote from sober responsibility.

"Let's take a drive, Pat," he said, maybe, one Saturday when they were in the office to help with inventory. And so they did and soon Patricia was pregnant. What a guy Greg was! went the talk. There they were, not even six months married, and Patricia was knocked up already. "What an animal!" Greg's friends said, admiring and laughing and leering; and wishing that they might have a go at sweet Patricia. Maybe Greg *had* inseminated his wife, who knows? But as the old saying goes, It's a wise child, et cetera.

EARLY MARCH

Patricia had a miscarriage, nobody knew why. Greg discovered that he didn't really care, but he drew on his small reserve of sociopathy and pretended to: tight smiles, and the like, bearing up. Patricia was relieved, and she, too, was brave.

As soon as she felt all right, it was back to the MG jive with Mr. Cool. The steering wheel of the damn car always hurt her neck, propped awkwardly, as she always seemed to be, as they fucked in one desolate spot or another in Canarsie or Coney Island. Patricia knew that all this was sordid, but her clitoris did not. So.

EARLY APRIL

I don't recall the MG owner's name. Paul will do, or you may come up with your own moniker—it should be redolent of wit and irony and sophistication, all slightly shopworn. He was a devotee of automobile rallies, and met clusters of other gasoline fans once a month or so to, well, "rally." Off they'd all go, with maps and clues and itineraries, gloves and scarves and Good Strong Coffee. They'd rush along the dark roads of Westchester or Nassau County, Jersey, and Staten Island, stopping to check clues by flashlight, and so on. I don't quite know how the winners of these tournaments were determined, but winning surely must have had something to do with the time it took to go from place to place. Or not. Perhaps there were no winners, which seems unlikely. This is America: the "love of the game" is but a quaint phrase.

There's Paul now in his duffle coat; hold your hat! He had

357

casually invited Patricia and Greg to (or on) a rally this night, an excursion through the dells and vales, copses and glades of Staten Island, in the vicinity of La Tourette Park. Paul and Patricia sat in the only seat of his gleaming green—racing green!—MG. Greg, what a sport, rode with another contestant, if that's the word. Paul and Patricia may have dallied 'neath a venerable elm, and in the magic moonlight made the panting beast. When all reassembled for coffee amid the hearty laughter of returned warriors, Greg noticed that Patricia's shirt was buttoned awkwardly: the second button in the third buttonhole, and so on. But perhaps it was but a trick of the light. Of course, that's what it was. He didn't think this phrase, "a trick of the light," but he knew it had to be so. That or a mirage, an illusion, a fata morgana—he was seeing things! He knew it was so. He *knew* it was so. He *knew* it was *so*. Patricia loved him and had said so on many occasions. Besides, Paul was an all right sort of guy and was also engaged, so he said, to a really *great* chick, presently in graduate school, and far, far away.

EARLY APRIL ET SEQ.

Patricia's father, Phil, was an alcoholic who owned a small electrical-repair shop. He was what might be called a professional male, what used to be known as a "real man." The contours and measurements of the latter were never clearly defined, but "real manhood" was usually determined by what its possessor (and his manly peers) was not, or by what they loathed or did not understand or were ignorant of. The last particulars were, well, numberless. In that sense, the "real man" was a series of negatives, denials, and blank spaces: of this fact, the "real men" were extremely proud. Such people are, certainly, still among us, but are very different from Phil, who, not to elaborate, would probably think of them as "a buncha faggots," funny haircuts, team jerseys, wooden slang, and all. So times change, but idiocy is always with us, like syphilis.

Phil, who never went so far as to think of Greg as a "faggot"— possibly because he refused to countenance the idea of his daughter being married to "one"—was, nonetheless, highly disapproving of him. The drunken, family-deserting shopkeeper was irritated beyond thought because Greg did not tell nor laugh at dirty jokes, did not ever want to go over to the Hudson in Jersey to see the burlesque shows (despite Phil's rapturous, manly descriptions of the womanly parts of Blaze Starr and Tempest Storm), blushed at sexual remarks made in mixed company, was bored by football of any variety or level of play, and, perhaps most sinfully, did not understand why Notre Dame, some college in the hazy distance, should be "our team." Nor did he ever ask. He was, as well, not convinced that God cared one way or another about anything at all, given a God in the first place. Phil, fragments and splinters of his childhood Lutheranism tucked here and there in his sozzled mind, was, but of course, devout. Sure he was. "Irritated" is the wrong word to use to describe Phil's feelings anent his son-in-law. "Crazed" or "rabid" will serve better.

But most profoundly, hidden deep under the many layers of Phil's blustering, beery inanity, he hated Greg because Greg possessed, yielding and complaisant, his daughter's body, the soft flesh that he didn't want to know he desired, although his wife knew this well. It might also be of interest to know that Phil had never once been sober when he talked to—mocked—Greg. It has little to do with this account, but years later, Greg came to see that Patricia was a female simulacrum of her father, good old Phil, complete with a petty contemptuousness for others, most especially him.

To Conclude

I had intended to go on with this story, since I know how badly things turned out for Patricia and Greg, but you surely do as well. I then thought that I might be able to invent a conclusion that would encapsulate their grim future, as well as stand up, so to speak, to the banal history prefacing it. But such a conclusion would be, as such conclusions are, abrupt if not solemn, ironic if not "psychological," or, unforgivably, given over to absurd changes in fortune. I'm constrained and somewhat chagrined to admit that this marriage and its subsequent dissolution is of a common sort, if slightly more painful than many.

In sum, Patricia and Greg lack, I think, pathos, but are caught in the toils of an undifferentiated misery. They often mistake this for desire unfulfilled, and feel that, with patience and a little luck, this amorphous hunger will be fed. Nothing like this will happen, for desire of this sort, or perhaps of any sort, is never satisfied.

A Certain Quantity of Conversations
Or, The Completely Altered Nightbook
Aleksandr Vvedensky

*—Translated from the Russian original of 1936–1937
by Thomas Epstein and Eugene Ostashevsky*

1. A CONVERSATION ABOUT AN INSANE ASYLUM

Three companions were traveling by carriage. They were exchanging thoughts.

FIRST. I know the insane asylum. I saw the insane asylum.

SECOND. What are you saying? I know nothing. How it looks.

THIRD. Does it look? Who saw the insane asylum.

FIRST. What's in it? Who lives in it.

SECOND. Birds don't live in it. Time passes in it.

THIRD. I know the insane asylum, the insane live there.

FIRST. That makes me happy. That makes me very happy. Hello, insane asylum.

THE MASTER OF THE INSANE ASYLUM. (*Looks into his decrepit little window as if it were a mirror.*) Hello, friends. Please lie down.

The carriage stops at the gates. Trifles stare out from behind the fence. The evening passes. Nothing changes. Consider the poverty of language. Consider impoverished thoughts.

FIRST. So that's what it's like, the insane asylum. Hello, insane asylum.

SECOND. I knew that's how it was. Just like that.

THIRD. I didn't know. Is it just like that.

FIRST. Let's go for a walk. They are walking everywhere.

SECOND. There are no birds here. Are there birds here.

THIRD. Not many of us remain and we won't remain for long.

FIRST. Write cleanly. Write boringly. Write aboundingly. Write resoundingly.

SECOND. Good, that's what we'll do.

> *A door opens. A doctor enters, accompanied by assistants. Everyone trembles with cold. Consider the conditions of place. Consider what happens. But nothing happens. Consider the poverty of language. Consider impoverished thoughts.*

FIRST. (*Speaking in Russian verse.*)
Please enter the insane asylum,
My friends, my ends.
It gladly awaits us.
We gladly await us.
We light a street lamp here,
The light hangs like a king.
Foxes run around here,
They piercingly squeak.
All is temporary here,
The flowers around us creak.

SECOND. I heard these verses through. They ended long ago.

THIRD. Not many of us remain and we won't remain for long.

THE MASTER OF THE INSANE ASYLUM. (*Opening his decrepit little window as if it were a part of the window.*) Come in, friends, lie down.

> *Three companions were traveling by carriage. They were exchanging thoughts.*

2. A CONVERSATION ABOUT THE ABSENCE OF POETRY

> *Twelve persons sat in a room. Twenty persons sat in a room. Forty persons sat in a room. Music played in the concert hall. The* SINGER *sang.*

Aleksandr Vvedensky

O you poets is it true
All your songs have been sung through.
And the singers lie in graves,
Just like misers they are grave.

The SINGER *paused. A couch appeared. The* SINGER *continued.*

The tree doesn't make a sound,
The night without honor flows.
Quietly the sun like science
Bakes the tedious groves.

The SINGER *paused. The couch disappeared. The* SINGER *continued.*

Clouds roll about, bored,
Horses gallop on a lark,
But no poems can be heard,
All is noiseless all is dark.

The SINGER *paused. A couch appeared. The* SINGER *continued.*

Probably the poets died,
The musicians and the singers.
Probably their bodies lie
Sleeping gravely like misers.

The SINGER *paused. The couch disappeared. The* SINGER *continued.*

O gaze upon nature

Here everybody approached the window and looked out on the paltry sight.

At the soundless forests.

Everybody gazed at the forests, which gave off not a single sound.

People now are sick and tired
Of the warbling of birds.

People stand around everywhere, spitting in disgust as birds warble.

Aleksandr Vvedensky

The SINGER *paused. A couch appeared. The* SINGER *continued.*

Turning crimson, the leaf falls.
The singers' cemetery palls.
Autumn. Darkness. Nightly chill
Settles on the speechless hill.

The SINGER *paused. The couch disappeared. The* SINGER *continued.*

The sleeping poets stood upright
And said, You're exactly right.
We lie in coffins, sung to rest,
Under the pall of yellow grass.

The SINGER *paused. A couch appeared. The* SINGER *continued.*

Music plays in the ground,
Worms with verses sing along,
Rhymes throughout rivers resound,
Beasts drink the sounds of songs.

The SINGER *paused. The couch disappeared. The* SINGER *died. What did he prove by that.*

3. A CONVERSATION ABOUT REMEMBERING EVENTS

FIRST. Let us recall the beginning of our argument. I said that I was at your place last night while you said that I wasn't. To prove my point I said that I spoke with you yesterday; but you, to prove your point, said that I didn't speak with you yesterday.

Both of them were majestically stroking their cats. Outside it was evening. A candle burned on the windowsill. Music was playing.

Then I said: come on, you were sitting there, at place A, while I stood there, at place B. Then you said: no, come on, you were not sitting there, at place A, and I was not standing there, at place B. To buttress my proof, to make it very, very powerful, I immediately experienced sadness, joy, and lament, and then I said: but there were two of us here yesterday, at the same time, at two

363

neighboring points, A and B—don't you understand that.

They both sat locked in a room. A sleigh rode.

But you too washed yourself over with the emotions of indignation, ferocity, and love of truth, and you answered: you were you, I was me. You didn't see me, I didn't see you. As far as those rotten points A and B go, I don't even want to talk about them.

Two persons sat in a room. They were conversing.

Then I said: (I remember) a groom walked on the cupboard, whistling; and (I remember) a mighty forest of flowers shook its wonderful crowns on that chest of drawers; and (I remember) a fountain babbled under the chair, and a vast palace rose under the bed. That's what I said to you. Then you smiled and answered: I remember the groom, the mighty forest of flowers, the babbling fountain and the vast palace; but where are they, they're nowhere to be seen. We were almost certain about everything else. But it wasn't like that at all.

Two persons sat in a room. They were remembering. They were conversing.

SECOND. Then we were at the middle of our argument. You said: but you can picture me at your place yesterday. And I said: I don't know. Maybe I can picture it, but you weren't there. Then your face temporarily altered completely and you said: how can that be? How can that be? I can picture it. I won't insist any longer that I was there but I can picture it. I see it clearly: I am entering your room and I see you—you're sitting here and there, and all around hang my witnesses, the paintings and the statues and the music.

Two persons sat in a locked room. A candle burned on the table.

You recounted all that very, very persuasively, I answered, but then I briefly forgot you exist, and the witnesses are mute. Maybe that's why I can't picture anything. In fact I even doubt the existence of these witnesses. Then you said that you were beginning to experience the death of your emotions but that nonetheless, nonetheless (and weakly now), nonetheless it seemed to you that you had been at my place. I too fell silent and then said that nonetheless it seemed to me as though you hadn't. But it wasn't like that at all.

Aleksandr Vvedensky

Three persons sat locked in a room. Outside it was evening. Music was playing. A candle burned.

THIRD. Let us recall the end of your argument. Neither of you said anything. That's the way it was. Truth strolled arm in arm with you like numeration. What was probable? The argument ended. I stood astounded.

Both of them were majestically stroking their cats. Outside it was evening. A candle burned on the windowsill. Music was playing. The door stayed tightly shut.

4. A CONVERSATION ABOUT CARDS

Well, let's play cards, *shouted the* FIRST.

It was early morning. It was very early morning. It was four o'clock in the morning. Not all who could have been there were there; those who were not there lay at home, wracked in their beds by terrible illnesses, while their crushed families encircled them, lamenting and pressing to their eyes. They were human. They were mortal. What can be done about it. If we look around, the same is in store for us.

Let's play cards, *that night nonetheless, shouted the* SECOND.

I like playing cards, *said* SANDONETSKY *or the* THIRD.

Cards cheer my soul, *said the* FIRST.

But where are our the one who was a woman and the one who was a girl? *asked the* SECOND.

Oh don't ask, they're dying, *said the* THIRD, *or* SANDONETSKY. Why don't we play cards.

Cards are a good thing, *said the* FIRST.

I love playing cards very much, *said the* SECOND.

They excite me. When I play I'm no longer myself, *said* SANDONETSKY. *He is also the* THIRD.

Yeah, you won't be playing cards when you're dead, *said the* FIRST. So let's play cards right now.

Why the gloomy thoughts, *said the* SECOND. I love to play cards.

And I too am cheerful, *said the* THIRD. And I love cards.

And I, how much do I love cards, *said the* FIRST. I am ready to play all the time.

You can play on the table. You can also play on the floor, *said the* SECOND. So here's what I am suggesting—let's play cards.

I'd play even on the ceiling, *said* SANDONETSKY.

I'd play even on top of a drinking glass, *said the* FIRST.

I'd play even under the bed, *said the* SECOND.

Then you start, *said the* THIRD. You start. Draw. Show me your cards. Let's play cards.

I'm ready, *said the* FIRST. I've played before.

All right, *said the* SECOND. I got nothing on my mind now. I'm a player.

I'll say without bragging, *said* SANDONETSKY. Who am I to love. I'm a player.

Well, *said the* FIRST, the players have gathered. Let's play cards.

As far as I can tell, *said the* SECOND, you've invited me and the rest of us to play cards. My answer is: I agree.

It seems that I've been invited as well, *said the* THIRD. My answer: I agree.

In my opinion the invitation also applies to me, *said the* FIRST. My answer: I agree.

I can see, *said the* SECOND, that we're all just about insane. So let's play cards. What's the use of sitting around?

Yes, *said* SANDONETSKY, as for me: I'm insane. Without cards I'm nowhere.

Yes, *said the* FIRST, if you please: it's the same with me. Wherever there are cards, there I am.

I go crazy from cards, *said the* SECOND. Play or be played.

Look, we've wrapped the night around our little finger, *said the* THIRD. Look, the night is over. Let's go home.

Yes, *said the* FIRST. It's been proven by science.

Of course, *said the* SECOND. Proven by science.

No doubt about it, *said the* THIRD. Proven by science.

They all broke into laughter and then headed for their near-by homes.

5. A CONVERSATION ABOUT RUNNING IN A ROOM

Three persons were running around a room. They were conversing. They were moving.

FIRST. The room is not running away anywhere. I am running.

SECOND. Around the statues, around the statues, around the statues.

THIRD. There are no statues here. Look, there are no statues.

FIRST. Look: no statues here.

SECOND. Our consolation is that we have souls. Look, I'm running.

THIRD. The chair is a runaway, the table is a runaway, the wall is a runaway.

FIRST. I believe you are wrong. In my opinion we alone are running away.

Three persons sat in a garden. They were conversing. Birds loomed in the air above them. Three persons sat in a green garden.

SECOND. When sitting in a garden
Wish upon a star,
Count how many of us
Will die before winter,

Hear the knocking of the birds,
The sound of human faces,
The roaring of beasts,
To stand and run the farewell races.

Aleksandr Vvedensky

> *Three persons stood on a mountain top. They were speak-*
> *ing in verse. There was neither time nor place for intense*
> *movements.*

THIRD. On a mountain of late
I thought about tectonic plates.
The earth is wrinkled, black and craggy
But terrifying is its empery.
Here's the air. Gray is its hair.
Hello air my neighbor.
I embrace this height.
God is within my sight.

> *Three persons stood at the seashore. They were conversing.*
> *The waves listened to them from far away.*

FIRST. I stood for long by the sea.
I thought about its deep.
I thought why does it sound
Like the musician Debussy.
I knew then the sea is a garden.
With its musical swells it seems
To summon me and you
To run around the room with dreams.

> *Three persons were running around the room. They were*
> *conversing. They were moving. They were looking around.*

SECOND. Here everything is as before. Not a thing ran away.

THIRD. We alone are running away. Now I will take out my weapon.
I will perform an act upon myself.

FIRST. How funny. Will you shoot yourself, drown yourself, or hang
yourself?

SECOND. Oh do not laugh! I am running so that I may run out faster.

THIRD. What an eccentric. He's running around statues.

FIRST. If you call all objects statues, then OK.

SECOND. I would have called stars and immobile clouds statues. As
for me, I would have.

THIRD. I am running to God. I am a runaway.

SECOND. I know that I killed myself.

Three persons left the room and rose to the roof. Why would they do that, you'd think.

6. A CONVERSATION ABOUT UNINTERRUPTED CONTINUATION

Three persons sat on the roof with arms folded in total tranquillity. Sparrows flew over them.

FIRST. Now do you see, I'm taking a rope. It's strong. It's already soaped.

SECOND. What's there to speak of. I'm taking out a gun. It's already soaped.

THIRD. And there's the river. There's the ice hole. It's already soaped.

FIRST. Everyone can see I am ready to carry out my plan.

SECOND. Farewell, my children, my wives, my mothers, my fathers, my oceans, my air.

THIRD. Cruel water, what am I to whisper in your ear. I think it can only be one thing: we shall soon meet.

They sat on the roof in total tranquillity. Sparrows flew over them.

FIRST. I am approaching the wall and picking a spot. Here, here's where we'll hammer in the hook.

SECOND. As the gun barrel caught sight of me
Death at once invited me.

THIRD. You are tired of waiting for me, congealed river. A little longer and I will approach.

FIRST. Air, give me your hand so I can shake it in farewell.

SECOND. A little more time will pass and I will turn into a refrigerator.

THIRD. As for me, I will turn into a submarine.

Aleksandr Vvedensky

They sat on the roof in total tranquillity. Sparrows flew over them.

FIRST. I am standing on a stool, lonely as a candle.

SECOND. I am sitting in a chair. There's a gun in my insane hand.

THIRD. Trees, the ones that stand covered in snow, and trees, the ones that stand in feathers of leaves, they stand far from this blue ice hole; I stand in a fur coat and hat as Pushkin once stood, and I that stand before this ice hole, before this water—I am an expiring man.

FIRST. I know all of that. I am throwing the rope around my own neck.

SECOND. Yes, it's all clear. I am inserting the gun barrel in my mouth. My teeth do not chatter.

THIRD. I am taking a few steps back. I am taking a running start. I am running.

They sat on the roof in total tranquillity. Sparrows flew over them.

FIRST. I am jumping off the stool. The rope is around my neck.

SECOND. I am pressing the trigger. The bullet is in the barrel.

THIRD. I have jumped into the water. There is water inside me.

FIRST. The noose tightens. I am suffocating.

SECOND. The bullet hit me. I have lost it all.

THIRD. The water filled me. I am choking.

They sat on the roof in total tranquillity. Sparrows flew over them.

FIRST. I died.

SECOND. Died.

THIRD. Died.

FIRST. Died.

SECOND. Died.

THIRD. Died.

They sat on the roof in total tranquillity. Sparrows flew over them.
They sat on the roof in total tranquillity. Sparrows flew over them.
They sat on the roof in total tranquillity. Sparrows flew over them.

7. A CONVERSATION ABOUT VARIOUS ACTIONS

An explanatory thought. It would seem what is there to continue when everyone died, what is there to continue. That much is clear. But do not forget, it is not three men that are acting here. It is not they that are riding in a carriage, it is not they that are arguing, it is not they that are sitting on the roof. Perhaps it is three lions, three tapirs, three storks, three letters, three numbers. What is their death to us, what is their death to them.

Nevertheless, the three of them were sailing in a boat, exchanging oars with every minute, with every second, with such speed, with such breadth that their amazing arms were invisible.

FIRST. He blew.

SECOND. He spat.

THIRD. It all went out.

FIRST. Light.

SECOND. The candle.

THIRD. Again.

FIRST. It does not work.

SECOND. The candle again.

THIRD. Goes out.

They began to fight, beating each other about the head with hammers.

FIRST. If we only had.

SECOND. Matches.

371

THIRD. They would have helped.

FIRST. Not really.

SECOND. It went out.

THIRD. Too much here.

> *They drink acid, resting on oars. But it is really opaque all around.*

FIRST. So light it.

SECOND. Light, light it.

THIRD. It's just like in Paris.

FIRST. You thought it was China.

SECOND. Are we really sailing.

THIRD. To faraway Lethe.

FIRST. Without gold or copper.

SECOND. Will we reach it by summer.

THIRD. Clip.

FIRST. Skip.

SECOND. Dip.

THIRD. If dead, then.

FIRST. Not for —————— .

SECOND. If mortal, then.

THIRD. Don't even look.

> *Thus they sailed in a boat, exchanging thoughts while oars flickered in their hands like gunshots.*

8. A CONVERSATION BETWEEN MERCHANTS AND THE BATH ATTENDANT

> TWO MERCHANTS *were wandering around a pool that had no water in it. But* THE BATH ATTENDANT *was sitting under the ceiling.*

TWO MERCHANTS. (*Lowering their heads like oxen.*) There's no water in the pool. I'm in no condition to bathe.

THE BATH ATTENDANT. Monotonous is my routine:
I sit up here like an owl
As sauna steam
And beefy air
Writhe above each cauldron.
I shall become
The prey of dark,
The child of the chaldron.
The ovens glimmer,
Candles fade,
As mercilessly steam is made.
Among damp bunks
Shoulders shine yellow
And boils the future
Slaughter's tallow.
They seek for birch
—————— money
Here hunters become meaner.
Within the dark
Scour howl bark
The father the horseman the swimmer.
And then the smoke shakes like a beggar
Inside this dark and godless place
Where every scoundrel's oily face
Loses its deathly swagger.

TWO MERCHANTS. (*Raising their heads as if struck dumb.*) Let's go to the women's section. I'm in no condition to bathe here.

THE BATH ATTENDANT. (*Sitting under the ceiling like a* FEMALE BATH ATTENDANT.)
When goddesses
Make their entrance
The sky congeals
In the distance.
They throw their furs down like wings,
They bare their skirts and other things
And turning naked in an instant
From their necks they dangle infants.

Soap dances wildly like Hope,
Sponge plunges down a slippery slope.
And her eyes' bright snow,
And her speeches' flow,
And the contour of nights
And the ovens' light
Are more frightening
Than candles' needy glow.
Here I sit among iniquity
Of multitudinous liquidity
That gushes from the open faucets
And rushes down the bodies' rapids,
Where bellies swell, recalling tyrants,
I may be a bath attendant but even I am sweating.
We female bath attendants now
Are weary and devoid of hope.
How happily that hook's screwed in.
I have a weapon. I have rope.
Let the naked ladies play,
I don't like them anyway.

TWO MERCHANTS. (*Staring straight into the bath like into waves.*)
This attendant must be sexless.

ELIZAVETA *enters. She undresses with the clear intention of
washing. The* TWO MERCHANTS *stare at her like shades.*

Look. Look. She is winged.
Yes, she's got thousands of little wings.

ELIZAVETA *does not notice the* TWO MERCHANTS. *She
washes, dresses, and leaves the bath.* OLGA *enters. She
undresses, apparently intending to bathe. The* TWO
MERCHANTS *stare at her as if into a mirror.*

Look, look how I've changed.
Yes, yes. I am completely unrecognizable.

Noticing the MERCHANTS, OLGA *covers her nakedness with
her fingers.*

OLGA. Merchants, aren't you ashamed to be looking at me?

TWO MERCHANTS. We want to bathe. And there's no water in the
men's section.

OLGA. What are you thinking now.

TWO MERCHANTS. We thought you were a mirror. We made a mistake. We beg your pardon.

OLGA. Merchants, I am a woman. I am modest. I cannot stand in front of you naked.

TWO MERCHANTS. How strangely you're built. You almost don't look like us. Your chest isn't the same and there's an essential difference between your legs.

OLGA. You speak strangely, merchants, can it be you have not seen our beautiful women. Merchants, I am very beautiful.

TWO MERCHANTS. Olga, you are bathing.

OLGA. I am bathing.

TWO MERCHANTS. So bathe, bathe.

> OLGA *finished bathing. She got dressed and left the bath.* ZOIA *enters. She undresses, which means she wants to wash. The* TWO MERCHANTS *are swimming and wandering about the pool.*

ZOIA. Merchants, are you men?

TWO MERCHANTS. We are men. We are bathing.

ZOIA. Merchants, where are we. What game are we playing?

TWO MERCHANTS. We are in a bath. We are having a wash.

ZOIA. Merchants, I am going to swim around and wash. I am going to play the flute.

TWO MERCHANTS. Then swim. Wash. Play.

ZOIA. Maybe this is hell.

> ZOIA *finished bathing, swimming, playing. She got dressed and left the bath.* THE BATH ATTENDANT, *who is also* THE FEMALE BATH ATTENDANT, *comes down from the ceiling.*

THE BATH ATTENDANT. Merchants, you have made a fool of me.

TWO MERCHANTS. How?

THE BATH ATTENDANT. By coming in fool's caps.

TWO MERCHANTS. But what does that matter. We did not do it on purpose.

THE BATH ATTENDANT. It turns out that you are predators.

TWO MERCHANTS. What kind?

THE BATH ATTENDANT. Lions or tapirs or storks. Or maybe even hawks.

TWO MERCHANTS. Bath attendant, you are shrewd.

THE BATH ATTENDANT. I am shrewd.

TWO MERCHANTS. Bath attendant, you are shrewd.

THE BATH ATTENDANT. I am shrewd.

9. THE PENULTIMATE CONVERSATION, ENTITLED: ONE MAN AND WAR

A bleak situation. A military situation. A tactical situation. Almost an attack or a battle.

FIRST. I am one man and the earth.

SECOND. I am one man and the cliff.

THIRD. I am one man and war. Here's what else I have to say: I composed a poem about the year 1914.

FIRST. I read it with no introduction of any kind.

SECOND. The Germans pillage the Russian land.
I lie
In cabbage
Unable to understand.
Shame on the Germans, shame on Kant.
Every gallant
Grenadier will avenge us.
Grand Duke K. R.
Plays God's sycophant.
Observing from afar
The Germans' actions,
I germinated
Like a star.

In sight of lawyers and lawmakers
I was tossed
From my nest
On my breast.

THIRD. Take a break. We need to think about this.

FIRST. Let's sit on a rock. Let's listen to gunshots.

SECOND. Everywhere, everywhere verses shed leaves like trees.

THIRD. I continue.

FIRST. What is it
What happened
I cannot accept
The Tsaritsa was praying
To gillyflowers
To garlands
To crosses
On graves
As she tore from herself the leaves
Of the innumerable infirm Russians.

SECOND. Have we really reached the communal graveyard?

THIRD. And here their remains are interred.

FIRST. Shots resound. Cannons make noise.

SECOND. I continue.

THIRD. Battling in sore
Battles
Not yet forgotten,
I saw
Representations
Of the unfortunate
Corpses of the dead.
Up till then
They were eating pudding.
From then on
Bombardments became their bedding.
But rattling
The sword
The bird

377

Aleksandr Vvedensky

> Glittering
> The bloody shirt
> The corpses
> In copses
> Like clouds
> The legs ran around like horses.

FIRST. An accurate description.

SECOND. Hear out the song or the speech of gunshots.

THIRD. You've made it all completely clear.

FIRST. I continue.

SECOND. How beautiful you are, O war,
  I love the cheek of wine,
  The eyes and lips of wine
  And the white teeth of vodka.
  For three whole years there was shelling,
  Pillage, bombardment, and yelling.
  Bayonets, flowers, guns firing,
  Bombardment, pillage, expiring.

THIRD. Yes, that's true, there was a war on back then.

FIRST. That year the hussars were beautifully dressed.

SECOND. No, the ulhans were better.

THIRD. The grenadiers were beautifully dressed.

FIRST. No, the dragoons were better.

SECOND. From that year not even the bone has remained.

THIRD. The gunshots wake. They are yawning.

FIRST. (*Looking out of a window shaped like the letter* A.) Nowhere do I see any writing that is connected to any concept whatsoever.

SECOND. What's surprising about that. What are we, schoolteachers.

THIRD. The merchants are passing by. Shouldn't we ask them something.

FIRST. Ask. Ask.

SECOND. Two merchants, where are you coming from.

THIRD. I was mistaken. The merchants are not passing by. They are nowhere to be seen.

FIRST. I continue.

SECOND. Why does the end come when we don't want it to.

> *The situation was bleak. It was military. It resembled a battle.*

10. THE LAST CONVERSATION

FIRST. I left home and walked on.

SECOND. Clearly, I was walking along a road.

THIRD. The road, the road was planted all around.

FIRST. It was planted all around with oak trees.

SECOND. The trees, they made noise with their leaves.

THIRD. I sat beneath the leaves and I thought.

FIRST. I thought about that.

SECOND. About my arguably stable existence.

THIRD. I could not understand anything.

FIRST. So I stood up and again walked on.

SECOND. Clearly, I was walking along a path.

THIRD. The path, the path was planted all around.

FIRST. It was planted all around with tormentor flowers.

SECOND. The flowers, they talked in their flower language.

THIRD. I sat near them and I thought.

FIRST. I thought about that.

SECOND. About representations of death, about its eccentricities.

THIRD. I could not understand anything.

FIRST. So I stood up and again walked on.

Aleksandr Vvedensky

SECOND. Clearly, I was walking on air.

THIRD. The air, the air was surrounded.

FIRST. It was surrounded by clouds and objects and birds.

SECOND. The birds, they were busy with music, the clouds fluttered about, the objects were standing in place like elephants.

THIRD. I sat nearby and I thought.

FIRST. I thought about that.

SECOND. About the feeling of life dwelling within me.

THIRD. I could not understand anything.

FIRST. So I stood up and again walked on.

SECOND. Clearly, I was walking in thought.

THIRD. The thoughts, the thoughts, they were surrounded.

FIRST. They were surrounded by illumination and sounds.

SECOND. The sounds were audible, the illumination blazed.

THIRD. I sat beneath the sky and I thought.

FIRST. I thought about that.

SECOND. About the carriage, about the bath attendant, about poems and about actions.

THIRD. I could not understand anything.

FIRST. So I stood up and again walked on.

*

TRANSLATOR'S NOTE

Aleksandr Vvedensky co-founded OBERIU, a small circle of avant-garde writers in Leningrad at the end of the 1920s. Most OBERIU members made a living from children's literature; few were able to publish any "adult" work. A series of scandalous poetry readings led to the 1931 arrests of Vvedensky and his main partner, Daniel Kharms, signaling the group's de facto dissolution by the authorities. After release, Kharms, Vvedensky, and friends met for discussions at each other's apartments. Without hope of publication or even circulation in manuscript, they created a collective body of work that in retrospect has become one of the most important developments in twentieth-century Russian literature.

The play translated here, whose Russian title is *Nekotoroe kolichestvo razgovorov (ili nachisto peredelannyi temnik)*, was composed after Vvedensky moved to Kharkov, Ukraine, in 1936. He lived there in near-total obscurity, most of his acquaintances being fellow card players. Arrested at the beginning of the war as a "prevent ive measure" by Soviet authorities, he died in transport, probably of dysentery. Kharms perished several months later, after a similar arrest in Leningrad. Their writings saw print in the land of their birth only after the onset of perestroika. —E. O.

NOTES ON CONTRIBUTORS

M. T. ANDERSON's novel *Feed* (Candlewick Press) was a finalist for the National Book Award and won *The Los Angeles Times* Book Award. He is the fiction editor of the literary journal *3rd bed* and lives in Boston.

JOHN ASHBERY's *Selected Prose* is forthcoming from the University of Michigan, and his new book of poems, *Where Shall I Wander*, will be published next spring by Ecco/HarperCollins. He is Charles P. Stevenson, Jr., Professor of Languages and Literature at Bard College.

MARTINE BELLEN's collection *Living with Animals* will be published next year by Spuyten Duyvil, and her chapbook *Malka's Secret Delivery* is forthcoming from G-O-N-G.

CAN XUE lives in Beijing and has published numerous short stories and novels. Her three books that have been published in English translation are *Dialogues on Paradise, Old Floating Cloud* (both by Northwestern), and *The Embroidered Shoes* (Henry Holt). She has a volume of recent fiction forthcoming from New Directions.

CHEN ZEPING is professor of linguistics at Fujian Teachers' University in China and the author of many books and articles in the field of Chinese dialects.

SANDRA CISNEROS's books include *Caramelo* (Knopf in English and Spanish), *My Wicked Wicked Ways* (Third Woman Press and Knopf), *Woman Hollering Creek/El Arroyo de la Llorona, The House on Mango Street/La Casa en Mango Street*, and *Loose Woman* (Vintage/Vintage Español).

JOSHUA COREY is the author of *Selah* (Barrow Street) and *Fourier Series* (Spineless Books). He lives in Ithaca, New York.

ROBERT CREELEY's most recent book is *If I Were Writing This* (New Directions). He teaches in Brown University's Program in Literary Arts.

THOMAS EPSTEIN writes on Russian twentieth-century literature and philosophy. He teaches at Boston College.

GRAHAM FOUST is the author of two books of poetry, *As in Every Deafness* (Flood Editions) and *Leave the Room to Itself* (Ahsahta Press), which won the 2003 Sawtooth Prize. He teaches literature and writing at Drake University.

FORREST GANDER's latest books are *The Blue Rock Collection* (Salt Publishing) and the forthcoming *Sound of Summer Running* (Nazraeli Press), in collaboration with photographer Ray Meeks.

KAREN GERNANT is professor emerita of Chinese history at Southern Oregon University. A new volume of stories by Can Xue translated by Gernant and Chen Zeping is forthcoming from New Directions.

PETER GIZZI's poetry collections include *Some Values of Landscape and Weather* (Wesleyan) and *Artificial Heart* (Burning Deck). He is also the editor of *The House that Jack Built: The Collected Lectures of Jack Spicer* (Wesleyan).

TAMMY GOMEZ has been recently published in the Austin poetry anthology *Terra Firma* (Agave Noir Press); in *Bicycle Love*, an essay collection (Breakaway Books); and online at vozalta.u33.infinology.com/cadavoz/tammy_gomez. She lives in Texas.

JORIE GRAHAM is the author of ten collections of poetry. Her newest book, *Overlord*, is forthcoming from Ecco/HarperCollins.

EVE GRUBIN's poems have appeared or are forthcoming in *The American Poetry Review*, *The New Republic*, *Barrow Street*, and elsewhere. She is programs director at the Poetry Society of America and teaches at the New School.

CHRISTIAN HAWKEY's first book of poems, *The Book of Funnels*, has just been published by Verse Press. He lives in Brooklyn.

FANNY HOWE's latest publications include *Gone*, *The Wedding Dress* (both University of California), and *On the Ground* (Graywolf).

MICHAEL IVES is a writer and musician whose work with the language performance trio F'loom has been featured on National Public Radio and the CBC. A collection of his prose "devices" entitled *External Combustion Engine* is forthcoming from Futurepoem Books.

ROBERT KELLY's newest books of poetry are *Lapis* (Godine/Black Sparrow) and *Scham/Shame* (a collaboration with Birgit Kempker published by Engeler Editions, Cologne). *The Language of Eden* is forthcoming from Black Square.

JUSTIN LACOUR is a recent graduate of the MFA program at the University of Massachusetts, Amherst, where he received the Glosband Fellowship in Poetry. His chapbook *Mr. Gravity's Blue Holiday* was selected by John Ashbery for the 2004 Philbrick Poetry Prize.

SARAH LANG was born in Edmonton, Alberta, Canada. This is her first appearance in an American publication.

ANN LAUTERBACH's seventh collection of poems, *HUM*, will be published by Penguin in spring 2005, along with *The Night Sky: Writings on the Poetics of Experience* (Viking). She teaches at Bard College.

KELLY LINK is the author of the collection *Stranger Things Happen*, published by Small Beer Press, which will issue a new collection of her stories next year.

NATHANIEL MACKEY's most recent publications are a book of poems, *Whatsaid Serif* (City Lights), and *Atet A.D.*, volume three of *From a Broken Bottle Traces of Perfume Still Emanate* (City Lights). *Paracritical Hinge: Essays, Talks, Notes, Interviews* is forthcoming from the University of Wisconsin.

BEN MARCUS is the editor of *The Anchor Book of New American Short Stories* and the author of *The Age of Wire and String* (Dalkey Archive) and *Notable American Women* (Vintage).

J. W. McCORMACK was born in Las Vegas and grew up in Tennessee. This is his first appearance in print.

T. M. McNALLY is the author of a collection of stories, *Low Flying Aircraft* (University of Georgia), and the novel *Almost Home* (Scribner). A second collection, *Quick*, is forthcoming this fall from the University of Michigan Press. He teaches at Arizona State University in Tempe.

RICK MOODY's books include *The Black Veil, The Ice Storm*, and *Garden State* (all Back Bay Books). He is currently working on a new novel.

PETER O'LEARY is the author of a book of poetry, *Watchfulness* (Spuyten Duyvil), and a book of criticism, *Gnostic Contagion: Robert Duncan and the Poetry of Illness* (Wesleyan). He is a longtime editor of *LVNG* and a contributing editor at *The Cultural Society.*

EUGENE OSTASHEVSKY is assembling an anthology of OBERIU literature in translation. A short book of his own poems, *The Off-Centaur*, recently came out from *The Germ.*

MICHAEL PALMER's most recent collections of poetry are *The Promises of Glass* and *Codes Appearing (Poems 1979–1988)* (both New Directions). His contribution to a multiple collaboration with the painter Gerhard Richter was published by the San Francisco Museum of Modern Art in the fall of 2002 as *Richter 858.* A new book of poems, *Company of Moths*, is forthcoming in spring 2005.

TOVA REICH's novels are *Mara* (Farrar, Straus & Giroux), *Master of the Return* (Harcourt), and *The Jewish War* (Pantheon).

FRANCES RICHARD's first book of poems, *See Through*, was published by Four Way Books in 2003. She is an editor at the art and culture magazine *Cabinet*, a founding editor of *Fence*, and teaches at Barnard College.

MICHELLE ROBINSON is a student in the department of American and New England studies at Boston University. This is her first appearance in print.

JOHN SAYLES's films include the recently released *Silver City*, as well as *The Return of the Secaucus Seven, The Secret of Roan Inish, Eight Men Out, Lone Star*, and *Matewan. New Hope for the Dead* was first performed in 1983 at the Manhattan Punchline and in the Seventy-Ninth Street boat basin.

GUSTAF SOBIN's collection of essays, *Ladder of Shadows* (a sequel to *Luminous Debris*), is forthcoming from Imperatore Press. His newest volume of verse, *The Places as Preludes*, will appear in spring 2005 from Talisman House.

GILBERT SORRENTINO's books include *Little Casino* (Coffee House), *New and Selected Poems: 1958–1998* (Green Integer), and *Mulligan Stew* (Dalkey Archive).

Originally from Kiev, Ukraine, GENYA TUROVSKAYA is a poet and translator currently living in Brooklyn. She is the author of *Calendar* (Ugly Duckling Presse), and her poetry and translations from Russian have appeared or are forthcoming in *6x6*, *Aufgabe*, and *The Germ*.

ALEKSANDR VVEDENSKY (1904–1941) was a Russian poet and one of the leaders of the short-lived group known as OBERIU. *Frother*, his play from the same period as *A Certain Quantity of Conversations*, is forthcoming in *The Germ*.

Carol Emshwiller's "fantastic"*
debut is the first in our new line of
Peapod Classic reprints:

Carmen
Dog

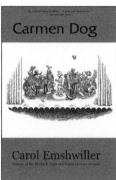

"A wise and funny book"—*The New York Times*

1931520089, $14

Carmen Dog is the classic feminist novel that inspired writers Pat Murphy and Karen Joy Fowler to create the James Tiptree Jr. Memorial Award.

Emshwiller takes a funny, sharp-eyed look at men, women, human and animal natures. When women start turning into animals and animals start turning into women, Pooch, formerly a golden setter, snatches her owners' baby and runs away from her mistress, who has become a snapping turtle. Pooch and baby end up in New York City, where there's a bad-tempered wolverine with expensive tastes on the loose at the Plaza, a pack of wolves in Central Park, a politically aware sasquatch, and a team of mad scientists at the Academy of Motherhood who are desperately trying to figure out what's going on. Meanwhile, the loyal and good-hearted Pooch discovers what she really wants: to sing *Carmen*.

"Carol is the most unappreciated great writer we've got. *Carmen Dog* ought to be a classic in the colleges by now. . . . It's so funny, and it's so keen."
—Ursula K. Le Guin, author of *Changing Planes*

*"Her fantastic premise allows Emshwiller canny and frequently hilarious insights into . . . both men and women."—*Publishers Weekly*

"Emshwiller has produced a first novel that combines the cruel humor of *Candide* with the allegorical panache of *Animal Farm*."—*Entertainment Weekly*

Peapod Classics: a new line of classic reprint titles from Small Beer Press.

www.peapodclassics.com

NOON

NOON

A LITERARY ANNUAL

1369 MADISON AVENUE   PMB 298
NEW YORK   NEW YORK   10128-0711

EDITION PRICE $9 DOMESTIC $14 FOREIGN

ahsahta press

LEAVE THE ROOM TO ITSELF
Graham Foust
WINNER OF THE 2003 SAWTOOTH POETRY PRIZE
SELECTED BY JOE WENDEROTH

In these poems, philosophy and pharmaceuticals gone lyric go shopping—and come home familiarly anonymous, hungry, and in love. Sports arenas, music television, home improvement, cosmetic surgery, weapons of mass destruction, and endless trips to the store are all scrutinized and celebrated by the voices that haunt and own this book.

ISBN 0-916272-77-X • $12.95

SPELL
Dan Beachy-Quick

"Taking a powerful, lyrical sweep through one of the country's most charged and versatile symbols, Dan Beachy-Quick opens *Moby-Dick* into yet more meanings and directions in this book-length reverie, perfectly sustained by his intricate sound play and impeccable phrasing. Intelligent, compassionate, exquisite, Beachy-Quick's is a unique voice in contemporary poetry."—Cole Swensen

ISBN 0-916272-78-8 • $16.95

SAVING THE APPEARANCES
Liz Waldner

These poems evince the mystery of the act of seeing, beauty of the natural world, and power of the longing that engenders its contemplation. "[N]o contemporary poet shows more wild individuality, more gusto ("truth of character...in the highest degree in which the subject is capable"—Hazlitt) than Liz Waldner. She has become one of the most convincing and most inspiring of our poets."—Stephen Burt, *Slope*

ISBN 0-916272-79-6 • $12.95

ISLAND
Charles O. Hartman

"*Island* is a brilliant book, holding equally in the closed curve of its shape the physical and metaphysical—all seen from the fortuitous vantage point of Charles Hartman's grand intelligence." —Linda Bierds

"If poets are lucky to study everything, Hartman's wide-ranging and inventive mind is one of the luckiest writing. His poems are our good fortune."—*Boston Book Review*

ISBN 0-916272-80-X • $12.95

COMING IN DECEMBER

THE AREA OF SOUND CALLED THE SUBTONE by Noah Eli Gordon
WINNER OF THE 2004 SAWTOOTH POETRY PRIZE, SELECTED BY CLAUDIA RANKINE

CUR ALIQUID VIDI by Lance Phillips

1910 University Drive • Boise, ID 83725-1525 • http://ahsahtapress.boisestate.edu

DELILLO FIEDLER GASS PYNCHON
University of Delaware Press
Collections on Contemporary Masters

UNDERWORDS
Perspectives on Don DeLillo's *Underworld*

Edited by Joseph Dewey, Steven G. Kellman, and Irving Malin

Essays by Jackson R. Bryer, David Cowart, Kathleen Fitzpatrick, Joanne Gass, Paul Gleason, Donald J. Greiner, Robert McMinn, Thomas Myers, Ira Nadel, Carl Ostrowski, Timothy L. Parrish, Marc Singer, and David Yetter

$39.50

LESLIE FIEDLER AND AMERICAN CULTURE

Edited by Steven G. Kellman and Irving Malin

Essays by John Barth, Robert Boyers, James M. Cox, Joseph Dewey, R.H.W. Dillard, Geoffrey Green, Irving Feldman, Leslie Fiedler, Susan Gubar, Jay L. Halio, Brooke Horvath, David Ketterer, R.W.B. Lewis, Sanford Pinsker, Harold Schechter, Daniel Schwarz, David R. Slavitt, Daniel Walden, and Mark Royden Winchell

$36.50

INTO *THE TUNNEL*
Readings of Gass's Novel

Edited by Steven G. Kellman and Irving Malin

Essays by Rebecca Goldstein, Donald J. Greiner, Brooke Horvath, Marcus Klein, Jerome Klinkowitz, Paul Maliszewski, James McCourt, Arthur Saltzman, Susan Stewart, and Heide Ziegler

$35.00

PYNCHON AND *MASON & DIXON*

Edited by Brooke Horvath and Irving Malin

Essays by Jeff Baker, Joseph Dewey, Bernard Duyfhuizen, David Foreman, Donald J. Greiner, Brian McHale, Clifford S. Mead, Arthur Saltzman, Thomas H. Schaub, David Seed, and Victor Strandberg

$39.50

ORDER FROM ASSOCIATED UNIVERSITY PRESSES
2010 Eastpark Blvd., Cranbury, New Jersey 08512
PH 609-655-4770   FAX 609-655-8366   E-mail AUP440@ aol.com

WATCHFULNESS

PETER O'LEARY

Watchfulness by Peter O'Leary
ISBN 1-881471-73-X $12.00

ONE OF THE BEST YOUNG POETS OF OUR TIME.
—RONALD JOHNSON

SPUYTENDUYVIL.NET
AND BOOKSENSE.COM

anarchy

MARK SCROGGINS

C   H

Anarchy by Mark Scroggins
ISBN 1-881471-74-8 $10.00

Annotations about the insults, both spiritual
and physical, that have terrorized history
from Sodom to the Twin Towers.
—Guy Davenport

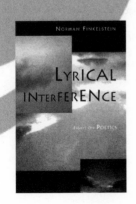

NORMAN FINKELSTEIN

LYRICAL
INTERFERENCE

ESSAYS ON POETICS

Lyrical Interference by Norman Finkelstein
ISBN 0-9720662-2-5 $12.00

HIS EMPATHY AND RESPECT FOR A
GIVEN POET'S PROJECT IS RARE IN
CONTEMPORARY CRITICISM.
—MARJORIE PERLOFF

MOTORMAN

DAVID OHLE
INTRODUCTION BY BEN MARCUS

Motorman by David Ohle; from 3rd bed
available through SPD, Amazon + 3rdbed.com

FICTION COLLECTIVE TWO

Real to Reel
by **Lidia Yuknavitch**

This third collection of fictions by Lidia Yuknavitch examines signifcance and meaning through a cinematic lense. With an intelligence that scalds every pretense and surface, her camera pans across subjects as varied as Keanu Reeves and Siberian prison labor. These are unforgettable fabrications by the writer and verbal cinematographer at her best.

Real to Reel
Lidia Yuknavitch
1-57366-107-4
$13.95

"Each story is a gem that could not have been written by anybody but Lidia Yuknavitch."
—Review of Contemporary Fiction

"This is not a book for the faint of heart or the weak of stomach. The skill of the writer is impressive and there can be no doubt concerning her formidable ability. "
—The Compulsive Reader

formally adventurous fiction

http://fc2.org

CONJUNCTIONS:42

CINEMA LINGUA

Writers Respond
to Film

Edited by
Bradford Morrow

Fiction and poetry inspired by the silver screen. Writers and artists include John Sayles, Frederic Tuten, Gilbert Sorrentino, David Shields, William H. Gass, Alexander Theroux, Lewis Warsh, Lyn Hejinian, Peter Hutton, Kristin Prevallet, Peter Straub, Robert Desnos, Luc Sante, C. D. Wright, Gerard Malanga, Joanna Howard, Eleni Sikelianos, Howard Norman, Joyce Carol Oates, Clark Coolidge, Donald Revell, Joshua Furst, Diane Williams, Peter Gizzi, Geoffrey O'Brien, Tan Lin, Laird Hunt, Bill Morrison, Thalia Field, Paul West, William T. Vollmann, Maureen Howard, Ann Lauterbach, and John Haskell, among others.

452 pages. $15.00, shipping included.

To order, please send payment to:

CONJUNCTIONS
Bard College
Annandale-on-Hudson, NY 12504
Phone: 845-758-1539
E-mail: Conjunctions@bard.edu